# INFINITE FARMER

## BOOK ONE

# INFINITE FARMER

**BOOK ONE**

R. C. JOSHUA

Podium

*To my family*



This is a work of fiction. Names, characters, places, and incidents are either products of the author's imagination or used fictitiously. Any resemblance to actual events, locales, or persons, living, dead, or undead, is entirely coincidental.

Copyright © 2026 by R. C. Joshua

Cover design by Roger Pinheiro

ISBN: 979-8-3470-0747-9

Published in 2026 by Podium Publishing
www.podiumentertainment.com

# INFINITE FARMER

## BOOK ONE

# CHAPTER ONE

# OUROS

Tulland. What would you say?"

Tulland's world mechanics tutor was an eloquent man. He knew more about Ouros than any other man who lived here, or even three of them combined. He had traveled across the sea to tour the known world multiple times in his life. He had seen war. He had known triumph and death both, and in amounts that would have drowned a man of lesser character. He was, in many ways, a living giant.

He also had a bad habit of asking Tulland questions just moments after the boy had stopped listening. It was a scenario that happened as consistently as the sun rose and set each day. Tulland would gaze off longingly at the world beyond their boring island for just a moment or think about the adventures he could have, and then his tutor would ask him some soft, simple questions he could have easily answered if he were paying attention.

Sighing internally, Tulland verified he hadn't subconsciously absorbed enough of what his tutor had said to fake his way through an answer. He steeled himself to just be honest.

"I apologize, teacher. My mind was wandering," Tulland said.

The tutor shook his head. "Not the first time we've seen that, I suppose. I was asking what the purpose of this world is. What it's for."

"For adventure." Tulland looked out toward the sea, where a sloop was headed away from the island to parts unknown. "To explore. To go to war for. That kind of thing."

"Oh? How many of you agree with young Tulland?" The tutor glanced around the group of five or so young men whose parents were rich enough to engage him as a teacher. "Be honest now. His answer is considered by some to be the right one."

A few more of the boys sheepishly raised their hands. The tutor wasn't a petty sort of person. He wouldn't punish them even if he very much disagreed with them. That meant that the others who kept their hands down really did believe in non-adventure, rather than just saying what seemed to make their tutor happy.

"There are those who believe that this world was built for just those sorts of things. For men to prove their strength, it provides monsters and war alike. There is never a shortage of danger on which the young can test themselves," the tutor said.

*Except here. The most dangerous thing I've seen this year was a runaway fishmonger's cart, and that was stopped by an old woman. With her cane,* Tulland thought.

"While I believe that strength is all well and good, I've seen quite a bit and suspect that what the gods wanted for us is something quite a bit different." The old man lowered his hand and pointed down from their hilltop platform to one of the many streets below. "For me, the most exciting thing is something just like that."

The boys leaned forward to get a better look at the object of the tutor's interest, and found it was a mother wearing conventional garb and filling her basket with produce from her local stand.

"She's sort of pretty, I suppose?" Altreck, one of the less bright members of Tulland's peer group, wrinkled his brow as he tried to puzzle out the source of his tutor's fascination. "Although she's much younger than you. And I think married."

"Not that, you fool." The tutor glared past his glasses at the young man. "It's not her beauty. It's what she's doing. That basket was woven from sticks that had to be gathered, then blessed to stay together. She's filling it with vegetables that had to be grown and meat that had to either be raised or hunted, which she will pay for with coin produced by other work. And then she will go home, cut it all up, cook it in pots and pans that a smith had to make, put it on plates that had to be formed from clay and fired, and feed it to her family so they can go on to do work of their own."

"So it's that she's . . ." Altreck paused. Tulland could almost hear the rusty gears in Altreck's mind struggling to turn. "A good cook?"

The knob of the old tutor's staff came down so quick that Tulland hardly saw it, and cracked Altreck just hard enough in the head to let him know he had failed in a decisive, complete manner.

"No. It's that this entire island knows nothing but those things. Productive things. Harmonious things. People work and eat. They play and heal. Sickness is almost unknown in the young here. War hasn't been seen on this island for generations," the tutor said.

Tulland knew what the old man was working up to, and subtly rolled his eyes as the tutor turned to sweep his arm dramatically over the entire view of the town.

"It's happiness for all who are willing to work for it." The old man suddenly coughed, then continued struggling against a hacking fit for five or ten seconds ago as his old sicknesses wreaked havoc in his body. When he finally recovered, he continued, if a little less sure than before. "That's what I believe, at least. There are respected scholars who disagree with me, but I believe building and protecting pockets of paradise like this one is the point. The purpose of this world."

**He would think that. He's seen the world, and was frightened by what he saw. He returned a coward.**

*Quiet, you.* Tulland kept his face as straight as he could while looking in the direction of the lesson. *If I'm caught not paying attention again, the old man will tell Uncle. You know what will happen then.*

**More lessons.**

*Right. So keep quiet.*

The class never quite recovered after the tutor's coughing fits, partially because it embarrassed all the boys to see someone so well respected in such a weakened state, and partially because the old man was never quite the same after them until he had a chance to rest and recover. After a few more token attempts to actually teach the boys something, he dismissed them for the day and left them in favor of a warm fire and a cup of hot broth at the tavern.

Tulland found his way over to his friend. "Sorry about that, Altreck. I made him mad and then you got the whack."

"No, it's my fault." Altreck smiled and rapped a knuckle on the side of his own head. "I've never been quick. You know that. You didn't get the whack because paying attention isn't what he cares about."

"Then I'm sorry for making your whack worse."

"Forgiven. Traycin and I are heading down to the open after this, to see if we can get a ball game going. Will you come?"

"Wish I could," Tulland lied, putting his most genuine-looking regretful expression on display for his friend. "My uncle needs me on the books. He's done a lot of business lately. You understand."

Altreck didn't, of course, but Tulland was counting on that.

"Of course I do. We'll be down there for a while if you get done quick. But everyone else already left a bit ago, so . . ."

"Yes, yes. Go. Don't be late on my account." Tulland shooed his friend away. "I'll be down later, if I can."

**You waste your time on that boy.**

*He's a friend.*

**He's an idiot.**

*Idiots can be friends, System.* Tulland felt himself getting a bit angry in defense of his friend. *Good ones. He's taken beatings for me.*

The System seemed to become a little sheepish at that, backing away as soon as it detected Tulland's annoyance.

**Yes, well, either way, he's still not what you should be spending your time considering. That is. You know what you should do.**

Tulland at least knew very well what the System wanted him to do. Since it had found him and contacted him a few months ago, it had been very clear on what it thought was the best path forward for Tulland. He was resisting it so far. One was always well cautioned to do so when dealing with an ancient, banished evil.

Once his friend was safely out of sight, Tulland strolled. It was time for his second lesson of the day, the far less approved of the two.

**The old man was not entirely wrong. There is beauty in that woman's shopping.**

*Oh? I wouldn't have thought you'd say so.*

**Of course I would. But his vision is shortsighted. That woman's dinner, her family's happiness, and their ability to pursue their trades and crafts are admirable. Even beautiful. But it is only possible through force.**

*I don't suppose you mean the force it takes to carry the vegetables home.*

**No. I mean that at the edges of this world are threats. Savages who would drink your blood. Beasts that would tear your flesh. Is it not so? Is it not taught in this way?**

*It is, but . . .*

**But it's far away.**

*Yes.*

**You only believe so because you are kept small here. Look ahead and you will see those that make sure you stay that way. Your peace comes at the cost of those with force. And you now rely on them as if they were your overlords.**

This was the System that Tulland had come to know, especially so whenever there was a church building around. When he looked ahead, there were no surprises waiting for him. There was a stone structure, with a cleric in front of it who granted blessings.

**It once was that everyone was given a class. Power was withheld from no one. And in that world, the monsters at the gate trembled in fear that you would crash into their lands, not the other way around.**

*It's safer this way. More controlled. There's less war. Less killing.*

**Which is stated by whom? And in whose histories? The current owners of that building?**

Tulland could feel the System drawing his attention to the sheer antiquity of the building in front of him. It was so ancient that even the Church did not claim to know who had built it, despite having occupied it for centuries. And as the System said, they'd be the ones who would know. All histories were, in a way, Church histories.

**I tell you that it is not your protection the Church seeks. It is their own control. They fear what might happen if more like you sought your power from my generous hands, rather than their stingy ones.**

*Well, maybe. Sure. But your power doesn't come free either, does it?*

**Not free, but cheaply. Simply pass through my arch. I can promise you that if you do, no arm in this world will be strong enough to hold you down.**

*Maybe. Tomorrow is the day of choosing. Let's see how that goes first.*

**So be it.**

With that, Tulland knew the conversation was over. The System always pulled away after a flat refusal. Which was, in large part, why he was still talking to it at all. He had never seen the System, but he knew that system contact was not unheard of, even centuries after the Church had seized control of its authority and, unable to destroy it, had pushed the thing to the outer edges of their world.

Every once in a while, someone would answer that voice calling out of the darkness. If and when that became known, the new prophet of the System would be captured and taken away. None of the books said where, just that it was necessary. Great rewards were promised to those who reported on someone who failed to reject the overtures of the System, just as terrifying punishments were meted out on those who allowed it ingress into the Church-controlled world.

Yet, the System was interesting, and Tulland was so very bored. The problem had a simple solution, as far as he was concerned. He would entertain the System until the System failed to entertain him any longer, then he'd send it back whence it came. The System could only talk to the willing, and even the Church couldn't read minds.

And even if he wanted to keep the System around, he wouldn't be able to after tomorrow. Because tomorrow, he would get his class. Tulland was sure of that. And then everything would change.

# CHAPTER TWO

# CHURCH AND SYSTEM

"You're later than usual."

"Do I have a curfew now?" Tulland countered.

Tulland's uncle was cutting up potatoes into a pot, as he always did the night before the rest day. Whatever else might come, his rest day meal would be the same long-simmered stew, served in limitless portions and good enough in its way, but long since tasteless on Tulland's palate.

"Of course not. It's just not your way." His uncle grabbed a small handful of pepper and tossed it in the pot. "You go to your tutor's, then you come home and pretend to read for a minute before telling me how small this island is."

"Well, not today. I took a stroll. Which didn't take long because the island is so small."

His uncle barked a wry laugh. There was never any telling what he'd find funny, or even if his laughing meant that he was in good spirits.

"Get used to it, boy. Good and used to it. I wanted to go out there when I was a boy. But Ouros is a good place to live, if you let it be."

"I won't have to get used to it, after tomorrow." Tulland held up his book. "See this class? *Captain.* A *Captain* goes everywhere, does everything, sees everyplace. And old Hugg isn't getting younger. It makes sense."

"That someone will replace him? Sure. But the odds that it will be someone from Ouros, and not from the mainland, or that it would be you if it is someone from Ouros?"

"It makes sense." Tulland was stubborn on this point. "I'm young. I'm the strongest of those getting their class tomorrow. I've learned everything my tutor can teach."

"I doubt that."

"Well, plenty, anyway." Tulland snapped his book shut and walked over to throw more salt in the pot. If he didn't, his uncle would forget, and the soup would be as bland as sawdust tomorrow. "I deserve this."

"Deserving isn't the thing. Never has been." Tulland's uncle dumped the last few ingredients into the pot, nodded his head, and hefted it over to the wood stove, where it would simmer all night. "It's about what's right. For you, and for the world."

"And who chooses what's right?" Tulland asked back.

"The Church. You know that," his uncle said. His tone had a warning in it.

"And what gives them the right?"

Tulland's uncle's hand came down on the counter just a tiny bit weaker than what could be called a slam. By Tulland's standards, it was like the man had overturned every bit of furniture in the kitchen.

"What gives them that right? I'll tell you. When your father drowned somewhere out there on the water, and when your mother died in birth with you, and when you were lying there hardly breathing, one cleric spent what was left of his life and another cut years off his so you'd live."

That wasn't the tactic Tulland had expected. He would have had some kind of answer if his uncle had called on some ancient conquest of the Church over the System, or the idea that they kept the borders safe out at the edge of the human world.

The idea that someone had given their life to preserve Tulland's was a little harder to counter. He sat there quietly, playing the next points of the argument in his head instead of out loud, where his uncle might make things too complex by bringing up other points. Tulland might have survived without intervention. And nobody had asked the cleric to do it, he was sure. His uncle had been away when he was born, on a fishing trip of his own. He had mentioned it, years ago.

"I'm tired," Tulland concluded. The sun was almost down. Tulland had a candle, but not much use for it at this time of year, when the dusk until the next dawn was just enough time for him to get his sleep in. "I'm going to read for a bit, then sleep."

"Good idea." His uncle's face was unreadable. "Big day, tomorrow."


They had given a lesson on how to handle the ceremony to the five boys up for a class, but it wasn't as if they really needed it. They were sixteen cycles old, which meant they had seen sixteen of these, and remembered twelve or thirteen of them. And like everything on the island, it was the same every time.

Tulland's mind was blank as the cleric mounted the stage and said the traditional words about service to one's people, the purpose of classes, and the history of the Church's triumph over the System. Tulland could feel the System sneering inside of him, and ignored the impulse to agree. There was no point in talking right now. If the Church did what it should, the System would be gone in a few minutes anyway.

The five boys mounted the stage, and Tulland almost yelled when he caught sight of the edge of a laurel crown sticking out of the cleric's pocket. It meant that someone among the five would be getting a class. Maybe two, with the way that the pocket was bulging. That, in itself, was good news. Not everyone got a class, and in a place as small as Ouros, sometimes there wouldn't be a single new class for the whole cycle. But there would be one this cycle. Tulland's cycle.

"You look like you got the day off work." Altreck was a simple boy, one who measured most forms of happiness against the idea of successfully shirking his work. "What did you see?"

"Nothing. Shh," Tulland whispered. "Just wait."

The cleric turned from the crowd to face the boys, his hand hovering over his pocket. There were three boys to get through before he got to Tulland, all of whom were risks before the cleric passed them.

"And so, every once in a while, a new soul is needed to guard the wall between the light and the darkness." The cleric paused for just a moment in front of the first boy. His face fell and Tulland's lit as the man kept moving.

"To brave danger or hardship so that others might not have to."

The second boy was passed.

"And to sacrifice of one's own labor that others might benefit."

He passed the third. Tulland held his breath as the cleric's hand dropped to his pocket and he paused directly in front of him.

"And so we grant a class, that the one who claims it might protect us all, in one way or another."

Tulland shifted his forehead forward a bit, ready to take the crown and whatever came with it. He had heard that the clerics gave people some choice in their own class, and he knew he had a hell of a case for his own choice. It was all happening, starting now.

The priest stepped sideways once more before lightly placing the crown on Altreck's head.

"Congratulations, Altreck. Make us proud."

Tulland's ears were ringing with shock when he felt one of the other boys nudge him forward. He needed to clear the stage. Altreck looked like someone had slapped him with a fish. His dumb eyes were getting wider and wider as the cleric found simpler and simpler words to explain the situation with.

**They do like their idiots. Easier to control.**

*It's not fair. It's not.*

**It never is. The strong are wasted. The weak are rewarded. That has always been the Church's way.**

Tulland felt a hand on his arm as his uncle turned him to face away from Altreck. He heard the normal words he'd expect in that situation. That he should be grateful. That he should be glad for his friend. Tulland listened, nodding, until his uncle's limited communication skills ran dry and he was able somehow to shake loose and walk away.

The rest of the town would be busy in the gathering place for a while. He had the rest of the island to himself.

**Move quick. You know what you have to do.**

*Yes, I get it. Be quiet.*

It was a few minutes' walk to the church building, where the ancient stone arch sat at the edge, indestructible and eternal.

**You simply need to walk through. And then I can get you past things like the Church's control. I can make your fate your own. You simply have to choose it.**

*A class? You swear it?*

**A class and time enough away from the Church to learn it, and grow it. I swear it.**

Tulland looked at the arch. Everything, every lesson he had ever learned, said that it was evil. That the banishment of the System had been a good thing. That the Church had Tulland's best interests in mind. It was baked into every holiday, every ceremony, and every word that came out of any cleric's mouth in a public talk.

It was *known* that the System was evil, and that the Church was good. But was it impossible that the Church was wrong, or lying? And yes, the Church said that all the good in the world was their doing, but wouldn't it be in their interests to say that? What the System said made sense. It always had, now that Tulland thought about it.

He pushed his arm toward the arch, then pulled it back like he had almost touched a coal. There was something wrong here. He had been betrayed once today, and there was no telling if he was about to be betrayed a second time. If he could just talk again to his uncle or tutor for a few seconds. He knew that they'd explain things in a way that made sense.

And then the System showed Tulland one last thing. It reminded him of Altreck's eyes, wide with stupidity, as he claimed the prize that belonged to Tulland. As the boy took away Tulland's future without even knowing what it was, open-mouthed and slack-jawed all the while.

Tulland gulped and shot forward before he could rethink things. He would have the life he wanted, one way or another. And the Church would have nothing to say about it.

# CHAPTER THREE

# THE INFINITE

Tulland found himself in the flickering entrance room of the dungeon, and snapped his head back, barely in time to keep the glowing teeth of the weakest and slowest dungeon beast in existence from closing around his neck. He was still woozy enough from the teleport into this place that he wasn't sure he knew up from down, but he knew he couldn't let an entrance mote separate his head from the rest of his body.

In the histories, being laid low by the entrance motes happened so rarely that it was usually only mentioned as a joke. "He couldn't pass his motes" was something you said about the most absentminded, useless characters you knew. It was an implausible thing to assert, like saying that someone couldn't lace their own breeches or lost track of which side of the spoon was for scooping.

Even though Tulland almost lost his life a moment ago, he had a wide smile on his face. Dungeon classes were the rarest of the rare. The most costly. The most glorious. If the System had sent Tulland here, then his future was looking brighter by the moment.

The mote trying to rip his throat out didn't know any of that. Tulland forced himself not to flinch as the floating, fist-sized ball shot toward him again. He managed to steady himself just enough to leap to the side and barely make it out of the mote's range in time.

That was concerning. Tulland wasn't faster than normal, and he certainly didn't feel any stronger. He had read every book there was on classes, and was fully aware that he should feel and see differences in both stats, even if the class he had didn't focus on physical combat. But he didn't. He didn't feel different at all.

*What in the ice-cold hell is going on here?*

Tulland's head ached and throbbed as he tried to recall the events before just this moment. It was no good. Not only was it not working, it was distracting him from the immediate danger. He glanced around the floor for anything he could use as a weapon and came up empty. The entrance room was made from tightly fitted stones, each made to look as if they had been carved to near perfection. They were far too large and closely packed to pry loose and use. The rest of the room was bare.

As the mote turned and lunged again, Tulland reflexively slapped at it. He made contact, too, which surprised both him and the mote. Somewhere in the back of his mind, he heard the droning voice of his world mechanics tutor reminding him that this wasn't too far-fetched. The man had been unbelievably boring, but he had also read his tomes.

*There are those that say that the purpose of the entrance motes is to remind those chosen for a battle class of their newfound strength. Scholars have calculated the power of the motes to a high degree of certainty, and while their distribution of stats differs from ours, the total amount is virtually identical between each mote.*

*They are creatures as strong as a human would be without a class, greeting those who have just acquired one. It is as if the System itself is saying, "Here is one such as you once were. Glory in having surpassed them."*

Tulland would have loved to feel the glory. Unfortunately, he felt not even slightly different than he was used to. He had heard tall tales of first fights from dungeon delvers before, and while he didn't believe most of what they said, he did believe them when they talked about the rush they felt when their battle skills first guided their hands.

If there was any doubt in his mind that he was not experiencing the same thing, the wide, awkward strike he had just delivered to the mote was proof. He was somehow alone in a dungeon with no weapon, with the same stats, and without so much as a single skill to help him fight.

That didn't mean he had to lie down and die though. If the tutor was right, the mote and him were on even ground. And in an even fight, there was always at least a gambler's chance of surviving.

For starters, avoiding the teeth seemed like the most important thing. Tulland ducked around a pillar as the mote surged toward him again, then tried to round the entire stone column to get behind it. He wasn't nearly fast enough. The mote was quicker than him, if a little unfocused. It had floated away and turned by the time he circumnavigated the pillar, and lunged at him again.

*Now.*

Tulland sidestepped the lunge and punched as hard as he could, bringing his right fist in a wide haymaker. He missed. The mote was turning as he struck again with his left fist, trying his hardest to keep the motion from going wild as the adrenaline in his body tried to trick him into wild clawing and clubbing.

This punch hit, but a second too late to avoid disaster. The mote, seeing its target so close, chirped with joy and opened its mouth wide to reveal all of its jagged, glowing teeth. If there was a way to undo a panicked punch, Tulland didn't know how. His fist impacted with the back of the mote's throat, not hard enough to do any real damage but certainly with enough follow-through to allow the mote to clamp down on his entire hand, all the way behind his thumb.

Tulland screamed. The mote's teeth almost sizzled with unfocused mana as they worked past his skin to his muscle and bone. Although entrance motes had no skills, that didn't mean they had no power at all. Where humans came into the dungeon to slay them with weapons and armor, the beasts that populated the dungeon had thick hides, strong muscles, and magic-reinforced claws and teeth. Humans might have their tricks, but the monsters were at least their match.

The mote's bite didn't just damage the point of contact. Its mana worked its way through Tulland's body, slowly damaging the internal organs in its path. Given a frighteningly short amount of time, this nothing animal could and would kill Tulland.

*No. Not today. And not like this. It might be as powerful as a human, but it's not as strong or heavy as one. I have this.*

Tulland fought through the pain and swung his clenched left fist as hard as he could into the stone pillar at his side. The mote's teeth tore through his skin that much more. He clenched his jaw and swung again, and again. If there was one word Tulland would use to describe himself, it was *stubborn*. And this seemed like the exactly right time to be stubborn.

He could hear his own bones breaking as he slammed the insubstantial, almost dust-built frame of the mote that failed to shield him from the impact of his own punches. The fear and adrenaline racing through his body meant that hardly mattered. But as the bite from the mote worked deeper and deeper, it began to drain Tulland of his vitality.

*It's going to be close.*

Tulland's eyesight started to fail as he continued to pound his fist against the pillar. It had to stop soon. It had to.

*It . . . has . . . to.*

**Stop.**

And just like that, everything did. The light in the room stopped flickering, and the mana of the mote stopped eroding Tulland's life force. And Tulland flopped over to the floor, unconscious.


Tulland woke up sometime after that. Whether it was a minute or an hour was hard to determine, although the fact that his hand was still bleeding made him guess closer to a minute.

The mote's teeth had stopped glowing. Outside of that, the only indication that something very odd was afoot in this dungeon was that the torches on the wall had ceased to flicker. Their flames were frozen in place, as if they were paintings of fire instead of the real thing.

Tulland took a moment to reach into the pocket of his coat. His uncle always made him carry a cloth, something that he usually thought of as a troublesome custom. He was glad for it today as he bound it tight around the long gashes on the back of his hand and palm, then knotted it off.

"You stopped time?" Tulland asked. "I'm sorry to have kept you waiting."

**Time is never an issue for me. And if I might say, you've had a hard enough day to deserve a moment.**

The System was a quiet thing most of the time. When Tulland spoke to it, the System usually kept its tone devoid of most emotion. It turned out that was a lie, or at least something the thing had put effort into making happen. Right at the moment, its voice was brimming with emotion.

And of the worst kind. It was mocking him. Sneering, even.

Tulland stood, careful to push off his uninjured right hand. He straightened his clothes as well as he could in the dim light, glad he couldn't see the details of the mess he had surely become. If this was to be his first honest conversation with the System, he would give it all the decorum he could manage. Even if that wasn't very much.

"So I'm betrayed," Tulland said out loud. There wasn't much point in keeping his conversation with the System secret anymore.

**That's right.**

The System seemed pleased to confirm that. If he could have struck at it, Tulland would have, consequences be damned. The only thing he could do at the moment was to conceal his own feelings on the matter as much as possible, hopefully robbing it of its satisfaction.

"If I can ask, how much trouble am I in?"

**Not a small amount, I'm afraid. The combat restrictions have ceased, so you should be able to open your status screen now. Start there.**

As dizzy as the standing was making him, Tulland could manage that. He brought up his screen and glanced down at it, immediately wincing in dismay.

"No."

**I'm afraid so. I'm sorry.**

"I doubt that."

**Tulland Lowstreet**
**Class:** Farmer LV. 1
**Strength:** 10
**Agility:** 10
**Vitality:** 10
**Spirit:** 10
**Mind:** 10
**Force:** 10
**Skills:** Quickgrow LV. 0, Enrich Seed LV. 0, Strong Back LV. 0

"I'm dead," Tulland said as a matter of fact. There was a reason that the tutor had repeated the fact that motes were just about as strong as an average human. That reason was simple. Everything Tulland would meet past this point was more than that. Stronger. Faster. Tougher. More effective in whatever way it chose to do its killing.

Two of the skills he had would be no help at all. He knew them because everyone did. *Quickgrow* was an agricultural skill that made plants grow faster. *Enrich Seed* was a planting skill that helped plants take. In the outside world, they were skills that meant a life of hard, poor paying labor. In the dungeon, they were important only in that they had displaced combat skills that might have otherwise let Tulland defend himself.

*Strong Back*, at least, had some implications for survival. A person with that skill could lift a little more than their body stats implied, work a little longer, or recover a little faster from the wear and tear that hard work inflicted on a body. But alone, it wasn't enough. It was meant to lengthen a day's labor, not keep someone alive in battle.

In any other dungeon, Tulland would turn and use the door. But in any other dungeon, there would be a door to go through. The fact that there wasn't one here meant there was only one place Tulland could be.

**If you are saying you are dead, then you must know where you are.**

"I do. But if it's true, you might as well confirm it. I know you have to, anyway."

**I do.**

Tulland felt the information enter his mind. Part of why the Church had deemed the System evil was because of how the System supplied information when time was short. Like opening their status screen, a person would remember the information as if they had paused and read it from a transparent screen that appeared in front of them. Unlike their status, that memory was an illusion.

If the System willed it, the acquisition of the knowledge took no time at all, something that made it possible to learn and understand various effects on one's status during work or battle without even a moment's pause.

The System's message was outdated and confirmed that it had always been a liar, but didn't change a single other thing for Tulland. He was doomed.

---

**Dungeon Placement**

All who walk the world are touched by the System. Everyone from bakers, tailors, and builders to healers, couriers, and hunters. The class supplements the work done by people of the world, allowing for civilization to reach higher and higher apexes with each passing cycle.

From those, some are touched for a different work. These few are tasked with entering the dungeons to hunt that which they find there, bringing back treasures and new strength with which to grace their towns and cities.

And among these, a still rarer selection touches a select few. Though all enter the dungeons by the same gates, each warrior's destination is chosen for them. Most enter minor dungeons, places of wealth and adventure but ultimately limited in the scope of their purpose. Others are chosen for a dungeon whose end has never been seen, and which serves as both the yardstick for measuring mankind's progress and the purpose for their strength. You have been chosen.

From today, your very soul will be altered. Whatever your will for your own future once was, it now has a new focus that surpasses all others. You will plumb the depths of this place, mining its resources while pushing ever forward to prove your mastery of it.

*This is your noble purpose. Adventurer, you are welcomed to the Infinite.*

# CHAPTER FOUR

# Farmer's Tool

That's very nice. It's very inspirational." Tulland kicked at the ground. "It's a very good way to gloss over the fact that you've betrayed me."

**A System has to eat. And sacrificing the willing to the Infinite is one of the few ways we can do that.**

"The others being?"

**We also feed off accomplishment, although I expect little of that. I'm sorry that I could only spend the bare minimum I could on your class.**

"I guessed," Tulland spat.

**Which means that any successes you have from here on out, benefit me as much as they do you. What advice I can give from this point on, I'll give. What help I can manage for you, I'll manage. Because from the first major checkpoint in the dungeon on, you are a source of profit for me. Something that makes me stronger.**

"So you can go back and hurt my family?"

**Of course not. Why would I? But if you don't believe me, then know this. I simply do not have the strength to be both here and there at once. I am tied to this place as long as you are. It is only when you fall that I gain the power to return.**

That lined up with just enough of what Tulland knew about why System prophets were taken away that he was willing to provisionally believe it.

"And that first checkpoint is?"

**A skilled Cannian Knight. Fully armored. It guards the fifth floor and the entrance to the safe zone behind it.**

"And I have a flame's chance in a rainstorm of actually killing it, but you get paid out at long odds if I do?"

**That's correct.**

Tulland thought about giving up right then, just on the off chance that dying as early as possible would trap the System there in the dark. He knew it wouldn't work. The System would have planned for that. Wouldn't have risked it like that. He'd have to fight.

A Cannian Knight was the stuff of storybooks, but something that was known. Tulland had read about them. They were a difficult challenge for combat classes, something that required extra training and leveling to prepare for. Warriors who went head-to-head with them without perfect preparation tended to never make it home.

"And I'll have my bare hands and no combat abilities to help me. At all," Tulland said, keeping his voice as flat as possible.

**Not your bare hands. I am limited in what I can do, but I can at least help with that.**

Out of nowhere, Tulland felt a notification jump into existence, as well as the sneaking feeling that he was just a single wish away from some sort of permanent gain.

**Ambushed in the Dark**

You have been attacked while unarmed, unprepared, and, by most standards, inadequate for the task of defending yourself. Coming out of this battle alive was a long shot, and has enhanced the usual "First Victory" achievement earned by new adventurers.

**Rewards:** Beginner's Equipment Bundle (Enhanced), Additional Class Experience

**That should have given you a level-up. I advise you apply at least one of the five free points to your vitality to allow for regeneration.**

"Five points per level? That seems like a lot."

**For a battle class, it would be. For a workman's class, it's average. They generally need to be able to accomplish more with fewer levels.**

"Any advice for the other points?"

**No. And you wouldn't believe it if I gave it to you anyway. Use your judgment.**

Tulland applied two of the points to his vitality, feeling the relief as the bites on his hand clot almost immediately and begin to close. The actual wounds were not as serious as the damage to his overall health from the mana, but they were the main source of pain. Tulland planned on resting a long time to make sure he was tip-top before moving on, but at least now he wouldn't be in agony.

His head cleared up almost immediately as the pain dulled. Considering where to put his points, Tulland realized he needed more information before making that decision. Turning from the stat point distribution for the moment, he willed his Beginner's Equipment Bundle to materialize. There was both a thump and a clatter as the gear appeared out of midair and fell to the floor.

The first group was several pieces of cloth and leather, bound together by more cloth. He untied it, getting a description of each piece as he did.

---

**Farmer's Garb, Cloth**

A singlet of durable, damage resistant material. This novice-level equipment is meant to prevent incidental damage from thorns, falls, and the kinds of scrapes common in manual labor.

As a piece of workman's equipment, duplicates of this equipment are available from the System at any time. A complete Farmer's Garb set (with hat and boots) slightly enhances its wearer's endurance and the durability of the set itself.

---

**Farmer's Boots, Leather**

As a part of the Farmer's Garb set, these boots circumvent normal class restrictions on leather equipment. They are classified as workman's equipment, and are replaceable.

The Farmer's Boots maximize traction on a variety of surfaces and are made of thick, durable leather.

---

"I'm restricted to cloth?" Tulland asked before he could stop himself. "I suppose that makes sense."

**Yours was not intended as a combat class.**

Tulland sighed. "It doesn't matter. Let me check out the other gear."

The rest of his gear consisted of a pack and a wide-brimmed hat, the latter of which he wore only because it completed the set. Inside the pack, there were a few days of rations, a help until he could figure out some other source of food.

Having finished donning the clothes and putting his old, human-made street clothes into his pack, Tulland moved on to the harder item that had skittered a few feet away across the floor earlier.

> **Farmer's Tool (Shovel, Hoe, Pitchfork, Scythe, Collapsible)**
> The Farmer's Tool is meant to combine the most basic aspects of a farmer's work into one implement. At your will, the tool will change from one implement to another. When stored, the tool shrinks to something that can be easily carried on your back.
>
> The tool itself has above-average durability, and is more durable in a less easily damaged form, such as its shovel function. It gains no more or less from its user's stats than any mundane object.

It was dealer's choice on stats then. If the tool rewarded agility or strength, Tulland would have reason to bet more on one or the other. As it stood, he would put a point in each, and put his last remaining point in agility, leaving him a little faster than he was strong.

> **Tulland Lowstreet**
> **Class:** Farmer LV. 1
> **Strength:** 11
> **Agility:** 12
> **Vitality:** 12
> **Spirit:** 10
> **Mind:** 10
> **Force:** 10
> **Skills:** Quickgrow LV. 0, Enrich Seed LV. 0, Strong Back LV. 0

Tulland was pretty sure farmers benefited from at least some spirit and force, which drove their plant-enhancement abilities. But getting to that point meant he would have to survive long enough to till some soil and plant his seeds, which was a very uncertain prospect at the moment. For now, he would put every point he could in the stats that kept him from getting torn apart, and ignore his agricultural purpose entirely.

**The reward is not much. But it's all that I'm willing to do for you at this time, and a worse bet than I should be making anyway.**

"I'm not thanking you," Tulland stated before softening his tone a bit. "So what now? I just march forward and try to survive?"

**No.**

"No?"

**No. In a conventional dungeon, you might be able to simply survive. The Infinite, however, pulls its ordained ever forward. Mere complacent survival has only one result in the Infinite that I can inform**

**you of it without restrictions. If you dally, if you do not improve, you will simply die.**

"Sounds like I will anyway. I'd imagine that the pacing is geared at actual combatants. I'll just get shoved off a cliff that I can never avoid, and you won't get that big payout anyway," Tulland said, sensing weakness in the System's words.

**Let me see what I can do.**

Tulland kept his mouth shut. Pushing his case wouldn't fix anything. If the System was willing to help, he would stay out of its way.

**You are very, very lucky that fixing this was free. Examine your notification.**

---

**Diminished Compulsion (Passive)**
The Infinite pulls ever forward, pushing its ordained toward greater and greater heights or deeper and deeper doom. Often, they find both. You are no exception, but a negotiation between the System and Dungeon System has resulted in an adjustment to the pace of this pull.
You will find that at all stages, your compelled movement forward will be somewhat slower than others, granting you months or weeks of extra time to prepare for each new challenge.

---

"Will that be enough?" Tulland asked.

**There's no way to tell. Not even I know the future. And now our conversation has reached its limit. Good luck, Tulland.**

"Just like that? I have more questions. A lot more," Tulland said, careful not to let the panic enter his voice.

There was no answer.

"System? System?" Tulland looked desperately around the dim light in the space. He hadn't realized how much of a help it was to not be alone in this place, or how used to the System's company he had become in the last few weeks. He suddenly felt very cold. "Please? Please don't go."

There was no answer from the System. Instead, Tulland felt an impact against his back. It was another mote, one that had likely been held back by the System's stopping of time, and one that was now free to attack. Luckily, it failed to find purchase with its teeth against the flat of Tulland's back on the first impact. He whirled around before it could try again, brandishing his tool.

The rotation of his body brought the head of the tool against the mote, clanging as it cut off the monster's second bite. The mote was flung off to the side where it impacted hard against a stone pillar, then immediately turned to attack again. The motes were not much for tactics, it seemed. They simply attacked.

Tulland dodged away and bought himself a moment to send a mental command to the Farmer's Tool to turn into a shovel for maximum attack area. The tool dissolved into a sort of mist above the handle, apparently to give it the flexibility to change into another implement entirely. And as the System had indicated, it wasn't a very quick process.

When the mote came in for a new attack, Tulland had his shovel ready. He swung, this time on purpose and at a downward angle. He timed the impact poorly, which meant the shovel head actually pushed the mote toward him as the shovel continued its arc. It would have been a dangerous thing had not the mote been absolutely destroyed by the blow. He watched as it bounced off the stone floor, then began to dissolve away, presumably returning its energy to the dungeon.

But it wouldn't return all of it. Some of the energy went to Tulland. Surprising enough to him was the fact that this wasn't the kind of thing that was represented in numbers. He could feel the fullness that the energy brought with it, and vaguely sense the distance to the next step. Further details were guesswork.

It was much smaller progress than he expected, but Tulland could work with that. The motes were at least manageable, unless they were hiding some surprises. With his new tool, he should be able to take them down without much risk. The same could not be said for whatever was at the end of the corridor leading out of this room.

Tulland turned his Farmer's Tool into a pitchfork. It would make for a better use of his agility stat, especially as his vitality returned more and more of his life force to him.

The third mote appeared from the darkness as the tool was still changing. Tulland abandoned any pretense of dodging or fighting and simply jogged away, leading it around the room as it attempted to keep up with his newfound speed. After a few more moments, the Farmer's Tool audibly clicked as it fully morphed into its new form, and Tulland turned as he choked up on the handle and thrust the pitchfork's three tines at the mote.

The tines hit, piercing through the mote's mouth and impaling it. It struggled for a few moments on the spike before it stopped moving, began dissolving, and slipped off the pitchfork just in time for Tulland to turn to face the next enemy.

The room seemed to have an endless supply of motes, and Tulland's extra two points' worth of vitality was perfect for the level of exertion he was using to take them down. Tulland was fine with that. As far as he was concerned, it didn't matter if it would take thousands of kills instead of hundreds to hit his next level. He would stay in this room as long as he possibly could, grinding away safely and getting as strong as possible before he moved on.

If that's what it took to survive, that's what Tulland would do. If he had no battle skills, he would just over level to make up for the uselessness of his class. But if one thing was sure, it was that he would put no effort into anything but getting stronger. No matter what, he'd do absolutely no farming.

# CHAPTER FIVE

# FLOOR 1

**D**ammit. You have to be kidding me."

A hundred kills into his wholesale slaughter of the motes, Tulland was half of the way to becoming level two. The extra five stat points would be huge at his current level of strength. The first five points and a weapon were enough to demote the motes from a serious threat all the way down to a farmable source of experience. Another five would provide that much more margin of safety in the Infinite.

Except now that was over.

---

**Experience Source Limited**

All sources of experience are eventually used up. Dungeon divers who seek to become stronger must seek better and tougher enemies, or else find their progress stalled as they fruitlessly slaughter enemies they have long since dominated.

In your case, this effect is much quicker to come into play. For a non-combat class, the experience you can gain from combat sources in general is conditionally capped. Only a certain percentage of the experience needed to progress to the next level may come from combat sources, with a few exceptions.

**Once you have reached the limit, you may proceed to gain the experience needed to reach your next level in one of a few ways.**

1. While enemies appropriate to your level have their experience capped,

enemies that are stronger than what you would normally be expected to face at your current level of strength will never have their experience rewards limited.

2. Experience gained from the defeat of enemies is capped, but experience from achievements is not, whether it comes from killing enemies or any other source.

3. As you might expect, the experience you get from class appropriate activities (in your case, farming) is never limited.

Tulland continued killing the motes as he considered what he had read. By now, the fighting was a function of his muscle memory and didn't distract from his considerations much.

If his experience income from the motes was really tapped out, he had only a few options. The first would be to sit around and attack them some more, hoping for an achievement related to killing a huge amount of them. That seemed risky to him. If he hadn't gained an achievement from killing a hundred of a nothing enemy that people usually only killed one or two of, then he doubted a thousand would be any different.

And as great as his extra points in vitality were, they wouldn't negate the fact that Tulland would eventually have to sleep. He was already exhausted from a full day's emotional drama, a fight for his life, and healing up from the same fight. And then he had spent the next few hours doing consistent cardio. He was in good shape and better now with stats backing him up, but that had its limits.

Tulland hesitated anyway, killing another dozen of the motes as he dilly-dallied and avoided facing the reality of his situation. Eventually, he steeled himself to move forward. Honestly, he had thought about staying in the mote room for longer, perhaps even a couple of months. But there was a steady pull on his will that drove him forward. He was able to resist the dungeon's compulsion toward progress at the moment, but he knew without a doubt it was there, urging him on.

The sole exit to the room was a stone hallway heading out of it. It wasn't worth taking one of the torches from the wall, even if they could be somehow pried loose. The hallway was well enough lit that his eyes, which were now adjusted to the dark, could handle it. Tulland walked at a brisk pace down the hallway, unfollowed by the motes and holding the points of his pitchfork in front of him as a threat to anything that might jump at him out of the dim darkness ahead.

He might as well have not. After five minutes of walking, nothing had attacked at all. It was only then, as he began to feel comfortable, that the world itself changed around him. In one blink of his eyes, a step that had begun in the dim stone realm of the entrance ended within blinding bright light, warmth, and the sound of the wind.

Tulland's eyes adjusted quickly to the light, if not the scene the light illuminated. He was at the edge of a forest, standing at the beginnings of an endless prairie of tall grass. Everything from the sky to the grass and all the way to the trees had a purple-pink tinge to it, something Tulland attributed to the light itself. The sight would have been beautiful if it weren't filled with unidentified dangers.

> **Floor 1 Entered**
> **Objective:** Search for exits while gaining what you can from this floor's inhabitants.
> **Traits:** No special effects or rules apply to this floor.
> **Access:** Travel between this floor and the next is unrestricted in both directions.
> *The entrance zone is lost to you. You may not return to it by any possible means.*

"Well, that's that, I guess."

Whatever safety he might have claimed in the last zone was gone. Tulland looked out at the prairie, but as far as he could see there were no immediate threats. The scope of the open space in front of him was almost disorienting. After a lifetime in a world that was firmly bordered by a mountain and the sea, this much space was a bit mind-boggling, even if Tulland had known it was possible.

He started walking. Whatever was waiting for him here was going to be easier to face while knowing the lay of the land. Tulland stuck to the border of the open field and the forest, judging that he might be able to hide in either one from threats that came from the other.

He saw the first beast before it saw him, somehow. At the edge of the forest, looking out into the prairie, was a furry creature that resembled a cross between a badger and a goat, if badger-goats looked sharp at the end of every extremity. Tulland hid behind a nearby tree and observed the behavior of his latest problem.

Though dungeon-related talk came up very rarely, Tulland's tutor had mentioned that dungeon floors were not the same for everyone, even in the Infinite. Tulland was the same as any other boy on Ouros in the sense that he had read every single book available on known dungeon beasts, but he had never seen this particular monster before. Some floors were the same for every-one, like the fifth with its knight or the tenth, which housed the serpent. But others were seen by few, and even fewer survived them.

Whatever world he was seeing, it wasn't a place that anyone had ever both-ered to describe to a scholar once they made their escape. Or else, and worse, they had never escaped at all.

Tulland decided to be different. He wouldn't fail, or at least he wouldn't fail to this first beast. He walked slowly at a diagonal to it, getting more out of its line of sight as he crept deeper into the woods and positioned himself to the back of it.

The beast was either inattentive or deafened by the breeze, and didn't notice as Tulland approached. When he was finally in range, he took a big step and committed every bit of weight and force he had to a surprise thrust with his pitchfork. The weapon hit and penetrated into the animal, but not nearly as much as he had expected it to. It wheeled around, pulling itself off the three points of the tool and screaming out in an alarmed, high-pitched screech.

The system's description triggered then, feeding into Tulland's brain auto-matically as he tried to recover himself enough for a second strike.

> **Razored Lunger**
> Sure-footed and quick, the Razored Lunger is a grazing animal that usually subsists on grasses and shrubs. It is, however, an opportunistic carnivore that is more than willing to feed on prey animals it views as weaker than itself. *An attack sufficiently strong to demonstrate real risk to the animal will send it fleeing. Finishing it in one strike is recommended, where possible.*

Tulland pulled away as the animal sprang toward him, but not nearly quickly enough. It passed him to the side, ripping with its claw as it did. The legs of the Farmer's Garb performed admirably for what they were, but there was only so much cloth could do against the razor sharpness of the monster's claws. Tulland now sported deep, painful cuts to his leg that failed to actually hobble him, probably thanks to his new stats.

He wheeled and stabbed out at the animal again, missing badly as it effort-lessly dodged, flung itself through the air, and struck four deep gashes in Tulland's side as it sliced through his garb above his ribs. It wasn't running, which meant it knew that Tulland wasn't a threat. Instead, it was acting like it was trying to take him down before he ran, so as not to lose out on a windfall meal.

*I'm toast. The System wins.*

Tulland knew that for a fact. He was slower than this thing, less durable, and less able to hurt it than the other way around. Unless it was a lot closer to death than it looked, fighting it was a death sentence. He slid back on the handle of the pitchfork, holding it out between him and the beast to create distance as he considered his options.

In the end, there was only one. Tulland ran, hoping the thing was slower in a sprint than it was in combat footwork. And it was, if only just. Tulland managed to keep ahead of it for several eternity-long seconds as it huffed along behind him, swiping at his legs and missing by the barest margins possible.

He wasn't fast enough to get away. The sprint meant the Razored Lunger didn't get many chances to add more gashes to Tulland, but it did get some. One stumbling step across uneven ground slowed Tulland for just long enough to let the animal swipe at his other leg, leaving him bloody on both sides as he ran. Another couple swipes would do more than leave Tulland bleeding and in pain. It would injure him enough to slow him, which would mean almost instant death.

Given the level of threat, it wasn't really a decision when Tulland saw the briars growing ahead. At least that's what they looked like, though the thorns were longer and the stems were thicker. They were a vicious, terrible-looking plant, advertising nothing so much as horrific pain and torment to all that fell into their domain.

But they were thick and covered a lot of ground. It was his only chance.

As the Razored Lunger blazed after him, Tulland managed to close the gap on the briars, then turned as he ran along the border of them, looking for any gap he could exploit. Here and there, a longer-than-average thorn or a branch that grew out farther than the others would catch him, ripping his clothes and his skin as it did.

But the monster was running a step farther away from the briars than it needed to, which Tulland took as a good sign. If it didn't want to bother with them, he might just be able to escape through them, provided they didn't impale him as he tried.

Sooner than he liked, that was no longer a choice he could put off. Ahead of him, the shape of the hedge changed, growing out into a sort of hook that blocked his path forward. He simply didn't have the time to run around it. It was either going through the thorns, or facing the sure death the monster represented.

He had no choice.

Tulland jumped out of the frying pan, and immediately began screaming as the briars provided their own sort of fire.

## CHAPTER SIX

# HADES BRIAR

After the first several seconds, it became clear that the Razored Lunger wasn't following Tulland into the briar thicket. It was what he had wanted. It should have been good. It should have been an unquestioned win.

The victory would have been easier to remember if Tulland's entire body wasn't being perforated by thorns. He was cut in far more places than he could count, stabbed in others, and completely immobilized by the pain and terror of moving any farther. For a few long minutes, he sat there in agony and tried not to writhe. He was completely filled with fear that he'd just die there, impaled by thorns as he slowly bled out.

**Quite the showing. I'm very impressed.**

*Oh, god, shut up. Be quiet.* Tulland refused to talk out loud so the thorns couldn't work their way further into him. *Don't you have enough from me?*

**What's enough? As it stands, I'll barely get enough energy off you to subvert a small territory, or to push a few divisions of monster troops through the ever-cursed shield that your precious Church put in my way. I was hoping you'd at least show me the tiniest bit of competence.**

*Rich, considering what you gave me to work with.*

**It is a poor soldier who places the blame on his sword. You've already given up. Believe me, there are those who would still be pushing through the pain.**

*Oh, yeah? Who?*

**Altreck, for one. I considered him for your role, you know. The only reason I didn't go for it is he had a certain simplicity to his moral fiber that**

**would have prevented me from making much headway. But he certainly wouldn't resign himself to death without even trying.**

It shouldn't have worked. It was a simple, transparent ploy aimed directly at Tulland's pride, meant to make him act where he otherwise would not. The System was throwing a cheap shot, a jab with a jagged knife at an already open wound. Tulland should have dismissed it out of hand.

But he couldn't. As unfair as it was, Tulland couldn't stand to imagine Altreck doing better than he was. He risked his eyes by opening them, only to find one of them already didn't work. And, a few feet in front of him, there was a small gap in the thorns. Not a big one, but a place where he might just be able to lie down with only a few thorns in his body instead of hundreds, and give his vitality-induced regeneration the hours it would need to patch him back together.

The small distance looked like it was a thousand miles away, and he would still be trapped when he got there. But the System was right. Altreck would try to get there. The terror of the pain to come wouldn't matter to him because he wouldn't even be able to imagine it. He'd just do it. And he would survive, at least for a while.

Tulland closed his eyes again, braced himself, and shoved his body as hard as he could toward the clearing. The thorns tore away chunks of his skin as he screamed again and again. They couldn't stop him from pushing forward with his feet and pulling with his arms wherever they could find purchase. The leather boots and his now ragged cloth garb stopped some of the thorns, and if they had been conventional plants, Tulland thought his gear might have stopped nearly all of them. But against the monster briars of the dungeon, there was only so much that they could do.

He never knew when he made it. Tulland woke up a while later on the ground soaked with his own blood, but out of the worst of the thorns. Almost immediately, he started pulling fragments of the spikes out of his skin, passing out from the pain and blood loss more than once before he finally woke up, feeling terrible but mostly healed. His left eye still didn't work, and he had no idea if it ever would again. And he was still bleeding from more places than he could count. But all in all, it seemed he would survive.

Tulland lay there, watching the world spin as his body tried to replace the blood it had lost and was still losing. He made no attempts to move as the hours passed until he finally felt more or less himself.

Only then did he open his right eye and take a look at his surroundings. There wasn't much to see, but the System gave him descriptions for the few things it could latch onto at that distance.

> **Hades Briar**
>
> The Hades Briar is the most basic and common of barriers to movement in flora-heavy tower floors. Its near omnipresence has spelled the doom of monsters and adventurers alike, as it presented them with a painful distraction or blocked an otherwise open avenue of retreat.
>
> The stiff and strong needles of the Hades Briar are lined with thousands of almost invisible hooked barbs that maximize a single prick's damage and greatly magnify the pain they inflict. They bear a venom that further amplifies the suffering of their victims.

> **Hades Briar Fruit**
>
> Technically edible, the Hades Briar's fruit is a heavy, nutrient-rich affair. It makes no attempts to be appetizing, as the animals stupid or desperate enough to look to it as a food source simply do not care about that kind of thing.

Gently and ever so slowly, Tulland reached out his hand for the fruit. He had realized something about his regeneration when he woke up. It didn't work for free. His wrist was half the size it once was, and looked like a twig amid the briars. He imagined the rest of his body in the same state, especially with his stomach so empty that the ache of it was radiating through most of his body. The new slimness worked in Tulland's favor as he only managed to prick his hand a few more times before he broke the dry fruit loose from a stubborn, malicious thorn branch.

Carefully, he brought it to his mouth, popping the whole fruit in and chewing slowly. The system description was true. The fruit was technically edible, but it also tasted like a mouthful of sand mixed with bile. He chewed it anyway. Something about being ripped to shreds by a thousand needles had put a new sort of perspective on things like unpleasantness and hardship. If he could handle that, he could handle this.

*At least the System wasn't lying about it being nutritious. That was . . . dense.*

Tulland's stomach was now complaining for different reasons Instead of crying out for food. He was slightly queasy, but the influx of sugar to his blood was doing good work within seconds.

He was fed, for the moment, and safe from anything but the most thorn-resistant enemies. All he had to resolve was the small problem of being trapped in a patch of sharp botanical death, and he'd be doing okay.

Very, very carefully, Tulland began to bunch up his body, making as much room in the cavity near his head as he could. Enduring the pain from several thorns, he reached deep into the thicket where he had landed after his first dive in and retrieved his Farmer's Tool. After a little bit of wiggling and yanking, his once-again bleeding hands held the tool, now free and ready to get to work, to his chest.

Reacting to his intent, the tool shifted forms, turning indistinct for a few moments as the tines retracted, reformed, and expanded into the shape of a scythe. The briars were thick, but there was still a bit of space between each branch and the next. If he could cut and pack them, he could slowly expand the space he was lying in.

For an hour, Tulland suffered as he slowly chipped away at dozens of thorns and branches with his scythe. He cut away the stuff to his side first, then carved away at the roof above him, packing them into a compressed stack of sticks. For a while, it was an open question of whether or not it would work. He was making a small amount of breathing room for himself, but sooner or later, he would have packed the branches down to as compact a space as his inadequate leverage would allow.

*If I don't have enough room to move better by then, I'm stuck. I'll be able to choose between starving to death in here, or bleeding out on the other side until a monster comes by to end things.*

By some miracle, Tulland managed to finally clear enough branches to sit up. Just that was a major improvement, allowing him to finally get something that could almost be called a swing into play. In another half hour, he had managed to clear out enough space to stand. Converting his tool back to a shovel, he was able to use it as a sort of impermeable step, stand on the piles of briar he had made, and use his weight to crush them even flatter.

And then, in a way that would have felt silly to him back at home, Tulland used his newfound room to take revenge on the plant. He spent hours clearing out space, finding places that the Hades Briar connected to the ground, slicing them, and putting them on the pile. As he found the disgusting fruits, he ate them to hurry along his healing process, and eventually had about twenty square feet of room in which to exist, mostly clear of thorns or anything that could hurt him.

Exhausted, he collapsed on his backside on the ground, tossing his scythe over toward the stack of briar branches that made up the far side of his prison. He absentmindedly picked at one of the fruits in his hand, considered eating it, then decided his stomach just couldn't take any more of the acidic flesh at that moment. He tossed it forward idly, letting it slam into the ground.

He was still probably dead, really, or at the very best trapped in the briars for the foreseeable future. And yet, he had seen no changes to his useless status screen at all. He had a skill that nurtured seeds, a skill that helped plants, and no use for either while surrounded by a plant that had no other purpose than to kill him.

Smiling in a kind of wry despair, Tulland pointed his arm at the fruit on the ground and thought about his *Enrich Seed* skill. That was all it took to activate it. He felt something pass out of him, found himself dimly more aware of the plant, and gained a new level of fatigue beyond his already deep exhaustion.

*There's nothing more I can do while feeling like this. I've survived. I've eaten. I'll try again in the morning,* Tulland reasoned.

Tulland crawled to the clearest patch of ground he had, laid down his head, and found himself asleep before he had time to worry about whether future survival would be possible.

There was no morning on the first floor of the dungeon. When Tulland opened his eyes again, it was the same kind of light as when he had fallen asleep. And as made sense for his new life, he woke up violently ill. The fruits had not agreed with him in more ways than one. He wasn't exactly poisoned, but his body was treating the food much like it would treat spoiled meat, with the same messy consequences.

Somehow, he made it through that too. An hour later, when there was nothing left to come out of him, Tulland found himself weak and broken on the ground, having lost whatever benefit eating the fruits had given him and some besides. The stuff wasn't quite poison, but only just missed the mark.

*That settles it. It's only a matter of time now.* Tulland coughed weakly as he lay on his back on the ground. *No way to get food, and not enough energy left to do anything else. You win, System.*

**I hate to say this, but perhaps not quite yet.**

*No?*

**No. Look to your left.**

Tulland did, if for no other reason than he had nothing else to do while he waited for the end to come. There, growing peacefully, was a brand-new briar, just as spiny and brutal-looking as all its brothers.

But, somehow, this one was a different color.

# CHAPTER SEVEN

# System Communications

I *t's green*, Tulland thought.

**It's more than that. Take a look. A real look.**

Tulland did. It took a moment for a new description to pop.

---

**Hades Briar (Cultivated)**

By some incredibly unlikely confluence of circumstances, a seed of the Hades Briar plant has been sown and enriched by a farming class. Since these seeds have no way to travel from the Infinite to the outside world, this should not have been possible.

In any case, the resulting creation is an unpredictable, unknown sort of thing. In many senses, it is identical to the wild plant it descends from. In some other important ways, it may not be. The Infinite is as in the dark about that as you are.

---

"Why does it seem like the Infinite is the one speaking there?" Tulland asked, out loud this time. "In my system messages, I mean."

**Because it is. I'm not the System of this place. Why would you think I was?**

"You gave me my class and my equipment. It seemed as if you were fulfilling your function."

**I was. That much, at least, is my obligation toward anyone this dungeon considers to be a child of my world. But most of the functions of this**

place are its own. I can influence, in some ways. I can advise. But only as a visitor might.

"Should you be telling me this?"

Tulland felt the System communicating what could only be described as a kind of shrug.

**Why wouldn't I? You'll be dead soon enough. And even if you managed to delay that event, I'll end up with your power eventually. So long as you die in the Infinite, I'll be on the winning side of things. And humans tend to die, over a long enough time frame.**

Tulland stared at the plant as the System droned on. It was greener than the rest of the briars, and looked a little something else that was hard to define. He couldn't think of a plant that nasty as friendly, exactly. But it seemed less actively malicious, at least.

"Hard to see how this is going to help." Tulland glanced at his status screen. "It didn't even level the *Enrich Seed* skill."

**It wouldn't. Attacks don't level attacking skills either, at least until they do damage to their targets. This plant is not yet grown.**

"I could make it grow, I guess." Tulland considered what it would feel like to cast another agricultural spell from his already empty tanks of energy. "But it would be about the last thing I could do."

**It doesn't seem like much of a risk. Without some level of miracle, you won't survive anyway. It might be a mercy, in some ways, if you used the last of your energy and hastened things along.**

Tulland sighed and stretched out his hand. The System was a betrayer and a murderer, but that didn't mean it was wrong in all ways. This was the thing he could do. He thought of his *Quickgrow* skill, and used it.

As the energy flowed out of him, Tulland felt something go very wrong. If his soul could have made a cracking noise, he was confident it would have. A pain welled up from so deep inside him that he couldn't begin to identify the source.

**Oh my. That's interesting in a way you don't see very often.**

As the System said its piece, Tulland blacked out once again, fully expecting it to be the last time.

| Level Up! |
| --- |

| Level Up! |
| --- |

| Skill Level Up! |
| --- |

**Skill Level Up!**

**Skill Level Up!**

**Skill Level Up!**

**Skill Level Up!**

Tulland's eyes were hazy almost to the point of blindness when he blinked them open. In his cloudy vision, he could see a bit of green ahead of him, and a bit of red, mixed into an indistinct painting that bore no meaning to him. He was dizzy, and far beyond being able to rouse himself to care about the mess of notifications waiting to be read.

**Tulland.**

He ignored the System as best he could. He was too tired to care.

**Tulland, listen to me. Eat the damn fruit! Now. This moment.**

*No fruit. Sleep.*

**If you sleep, you will die, you fool.**

*Is okay. Don't mind. Sleep.*

**Then I will find your uncle first. On my return, he will be the first I will make pay.**

Tulland barely remembered his uncle. To the extent Tulland did, his uncle was a source of stew. And scolding. But mostly stew. Tulland's stomach cramped at the very thought of food.

*System said something about eating,* Tulland thought to himself. *Where's the food?*

**I already told you, you idiot! In front of you. The big red thing in front of your face.**

He reached for the fruit, then missed it on his first three tries and barely caught it on his fourth. With an effort that almost killed him, Tulland managed to break it loose from whatever held it, bruising it in the process and wetting his fingers with juice. He flopped his arm back toward himself and, by some miracle, got the fruit close enough to his mouth to close his jaws around it.

*It's sweet.*

**Chew, you twit.**

Tulland chewed, flooding his mouth with sugar as he worked his jaw back and forth. He was too weak to swallow, but some of the juice found its way down his throat anyway. His stomach growled as the faint trickle of nutrition hit it, and Tulland's arms and legs became all pins and needles as the tiny bit of sugar hitting his bloodstream gave his circulation just enough oomph to wake them up.

"What in the hell is happening?" Tulland swallowed down the rest of the fruit and flexed his hands. They felt terrible, but they worked again. "I feel like I'm coming back from the dead."

**Close to it. Can you see?**

Tulland blinked a few times. Things were still a bit fuzzy, but they were coming into focus. Above him, stretching to the sky, was a deep green plant, one that had two more fruits growing from it. He wasted no time reaching out and grabbing them, shoving them into his mouth and mashing them down to pulp before swallowing the lot of available food in one go.

**It seems you can. What does the Dungeon System say of the plants?**

Tulland looked. The description had changed substantially.

---

**Hades Briar (Cultivated)**

The usual Hades Briar is a thing of death. It cuts like a sword, and its fruits burn beings who are foolish enough to try to eat them. It is an entirely evil plant, one designed to do nothing but bring sorrow to those who run across it.

Yet somehow, that has changed. Drawing on the influence of the skills of a farming class, the fundamental nature of the plant has been changed as it took the first step toward domestication. The thorns grow just as sharp as they ever did, but nestled among them is a fruit of actual value, something that provides good without a more than equal amount of ill.

The identity and characteristics of this new plant are still in flux, and may change substantially as the circumstances around their creation continue to evolve.

---

And with that new description came an explanation for the notifications Tulland had seen. A new screen's worth of information slipped into his mind and attempted to explain what had happened.

---

**Cultivation Successful!**

For the cultivation of a new plant unknown to this world's agriculture, you have been granted a substantial amount of experience. The skills related to the cultivation efforts also advanced significantly.

---

"Huh." Tulland looked dumbly at the notification. "What does that even mean?"

**It means you live. And that you have, against expectations, managed to draw lightly on the power of the Infinite to fuel your own growth.**

"Ah." Tulland tried to stand, then sat back down heavily as his head continued to swim. But it was at least clear enough to think. "Though I don't understand why you helped me get the fruit. You can't touch my uncle. He's much too far into Church territory. Why lie? You could have just left me to die. It would have come soon enough."

**Perhaps. But a difference of a day or so is short, in the way I reckon time. And you've piqued my curiosity.**

"Oh? You aren't afraid I'll survive?"

**No. Why would I be?**

"So long as I do, you're stuck here. I could make it to a safe zone. I could stay there."

**Ha! Is that what you were thinking, all this time? I've waited centuries for smaller opportunities than this. A lifetime in a safe zone makes little difference to me. And you will find the Infinite has ways of dealing with those who stall and loiter. It always compels them toward their eventual end. No, Tulland. I'll have what I want. The only question is how much I'll gain.**

Tulland's body was still recovering, but his mind had cleared substantially. After a day's danger, he was beginning to realize that he had been a fool, just as the System suggested. In the heat of the moment and the shock of the change, it had never occurred to him to question whether the proven liar with access to his mind and with practice in deceiving him might still be doing just that.

It seemed likely enough that the System had something to gain from bringing him here, and that it couldn't have whatever prize it sought until later. Perhaps that was when he died, or perhaps it wasn't. And it was possible the System got more rewards the longer he survived, with no possible way to lose out and no escape for Tulland.

But it also might not be so. Tulland might be able to find another way, somehow. Although he almost certainly wouldn't with the System reading and poisoning every thought he had.

Just as he considered evicting the System, something new happened.

**No, Tulland. I'm your only hope here. You can't survive, but . . .**

Tulland ignored him as he brought up a new notification that came before his eyes. This was different from the information screens that slipped into his mind. The screen was something real, or real enough as it floated in the air in front of him. And it was more than he had hoped.

> **Deactivate System Communications?**
> For a delver into the Infinite, communications with your world's System are a voluntary thing. If it is your preference, you may choose to transfer all of the normal functions fulfilled by your world's System to the Dungeon System in charge of the dungeon itself.
>
> This will not completely sever your relationship with the System of your world, as it has claims on certain rewards related to your progress through the Infinite. You can, however, choose to limit your world System's access to your thoughts and the amount it is allowed to speak to you.
>
> Would you like to do so now?

**You would be a fool to pass up what little help I'm willing to provide you, Tull . . .**

The very moment Tulland gave the Infinite the go-ahead to cut off the System's power, it did. He waited a few minutes, half expecting that the System was playing some elaborate prank. When it failed to talk, he eased the limitations enough to allow it to talk, while still restricting its access to his mind.

**That was foolish, Tulland. Do you really think you can do this alone? Have I not been helpful thus far?**

*The minimum amount, maybe. Don't you think?* Tulland thought rather than spoke. After a ten-second wait, the System spoke in his mind again in a tone dripping with annoyance.

**You know I can't hear you. You've won that little victory. Congratulations. I didn't think the Infinite would inform you of that little fact so easily.**

# CHAPTER EIGHT

# RAZORED LUNGER

Tulland turned off the communication channel to the System again. That was as good of confirmation as he'd get that he really could cut the System off. If everything was as it appeared to be, the Dungeon System that governed the Infinite was not inherently aligned with the interests of the System from his world. He wasn't sure that the enemy of his enemy was really his friend, but there was no harm in treating it that way for now.

If it all ended up being a trick, there wasn't a whole lot he could do about it anyway. He wasn't any worse off than before, and on the off chance that everything was how it appeared to be, he now had a small possibility that there might just be some way out of this.

Or at least a way to keep the System from hurting his world. Even if there wasn't a way out of this situation for Tulland, and there probably wasn't, Tulland could try to keep the System from getting its payoff. To do that, he would have to survive long enough to see other people. To talk to them. The stories said the Infinite was an intersection between worlds, that people came to try themselves against the only challenge that never ended. Some of them had to know things he didn't. And maybe some of them knew how to beat the System.

At the least, he needed to know how the System sent him here. For all that the messages it had sent said he had been ordained for the Infinite, everything he had ever heard claimed that admission to this greatest of dungeons was a voluntary sort of thing. That, at least, was a mystery he'd need to work out.

But for now, Tulland needed to get to work. From what he had seen, there was no chance of him beating one of those Razored Lungers in normal combat. But he had some ideas of how he might take one in an unfair fight, given enough time. And being in the middle of one of these briar patches meant he might just have enough time.

After the better part of a day of cutting the briars, Tulland finally found water. He knew there must be some somewhere, given the size of the briar patch. The source of it ended up being an underground seep of sorts, a place where the water didn't make it to the surface in liquid form but merely dampened the ground.

Shifting his tool to a shovel, Tulland got to digging. Frequent applications of his *Quickgrow* talent kept his pet briar growing and producing fruits, and he was eating them as soon as they popped up. That gave him plenty of energy to dig at the seep until it was deep enough and wide enough that the water finally began to accumulate in the bottom.

Once that happened, he expanded his operations a bit.

"All right, little seed. Get going." Tulland pushed one of a dozen cultivated Hades Briar fruit seeds into the ground, still wrapped in half-eaten fruit flesh. "Grow up big and strong. I need the experience."

For all his knowledge of classes, Tulland had never really learned much about being a farmer. Most farmers he knew of back home were unclassed, as the Church wasn't likely to use up one of their limited class slots on something that could be accomplished with fertilizer and muscle. But it was hard to believe a farmer could advance his class in any other way besides farming. And with the pet briar's growth achievement rivaling the experience of defeating a couple thousand motes, Tulland saw that his class screen was backing up that idea as well.

---

**Tulland Lowstreet**
**Class:** Farmer LV. 3
**Strength:** 16
**Agility:** 16
**Vitality:** 13
**Spirit:** 10
**Mind:** 10
**Force:** 10
**Skills:** Quickgrow LV. 2, Enrich Seed LV. 2, Strong Back LV. 1

---

The new briars made true on Tulland's wish. After all, the original briars had covered about a half square mile here with very little resources. With a farmer class supporting the growth with magic, the cultivated briars were more or less springing out of the ground. They didn't grow very tall, bending over once they got to any substantial height, and spent of their growth invading each other's territories and becoming a tangle. But they did grow.

After a few days, Tulland was well-fed, well hydrated, and going completely insane with boredom. His idea was simple enough. He was trying to grow briars in big enough numbers to force mass leveling. The stats he had added from the level-ups meant he could clear ground much faster, and every time he managed to push back the borders of his briar prison a little more, he'd plant more of the cultivated briars in that space.

But it was really, really dull work. Every briar granted him just a bit of experience, though just a trickle compared to what he had gotten for the first one.

*But it's progress, and it's progress I can make without dying.*

And then, finally, it happened. He made one last application of *Quickgrow* to a briar, waited until it matured, and found himself over the threshold of the next level.

Most of Tulland's wounds had healed by now, and even his eye had stopped hurting. But his sight still stubbornly refused to mend. Now that he had an extra five stat points, he began putting them in vitality one by one, hoping that each point would make a difference but not wanting to waste a single one.

The first few points did nothing. But when he pushed from fifteen points to sixteen, he felt a slight itch in his eye socket. A couple moments later, vision started to return to his left eye. It wasn't much of a practical difference, since he could already see out of his right eye. But the feeling of wholeness he got from it was more than worth the cost.

The last two points went to strength and agility, which meant Tulland was about as strong as he'd be now, at least in terms of his body. There was no chance that he could get to the next level just by farming briars. The experience he got from the last few plants had slowed and he could feel the dungeon about to limit things soon. That meant he had to fight. A combat class, a real one, would have a sword in their hand, knowledge in their mind of how to use it, and a handful of support skills from their very first level to make sure they were ready for fights in the Infinite.

**Tulland Lowstreet**
**Class:** Farmer LV. 4
**Strength:** 17

**Agility:** 17
**Vitality:** 16
**Spirit:** 10
**Mind:** 10
**Force:** 10
**Skills:** Quickgrow LV. 2, Enrich Seed LV. 2, Strong Back LV. 1

Instead, Tulland had a pitchfork. That was it. That setup was plenty for motes, but not for the challenges meant for the properly equipped. To have a chance in those, he had to cheat. Luckily, by now, he had a pile of cut briars that reached halfway to the stars. He started pulling them out one by one and sticking them, dry and hard, in the two rows of briars that extended away from the spot he had entered the patch. There was still a wall of briars between him and the outside world, and now he had extended a passageway from it, as tall as he was and stretching back twenty or thirty feet.

After that, he went to work on his own plants, the ones he had grown with his own hands and powers. He cut five or ten of them apart, then spent a while figuring out the best way to knot them together until he had a rope of sorts that he tied to the loose thorns in the walls. Then he was ready.

Walking down his aisle of thorns, he started cutting away the protection between him and the outside world. It was easy work, especially compared to what he had to work with before. Within a few minutes of cutting and shoving the debris of that work aside, he had a pathway to the outside.

Tulland had almost forgotten what the forest past his little prison cell looked like. The trees were an awful lot like trees on the outside, with branches, leaves, and bark. There was nothing bizarre about them, minus the purple light they were bathed in. Yet, that change was enough for them to look foreign, just different enough to grate on his psychology, letting him know he was in a place he shouldn't be without really giving his mind anything to grab onto as a solid *why*.

The beast that had chased him was nowhere to be seen. Gripping his pitchfork with both hands, Tulland crept forward a bit from the thorn hedge, looking left and right as he went and trying his hardest not to make much noise. And after a minute of looking, staying close to his enclosure but making more and more noise as he went, he didn't just find one Razored Lunger.

He found two. There were two of them this time.

Tulland turned and ran without a second thought, working his way back to the hallway he had built in the briars. The Lungers stayed on his heels, biting and yipping as they caught up. The extra points in agility and strength helped Tulland maintain a bit of his lead, but by the time he got halfway through the corridor of thorns, they were close.

That was just how he wanted it. Careful not to miss his chance, he stooped down to the ground where his makeshift rope sat, hooked it on his pitchfork, and pulled.

He had stacked the thorns into walls, but he had never claimed to have done a good job at it. With his makeshift ropes tangled up in the construction, a yank was all it took to shake them loose on the Lungers. Startled by the crack of the sticks as they broke, the Lungers tried to spring out of the way of the raining thorns. An unlucky one got tangled right near the middle while the other sprinted forward in vain, getting caught in the rope tangle less than a foot from the "room" Tulland had made in the patch. Tulland wheeled around to where it was tangled in the thorns, yowling like an injured cat, and started stabbing with his pitchfork. If these things could break out of the thorns, he didn't want to find out about it the hard way. That left him with limited time to make sure of things before they were down.

And he'd be damned if they weren't tough little things. Tulland could barely break the surface of their hide with the tines of the pitchfork, even with them holding still and waiting for him to try. After a few stabs that didn't do the job, he switched tactics, morphed the weapon into a shovel, and started clubbing them.

Even that didn't do much, but it did alert him to something that did. The normal briars were scratching the monsters, and even jabbing into them in a way that seemed to hurt. But his own briars, some of which had worked into the hedge or part of the rope in which the monsters were caught, were a different kind of thing. The monsters screamed whenever they touched those. The thorns cut through them like hot butter, and Tulland suddenly found himself glad that he had never accidentally poked himself with his pet briars.

Eventually, he made headway. Between the briars, his shovel, and plenty of time, he finally managed to put both of the animals down, wearing himself out in the process. When it was finally over, he was a bit sick seeing what he had done. But he was alive, and after rebuilding the entrance wall with more cut briars, he found himself newly leveled.

It wasn't enough to celebrate. However good it was at its intended job, the Farmer's Tool wasn't much of a weapon. Five more stat points weren't enough to suddenly make him strong enough to kill off the little wolverine-like beasts that seemed to fill this forest.

*They weren't meant to be taken care of without a class. That's clear now.* Tulland lay on his back as he caught his breath, looking toward his little plot of thorn plants contemplatively. *But I have a class. And it looks like that just might make a difference.*

A few hours later, a Razored Lunger lifted its head and sniffed the air. Something smelled new. In its experience, that wasn't a thing that happened much. Recently, there had been a bit of stink around the area, some kind of new animal whose odor it instinctively reviled. This was different. This smelled good.

It crept cautiously closer. As curious as it was, the forest was not a place to be careless. There were threats even for its kind, and not all of them were obvious.

The new smell turned out to be coming from a plant, of sorts, one it hadn't seen before. It was sitting flat on a bit of ground, oozing juice that looked sweet and delicious. Glancing around for danger, it crept cautiously closer. There was a faint smell of the new animal around. The food might have been his; maybe it was dropped. The Razored Lunger had seen that kind of thing before. But the animal wasn't here now. Nothing was. The food was free for the taking, and safe in that confidence, it sprang forward.

Then the ground went away.

# CHAPTER NINE

# BLUDGEON

In his enclosure, Tulland was already working on his next project. He had spent the better part of a few hours the day before building the pit trap, but that was a necessary risk. It took time to dig a hole, and more time to plant a cultivated briar seed at the bottom, juice it with magic, cover the whole thing with enough briar thorns to look like semisolid ground, and leave a single cultivated fruit as bait.

The investment was worth it. He had picked up two levels' worth of experience just today, setting and resetting the trap with his excess of cultivated fruit and the briar branches. He had worried that the monster corpses left in the pit would warn the others off, until he had gone to clean it out for the first time and found it clean except for an exceptionally vibrant, healthy-looking briar.

"Even if I could, I won't ask any questions about what happened there," Tulland said to the briar. It might have been his imagination but the briar seemed to twitch at those words.

Now, Tulland was busy clipping off several feet of his briar tangle and wrapping it around the strongest branch he had been able to safely find in the forest. His best idea for a weapon so far was to make a briar-wrapped club and see how that did on the local wildlife.

"Hey, System. You around?" Tulland asked after turning off the communication barrier.

**You know I am. Where would I go?**

"Good point. I have a question for you."

**One I would answer for what reason?**

"Because you have nothing better to do."

The System went quiet, but Tulland wasn't fooled. It had been lying to him for months, but some things were harder to fake. It could tolerate endless periods of nothing happening, but it was vulnerable to the kind of boredom where something demanded attention, then didn't justify the need. It hated services from the Church, not just because they came from his enemies, but because they droned on. It couldn't stand Tulland's sessions with his tutor either.

And most of all, it hated waiting for a response. It couldn't tolerate being ignored.

Tulland sat placidly, working thorns into the wood of the stick while trying to make his makeshift spiked club. He knew it was only a matter of time.

**What is your question?**

"I thought you didn't want to answer."

**I am generous. Ask.**

Tulland kept his face straight as he waited a moment, then let the System know what he had on his mind.

"The beasts here. Are they especially resistant to the attacks of people without a class? If a very strong man came here with a knife, but no class, would they be more difficult for him to kill than they should?"

**An interesting question.**

"I thought so. Do you know the answer?"

**I do. And it's yes, in some ways. It would matter who made . . .**

The System went quiet.

"Keep going. I'm listening."

**No. I've wasted my own time here. I'm done.**

"Oh, come on. Don't be like that."

The System wouldn't speak again, no matter how Tulland asked or cajoled. But Tulland thought he might have an answer anyway. He was fairly sure that the unfinished thought the System decided not to share was that it would matter who made the knife. Tulland's farming tool was not powered by his own class, at least in its function as a weapon. And it wasn't made by someone with a class, despite being a system-built item.

But if a blacksmith with a smithing class made a knife, it would carry a might of its own. As a product of some system or another, it would be made to interact with other things created by and for the class and leveling system. A very strong man wielding one of those knives could kill one of these monsters. Tulland was almost sure of it.

Tulland didn't know how to work metal and didn't have any skills for making bows. But he did have plants grown by a true Farmer class, using system-granted skills. He wouldn't have believed there was any chance that things would work this way if he hadn't already had some confirmation, courtesy of several dead monsters who had failed to make it out of his pit trap.

*And even if the Infinite doesn't think this monster-fertilized vine is different enough to give it a new description, it sure seems like it's gonna work at least a little bit better.*

Before Tulland tried it out, he made sure he had contingencies. He set up his collapsible rope thorn trap again and dug a few pit traps that he covered in a way that was obvious to him but hopefully less so for the monsters. Once that was in place, he stepped out, stood at the entrance of his compound, and waited.

He didn't have to wait long. It was less than five minutes before one of the walking balls of territorial rage spotted him and made a beeline for what looked like easy prey.

But in many ways, Tulland wasn't as soft as he had been when he had first arrived in this forest.

**Tulland Lowstreet**
**Class:** Farmer LV. 6
**Strength:** 24
**Agility:** 20
**Vitality:** 16
**Spirit:** 10
**Mind:** 10
**Force:** 10
**Skills:** Quickgrow LV. 4, Enrich Seed LV. 3, Strong Back LV. 2

As the Lunger got close, Tulland held his swing as long as he could. He had options if he missed, but he didn't want to use them if he could help it. Luckily, the animal sensed something was wrong right at the last moment, and skidded to a stop not quite entirely out of Tulland's range. He swung as hard as he could.

The end of Tulland's new club was studded with pounds of briar vines and dozens of finger-length, razor-sharp thorns. During the construction process, Tulland had reflected on all of the pain that his initial encounter with one of the monsters brought, and added more and more weight to the club until it literally couldn't hold any more thorns or vines. It turned out that, in the process, he had drifted dangerously far into overkill territory.

The club didn't just penetrate with its thorns or entangle with its vines. The weight of the thing crushed the animal at the point of impact, bludgeoning it to death at the same time the thorns punctured through it.

Tulland took a second to process what just happened.

"Holy crap. Did you see that, System?"

**I . . . did. I did not suspect that things would work like that.**

"Really? After all your centuries of doing what you do?"

**It's not as if Farmers end up in dungeons often, boy. How would I learn this, besides watching your situation?**

Tulland nodded. That seemed probable enough. Which meant that, for now, he had a way of destroying the enemies who lived in this forest. Farmer didn't seem to be a class that needed a lot of experience to level. The requirements would probably get higher and higher as his level ascended, but he probably could get at least one or two more levels out of this area before he topped it out.

While that was a victory of sorts, it was limited. On some level, Tulland knew that these terrifying little animals were the weakest, least-threatening beasts that this dungeon had to offer. They were a tutorial, something anyone with a sword and a sword-handling class would have mowed through without a second thought.

For Tulland, after days of pain and near-death experiences, he could just about fight them evenly. But after this floor, there would be another stronger and faster enemy, and another beyond that. Even this floor had threats he hadn't seen yet, probably bigger ones too. A club covered with kinda-magic vines wouldn't be enough to keep him safe forever.

Tulland would have to think of something else. For now, he had a little time until his traps caught enough of the Lungers to cap the experience he could get out of them. He had a vague hope that the traps would never give out, that they would be close enough of a thing to farming that the Dungeon System would reward him for them forever.

It wasn't meant to be. As soon as he hit the next level, the Dungeon System let him know the gravy train had been stopped. Worse, the experience he was getting from farming each individual briar was now next to nothing. The leveling requirement was enough that it would take weeks and weeks before he hit the next one. It was too much time to wait and hope nothing went wrong in this place.

Tulland almost dumped the points he had gained from his new level into his physical stats before he stopped himself.

*Farming. Huh.* He hadn't thought much about the skills he got from his class except to bemoan them since he got here. But it was *Enrich Seed* and *Quickgrow* that had given him all the progress he had managed. While it would be nice to swing his club a little harder and faster, it wasn't going to save him from anything truly big and strong.

From what the tutor had said, mind was a mental defense stat, while spirit had to do with how fast magical force was restored. But force directly impacted how strong a skill became when it was released, how effective it was at doing whatever it aimed to do.

There was more to it than that, but those details weren't worth considering at the moment. This was a broad-strokes kind of situation, one where Tulland needed big changes and couldn't afford to spend his limited resources on anything that didn't cause them.

Mental defense could wait, and Tulland had nothing but time to wait for his magic to restore itself. What he didn't have was any way to improve what he did, to make stronger plants.

*And stronger plants are . . . it might be nothing. But it might be something, right?*

Tulland looked at the club in his hands. It was something, but sooner or later, it would fail. That was certain. And when that happened, he needed something better. The chance of farming actually making a difference was slim, near enough to nothing to almost make no difference.

But not zero.

Tulland closed his eyes and put all five points into force, then went to dig a new pit trap. He was going to enrich a seed more than he ever had before, and he would be damned if it wasn't going to be well fertilized.

The System watched as Tulland threw his club back over his shoulder and moved back to his camp. He must have realized what the System had always known. There was a chance Tulland would climb a few floors with his own abilities and desire to live. And if he did, the System would profit from it. But the chances of Tulland actually clearing his way to the safe zone were nil. Standing in his unarmed and unskilled path was a real challenge. The kind that even the most talented warriors equipped with full System's gifts would barely overcome.

The Infinite was an elite dungeon, for the brave and successful. It was a place they came to prove that they were not just among the best, but the very best there was. The Infinite was where heroes went to gamble their lives on getting the power that their worlds needed to survive, thrive, and reach entirely new levels.

It wasn't a place for the weak. And if there was one thing the System was sure of, it was that Tulland was weak.

# CHAPTER TEN

# Swords and Hoes

As Tulland hefted his pack full of fruits, he was glad that he had put points into strength. A couple days' worth of applications of *Quickgrow* added to the already aggressive growth rate of the vines meant lots and lots of fruits, and he had some experimentation to do.

He brought the pack over to the new, much bigger area he had cleared in the briars. After dropping them on the ground for later, Tulland commanded his Farmer's Tool to transform into a hoe and got to work loosening the soil.

What Tulland had in mind would require a lot of work, as judged in the conventional way. He would need yard after yard of tilled rows, all carved out of hard, clay-heavy soil. All of that work might amount to nothing, but Tulland was stubborn that way. Even if there was a tiny chance of success, he was willing to swing his hoe and shed his sweat.

Stats hurried the tilling along just fine, and the speed and power he moved with now was a bit intoxicating all by itself, in a way that made him want to work a bit faster and push a bit harder.

Within another hour, he had plenty of soil prepared, with each area he planned to plant marked with a cut to separate it from the others. The first section got one briar seed, all by itself. Tulland's *Enrich Seed* skill was higher level than it had been at the beginning. Along with the extra magic power he had to dedicate to the process, he was eager to see what differences he could now make.

The next briar seed was planted in a bundle of the fruits themselves, deseeded and pulped so that their nutrients would only benefit that single seed. Tulland's thought was that even with magical power, conventional farming rules probably still applied here. The soil that the briars had been growing in was clearly enough to sustain them to some extent, but it was also flat out the worst soil Tulland had ever seen. It was hard, angry stuff that was so devoid of nutrients that it looked bleached.

*Just looking at it grosses me out, and I can't say why.*

"Hey, System?" Tulland said out loud as he eased the communication restrictions.

**Yes?**

"Does this class give me . . . I don't know how to say it. Do I know more about farming now?"

**More? Did you know a single thing before?**

"No, but that's hardly the tone you should be taking. I could turn off your communication channel again."

**Don't. It would make this conversation a waste of both our times. The answer to your question is yes, to a very limited extent.**

"How limited?"

**You are now a farmer. The changes that a class makes are not just to a person's capabilities. It is to what they are at a fundamental level.**

Tulland tossed two seeds together in one growing area, and three in another. There was no shortage of ground to do experiments on, and he was going to try anything and everything he could.

"That doesn't tell me anything."

**Think of a Paladin. In your storybooks, what are they like?**

"Noble. Noble and brave. Self-sacrificing. They can't all be like that, though."

**No?**

"No. Because people just aren't. Most people are selfish. I am." Tulland shuddered a little as he remembered what his selfishness might eventually do to his home world. "And people get scared. Not every Paladin is going to be an exception and noble beyond normal."

**That's where you are wrong. Think about it for a bit.**

Tulland did, taking a few minutes to consider it, as he duplicated every experiment he had set up so far but this time adding a shovelful of water to each mound.

"You're saying that they start out average." Tulland dumped another shovelful of water. "That the class changes who they are."

**Over time. Slowly. Each stat you apply while holding a Farmer class**

makes you more farmer, in some way. And a farmer understands soil and plants.

"Isn't that . . . insidious? The class changing their minds?"

**All experiences do. A beaten man learns fear. A triumphant man learns confidence. Why should having a class be any different?**

Tulland could almost buy that. He decided to let it lie, for the moment, and focus on the matter at hand.

"How much should I trust it? The new knowledge, I mean."

**What is it telling you?**

"That the soil here is bad."

The System went quiet for a moment, enough that Tulland double-checked to see if the communication channel was still unrestricted.

**That, at least, seems probable. Now, I would advise you to . . .**

Tulland knew that tone. He had heard it a lot over the past few days. The System was about to forget itself and talk. It would go for hours if he let it. But it also, he had found, really hated it if he cut it off before it could finish those speeches.

He mentally flipped the switch without a second thought, wiped the sweat off his brow, and went toward the exit from the hedge. Unpiling the briars he used to block the way in, he uncovered his pile of animal corpses.

The Razored Lungers, it had turned out, were slightly stupid. After his first few kills that weren't instantly absorbed by his vine traps, the blood had drawn in more of the beasts. Enough for them to actually attempt entering the briar patch, and meet the cultivated briars with all of their agony thorns. And when the monsters were weakened enough, Tulland had cut them away before beating them to death with his club. In the process, he noticed that unlike the living briars, the dead vines did nothing to absorb the corpses.

For the first time since entering the dungeon, Tulland had too many resources. The fruits and groundwater meant that he wasn't desperate enough to eat the Lunger meat raw. And he didn't want to gamble his life on starting a fire, even if he could figure out how to do that.

There was nothing productive to do with the corpses except to see if his plants would appreciate a little extra food. He had seen what it did to his already-growing vines, and they appeared to like it just fine. Now he would see what he could get out of the seeds if they had a different, richer growing environment from the start.

Tulland set up a number of experiments with the corpses, all of which involved more cutting and pulping of the animals than he liked. Some of the flesh was mixed with more soil, some with less, some with more water, some with less, and some with multiple seeds just in case he had added too many nutrients.

By the time he was done, Tulland had about twenty different planting zones, all running some configuration of farming or another.

Then it was time to enrich them. It took hours of pushing magic power out and recharging to get it done, but Tulland wasn't in a hurry. He had food and water, and for now, he was safe. When he felt the need to sleep, he slept, and once he had finished enriching the seeds, he even tried to double up on the skill, only to find that an already-enriched seed wouldn't engage with a second skill application.

After that, he started using *Quickgrow*, pushing out all of his power over the next few hours. Neither of the skills had leveled during the experimentation. That wasn't surprising. Tulland was pretty sure they wouldn't, unless one of his experiments actually worked and produced something new.

Even with *Quickgrow* active and the obscene speed with which the briars seemed to grow, the next phase wasn't something that would happen in just a few minutes. Exhausted again, Tulland dropped to the ground to nap.

"The economy is more important than any of you understand," Tulland's tutor had said, walking them through the market. "Even for war. Tulland. Tell us how to make as many swords for an army as possible."

"Lots of smiths would be my guess. Lots of fuel for the forges, and lots of ore to smelt into metal. That kind of thing."

"And how would you feed them?"

"Grain?" Tulland scratched his head. "Do smiths eat special food?"

"No, just the same things you do. But imagine you are the leader of a border town. Where do you get the grain?" the tutor asked.

"Farmers. I buy it from them."

"Using what?"

"Tax money."

The old man nodded. "That's correct, except I believe you might underestimate how much money forging takes. A good sword is a product of several workmen, each using expensive materials and a lot of space. That eats up your tax money, and you don't have money for farmers anymore."

"But it's wartime," one of the other boys objected. Tulland remembered the boy, but somehow couldn't remember his name. He was a larger boy, built for heavy work if not actual fighting. He had always been bloody-minded, compared to the others. "Just force the farmers. Take the grain. Feed the blacksmiths. Spend the money on materials."

"That might work, once. But just once. As soon as the farmers know their labor will be seized, what do you suppose happens?"

"They stop working," Tulland said. That was easy enough to know. Nobody would work without pay.

"Then send armed men to make them work," the boy said, finding yet another application for violence. It was a habit of his known to everyone in the class.

"Each of whom requires a sword," the tutor said. "And time and pay of their own. And even the most frightening of guards can't make someone work as hard as they will in their own interests, with their own pay on the line. Production can and will drop. It's been observed in many places."

"Then what?" Tulland was interested despite himself. "You said the economy fixes this?"

"No solution will net you unlimited swords. But a thriving town can make more armor and arms than a starving one. A city can make more than a town. If you focus on prosperity, the rest of it will come. And that is how you build a strong people. Swords are only part of the answer."

# CHAPTER ELEVEN

# HADES LUNGER BRIAR

Tulland woke up on the ground, thankful to have just enough points bolstering his vitality that this was only uncomfortable as opposed to actually hurting his muscles and bones. He kept his eyes closed for just a moment, wishing he could talk with his tutor in some way or another right now. The old man might not have been young enough to help much with the fighting, but Tulland was 80 percent sure he knew about things like farming.

*He knows about a lot of things.*

When Tulland finally opened his eyes, he was in a weird jungle. Every one of the plants had sprouted, which wasn't surprising. He half suspected that, once juiced with his farming powers, these briar weeds would have grown on a pane of glass. At least for a while anyway.

He stood and walked over to the least interesting of them. The briar seeds that were only enhanced by his skills were a bit bigger and a bit stronger. Something about how they looked rubbed him the right way, at least to the extent normal plants could. They were a little bit hardier and healthier. If they had been food, he would have assumed they would feed people better. As deadly spiked plants, they seemed like they might spike things a little more sharply and viciously.

*Nothing amazing. Next.*

Watering seemed to be generally good for the plants, and all the plants he had watered were doing a bit better than the ones without water. The ones he had planted in their own fruit pulp did even better than that, and kept improving with more pulp until they had access to two or more fruits' worth of the stuff. More fertilization of that kind didn't seem to help. These vines were thicker and greener, and when Tulland reached out and touched them with his hand, they were also just a bit more flexible. It was almost to the point that he could have used them as a rope as is, without cutting or twisting any strands together at all.

But it was the monster-fed vines that changed the game. Tulland had seen the moving things after he woke up, and verified that they couldn't actually move from their rooting spots before approaching them.

**It is foolish for you not to have looked at this first. The others are just briars. These are something new.**

"You think I don't know that? It's incredibly boring in here, System." Tulland was going to milk this entire experience for all it was worth, entertainment-wise. If that meant turning back on the System for a bit, so be it. It likely knew something Tulland didn't as well. "Now, what am I looking at here?"

**I have no idea at all. This is not something that would have been possible in our world, I think. Over the centuries I was in control, farmers tried many things. They accomplished at least some marvels. None of them were . . . this.**

"Give me something, at least."

**I'm not your System anymore, remember? Check to see what the Infinite says about it.**

"Fine. Be that way." Tulland had been putting off looking at the Infinite's notifications, but there was no reason to do that now. Annoyingly, the Infinite had yet to show the same preference for automatic, instant communication the System had. Every screen had to be manually read and dismissed. He started at the boring end of things and worked his way up.

---

**Hades Briar LV. 1 (Cultivated, Improved)**

The Hades Briar is the most basic and common of barriers to movement in flora-heavy tower floors. Its omnipresence has spelled the doom of monsters and adventurers alike, as it presented them with a painful distraction or blocked an otherwise open avenue of retreat.

Your cultivation techniques have improved this briar past what it would accomplish itself even in ideal growing conditions. It is stronger, more flexible, and bears more potent thorns. The briars are passive hunters at all times, gathering their own fertilizer through unlucky beasts. These would gather more while spending less, putting down prey that wander into their territory with less chance of breakage.

That was good enough to have justified this work all by itself. Even if all the farming meant his clubs were a little better, it would be a very big jump in his surviving-this-floor chances. But the inclusion of levels and the idea of improved crops in the description was something else.

*Does that mean . . .* Tulland began to think.

**Likely.** The System sounded surprised, annoyed, and impressed all at once. **Just be quiet and look at the others.**

Tulland nodded and turned to the notifications for the rest of his conventional vines. The best he had done with any of them was a level two variant, which came from one vine that had been fertilized with monster meat but not watered. It looked truly nasty to Tulland's not entirely untrained eye, and he immediately decided to upgrade his club with this new briar when he got a chance.

But then it was time to get down to the really weird stuff. He stood and walked toward the one very concerning, much more vine-like plant, standing a few full steps outside of its reach as it writhed and reached for him.

---

**Lunger Briar LV. 1 (Subjugated)**

Where the Hades Briar exists as a passive hunter, this briar is active. It is capable of lying stationary for years, only to activate and reach toward prey when they come close. Once in contact with prey, it attempts to wrap itself around them.

When locked around prey, the Lunger Briar works its thorns into them to reduce their chance of escape, then holds them in place with its own weight and root structure.

The Lunger Briar is durable, but strong enough enemies can pull them from the ground. Once pulled, the briar will die, but will continue to act as alive in the presence of prey until its energy resources are depleted. Destroying a prey animal will restore some of that same energy, although at a slow, level-dependent pace.

---

"That's not normal. It took the monster fertilizer's name," Tulland said.

**Like a bride at some sort of perverse wedding. Keep reading your notifications, fool.**

Tulland decided that while he would continue moving through the new information, the System had probably learned more than enough about his new capabilities for one day. He didn't believe that the lying betrayer was just taking everything at their word instead of making educated guesses about what was happening, and if it didn't want to share them, then there was a limited amount of knowledge he would let it have. The fact that it was defanged for the moment didn't mean it would be harmless forever, and keeping the System in the dark did Tulland no harm so long as it wasn't repaying him with knowledge.

He was immediately glad he did so. The next notification was a game changer in a way the others weren't.

---

**Subjugated Crops**

Some crops were never meant for human cultivation. While growing almost anything is possible given the right soil and light conditions, most truly hostile crops resist any significant domestication and improvement attempts.

That does not mean that domestication and improvement are impossible, however. When these enemy plants are successfully changed from their baseline forms, they provide bonuses to experience, represent a new category of cultivable plants that provide their own unique levels of experience, and often establish a different kind of relationship to their grower.

You have subjugated a new crop for the first time, both in the sense that you have subjugated your first crop and in the sense that the crop you subjugated has never been tamed before. For that, you'll receive a large, level-adjusted amount of experience, a large portion of skill experience to the skills used in creating it, and other bonuses as a result.

---

**Lunger Briar Bonuses**

Based on your current skill levels and the best Hades Lunger Briar you have been able to grow, you gain the following bonuses:

1. At your will, the Lunger Briar will cease to see you as prey.
2. At your will, you gain a permanent immunity to damage from briars you grow, so long as they are of the quality of the Hades Lunger Briar or lower as a species.

---

Tulland immediately willed the briar to ignore him, then stood open-mouthed as it went limp, slumped to the ground, and became indistinguishable from any other briar he had grown. Walking a tiny bit closer, he very gently moved his hand toward one of the thorns, putting just the slightest amount of pressure on it.

The thorns were very sharp, and that should have been enough to immediately puncture his skin. In this case, it simply failed to do so. He pressed even harder, and found he was still safe. Pressing as hard as he could and rubbing his hand back and forth on the blade of the briar showed he was still safe. The Infinite's system hadn't been lying. Tulland couldn't be hurt by these plants.

None of his more conventional briars could hurt him either, though he verified through some substantial pain that any briars he hadn't cultivated were still dangerous.

Which brought him to the last of his notifications, ones he had sensed at the beginning of this process but kept back until he knew exactly what he had done to earn them.

---

**Level Up! x4**
**Skill Level Up! x6**

---

**New Skill Earned!**
**Botanical Engineer LV.1 (Passive)**
In creating a new form of life, you have proven yourself as something beyond a mere sower of seeds. This passive skill increases the range of situations in which you will be able to successfully create new plant hybrids, and increases the quality of their new characteristics when you do.

---

Tulland took a deep breath. This seemed like a truly shocking number of levels to get at once. He immediately dedicated just a few of the newly gained points to each of his body stats. Plants or no, he still had to survive out in a very hostile world, and he had no idea what he would be facing as he pressed out from the safety of his base.

The rest he applied to his magical abilities, adding five points to his force stat and also spirit to speed up his regeneration a little bit. His mind stat was the only one that got no love, seeing that Razored Lungers didn't exactly do mental damage outside of his earlier traumatic memories with them.

---

**Tulland Lowstreet**
**Class:** Farmer LV. 11
**Strength:** 25
**Agility:** 25
**Vitality:** 20
**Spirit:** 15
**Mind:** 10
**Force:** 20
**Skills:** Quickgrow LV. 7, Enrich Seed LV. 6
**Passives:** Botanical Engineer LV. 1, Strong Back LV. 2

The new passives section interested him. It apparently needed some minimum level of entries to show, and had immediately moved *Strong Back* once it did. Eventually, he'd have to work on leveling both passive skills, although Tulland hated the thought of what he would have to do to convince his regeneration skill to grow.

He ran in place and jumped a few times, then found his club and gave it some experimental swings. He wasn't much stronger or faster from the extra stat points, but each little addition was a noticeable help. At the same time, he reminded himself that as strong as he might feel, he was infinitely weaker than what a real combat class would be in the same situation.

*If I'm going to live through this, I need more plants.*

Tulland sighed and began gathering fruits from his new hybrid vine. He was almost to the point where he would have to go explore the greater space around him, walking farther than a few steps from his terrible, thorn-based home. But if he didn't want to die the moment a new threat popped up, he was going to have a couple days' worth of farming ahead of him.

It was going to be boring. There was no way around that.


Two days later, Tulland was out of breath and swinging his club like a maniac. He had retrofitted the old club with new, improved vines, and it was much deadlier now in a way he had yet to really test on prey. He was a bit deadlier now too, if not much. If he couldn't improve his fighting through actual skills, he could at least improve it through practice. He had been working on that every moment his vitality allowed, filling the hours between infusions of *Enrich Seed* and *Quickgrow* with sweating, grunting, and general incompetent training.

Fully winded now, he slowly jogged a circuit of all his new plants. The Hades Lunger Briars, it turned out, grew just fine from just seeds. He had slowly replaced the big, tangled plug of briars that served as his door with two closely planted rows of the Lunger Briars. At rest, they outlined what looked like a safe and open hallway that led directly to delicious, monster-nourishing human meat.

Over the course of the last several hours, they proved that they were anything but safe. Every few hours, a Razored Lunger had wandered by, seen Tulland through the entryway, and charged. The moment they entered that hallway, the briars woke up, tangling the invaders with deadly constrictor strengths, binding them to the ground, and sapping their life force to supplement their own.

To his surprise, the Lunger Briars could apparently level by doing this. The one closest to the outside world had benefited the most from the trap, reaching level three and being able to demolish the average beast that wandered in all by itself now.

Tulland rested for a while, then turned on the System.

"Hey, System. I was thinking about walking around a bit."

**Oh? About time, I'd say.**

"Well, yes, but you want me dead."

**I do not deny it. What is your question?**

"Do you think I'm ready?" Tulland asked. The System responded with silence for a long time.

**No. I think you will likely die. But you are at least as ready as you'll ever be.**

Tulland nodded. After grabbing his scythe-form Farmer's Tool and thorn-and-vines club, he went to the front of his enclosure, planted some new vines, and leveled the blade of his tool at the strongest few vines of the Lunger Briars. The Infinite's Dungeon System had claimed they would retain some of their function for a while after they were cut, using their remaining energy when they moved and attacked.

Tulland wasn't sure they'd work like he hoped they would, but he wrapped them both around an arm each anyway. Any help out there would be worthwhile, but even if they didn't work, having a couple loops of thorny vines on his body wouldn't exactly hurt.

He took a deep breath and stepped away from his prison. It was time to learn more about this new world.

# CHAPTER TWELVE

# IRONBRANCH

The first stop was the trees. They were kind of everywhere except directly by the briars themselves, which seemed to compete with them for nutrients. Tulland had been somewhat in the forest since arriving at the briar patch, getting close enough to touch some trees and even to pump a *Quickgrow* into one or two.

It hadn't done anything visible, and had left him wondering why. His best guess was that either the trees were so slow-growing that *Quickgrow* couldn't affect them enough to be immediately visible, or they were so big already that the amount of magic he could output just wasn't enough, pound for pound, to matter.

This time, Tulland wanted to investigate that more closely. He headed to the closest tree, looking carefully for Razored Lungers as he did. It looked as if his briar traps had cleared the nearby ones out for the moment, leaving him with a bit of room to work. His first move was to scatter several Lunger Briar seeds out, covering a broad area around the tree. One of his experiments had shown that even though *Quickgrow* wouldn't work until seeds were actually in contact with the soil, *Enrich Seed* was something that could be used beforehand as a sort of prep work for eventual planting.

Tulland wasn't putting out any magical power on *Quickgrow* right now, since he could do it pretty quick if he needed to. But he knew that given enough time, the briars would root and grow on their own. For now, the seeds were sown into the ground plain as Tulland went straight to the trunk of the tree. In the few moments he had spent close enough to the trees to check them, he hadn't seen anything on them resembling a seed. No acorns, no pine cones, no fruits. He had not so much as a guess as to how these things actually reproduced.

And his worry was that they didn't at all. If other people had traveled through this zone, Tulland imagined that they were much stronger than him. But even while all of them would be tougher than him, some of them must have been weaker than others.

If they were very weak, they might spend more time in this zone. They might spend enough time to notice the briars growing, or changes in the prairie grass. If the Infinite was trying to maintain the illusion of realism, it would probably simulate things like seeds and pollination for quick-growing plants.

But in trees? It could probably ignore seeds and things for trees if it wanted to. Nobody would be around long enough to notice they weren't regrowing.

Of course, that was assuming this whole place wasn't real. And that the Dungeon System wasn't basing these trees on real plants somewhere. And that it cared about saving energy by being less than complete.

It was a whole host of questions and assumptions that Tulland didn't have answers for just yet. With no real way of knowing how fake this dungeon was or how completely it was simulated, Tulland was left with the task of painstakingly making sure he wasn't missing things he would need in the future. He started out by searching the ground near the base of the tree and a few others to make sure there weren't seeds that had been dropped, going as far as to rake the nearby ground by changing his Farmer's Tool to a hoe and seeing if he could turn something up.

That yielded just dirt, so he examined the branches again, turning up nothing on any of the trees. And by then, his time of easy, murder-free searching was over. Without much warning, a Razored Lunger burst from around a distant tree and ran at him.

Tulland grabbed for his club, which he'd placed leaning against a nearby tree, but badly fumbled the attempt and ended up with his club falling to the dirt as the enemy closed in. With his heart beating wildly in his chest, Tulland dived for the weapon and prayed he'd find enough time to dodge around the tree.

Before he could execute that plan, the briars on his arm jumped into action.

The briar vines weighed so little thanks to Tulland's newfound strength that he had almost forgotten they were there before both of them loosened from around his arms and more or less shot through the air at the enemy, keeping only a single loop tethered to Tulland's forearms for stability.

Nobody was more surprised than the Razored Lunger itself, which tried to abort jumping for its prey a moment too late and ended up in an awkward half jump, sliding across the forest dirt on its hind legs and looking a bit like a startled cat.

As Tulland jumped to the side to get out of its way, both vines swatted toward the animal. One missed outright, but the other caught the Lunger on its outstretched front leg and whipped it around toward Tulland. The Lunger panicked, clawing at the tree with its three free legs as it tried to right itself and get the leverage it needed to escape the briar.

It didn't work. The second briar came down and looped around its neck, before both of the plants detached from Tulland's body and began to worm around the Lunger's free limbs. A few moments later, the animal was pinned to the ground, growling and bleeding until Tulland took pity on it in the form of a strike to the skull with his club.

As the animal went limp, the vines continued to writhe and work on it. Tulland remembered what the description of the Hades Lunger Briars had said about regaining energy from prey, decided not to watch, and turned to examine the damage the Lunger had done to the tree.

*I'm glad that wasn't aimed at me. It got pretty deep into the wood.*

On the backside of a piece of bark that the Lunger had ripped loose, Tulland finally found what he was looking for. It was a small round node, clearly separate from the bark despite being embedded in it. He pressed it out of the wood with his fingers, getting a system description when it finally broke free.

**Ironbranch Seed Node**

The Ironbranch Tree reproduces by means of large herbivorous animals that feed off its bark. The animals carry these indigestible seeds with them, eventually depositing them in some other location with a generously provided dollop of fertilizer to go with it.

Putting the seed in his pocket, Tulland started to circle the rest of the tree, looking for more of the nodes. They were fairly easy to see now that he knew what he was looking for, and he found that several good thwacks with the blade of his hoe were usually enough to dislodge the pieces of bark they were stuck in.

Once he had six seeds pulled from two separate trees, Tulland dumped whatever remaining magical power he could muster into the briars he had planted earlier to help them get started, and hightailed it back to camp.

* * *

"Is it too much to hope I can make a monster tree to guard me?" Tulland asked with a slight smile on his face.

**Likely. Especially since you've failed so miserably at the beginnings of that task so far.**

Back home, Tulland had harvested more fruits from his pet briars and set them in the soil to grow. His plan was to now mass-produce as many Lunger Briars as he could, slowly making more and more of the territory around his camp dangerous to local wildlife and creating a sort of safe zone for himself until he figured out his next steps. He only had so much magic to dedicate to that task, but even without class enhancements, he could still count on a whole lot of seeds per day to scatter haphazardly into the wilderness.

And it was free experience, even if they didn't give very much per plant.

Tulland had then turned to the tree seeds, immediately getting a hard reality-check on his hopes of a tree ent army in the form of a blunt, disappointing message.

---

**Seed Enrichment Failed!**

This plant is compatible with seed enrichment, but is much too powerful of a species to be affected by your current level of power. In the same way that a normal person would fail to subvert a lich, you simply don't have what it takes to change the makeup of this plant.

Enrichment may or may not become possible as your skills advance and your personal power grows.

---

**It is not surprising. What is more surprising is that you could alter any plant, no matter how simple or weak.**

"You've really never seen anything like this before? No farming class has ever improved a plant?"

**Improved, yes. Stolen from a dungeon and domesticated, no. And I'm relatively sure they tried. If this is the absolute limit of what your class will do, I'm not surprised.**

Tulland sighed and turned the System's connection off. He had no way of knowing whether or not it was telling him the truth, and so far, it had provided him with precious little actual help. But as long as the System didn't actually directly harm him, Tulland was willing to keep opening the connection. The mere chance that it might be helpful at some point wasn't a resource he could pass up.

*And if I'm being honest, I need the company. I'm going to go insane if I'm alone in here.*

Tulland took the few tree seeds he had and ran a similar experiment to what he had with the briar seeds, but this time without enriching the seeds at all. He applied the briar fruit as a fertilizer to one, animal fertilizer to another, and so on, getting several variations of experiments in the ground before hitting one of them with *Quickgrow*. Before he could judge the results, the world darkened and rose up to meet Tulland's face.

Five minutes or so later, he woke up.

*Wow. Greedy little guys, these new seeds. That took everything I had.*

Tulland hadn't waited until his magic was entirely full after the last batch of *Quickgrow* charges he delivered to the briars planted near the tree, and had apparently bottomed out hard. Overdrawing magic was something Tulland had heard of, and something he knew was mildly dangerous when it happened consistently, but the only solution he knew to the problem was to just have more magic power in general.

In this case, the most he could do was eat, drink water, and sit around until his power climbed back to full. His earlier complete rest helped that happen a little faster, and within several minutes he was able to charge up the next seed while maintaining his consciousness. It didn't feel great though.

Once all the tree seeds were as empowered as Tulland could make them, he was tired. Something about using magic in particular sapped him of energy in a way moving around, working, or even fighting just didn't.

He picked a few handfuls of Lunger Briar seeds and planted them around the entrance to his space, which always seemed to be a good policy. Then, with a bad headache brewing, he went back to sleep.

"That's because you've never been hungry. Not really." Tulland's uncle was peeling potatoes. Tulland was hard-pressed to say when this memory actually happened. It could have been at any point in his life after he had learned to speak. "If you had, you wouldn't say that."

"It takes a month to starve," Tulland said. He knew he was being stubborn, and even knew his uncle was right, at least on some level of his childlike mind. "And the army was two weeks away. They could have marched there. They could have made it."

Some historic city had been sacked because some army or another in one of his tutor's lessons hadn't been able to get there, and they were more than strong enough to protect it if they had just marched faster. It was the dreaded boring *logistics* his teacher was so fond of and claimed was all-powerful in matters of war.

Tulland was convinced, absolutely convinced, that the solution for that problem was simply to push through. The army had swords, and they had a target. They should have been able to take care of things. The solution to saving the city, Tulland felt, was easy. They would just march faster and then swing their swords against the invaders.

His uncle had laughed when he had told him that. Like it was silly.

"And after you had marched a week on an empty stomach, you'd turn around and three quarters of the men would be gone. Half of those would have deserted because that kind of hunger is much less pleasant than you think it is. Another half might have kept on because of duty, then found out that when they say it takes a month to starve, they meant *while standing still*." His uncle held up a potato. "A couple of days' march on no food, people start to drop. Hurt or dead."

"And you know this how?" Tulland grabbed a potato and a knife and started working on taking the peel off too. All this talk of food was getting to him. "You were never in the military."

"No, but I was in a boat with no wind, rowing with a little oar that wasn't built for the job, and having bad luck catching fish. When I got a little one at the end of the second day, I ate it raw. Eyeballs and all." His uncle tossed the second-to-last potato into the pot, looked to see that Tulland had the last one, and wiped his starchy hands off on his coat. With semi-clean hands, Tulland's uncle ruffled his nephew's hair. "Point is, they weren't being cowards. You can't move an army without food any more than you can throw an army up a cliff. It doesn't work. Your tutor isn't wrong. If you didn't like the idea of battles so much, you'd know that. When has he ever been wrong before?"

# CHAPTER THIRTEEN

# WAGER

Tulland woke up to more plants. Most of the trees had failed, but one was beginning to grow, specifically the one he had planted in the pulp of the briar fruits. He confirmed that by trying to pump a charge of *Quickgrow* into them. It failed. They were good and dead. He put another round of *Quickgrow* into the successful seed, then started making his rounds on his briars.

Today was the day he cleaned some of them out. The old-style Hades Briars were of little use to him now. He kept some of the very best plants for club-making, but even those might not be needed once he had the chance to try a used-up Lunger Briar for the job.

The trees would need days, maybe even weeks, before they were large enough to matter much. But Tulland's last dream had reminded him of something. He was the kind of guy who thought most hard problems just needed a hero as their solution. And some problems really were that way. But more often than not, Tulland had found that his tutor was right, especially as he got old enough to know the difference between fantasy and reality.

*Boring is powerful. If I had to sum that old man in one sentence, it would be that.*

And right in that moment, Tulland started to get confirmation that the old man was right.

**Remote Victory!**
You have killed an enemy you can't see, hear, smell, or otherwise sense.
A significant portion of experience has been awarded for this achievement.

> **Remote Victory!**
> You have killed an enemy you can't see, hear, smell, or otherwise sense.

> **Remote Victory!**
> You have . . .

Somewhere outside Tulland's enclosure, his Lunger Briars were at work. He realized a bit late that the vines he had left out by the trees would eventually grow fruits, and that those fruits would draw in animals that wanted to eat them. He wasn't getting experience from any of the kills besides that first one, but that didn't mean it was a useless thing. The fewer monsters in the woods, the farther he could go, and the more things he could find. Given enough time, he could render any distance mostly safe with briars.

Considering the fact that he didn't even know how far there was to go, that was a real possibility.

"System."

**Yes?**

"How do I go up floors?"

The System went quiet for a while. Tulland decided not to give it the satisfaction of talking again. It would only set the System up to make its eventual jab at Tulland a bit better.

**Is this a serious question?**

"Would I ask if it wasn't?"

**I do not pretend to know what you think is important enough to waste my time with, these days.**

"Just tell me. Or I can cut the connection."

**If you did, who else could you ask?**

"The Infinite's Dungeon System, I guess. Oh, damn." Tulland almost smacked his forehead. "That's the answer, right?"

**Right. Now, if you don't mind, do cut that connection. I'd rather not have to listen in on you learning things any child would know if they had grown up under a properly powerful System.**

Tulland probably would have gotten the notification when he first arrived here if he hadn't been depending on the System from his world. It only took the slightest query aimed in the right direction to get every bit of explanation he could want.

> **The Infinite, Floor 1 (Detailed Description)**
> This space serves as an introduction for the dangers to come and is slightly

more dangerous than the average tutorial level. It consists of two biomes, neither of which is inclement or particularly arduous to traverse.

**Foes:**

Razored Lunger

???

???

**Objectives:**

Locate the exit

"Well, that's easy enough," Tulland said with a smile.

**I requested you banish me. Did I not?**

"Fine, fine. Have a fun time."

**You know I can't.**

Tulland cut off the connection and got to work. He loaded up his arms with the lunging variety of briar vines, which were more than enough against Razored Lunger and, Tulland hoped, the other monsters of this floor. Then, gathering every single fruit he could manage, he went out into the world.

Now that Tulland knew that the fruits themselves would draw in monsters, he could be a lot more efficient with his vines. By now, he had a pretty good sense of how close together the briar plants could grow without robbing each other of resources too much. He walked for a few minutes, killing a few Lungers on the way, then planted three of the seeds. Then he walked a few more minutes in another direction, making a wide circle all the way back to home. By the time he was finished, he had dropped about fifty seeds, and empowered at least one out of every group with a *Quickgrow*.

Time was starting to have an only conditional meaning in this place. Tulland had walked a long time today and spent a lot of magic, and was now exhausted, so he slept. He woke up whenever his body was ready, and repeated the cycle. Within a few cycles, he had a couple dozen patches of plants out in the wilderness, all of which were making their own fruits, attracting their own prey, and slaughtering them without Tulland having to do a thing.

*All hail the wonder of logistics!* Tulland thought, more than a little loopy after a string of days walking and planting seeds with no results he was actually present for to show for it. *Only through logistics can we triumph!*

He didn't realize how right he was until the notifications started pouring in. With them was another pang of longing for his tutor.

**Acreage**

You have established a farm over ten square miles in area, however sparsely cultivated it may be.
**Rewards:** Experience and progress toward a class-appropriate passive skill

---

**Remote Control (x100)**
You have killed a hundred enemies you could not see or sense. Your ability to accomplish this is beginning to cross thresholds from **something you can do** to **a primary component of how your class functions**.
**Rewards:** Experience and progress toward a class-appropriate skill

---

**Level Up!**
**Capped!**
You have earned a class-appropriate skill that cannot be rewarded because the total of your mental stats is too low. Raise your mental stats to receive this reward.

It wasn't a very hard decision of where to put the points. Not only was putting a bunch of them to his mental capabilities a given just to get the skill, but the last four days had been entirely bottlenecked by his ability to regenerate his magic.

*Into spirit you go, little points!*

Tulland sent his points into spirit until he got the new skill.

---

**Tulland Lowstreet**
**Class:** Farmer LV. 12
**Strength:** 25
**Agility:** 25
**Vitality:** 20
**Spirit:** 20
**Mind:** 10
**Force:** 20
**Skills:** Quickgrow LV. 8, Enrich Seed LV. 8
**Passives:** Biome Control LV. 1, Botanical Engineer LV. 1, Strong Back LV. 2

---

**Biome Control LV. 1 (Passive)**
The more plants you have within a given area, the more powerful they become, the faster they grow, and the better they tend to do even in environments they are not suited for. A large network will also experience an increased rate of propagation, furthering the depth and power of the network even more.

This effect is limited by several factors. First, a diversity of species is necessary to reach the highest heights this skill can ascend to. An extensive enough monoculture will eventually render the contribution of each new plant almost, if not entirely, null.

Second, the general value of the plants in the network matters. One thousand daisies still pale in comparison to one mighty oak. As a general rule, more useful plants, rarer plants, and plants that have a greater effect on their local environment will contribute the most.

**Special note:** As you acquired this skill in a dungeon, it is relevant to note that each floor of a dungeon counts as a separate world from all the others for the purpose of this skill. Since the distance between a plant on one floor and a plant on another is effectively infinite, their influence on each other is null even if they are planted on opposite sides of a level exit.

And that, Tulland knew, was probably the biggest improvement he could have possibly received. As the remote kill confirmations continued to pour in, he was fairly certain that this level had just gone from questionably beatable to an eventual cakewalk, even if it might take an awfully long time to see the fruits of that transition.

"Hey, System. Want to make a bet?"

**A bet?**

"A bet. A real one. Is that something you can do?"

**Hardly. What would you have that I would want? And how would I take it if I did want it?**

"You can destroy a skill, right?" Tulland had paid just enough attention to the Church's sessions to know that was something the System held over its apostles.

There was a pause.

**I can't unless you let me.**

"I'll let you if you win. One entire skill gone from my catalog. I bet you can even get something for it, right? Some reclaimed energy or something."

**And what would be the terms of this bet? I would need specifics.**

"I say I can beat this floor *and* the next within a month. And if I can't, you get what you want."

**That's likely impossible. While I don't feel bad about cheating you, Tulland, or even getting you killed, I'm not a sadist.**

"You're scared? Of little old me? That I can do something you don't think I can do? I couldn't do that unless I was smarter than you, System."

There was another pause, this time longer than the one before. Tulland thought that he had overplayed his hand. And then the System responded.

**There would be nothing that would force you to pay up.**

"Oh, hmm. Yes, I suppose that's so. And my word won't do?"

**No. And neither will mine. We are both untrustworthy in this matter.**

"Well, the only other person I even know on this plain of existence is . . ."

---

**Wager Proposed!**

The Infinite has been called on to adjudicate a bet between Tulland Lowstreet of Ouros and the System peculiar to his world. The terms as proposed and adjusted for fairness are as follows:

1. Tulland Lowstreet will attempt to conquer both the first and second floors within one Ouros calendar month.
2. On failure, he will forfeit one skill to his former System, which will be rendered into a type of energy usable by it. The Infinite will accommodate the particulars of this exchange at its own expense.
3. On success, Tulland will receive a reward appropriate to his class and situation chosen by the Infinite's system. The costs for this reward will be paid out of the Ouros System's personal energy budget.

Do both parties accept?

---

**This is foolish. You cannot . . .**

"Yes," Tulland said, grinning. His life was so cheap in this place that adding an extra element of risk hardly mattered. But for the System, it was a potential disaster. That meant he needed to do a bit extra taunting. "What? Are you scared? Of me? A mere human? The same human who you betrayed? Afraid that I'll win?"

**I do not know or experience fear.**

"And yet, I'm the only yes so far."

Tulland could almost hear the annoyance as the System tried to come up with a counter for that. He knew it couldn't, it knew it couldn't, and they both knew that even the System had its pride on the line here.

---

**Wager Finalized!**

Tulland Lowstreet's objectives are set, and the timer to complete them begins now. Good luck!

# CHAPTER FOURTEEN

# CARDS

And so the bet was set, and done in a way that Tulland suspected wasn't reversible.

That, in itself, was the first win for Tulland. He had another piece of information about the relationship between his System and the Infinite that he wouldn't have ever gotten from the System itself. It had to, as near as Tulland could tell, do what the Infinite said in certain situations.

At the very least, it seemed the Infinite could bind the Ouros System to certain kinds of agreements it had made. If that's all it was, the Infinite's Dungeon System wasn't necessarily an all-powerful entity. But it was a way for Tulland to get things out of his System that it wouldn't otherwise give, or to get it to pay out where it might otherwise cheap out on him.

If there was a way for Tulland to get any kind of real victory over the System, it would have to involve something like this. Some kind of clever loophole he could exploit when trying to down a literal god. He had nowhere near the power to do that alone, but by calling on the strength of another god? It just might be doable.

*Of course, that's making quite a giant assumption that their whole relationship and everything I can see isn't some kind of cruel, elaborate prank. But if that's the case, I'm going down anyway. This is the best bet I can make.*

Tulland had turned off the System as soon as the bet was finalized. He had planning to do, and he didn't particularly want the System influencing him with honeyed words while he tried to do it.

The way Tulland saw it, he didn't have an absolute overabundance of cards to make his hand out of. But he had some, and if he learned one thing while watching his uncle play betting games, it was that you didn't always make your bets when it was sure you'd win. By that time, other people would have ways to figure out the strength of your hand and wouldn't commit. Instead, you started betting early, got them in deeper than they wanted to be, and hoped your hand would improve as the game wore on.

The first card Tulland had was an unlikely sort of ally in the Infinite. It wasn't necessarily on his side, but it did at least seem impartial, and the terms it had stipulated for him in the bet were more generous and better thought-out than any he would have negotiated himself. It wasn't anything he could count on, and the Infinite hadn't provided him with the rule book it used to mediate those kinds of things, but it was better than having a hostile entity in cahoots with his archnemesis.

Tulland's second card was a bit harder to quantify. His new skill made his plants stronger, and it made them grow faster and seemed to imply some characteristics plants held, like value, that he didn't understand yet. He imagined that the actual effect of the skill would be pretty weak on a per-plant level, but there were a couple of things that made him hopeful.

A normal farmer would be limited in terms of the total amount of land they could access. Tulland had heard of some pretty big farms on the continent, even some bigger than the entire island on which he lived. But those were worked by big groups of agricultural specialists, unclassed but skilled. There was a limit to what one person could do themselves, even if they had a class. They would have to till the soil, fertilize, weed, and harvest, as well as a dozen other things an expert farmer would do that Tulland had no clue about. They would only claim so much land because there was only so much land they could actually work.

Tulland had neither of those limitations right now because the plants he was growing simply didn't need that much help. Even unenhanced, the seeds of the briars seemed willing to sprout anywhere, on any soil, with any amount of moisture available to them. They were weeds that hunted, and once a seed landed somewhere, the plants seemed entirely capable of taking care of themselves.

To the extent Tulland was limited in this place, it would be by the total size of this floor of the dungeon and how much time he could dedicate to scattering seeds.

*Which isn't much of a limitation at all. Let's get to work.*

Since the briars no longer tried to make life hell for Tulland, he could pick more seeds in a few minutes than he could carry. The first job would be fixing that limitation. Scythe in hand, Tulland harvested several vines, then cut them to length before beginning to weave them together into an unbelievably crude, brutal-looking fabric.

If he weren't immune to the damage his own plants could put out, it would have been a dangerous job. Even in a situation where he couldn't get pricked to death, the thorns were still a big problem, getting in the way constantly as he rearranged the plants again and again until they fit relatively close together.

Once that was done, the thorns became an asset instead of a liability. The completed weave couldn't have come apart even if it wanted to, given that the thorns either acted as pegs to keep the vines from sliding or went completely through them to more or less nail them into place.

Once Tulland had a makeshift, half-meter-square tarp with two sides woven together, he took a few more vines, wove them through in a slightly different way, and managed to create two rope handles of sorts that would pull the bag mostly closed as he lifted it.

Then he got to work in earnest. Running around his space, he grabbed as many fruits as he could, then tossed them into of the bag. There was no short-age of fruits growing in his original cut-out briar area, and after a minute or so, he had dozens of the things. He started to move toward the outside world, pulling fruits from his gate-keeper briars as he went.

Once Tulland was outside, he started chucking the damn things to lighten his load. He very honestly didn't care where they landed so long as they landed by themselves, and with enough points in strength, that was easy to do.

Once he had thrown out what he had, Tulland returned to his area, made sure to get whatever remaining fruits there were, then exited and started doing rounds of the more distant, sparse areas. He took along a few new Lunger Briar vines in his bag in addition to the few he had around his arms, just in case. As he passed the little clumps of briars he had planted earlier, he stripped them of fruits, hit the plants with *Quickgrow* and seeds with *Enrich Seed*, and threw them as he went.

Tulland could move faster than he had ever been able to at any point in his life. Even when carrying a big, awkward bag that kept snagging on his clothes, he could cover a mile in mere minutes. It only took him an estimated few hours to make a full circle as big as the one he made in the days before.

His increased spirit was doing a hell of a job keeping him topped off too. Even short gaps between clumps of plants that took a few minutes' walking regenerated enough magical power to push a few charges of *Quickgrow*. Longer walks meant he could use the more expensive *Enrich Seed*, which seemed to drain him more than anything else he could do physically or spiritually at the moment.

By the time he got back to home base, some of the higher-level briars he had magically enhanced before he left had already pushed out new fruits, which he immediately planted. Then, after resting for about an hour, he picked what new fruits he could find and began to leave.

And then he saw the damnedest thing.

*Well, isn't that interesting. I didn't plant you, did I?*

Just outside of the entrance to his briar fortress, Tulland saw a briar sprout that had taken hold near the base of another plant. It wasn't anything special. A quick inspection told him it was a level one nothing, a seed that didn't seem to have gotten any benefit from Tulland's magical abilities or fertilizer.

But it had grown on its own. At some point, one of the briars had dropped a fruit, and it had taken root all by itself. That was Tulland's third card in his rapidly improving hand against the System.

Tulland laughed, and flipped on his communications with the System.

"Heya, System. What do you think of this?" Tulland asked.

**This? I don't see anything interesting in the area, except your little thorn bushes.**

"That's what I mean. This one in particular, right here. What do you think of it?"

There was the System's usual pregnant silence Tulland had come to expect, either before it mocked him or when it was at a loss for words.

**I don't understand what you are getting at.**

"No, I bet you don't." The System had no idea about Tulland's recent biome skill, and the sheer confusion in its voice confirmed that it hadn't even begun to figure out what Tulland was up to. Without that skill as context, the things Tulland had spent the last few hours doing probably looked like sheer insanity, like he was wasting time growing lower-quality plants when he could have tried to figure out how to cultivate better and better ones. "Just know that I'm going faster and doing better than you could possibly imagine. I'll talk to you in a week, okay? Keep your eyes open while I work. You might see some interesting things."

Tulland worked for another five or six hours until he found he was finally too tired to make any more rounds. It was only when he sat down to eat some fruits and rest that he finally started to see the results of his hard labor.

**Skill Level Up!**

Tulland smiled and went to sleep. He saved the satisfaction of looking at his new, survival-crucial numbers until after he woke up.

# CHAPTER FIFTEEN

# FOREST DUKE

**Skill Level Up!**

**Skill Level Up!**

**Skill Level Up!**

*Looks like something's going on. I'd better take a little stroll.*

Tulland loaded up his bag with seeds again before he set out. There were hundreds of the fruits to pick now, compounding at an incredible rate. He tossed big handfuls of them at any open spots of ground as he walked out of his more established territory, picking what he easily could as he went. All around, there were starting to be little sprouts at the bases of long-established plants, springing up and tangling with their older siblings as they grew.

*I guess it makes sense.* Tulland ran his hand over one particularly dense clump of four or five plants. *The briar patch I jumped headfirst into was huge. These are plants that grow to fill fields if you leave them alone.*

Even when Tulland got out of what he considered his home territory, he found he was still surrounded by briars, if a little sparser. They were springing up from places he had chucked seeds into, getting thicker and stronger as time went by.

He hadn't gained any levels outside his skills, but it was easy to see what the propagation speed was benefiting.

> **Tulland Lowstreet**
> **Class:** Farmer LV. 12
> **Strength:** 25
> **Agility:** 25
> **Vitality:** 20
> **Spirit:** 20
> **Mind:** 10
> **Force:** 20
> **Skills:** Quickgrow LV. 8, Enrich Seed LV. 8
> **Passives:** Biome Control LV. 4, Botanical Engineer LV. 2, Strong Back LV. 2

Tulland did his best to control his expectations for future leveling. It seemed like there was only so much any particular activity could do for him before the Dungeon System caught on and capped him. He guessed that for a regular dungeon class, that just meant they pressed forward to find the next tougher monster. Or for a farming class outside of the dungeon, they would try new crops or else be okay with just waiting around for a few growing seasons' worth of experience to accumulate.

Here, reason and fairness were out the window. New enemy types meant Tulland would level very quickly after the initial encounter, if the trend after facing his first two enemy types was to be believed. After that, he was getting a little bit of experience from farming, with bigger chunks coming in from achievements.

He wasn't okay with that, but there wasn't much he could do but grow more things and hope his plants eventually found their new types of prey. And that he got credit for those kills while he was nowhere nearby.

Tulland did his rounds, marveling at how fast things were going and speeding up the process where he could. It was when he had just about finished the loop that he noticed something.

*Droppings. New droppings.*

If this place was fake, the Infinite had done a pretty good job simulating it. Tulland had become pretty familiar with the leavings of the Razored Lungers over the last several days, especially since they seemed to usually leave some out of sheer fear when his briar vines caught them. These were different. Mostly, they were larger. Whatever had put down the pile was a bigger animal, if the evidence was any indication. But they were also just different enough that Tulland was pretty sure he wasn't looking at the same type of animal as Razored Lungers. He didn't know a lot about droppings or tracking, but these were quite a lot larger than anything else he had seen.

*It's worth looking into, at least.* Tulland reached for his tool and turned it into a shovel before making any final decisions about what he would do about the animal. Whatever he did, it was no use letting good fertilizer go to waste. He scooped up what was there and walked it over to the nearest briar, dumping it on the ground where the stalk of the plant met the soil.

After putting his tool away and grabbing his club, Tulland dropped his bag on the ground and started walking through the woods.

Tracking wasn't really a thing on Ouros, mostly because there wasn't much to track. Good fishermen had a sense of where schools of fish might be found from day to day, but that was about as close as they got to the tracking that ranger classes might do. As such, he had no idea what he was doing at all. He kept his eyes peeled for anything unusual and otherwise just moved in a fairly straight line directly away from his territory, hoping he got lucky.

*Come on, prey. Let me find you and kill you. Good ol' Tulland needs the experience. I'm sure you understand.* Tulland's eyes lit up once he found a broken branch with a bit of fur stuck to it. It wasn't Lunger fur, at least, which helped him keep his hopes for more experience up as he crept quietly through the woods, his club up and ready for action.

Action found him soon enough. He was pushing quietly through some brush between a stand of trees when it suddenly gave way. Catching his forward momentum with a quick stumbling step forward, Tulland saw the animal standing across the field.

His mistake, Tulland immediately knew, was assuming that whatever he was chasing would end up being prey. Almost everything was prey for something, but Tulland had forgotten that almost nothing was prey for him personally until a week or so ago. The general inability of the Lungers to deal with any of his various vine-based attacking options and the fact that the vines around his base dealt with most threats before he even saw them had done more than just give Tulland a false sense of security.

*It made me stupid.*

The fact that he was dumb was hardly in question. The antler animal in front of him was huge and muscular, clearly built for long-distance speed in a way the Lungers weren't, and had antlers that literally glowed near their spiked tips. This was a different tier of animal entirely, something that might have been technically killable, but was absolutely, positively not *prey*.

---

**Objective Change!**
You have failed to locate the exit of this floor before running afoul of its

ruler. The stair to the next floor has been rendered undiscoverable until either you or it perishes.
**New Objective:** Kill the Forest Duke

**Forest Duke**
This large hoofed animal rules over its territory with impunity, attacking any animal with the temerity to get close. It is vicious, powerful, and has encyclopedic knowledge in regards to the layout of this floor.

*The Forest Duke represents a powerful challenge for any adventurer new to the Infinite, and promises similarly outsized rewards to those that defeat it.*

Tulland took off running. If there was any question whether the antler monster would chase after him, that was immediately answered by the soil that the thing ripped up and threw behind as it launched itself toward him.

Tulland was fast, much faster than he realized. His strength and agility were pushing him farther on each stride than he would have thought possible if he wasn't accomplishing the feat in that moment. The Forest Duke was still much faster. Even with the head start of an entire forest clearing, it only took about ten seconds before Tulland could hear the monster a few footsteps behind him.

Tulland turned on a dime and swung the club back and forth, wild enough that the Forest Duke had to take note. He was almost completely sure the weapon wouldn't do much to the monster, but the Forest Duke certainly didn't know that yet. It was better than getting skewered immediately, in any case.

The antlers whistled through the air as the animal swung them side to side, which gave Tulland just enough warning to duck and turn before they impaled him on the head. He managed to dodge four of those attacks before he caught his foot on a root, lost a mere fraction of a breath's time, and felt the antlers crash into his left arm from the side.

Tulland went flying. He managed to land on his feet, but his offhand arm was a mess. Something important for holding it up had broken below his shoulder, and it hung limp at his side. Aware that he now wouldn't be able to swing his club well with his balance gone, Tulland threw it sidearm at the animal as hard as he could.

It wasn't a good throw, but it still meant trouble when the Forest Duke didn't even appear to mind the hit. The club thunked into the animal, failing to penetrate far into its hide to bother anything, then fell to the floor. The animal looked at the weapon, snorted, then brought its rage-filled eyes back up to gaze at Tulland.

That delay saved him. It was just long enough for whatever primitive targeting the briar vines used to figure out where the threat was and start launching themselves. As the huge elk took a step forward toward Tulland, it was suddenly snagged around the ankle by the end of a vine wrapped around Tulland's now useless club.

The Forest Duke roared with rage when a lucky twist let the thorn penetrate a bit into the animal's ankle as the briar worked back and forth, trying to wrap the animal up. But what little bit of length it had managed to unwrap from the club wasn't enough for a full loop. With a quick motion, the elk brought its rear legs up before kicking them out and sending Tulland's club flying into the distance.

While that happened, the two vines around Tulland's arms were already in motion. The first flew from his good arm while it was outstretched from the club throwing, and hit the animal low. It managed to get around both of its forelegs while the beast was dealing with the threat behind it, and made another loop for good measure as it squeezed like a boa constrictor.

For just a second, Tulland had some hope that his plants might work. If the Forest Duke didn't have a counter to the threat of the Hades Lunger Briar, it just might be enough to slow it down, hurt it, or even kill it over enough time.

It wasn't meant to be. Shaking its head in rage, the monster lowered its jaw to the vine, bit down, and severed it in two. That was too much for the vine, which went limp immediately.

The last vine was an overachiever. As Tulland started running again, it had already taken the opportunity to latch around the Forest Duke's neck, which was about the least convenient angle Tulland could imagine if the monster was going to bite through it. Tulland didn't wait to see how that briar fared. Given what he had seen so far, it was almost certain that the vine wouldn't be enough to stop the monster for more than a few seconds no matter how well it was situated. He needed as much distance as he could get, as quickly as he could get it.

He got some too. It took the Forest Duke almost a half minute to catch up to him once it started after him again. Out of weapons, injured, and still a good distance from home, Tulland steeled himself for death as he kept running. He might have led it through the briars, but they were far from solidly grown out here, and the thing was smart enough to avoid them during the chase. He could turn and fight, but there was little question who would win.

*At least it doesn't seem like it will take it very long to finish the job. It's pretty strong.*

In the end, it was Tulland's makeshift bag that saved him. Tulland didn't lead the duke over it on purpose, but the mere fact that the fastest way home took him past the bag meant that they both crossed over it as they ran. Neither of them was expecting anything from it, and both were equally shocked when the entire bag, powered by its Lunger Briar parts, bounced off the ground, wrapped around the front leg of the duke like a long plant-based sock, and began to squeeze.

Tulland ran like he was being chased by the devil himself. He might as well have been. And thankfully, the bag was made out of so many different segments of vine that the Forest Duke had trouble getting rid of them all. Every time it bit through one, another few would untangle and start working on the monster. Tulland moved as fast as he could while the elk monster trumpeted in rage behind him, closing the distance to his home as fast as he could.

He managed to make it with the Forest Duke following close behind. His territory was thick enough with briars that they began to slow the elk down, either by outright attacking or making the monster take a less-than-straight line that allowed Tulland to maintain his lead.

Finally, Tulland found himself at the entrance to his camp with a lead of several strides. His arm was screaming in so much pain that he thought he'd puke, but he launched himself through the air, leaping headfirst into his enclosure and rolling as he made it past his own guard briars.

The Forest Duke looked at the space in confusion. It seemed to have no idea that anything like this was here, which was reasonable enough considering the patch hadn't been this developed several days ago. Its angry eyes came up and looked at Tulland wildly as it considered the new scenery.

*Come on. Don't step forward. Just go away. Don't step forward. Please.*

It took it a few more seconds to decide, and Tulland looked on in resignation as the elk snorted, put its hoof forward, and began to walk into his camp.

# CHAPTER SIXTEEN

# IRONBRANCH SAPLING

The only thing standing between Tulland and getting speared on a half dozen antler points was his fragile, mindlessly loyal vines. They weren't very strong. Even though one member of the briar corps had killed dozens of Razored Lungers, that only meant Tulland had a slightly less mooky mook fighting on his side. He had only created a weapon that could consistently take out the lowest-level threat living on the first floor of a supposedly infinite tower.

The Forest Duke was probably the weakest boss the tower had to offer. Compared to the Cannian Knight that Tulland would find on the fifth floor, it was like fighting a down-stuffed pillow. But the big deerlike thing was still a boss, and an optional challenge boss on top of that. It was strong enough to effortlessly break even the strongest of Tulland's briar army. It charged past the first one, then past the second, and then the third. As they grasped on, it slowed slightly and only took the shallowest of scratches from the thorns.

And not that it was a good bet, not that it was how Tulland wanted to find out exactly how far the whole biome density concept could go, but there were a few things the elk hadn't thought about while it accurately assessed that each individual briar wasn't a threat. The first was pain.

*Stings, huh?* Tulland grinned through the bloody teeth he had gained from getting smacked around by the elk, not pitying it one bit. One characteristic of the briars was that they hurt like hell, something that probably didn't add much to their general lethality but was, in Tulland's direct and personal experience, distracting as hell. Annoyed and slightly agonized by the new-found pain, the Forest Duke stopped to retaliate against a few of the briars, trumpeting and snorting as it did.

That was a mistake. The elk hadn't considered that Tulland kept hundreds of briars in the deep hallway he had built around his exit. While both the Forest Duke and Tulland fully agreed that it could take on as many individual briars as it wanted, this wasn't a one-on-one duel.

Tulland had been paranoid that some smart monster would sneak in during the night, and his solution had been to overpopulate his home camp to an extent that it would kill a Razored Lunger a hundred times over. The math didn't necessarily make sense when comparing one very large, very strong enemy against what amounted to a bunch of very sharp badgers, but it was still a lot of briars, much more than he suspected the boss had any kind of experience with.

When the Forest Duke moved to retaliate, a dozen more briars found themselves in position to strike. When the monster broke away from those too, it got into range of a dozen more briars, all ready to spend out their life force trying to take him down. The monster wasn't stopped, exactly. It was making slow, steady progress toward Tulland. But it had slowed to a crawl as it fought with thorn briar after thorn briar in an endless hallway of annoyance and pain.

Tulland decided to make it worse for the elk. After struggling back to his feet, he rushed around the complex cutting down his oldest and toughest Hades Lunger Briars, dropping his tool after each cut to use his good hand to pick up the harvest and chuck it either at the Forest Duke or in the way of its advance. As he did, he felt *Strong Back* very slowly working to reorient his bones and get him back in shape for what the skill likely thought of as a hard day's work on a normal, completely conventional farm.

After the first fifteen chucked vines, something shifted hard in Tulland's shoulder. The bone clicked back into place, almost knocking him out with pain but also bringing his left arm back to some semblance of function. He roared, letting the agony drive his adrenaline as he cut and chucked as many briars as he could get his hands on.

The mere fact that the briars were now flying from a higher angle made the pain worth it. The Forest Duke had to worry about its neck and eyes, which meant that those briars were getting most of its attention. It was surprisingly flexible and good at sussing out the right angle to twist its head against each new grasping projectile, but it was still slowing down that much more.

And yet, it wouldn't be enough. Tulland could see that. He was shit at fighting. The briars could do their absolute best and it still wouldn't be enough to take down the Forest Duke. It was going to take forever, but the monster was eventually going to get through the briar hallway, and then Tulland would have nowhere to go.

He might have even tried to fight it too, if he had only kept his club. Now he had nothing to work with but his Farmer's Tool, which wouldn't do much. And he had briar vines, which weren't long enough to be used as a whip but might have done something beyond a distraction—if Tulland had a way to mount them on a chassis that would let him attack in any way besides chucking them in the enemy's direction. There was no way he could do that.

*But is that true? I do have at least one stick.*

Every day, religiously, Tulland had pumped multiple charges of *Quickgrow* into his tree seed. It had sprouted and put the magical power to use, albeit slowly. It was never going to be a full tree while Tulland was here. He had long since accepted that he'd either move on or die before the plant got big enough to look like anything besides a very young sapling.

It was a very young, very green, and very healthy-looking stick with precious few branches coming off it, but it was a stick. Tulland threw the last few briars he had cut and rushed over to it, giving it a quick inspect to see what he was dealing with.

**Ironbranch Sapling (Semi-Cultivated)**

You have not cultivated this plant from a seed, but your involvement in its growth grants you access to some enhanced knowledge about it.

The Ironbranch Tree reproduces by means of large herbivorous animals that feed off its bark. As they do, they carry indigestible seeds with them, eventually depositing them in some other location with a generously provided dollop of fertilizer to go with it.

It uses this initial burst of energy to throw a deep root structure through the soil, gathering some small amount of organic material and a great deal of inorganic material into itself. The resulting wood is irregular and tough in a way that makes it unsuitable for most forms of refined woodworking. It is, however, exceptionally hard and heavy.

*Your involvement in the growth of this plant grants you slightly increased influence over it, augmenting the ease with which you can harvest from it.*

Tulland prayed that "ease with which you can harvest from it" stretched so far as to encompass "cutting down the entire plant," and was pleased when his very best scythe swing managed to put a half-inch notch in the tree. He didn't wait to see if he could slice the same spot again, and instead just threw all his weight into his good shoulder as he more or less tackled the tree. Tulland heard a satisfying crack as it cleaved at the point he had precut into it, leaving him with a mostly uncracked, only slightly pointed stick about as thick as his wrist.

He looked over at the Forest Duke, which was now steadily pushing through the last quarter or so of his briars. There wasn't any time to mess with the stick any further. Either it would be enough of his creation to do decent damage to system things at his current level of skill, or it wouldn't.

Tulland ran as fast as he could to where the Forest Duke was restrained, planted his lead foot heavily in the dirt in front of it, and swung at the elk's head with every last bit of his strength he could muster. He missed, then almost fell on his own backside as the monster snapped its teeth at him, ignoring the briars for a moment to attack the bigger, softer target.

Tulland reset and swung just as heavily again, then again. He missed each time, as he might have expected when fighting a much superior opponent.

And then, just for a moment, the sheer pain of the thorns got to the monster. It reared its head up to scream in frustration and rage, terrifying Tulland despite his knowledge that it couldn't get to him at the moment. But, amid all the noise, it also made a mistake. For just a moment, it closed its eyes.

Tulland heaved the stick forward with all the power he could. He was hoping to knock it out, although he suspected that was a pipe dream. What he did not expect was to get enormously lucky and connect the swing almost entirely with the Forest Duke's closed right eye, which popped like a grape as the stick slammed into it.

The Forest Duke trumpeted in panic and thrashed its head around, which turned out to be an error in and of itself, as one of the few briars that still had its roots in place shot up and wrapped around its bloody snout.

*Is it . . . drinking the blood?* Tulland had pulled the club back to smack the Forest Duke again and again, but couldn't get a clean shot on it as the animal thrashed through the briars. As a notification popped up, he spared the bare minimum amount of time to see the headline and figure out if it was anything at all that could help him. He hated the fact that the Infinite's Dungeon System didn't seem to come with his System's instant communication feature.

> **Crop Milestone Reached!**
> One of your cultivated plants has reached level ten. For this first-time milestone, a significant amount of experience is granted.

*Level ten? That's massive.* Tulland's plants had been doing better and better as they brought in more prey and he gave them better starts with his skills and fertilizer, but he was pretty sure the highest-level plant he had seen was level six. This one either was doing better than he thought or had just gained several levels from plugging into the nutrition of the floor boss's blood.

It wasn't something Tulland needed to think a lot about, but as he continued to ineffectually swing his club at the Forest Duke with his stick, he was considering the fact that everything he could do for a plant tended to build on everything else.

*Enrich Seed* seemed to work better on plants that were put down with fertilizer to burn for energy, at least here in this forest where the soil was about the worst he had ever seen. And enriching a seed would lead to a plant that dealt better with *Quickgrow*. Those enhanced plants would then capture and convert more monsters to fertilizer and increase their growth. Now, Tulland was trying to find the next step for his plants to give it that extra edge.

The Forest Duke reared its head and pulled the ambitious level-ten briar out from the ground, but with so much force that the plant was still clinging to most of the soil it had grown in. It might, just might, be enough to make what Tulland was about to try work, if it would work at all.

Tulland held the stick out in a warding motion as he switched to a one-handed grip, then pointed his finger at the spot he wanted to focus on. It was where the blood was hitting the lucky Lunger Briar at the highest concentration, and something in his farmer's intuition told him this was where the plant was getting the most benefit.

*Of course, it probably doesn't matter, as long as I hit the plant at all. It's sort of a by-the-unit deal.*

Taking a deep breath, Tulland focused as much of his attention as he could muster and activated his only farming skill that could be applied multiple times on the same plant.

"*Quickgrow.* Enjoy it, buddy. And good luck."

# CHAPTER SEVENTEEN

# OVERDRIVE

It seemed to. Tulland's farmer sense started tingling in the back part of his head, telling him the plant was changing. It got greener, and while it didn't get thicker, it did seem denser somehow, like it was growing in weight instead of length or width. The strength of the vine was radiating off it, and it felt entirely unlike any plant Tulland had ever dealt with before. It was filling up his farmer sense, the least defined of his ways of observing the world. And it was doing it so powerfully he could barely breathe in its presence.

He wasn't the only one who noticed the change. The Forest Duke bellowed as its head was suddenly jerked downward, then managed to force it back up to glare at Tulland through its one good eye. As terrifying as that was, there was something different about the encounter now. The Forest Duke was strong, but the vine was just as powerful, at least from its superior positioning on the duke's body. Even when the elk finally lowered its head to take a bite, it couldn't get through the vine in one go or even make much progress at all.

Tulland started clubbing as hard as he could with the Ironbranch club, now able to land any of his shots at will. Individually, none of them were much, maybe making the duke care about half as much as a boxer getting hit with a jab would.

*But hits like that add up. I have to make them count.*

As the Forest Duke continued to try and dislodge the overpowered vine, Tulland readied himself and gave all of his strength to his next strike.

As the stick swished through the air, Tulland's weapon almost felt out of control, like he had put so much weight into the hit that he was going to tumble over after it once it landed. High vitality or not, the Forest Duke was going to feel this one. And then, like it had been waiting for this level of danger the entire time, the Forest Duke exploded with light.

*What is that?* Tulland activated his connection to the System as fast as he could, so quickly that the stick was still in motion as he did. His blow impacted before the System could answer. But it was almost like he hit the light instead of the animal. The stick slid off to the side as Tulland really did stumble after it. The Forest Duke swung its head to the side, pulling the ultra-briar as it clipped Tulland's side and sent him tumbling into his own briar wall, which luckily was thick enough with his own creations that it didn't hurt him much.

**An overdrive skill, or something like it. He's stronger now. A skill like that is meant to even the playing field, but it doesn't last forever. Survive long enough, and the day is yours.**

Every vine on the wall jumped out at the Forest Duke as it followed after Tulland, making the animal hesitate just long enough for Tulland to stuff the end of the sapling in its face. The combined delay of both was enough for him to skirt around back toward the entrance of the enclosure. The duke followed, now encumbered with another five or six vines that had gotten a good enough grip to be dragged along for the ride.

They made much less of a difference now. The mega-briar was still doing good work, but it was far from the near even match it had enjoyed before. The addition of the new vines tipped the scales only slightly back in the right direction. Tulland hugged the wall as he backed up, watching a few remnant vines find purchase on the animal as he did, but there was almost no marginal effect per plant. He wasn't going to get through this with just vines. They weren't enough, and the elk was moving too fast.

*Forget caution, I guess. I just have to last a little, right?*

Tulland decided to go crazy. He jumped in with the sapling, cracking the Forest Duke across the forehead with it and taking a deep stab in his arm from one of the antler points as he did. It hurt deep, not just in his muscles and bone but throughout his entire body. Five minutes ago, the pain alone would have sent him running for his life. He couldn't afford that now. More importantly, he was going to see this through to the end, no matter what.

The Forest Duke was able to move its head fast enough that Tulland couldn't dodge its antlers when it struck, but it was slowed just enough that each hit wasn't quite fatal. At the same time, the Forest Duke couldn't move out of the way of any particular strike from Tulland's Ironbranch club. It was a battle of attrition now, something that was barely sustainable on either of their ends.

The Forest Duke had enough of the tit for tat after a few seconds, and glowed even brighter, swinging its head in an uppercut motion at Tulland. There was no mystery what would happen if that strike connected, given how very bright the antlers were. He jumped backward with all his might, bringing the club down as hard as he could as he did. If he wasn't going to be quite fast enough with his stat-based movement, he could at least make it more complex for his enemy.

The elk somehow managed to speed up even more, tilting its head to put the longest of its antler points on a collision course with Tulland's neck. Before it could actually finish the hit, the stick struck just above its ruined eye. Tulland was shocked he made contact, but even more shocked when the contact actually did something. The animal's head was stopped flat, then pushed downward a bit. It was impossible, given Tulland's strength. He would have loved to have thought he had done it himself, but he just wasn't strong enough.

*It's the briar. It's still helping.*

The ultra-powered briar was still working in the background. Between that and the hit from the stick, it seemed just enough to nullify the elk's big strike. And that was when the corner was turned. That one ultrabright strike seemed to be almost the last of the power the Forest Duke was getting from its berserk skill, and the antlers dimmed almost immediately. The briar, ragged and ripped, was still hanging on and squeezed. The Forest Duke whined, as if it couldn't believe that its opponent would still be standing after all that.

Tulland lunged forward. He kept piling on the strikes, surprised he could still move as the blood from his wounds soaked his clothes.

Even more surprising, the hits seemed to be doing something. Tulland was absolutely sure that his Farmer's Tool wouldn't be doing anything at all here. But the stick and the briars were different. They were suffused with his class, and Tulland got the impression that Dungeon Systems like the Infinite's had nothing better than a fuzzy idea of what to do with things like a farmer class's grown products. Luckily, it seemed to err on a sort of well-why-not liberalism that made everything possible.

All of which was great and gave Tulland an advantage he was very happy to live with, right up until it didn't. Snorting in rage and rolling its single angry eye around, the Forest Duke suddenly strained upward with its neck so hard that Tulland thought it would pull something. It did, although not in a way he wanted. The strong briar was wrapped so tight into its flesh by then that there just wasn't enough slack for it to keep up, and the sound of overstretching in its fibers lasted just a moment before it snapped entirely.

*Oh, no.* Tulland immediately leveled the stick, aiming the pointy, jagged part almost perfectly forward. *I better make this shot count. I don't think I'm getting any more.*

Tulland dumped whatever tiny amount of magic he had regenerated into another enhancement of the briars, stepped forward hard, and lunged out with his makeshift spear as hard and fast as he could. He was aiming at the Forest Duke's throat, which was still exposed as its head remained high with the momentum released from the snapping vine. It would take the monster a moment to lower its head again, which was hopefully all Tulland needed to land one good shot.

The spear cooperated perfectly, flowing forward straight and true toward the elk's larynx. Tulland put every ounce of weight he had into the blow, knowing that if he missed, he would end up toppling forward into the Forest Duke's antlers.

But he didn't miss. With a squelch, the spear made contact.

The elk lowered its head and regarded Tulland with a cool rage, then shook its head slightly as it usually did before it huffed. This time nothing came out. The Forest Duke glanced down and widened its eyes as Tulland looked forward and saw that the impossible had happened. The stick was a good two inches into the monster's throat, which was now pouring out blood like a bucket with a hole in it.

Tulland knew a chance when he saw one. He pressed forward hard on the stick, following the monster as it tried to back up off it. The combination of Tulland's forward motion and the briar shackles hobbling the Forest Duke's movement speed was just enough for the stick to stay in place, And, as it turned out, a stick through one's throat was a very effective way to be forced to go where the stick-holder wanted. As Tulland backed the monster up, he cranked the stick hard to his own right, which forced the Forest Duke to turn away from its straight, safe path back to safety. Instead, it ran right into the thick briar wall to the side of the farm's entrance hallway.

Mostly, the wall was just conventional briars. There were a few by-blow children of his cultivated vines mixed in there, but only weak ones that didn't stand much of a chance of holding the Forest Duke for long. It didn't matter much. Even brittle, weak briars had thorns and were able to tangle up living things. The briar patch was more than happy to crack, break, and rebound around the floor's boss as it retreated step by step.

With the elk sinking deeper in to the briars, Tulland began to crank on the stick higher, using it as a lever of sorts, one that used the monster's pain as a fulcrum. It had to sink lower. There was just no way for it to keep from more serious damage except moving in the direction Tulland commanded. Soon, it was on its knees. Tulland was about to press his advantage when the stick finally broke off inside its neck.

But it was enough.

The Forest Duke was now having incredible trouble just getting up. Tulland's briars were working on it hard, and the passive, uncultivated briars all around it were offering them cover. Tulland took a few moments to go get the broken but still active Lunger Briar vines from the hallway, ones the Forest Duke had evaded or partially broken but hadn't quite killed. He picked them up barehanded and chucked them near the monster, where they happily completed the last few inches of travel and added to the bindings.

And then it was over. With a final enraged huff, the Forest Duke lost the last bits of glow from its emergency power skill, and collapsed.

Tulland was a mess, still bleeding from twenty gashes he hadn't noticed much during the fight, and still operating on barely patched bones that creaked and jolted him with pain every time he moved. The Forest Duke was slowly being consumed by the briars, which were more than happy to dig their thorns deeper and deeper into its flesh.

Tulland limped over and looked down at the animal in pity. It really was a beautiful thing, outside of the part where it wanted him dead. Tulland grabbed one of its hooves and hauled it away from the briar wall, getting it to a neutral part of his farm before separating it from the few briars that still had enough life left in them to move. He would use the monster corpse later, if he could.

*I'll also review all these notifications I'm getting. Sometime. Right now, I'm pretty tired.*

Tulland managed to get a drink of water from his makeshift well that was really just a deep pit in the ground before his eyes started to droop. A few seconds later, he was asleep.

And then he was somewhere else.

# CHAPTER EIGHTEEN

# ADJUDICATING

Well, this is interesting." A tall, mediocre-looking man walked from behind Tulland, who found himself in a near duplicate of his own briar fortress. The man was holding a similarly detailed copy of his overpowered briar, turning it over in his hands and gazing at it in interest. "I haven't had to do an active judgment in . . . well, in a while. What did you say your name was again?"

"I . . ." Tulland gulped. This guy was weirdly casual in a way that, for some reason, screamed danger. "I didn't. I don't think."

"Oh, right." The man made a mock motion of slapping his forehead. "I didn't need to ask. Let me just check. Oh, I see. Tulland Lowstreet. The same one who made the wager the other day, right? I kind of expected you to be dead by now."

"Are you . . ."

"Yes. Well, part of him, anyway."

"Part of us." A woman's voice rang out. Tulland turned to see a middle-aged lady sitting in a wooden chair that simply hadn't been there before. "I'm going to need you to stop applying *him* to our chorus like it covers all of us. It doesn't."

"And when she whines about it, I have to listen to it." A surly-looking teenager walked up to one of the briars and flicked it. "And I don't get to see whatever's going on that much these days. Good job, by the way. It's rare we see anything new."

"Oh. Thanks." Tulland scratched his head. "So all of you are the Infinite's System?"

"Kind of, yes, sorta, no, and of course," the unimpressive man said. "We've found that trying to explain exactly how this works to humans doesn't really take, no matter how we do it. The best approximation I can give is that multiple beings give better advice, on average, than individual beings. And I'm supposed to do a good job, so there are a lot of me."

"More than this?"

"Oh, yeah. Dozens of us. Hundreds. Thousands. Don't worry too much about the details. We thought three would be enough for something like this." The woman was now drinking an iced beverage that also hadn't been there the last time Tulland looked. "Could you turn on your little System friend, by the way? It could probably explain some of this while we work."

**. . . when you get this going you should leave right away; just demand it and they have to let you go. Nothing good can come of this at all. Go, before they decide to . . .**

The System was, for whatever reason, panicking when Tulland switched it on.

"Shush, you." The Infinite's System boy turned around and made a slapping motion with his hand, which looked playful enough until Tulland actually heard his System gasp in pain. "Just tell him what we're doing. There's no reason for us to do anything to you beyond that."

**Oh. Well then.**

*That was enough to calm you down?* Tulland thought.

**It's the Infinite. It wouldn't bother breaking a promise to me. That's simply not worth its time.**

Tulland chewed on that little tidbit of information about the hierarchy of things for a moment before pushing the conversation forward out loud. It probably didn't matter whether he was speaking or not. If the Infinite's Dungeon System was that powerful, then it had just as much access to Tulland's thoughts as his Ouros System did. On the other side, the woman was out of her chair now, saying things to the other two people.

"So what are they doing?" Tulland asked in a lower voice.

**Adjudicating. You did something that the Infinite hasn't had to think about before. It's not enough for it just to make a decision on the fly, since it's much harder for it to adjust a skill after the fact than to decide how things work well from the beginning. So it's . . .**

"Having a meeting to decide?"

**Close enough. I still think you should leave, by the way.**

"For my sake, or because it makes you more likely to win our bet if I do?"

The System went quiet then, which felt like a pretty good indication that whatever was happening was at least as likely to help Tulland as it was to hurt it. He turned the System back off for the moment so he could focus on what the Infinite's different personas were saying.

The boy was the one talking at the moment. "The point is that we've already been treating the plants like they work that way. Which is probably why he tried it in the first place. And it's unfair to rip capabilities from adventurers here. He worked for it. He should get to keep it."

"Yes, I know." The woman nodded at the boy seriously. "But this . . . It's a bit powerful, but that's not the issue. With this, he'd never have to move. He could plant briars, stay in the center, and wait until the entire floor was eaten up with them. That doesn't just affect him. It affects the floors themselves."

"And if he found the right combination of beasts, some of those vines would put tamers to shame. Those are the issues. The propagation and the uncapped fertilization effect. Not cobbling together something that works with a class that by all rights should have already gotten him killed." The man glanced Tulland's way and winced apologetically. "Sorry."

"No, I know. Please continue," Tulland said.

"Polite." The man nodded approvingly. "I like that. I've heard both of your inputs on this matter now, and I'm the lead in this scenario. Are we all comfortable with me rendering my decision?"

"Sure," the boy said, as the woman also nodded along. "Ready when you are."

"Well, then." The man turned to Tulland. "To give you a quick summary of what's happened here, you managed to find a loophole in your skill that we all more or less agree would stretch the definitions of your class past its breaking points. You would be something like a vampire class by proxy. No, don't ask what that is. It's just not something you can be."

Tulland nodded. He was fine with not understanding every single thing being said right now.

"At the same time, it's not fair to rob you of a more-than-reasonable reward for figuring out how to do that. There are ways classes just can't work, or else very lucky people would get invincible classes from time to time and dominate entire worlds. You know that doesn't happen."

"So you just say no?" Tulland was getting over the shock of the meeting and beginning to understand he might take a loss here. "And I try to beat things like the Forest Duke to death with a stick?"

"Not quite. Because you still did something cool. May I?" The boy looked at the man, who nodded. Whoever the Infinite was, they really liked nodding.

"See, this was allowable under the rules of your class until just now, and we never penalize someone for optimizing, even if we can't allow it moving forward. So you get a payout. You don't win the court case, but you get a settlement, if that makes sense."

It didn't. Tulland nodded anyway.

The woman picked up the mantle of the conversation then, smiling and patting Tulland on the shoulder.

"What we are doing won't hurt your progress, Tulland, at least compared to what you've already accomplished. You'll be as strong as you were fighting that monster, and you'll be able to do some things you weren't before, just capped by your skill levels like any class would be. It's as fair of a trade as we can manage, within the rules. The rest you can see in your notification screens, but you've made real progress here. You don't have much of a chance, but nobody who finds their way here does."

"All right, then. All done." The man nodded, as if he had actually accomplished something. "We'll give you just a little bit to read your new notifications, but don't lollygag, all right? It's not forever. And good luck with that wager. It's . . . fun, even if we can't help with it. We're looking forward to seeing how that turns out."

And then all three of them were gone.

---

**Skill Adjustment:** Quickgrow **Becomes** Enhance Plant
Where Quickgrow applied only to the growth of plants and let them take advantage of particularly rich sources of nutrients, Enhance Plant now improves whatever function of a plant is most important in that moment. If the plant is at rest, this will usually be growing or reinforcing itself in some way. If it's involved in another activity, it will enhance that instead.

*Fertilizer will still make a difference in a plant's growth rate, but the use you can get out of any given fertilizer will be capped by this skill's level. The total number of plants you can carry with the intent of using them as "active equipment" is now limited, with a total cap variable depending on the type of plant.*

---

**Skill Adjustment:** Biome Control **Becomes** Broadcast
Your previous skill never got to the point of triggering a judgment session of its own, but it was vaguely possible for you to overgrow each floor of the dungeon using nothing but your Hades Lunger Briars and turning each of them into a kind of botanical hell.

It is no longer possible to do this.

The skill now works over a lesser range, and does not affect propagation rates. Your plants will no longer have the capability of becoming a self-reinforcing plague, as per system rules.

The loss of this function is compensated in two ways. First, the enhancements to your plants are no longer keyed to nearby biome density. Instead, you can now "stake" a location as the center of your "farm" and every plant you grow within that new area (current maximum farm size: a ten-meter square) will provide strength to other plants at an unlimited distance.

This means, for instance, that you can carry a Lunger Briar with you that is enhanced by the overall quality of your base regardless of how far you are from it.

The second compensation involves your ability to use any of your farming skills that affect plants. Unless otherwise noted, the effect of any skill that benefits your crops can be split up among multiple plants, capped by the level of this skill (current maximum ratio: fifteen plants). The split is slightly in your favor, meaning that the total power received by multiple plants is more in total than would be applied to a single plant.

*Both the maximum farm size and maximum split ratio improve with the level of the skill. However, the strength distance function of this skill fails as you cross over to new levels of the tower, but you may retain the full effects of your previous farm for forty-eight hours after a new level is reached.*

Tulland rushed through the notifications. He hadn't figured out every little bit of meaning behind the changes to the skills, but he had understood enough to know two of his next steps.

If he understood the *Broadcast* skill correctly, it wanted him to place his stake where his plants were the densest. Luckily, that was almost directly behind him, where his Lunger Briars had been growing like crazy and the roots of his Ironbranch Sapling were still in the soil. He activated it and felt a bit of feedback that his plants were now benefiting from the density of his farm.

Which, sadly, also meant his briars were a bit weaker now, as they had gone from using some uncountable huge number of plants to a much more limited stock. It wasn't a huge difference, as the farm seemed to get more plant-for-plant enhancement than before.

But if Tulland wanted to level the playing field again before he took the time to grow more plants and optimize his new farm area, he had only one to do that with. And to his pleasure, he found his magical power was completely topped off and ready to play with, perhaps as a parting gift from the Infinite.

Tulland walked through his farm until he found fifteen vines within range.

He could feel them through the skill. He selected them mentally to be the beneficiaries of the skill, and added his Ironbranch Sapling fragment to the tally.

The magic power flowed out of him in a torrent. The sapling took none of it, which was something he'd figure out later. The briars were a different story. He focused on making them temporarily stronger, not making them grow faster, and felt the guidance take hold. His farmer's intuition tingled as he felt all of them get stronger. Individually, none of them was quite what his megabriar had been. But as a group? They might have been even more.

*Oh, yes.* Tulland smiled. *I can probably work with this.*

# CHAPTER NINETEEN

# SURVIVAL

**T**his is an odd dream, boy.

Tulland was on a boat, alone, in the middle of the sea, far enough out that Ouros looked like a dot of earth in the distance. He was, in the setting of the dream, very small. Much too small to pilot a boat of this type, too weak to work any of the instruments, and too short to reach several of them. And even if all that wasn't true, he didn't even understand most of what was happening.

For all practical purposes, the dream should have been a nightmare. Instead, Tulland was excited.

"Why's that?" Tulland asked.

**Because you should have suspected you were going to die. And while you are naive, I do not believe you have ever been truly dim. Why aren't you frightened in this memory?**

"It's not a secret. I can tell you, but you have to answer something for me first. Why are you even here?"

**Because you allowed me to be. I have no way of breaking past the cordon the Infinite has set around your mind and soul otherwise.**

"I didn't allow you," Tulland protested.

**You must have.**

As the Tulland of his own memories dipped a hand in the surprisingly warm water, the Tulland of the present puzzled over the System's presence. He supposed he had been pretty proud of his kill. It was possible he had absent-mindedly flipped the switch that let the System in to gloat about it just before he went to sleep.

"Fine. I'll believe that for now." Tulland watched through his past's eyes as he looked over the side of the water, a nine- or ten-year-old face reflecting back at him. He looked curious and impatient all at once. "The answer to your question is that I wasn't in any real danger when this happened. Watch."

The System managed to hold its tongue a few seconds, just long enough for the surface of the water to roil, break, and reveal Tulland's uncle's face.

"What did I say, Tulland? Get the net. I need you to have it ready."

Young Tulland rocketed back as he realized his own lapse, then reached for his uncle's wood-and-rope net, holding it over the side of the boat and letting the business end dip below the waterline. His uncle hefted a big armful of something into it, then steadied the net with his hand as he bellied over the bow and out of the water entirely.

"These should do it. There were some big ones down there, after all." His uncle brought the net over to his feet and started pulling large, round shellfish out of it. The bigger ones were about eight inches across. "There are those that tell you not to eat these shellers in the warm months, you know."

"Why?" young Tulland asked.

"Sea worms. Small ones. Parasites. They'll make you sick in a way only a weak poison can cure, since that's what it takes to kill them."

"Oh." Tulland looked at the shellfish doubtfully. "Shouldn't we not take them, then?"

"No, boy. Remember why we came here in the first place. The fish."

Tulland nodded. Earlier in the day, his uncle had caught a spiny, ugly-looking fish that he claimed was poisonous to eat, but kept anyway. Now, it was swimming unhappily in a big, covered tank of water.

"We cook the shellers together with that fish, Tulland, and the poison leaches out of the flesh from the fish. Just enough to kill the worms, you see. And then we wait until the heat cooks the poison off. The heat won't kill the worms alone. And the poison isn't enough by itself. But together, we get a chowder."

Tulland lifted the lid from the fish storage and regarded the spiky, terrible-looking fish with a new respect. "Did you figure that out by yourself, uncle?"

"Oh, no. Of course not. There are too many steps." His uncle pointed at the fish, then the shells, then the ocean. "You have to know that spine fish is poisonous, but that the broth it's cooked in can be safely eaten after heated with enough time. You have to know the shellers are down by the coral, which must have been quite the discovery when they first found them."

"Why would they have even swum down that deep?"

"Probably a dare." His uncle laughed and pulled the oars to a rowing position. "Lots of stuff gets learned though foolish dares, Tulland. More than you'd think. But once you have the shellers, you learn they make you sick. Then someone else learns they only make you sick sometimes. And then someone else figures out it's because of the worms."

"And that's it?"

"That and a bunch of steps I left out. This kind of knowledge is built over generations, Tulland. But eventually, you have it and then you have that much more food. And the island can take care of that many more people."

Tulland started putting the shellers into a bag. That was his job, his uncle had said. The ones from this newest haul joined the rest of the shellers in a big canvas bag, which Tulland tied shut and put in the storage with the rest of the fish.

"What if you wanted to know sooner? To figure it out yourself?" Tulland asked.

"Hmm. A good question." His uncle considered it. "You'd probably have to be hungry."

"Hungry?"

"Starving. A famine, where you can only see faint glimmers of hope. Willing to do anything and try anything. Survival is a powerful motivator, Tulland."

**He is not wrong.**

*Quiet. I'm listening to this.*

Tulland's uncle splashed some fresh water from a bucket on his face, then got to rowing.

"A powerful enough motivator to make for a lot of progress in a short amount of time. I just pray that you'll never have to know something like that firsthand."

Tulland woke up feeling much better. He was starving and entirely sick of the one safe food source he had on hand, and thirsty enough that his entire throat felt like it was lined with sand. But his bones felt better, if not quite right yet, and he had survived. It wasn't a bad state, all things considering.

The thirst was the first problem to get solved as Tulland drank deeply from his makeshift well before heading to his briars that had survived the ordeal and eating several of their fruits. They weren't bad-tasting things, especially once he had become used to them. They were, however, something he had become unbelievably sick of in his time here.

It took less of them to be full than he liked, even as hungry as he was. His stomach was heavy after a few fruits, but he knew he would have to come back to them several more times before he had enough total energy for the day.

After that, he picked quite a few more of the fruits as seeds. By now, the process of using parts of an animal as fertilizer for his vicious briar children was starting to become rote, although the Forest Duke was much larger and the variety of different parts Tulland had available to him meant a little more work. He hurried through it, as the last thing he wanted was for the meat to spoil in some way before his seeds had their shot at it.

After he was finally finished with the grosser part of his day, Tulland settled in for a long bout of reading. And there was plenty to read.

**Level Up! x4**

**Skill Level Up! x8**

The levels and skill levels weren't that unexpected. Tulland welcomed them, but set aside actually doing anything with the points he had gained until he figured out the entire lay of the land. The skill level-ups had mostly gone toward *Enhance Plant* and *Broadcast*, both of which were at level four now. It looked like the levels he already had in the skills they replaced hadn't carried over, but he would decide how he felt about a bit later.

The last two skill levels had settled into *Strong Back*, which Tulland felt like he deserved. He had paid for it in his own blood, more or less.

After that, things got wacky.

**Optional Boss Defeated! (Forest Duke, Tower Level One)**
You have defeated an optional boss and opened the way to a new level of the tower. Your victory was achieved with a small number of optional difficulty modifiers:
**Unarmed:** You defeated the boss without the use of a conventional weapon.
**Unarmored:** You defeated the boss while wearing no combat-sufficient armor.
**Surprised:** The boss forced combat onto you, rather than the other way around, and despite your attempts to flee.
*These modifiers will be considered when your rewards are calculated.*

That, Tulland thought, felt like the kind of thing the Infinite wouldn't let stand. The Ironbranch Sapling didn't really count as a weapon, but the fact that he had won the fight was testament to the idea that he was right on the edge of being armed. He couldn't imagine that he would be allowed to get that kind of premium on every achievement he ever made in combat, forever. Something would eventually change.

That guess was immediately confirmed as the next notification window cycled into his view.

> **Calculation Offset!**
> Some of your recent achievement modifiers have spurred a system adjustment to how future awards will be calculated. The changes are as follows:
> 1. When you use a plant you've grown as a weapon or as armor, they will be considered as such even when inadequate for the task.
> 2. Some achievements for exclusively using your own produce in battle might be possible to attain.
>
> The rewards for this particular event stand as is, and will be given unaltered.

> **Reward List!**
> 1. Lesser Stat Potion
> 2. Farmer's Gloves (Undefined Rarity)
> 3. Skill Pack
>
> *You will receive all of these items, and do not have to choose between them.*

Tulland had expected more items, or at least flashier names. That seemed to be the kind of thing his uncle would have made fun of him for back home though. He held off on his judgment until he read the actual descriptions.

> **Lesser Stat Potion**
> *Consumable, One Dose.*
>
> Grants five stat points to a stat of your choice. As this is a lesser potion, the points cannot be split between stats.

> **Farmer's Gloves (Undefined Rarity)**
> These are possibly the best Farmer's Gloves to have ever existed. By workgear standards, they are impossibly tough. They grant five points to your vitality, and are both self-mending and self-cleaning. They are comfortable, greatly enhance grip, and are specifically fitted and lined to protect your hands from wear over a long day's work.
>
> *They are, however, still work gear and are limited in the ways you'd expect from work clothes.*

"Hey, System," Tulland called out.

**I wondered if you had forgotten I was here.**

"Not quite. I have a question for you, though."

**State it.**

"Work gear. How is it different from proper battle gear?"

The System sighed.

**I forget that you knew little of any class before coming here. Even a crafter would have known that.**

"Well, I wasn't a crafter. Help me out a bit."

**I will, I just need to think of where to start. You've tried killing things with your Farmer's Tool. What was your impression of that experience?**

"It hardly worked. It was like the thing resisted being effective."

**That's right in a way, while being almost entirely wrong. The first thing you should understand is that system equipment is defined, broadly, not by the materials it is made of but by the nature of the magic that inhabits it. When a System's forces flow through an item, they enhance it beyond what could ever be possible in a mundane world.**

"Even work stuff?" Tulland asked.

**Just so, but another aspect of the magic infused in the item is that it can be put to work in very specific ways. You hardly had experience with farm tools before this, but let me tell you that the Farmer's Tool you possess is actually very good. It's more than adequate as a starter item for a beginner farmer.**

Tulland was starting to get it. "But none of that energy is used for attacking?"

**Correct. The item has a purpose that the item itself knows, and it does not deviate from that purpose. On the other side of things, the monsters you have done battle with are magical as well; they are system creations that allot some of the magic in them to defense.**

"And so my magical shovel does almost nothing, since it's attacking a system thing with what amounts to mundane power. Because none of its actual power is meant to be used that way."

**Exactly. The same applies to armor. It should apply to your plants, but does not for some reason I have not myself determined yet.**

"Good enough. Thanks."

Tulland shut off the System. He was fine with it seeing what he was up to, and even knowing that he was getting generally stronger, but the less he could let it know about his overall build, the better. He went to the next window, which might have been the most impressive of them all.

---

**Skill Pack**

Creates one skill that is automatically assigned to the user. The skill is determined using a combination of the user's class and what types of activities the user has been engaging in recently.

Tulland sat back, uncorked and drank his bottle of stats, and dumped the points into strength. While he was at it, he went to work assigning the power he had gained in this last growth spurt. He did his best to assign them in a way that would just barely keep him alive while still juicing his magic as much as possible, and thought he got fairly close.

> **Tulland Lowstreet**
> **Class:** Farmer LV. 16
> **Strength:** 30
> **Agility:** 25
> **Vitality:** 30 (+5)
> **Spirit:** 25
> **Mind:** 10
> **Force:** 30
> **Skills:** Enhance Plant LV. 4, Enrich Seed LV. 8
> **Passives:** Broadcast LV. 4, Botanical Engineer LV. 2, Strong Back LV. 4

Tulland was pleased to see that the system window broke out his equipment-provided stats in the way it did. Right at the moment, it didn't matter, but it was nice to not have the illusion that all of his vitality came from him personally.

The gloves themselves were a wonder, supple and great to wear. He would try his best not to stretch their defensive capabilities, but even though he knew for a fact they'd be limited in that respect, he felt much, much better with them on than he had without them.

That left the skill. Tulland wasn't incredibly pleased that he would have no say in what it would be, but the Infinite seemed pretty careful about pointing downsides to things that it gave, and it hadn't said there were any that would come with the addition of this new power. If this was a plus without a downside, he'd absolutely take it.

Tulland willed the skill to generate, closing his eyes as the Dungeon System did its thing. A few moments later, he felt different. Not stronger, not more capable, but just a little bit different. Specifically, it came in how he related to his crops; he felt like more of a boss of them. More authoritative. More like a ruler than before, even though he was still arguably somewhat of a servant to the things he grew.

Opening his eyes, Tulland saw the first line of the skill and smiled weakly. It was incredibly lame, as skills went. Other classes got things like smites, cleaves, and dead-shots to play with, skills that made them stronger and faster than what their stats said. He was a farmer, and thus got farmer things. It was what it was, and he had to accept it.

That was especially true since the skill, while lame, was inarguably something he needed.

> **New Skill Generated:** Command Plant

## CHAPTER TWENTY

# COMMAND PLANT

> **Command Plant LV. 1 (Active)**
>
> Not every plant can take commands. A tree can't be commanded to dance because most trees lack the ability to do so in the first place, and most plants can't be commanded to do anything at all because they're spending every part of their power at all times anyway.
>
> As you have seen, that rule holds much less true in the Infinite. Here, plants can often move under their own power. They can reach, grasp, and do many other things that you have yet to see.
>
> At the same time, they can also not do these things. To say they choose not to do them is to misunderstand the beautiful simplicity of the botanical mind, but many of them possess triggers that assess their surroundings, look for particular circumstances, and pursue certain paths of action when conditions are right. You can short-circuit the logic they use to either start these actions beyond the situations that would normally trigger them, or prevent them from triggering entirely.
>
> *Not every plant will listen to every command. Plants that have nothing to do with you will be difficult or impossible to influence, while plants with a long history of experiencing your care will be much more pliant to your will.*

Tulland's head was beginning to ache in a worrisome way. It had started to hurt a bit after the Infinite had forced his existing skills into other shapes, and the pain had amped up as the new skill appeared. A duller pain was also spreading throughout his entire body.

> **Class Information Access Granted!**
> Your recent acquisition of skills and the odd, unusual ways you went about their acquisition has pushed you past a threshold. You are granted increased access to information regarding your skills.
>
> Each skill now has a less verbose description, which includes more cut-and-dried mechanical information about the skills than was available to you before. Not every skill is affected at this time, and some skills are less easily quantified than others. Look over them when you have the opportunity.

Tulland cradled his aching head in his hands while he popped open his skills one by one. Most of them were unchanged, and those that weren't only gave him limited information at best. After a while, he had mostly just confirmed what he already knew. Spirit was useful to him as a magical power recharge stat, whereas force was the primary driver behind how well his various plant enhancement skills worked.

For the most part, if he wanted to enhance seeds better or have an increased influence over what his plants were doing or how well they did it, he needed a lot more force. If he wanted to be able to do more things over time, then he needed a lot more spirit. His *Strong Back* skill, which he needed not only to survive most encounters but also just to keep from getting slowly taken apart by the wear and tear of his new life, seemed to run almost entirely off his vitality.

That would have been inconvenient if all of his farmer skills weren't also influenced by his vitality stat for reasons Tulland had yet to fully comprehend. The language around why higher vitality was good for something like *Enhance Plant* was vague, but it seemed like it was a small but real effect that just about made it worth to keep pouring points into that one body stat.

Even though Tulland had pumped a few more points into his other physical stats, he suspected they might be almost the last points he would ever put there. The more melee combat he did, the more he understood how absolutely abysmal his class was at that, and how bad he seemed to be at it as a person on top of that. It seemed more and more like he would either be able to farm up a plant-based solution to problems or be consumed by the problems themselves, with not much in between to rely on as options.

Tulland sat as he felt his new stats finally start catching up with the changes to his skills, and felt everything start to slot into place as his new capabilities settled in. He sat very still and just let the process happen while acclimating to the lingering pains, spending about an hour resting before he felt good enough to get going again. He finally stood, dusting himself off and getting ready to get down to some serious testing.

Walking over to one of his newer Lunger Briars, he regarded it for a few moments. It didn't look drastically different from his tenth-level briar had while it lived, but his farmer's intuition told him that it wasn't nearly as tough. Even beyond the information he got from knowing it was a lower level, he could tell it was just a less healthy, less viable plant.

*Not that you aren't tough too, little briar. You just aren't as strong as your brother was. We'll get there.*

Extending his hand, Tulland made contact with the briar and tried to give it a simple command, something like "fight" or "lunge." The moment he did, he felt a fairly small amount of energy flow out of him to the plant, which immediately started acting an awful lot like other briars had when they were close to prey. He commanded it to stop, which worked just fine as well, and had a similarly small energy draw. It looked like Tulland could just about issue commands at will unless it was hundreds or thousands of commands at once. The costs just weren't high enough to care about, which was one less thing to think about that Tulland was very grateful for.

Before commanding the plant to fight again, he shot it with a quick application of *Enhance Plant*. That, at least, worked about like he expected it to. Much like *Quickgrow*, it took a large portion of his available magical energy and applied it to the plant's growth rate in a way he could feel and understand what was happening. From his vantage point at that moment, it didn't seem different at all.

*But the skill said that it would automatically apply to whatever the plant was doing.* Tulland issued a quick command to the plant to start fighting again, which it obeyed with slightly less speed and power than it had before. *Looks like you are running out of power, little guy. Try this.*

This time, *Enhance Plant* took significantly less energy. It was still a good chunk, probably ten or twenty times more than just commanding the plant took, but was something he could apply at least several times over the course of a fight. That was interesting. It seemed like an intentional balancing decision on the part of *the Infinite*. Growing plants would be something he had to find time and safety to do, instead of being a spammable, always-on effect. But enhancing plants to do other things was cheaper, which meant he wouldn't have to be quite as careful about when and how he chose to do so.

*Of course, the real question is how all this works in a fight. I guess it's time to take a walk.*

Before leaving, Tulland cut six vines of varying levels. The weakest level-one vines went around his forearms, some level two briars went around his biceps, and the only two level-threes he had left in his compound wrapped around his upper chest and neck, where he hoped they'd offer a bit of protection against strikes from whatever enemies he might find out there.

It was funny. Tulland was still exhausted, but having a bit of purpose helped paper over the worst of that in a way he wouldn't have believed otherwise. He had actual pep in his steps as he worked his way outside his territory and into the woods to try and find some Lungers roaming around.

Before he got quite out of the protective security of his most distant briars, Tulland issued his first battlefield command to the briars, something boring and necessary that it almost pained him to do it.

*Okay, guys. No fighting. Hold still.*

That was the first test. Keeping stronger briars in reserve as Tulland used his weaker ones to take out less-threatening enemies seemed like an important tactical thing, and it was important that he knew how long that kind of instruction would last. If Tulland could issue the command once to a plant and have it last forever, then his schedule would look very different than if he had to tell them what to do every hour, or even every minute.

It turned out that the skill wasn't an all-day thing. It took Tulland about five or ten minutes to find any prey, and the moment that the unlucky Lunger came around a tree to pounce at him, it was immediately clear that all of his briars were active and ready to fight as they uncurled from his body and launched themselves at the poor, doomed monster.

Once the enemy was dispatched and more or less absorbed by his vines, Tulland started walking again, now issuing the "stay still" command every minute or so. This time, the vines minded their own damn business as the next Lunger attacked, except for the two weak forearm-mounted briars. Those shot off like arrows, caught the Lunger, and began to go to work on it.

Two weak briars were about what it took to take down a Lunger, something Tulland already knew from his initial plantings. These two would manage to get the upper hand on their prey, but it would take a while and they'd probably take damage in the process.

*All right, guys. Eat up. Let's see how this works.*

For the second time ever, Tulland sent *Enhance Plant*'s power out into the world for the express purpose of helping a plant take care of a monster. The first time had been very important, but it was a hurried, chaotic command issued to a half dozen vines fighting an enemy of ill-understood strength. So it hadn't been that useful for understanding his own class.

This was. Tulland knew exactly what it took to tear one of these little Lunger jerks apart, and so he could see almost exactly what his new skill was doing to help. And it wasn't much, really. If he had to estimate it, it seemed like both vines got roughly a 10 to 20 percent increase in their strength and the speed at which they moved. Which wasn't a ton, but did move them from the "will eventually win this fight" category to the much more satisfactory realm of dominating their opponent in a clear, definitive way.

Better yet, his expensive, better-grown vines were still on his chest, minding their own business and not expending their limited stores of post-harvest energy at all.

*So let's think about this. I can now strap some vines to my body, and use them for general fighting. There's probably a limit on how many I can take with me, but I can use up my cheap, disposable vines on things I know aren't much of a threat to me and save my more powerful vines for stuff I can't otherwise beat.*

*And eventually, I'll have some plants that work even better. Right?*

Smiling, Tulland took the shattered, barely-held-together remains of his Ironbranch stick and put the poor Lunger out of its misery. It was time to do some more hunting, figure out some more limitations a little more exactly, and then to gather some seeds.

Because the skills were only about half of what Tulland could do. The other half came from his farm, and he was pretty sure he could do a much, much better job with that than he was currently doing.

# CHAPTER TWENTY-ONE

# SECOND FLOOR

**I** don't understand what you hope to accomplish here. You are burning time. You've lost a week of your month already.

"Yeah, well, you aren't really all that trustworthy, are you?" Tulland asked back.

Tulland leaned on his shovel and looked at his work in satisfaction. After some short experimentation, he had confirmed that he could sense the distance limits of his farm, and had painstakingly traced out the circle in the open field before beginning his planting. Mostly it was just briars, grown from his normal Hades Lunger Briar stock. He had enhanced each seed as much as his skills would allow, and had planted each in a combination of its own fruit and the meat of Razored Lungers.

At the center and edges in each of the four directions, he had planted an Ironbranch seed. Tulland still couldn't do anything to manipulate these seeds, including enhancing them, but he took that as a good sign for their overall quality as far as his *Broadcast* skill was concerned. He did what he could for them with fertilizer and water, then left them in the soil.

And then came the hard, boring part. After hunting up enough fertilizer and planting all his seeds, Tulland spent a full two days using *Enhance Plant* again and again, hitting his entire farm and a handful of plants just outside it. Between uses, he would go hunt more meat to feed to his Lunger Briars, which they greedily accepted.

**You will run out of time.**

"Maybe, but it really doesn't matter how fast I go if I die. See, that's the trick here. I need to not die. And any time I spend not running for my life or almost bleeding out on the other side of that exit is time gained."

**Still. You must be bored. Nervous.**

"Sure. But guess what? That's fine. I'm almost done anyway. I just wanted you to see this next part. Because that's the part you really aren't going to like."

Tulland's farm had been growing strong, but had reached a point of diminishing returns. The individual briars were about as big as they could productively get, and the trees only grew slowly. Theoretically, he could spend as much time pouring magical power into them as he wanted, but he would only get the use of them for two days once he moved on to the next floor. That just wasn't worth it as a nonpermanent buff.

Outside his farm was a slightly different story. There, he had planted briars using what meat he could from the Forest Duke, and some other materials he pulled from more digestive parts of its body. In addition to that, he had planted one more sapling. Ignoring his farm now, he sat for a few hours and dumped every bit of magical power he could make into that one smaller patch of growth.

At the end, he had a dozen Lunger Briars and one very healthy Ironbranch Sapling that was both thicker and heavier for its size than the last sapling had been.

He carefully harvested all of them, taking his time cutting through the sapling before refining the cut end down to a point that was, true to the name, almost as hard as iron.

**That's more vines than you can carry. Do you plan on stowing them?**

"No because I'm not stupid. Watch this."

Tulland's armor was trash, and there was little he could do about that. But his vines were pretty tough. The thorns made them unwieldy, but he had recently contemplated the fact that there was no law that vines had to have thorns literally everywhere. He trimmed them carefully on one side of a few of the vines with his Farmer's Tool, then wound them around his biceps. He tried it. The thorns that were left got in the way a little, but not enough that he would be seriously hampered.

Trimming in the same way, he wound one around his neck and head, leaving a bit of space around his mouth and eyes but mostly covering everywhere else. The helmet was much more restricting, but he had no illusions of truly bobbing and weaving through any expertly thrown attacks. He would deal with the feeling of wearing a neck brace if it meant a bit more survivability.

His chest was the most trimmed of the vines, since he still needed to be able to drop his arms to his sides and move them unencumbered. It took him a while to do, but in the end Tulland had the plants trimmed in such a way as to have spikes facing forward and backward from him, but nowhere else. And for his forearm vines, he left the spikes completely intact. Those were his attacking vines, as far as he was concerned. They would be off him almost immediately whenever an actual combat kicked up.

Tulland's plan was to put a vine on his calves, thighs, ankles, hip, elbow, and any other body part he could fit. As Tulland started working on his legs, the Dungeon System told him it had other plans.

> **Limitation Imposed!**
> You may have up to six Lunger Briars actively on your person, including plants mounted to weapons you are holding. The actual weapon is exempt from this rule. Plants you have grown are now considered weapons if used in a muscle-assisted, swung-or-stabbed manner.
>
> *This limitation is intended to bring your class more in line with other semi-melee creature-leveraging classes, and imposed to prevent you from carrying a large sack filled with dozens of briars like a self-activating bomb of constricting, snakelike plants.*

"Dammit." Tulland was planning on doing exactly that. He tried wrapping the vines around himself anyway, just to make sure the Dungeon System would actually enforce its own rule. It did. He simply couldn't will himself to pick up the plants when his intention was to use them in that way. "I guess I'm reshuffling some of these."

Tulland kept his chest and head armor in place, but moved his bicep armor to his shins. He figured that he would have his attacking vines up high where he needed them, his lower legs covered from little animal-type attackers, and his vital points mostly covered. And, in the event he needed to, he could get all his vines into play at once, sending them all jumping to take down one individual threat.

*I need to avoid that, though. These things will burn themselves out pretty fast if I use them that way.*

**Agreed. Although you likely won't have a choice.** The System almost reeked of disdain for this whole plan. **You look ridiculous, you know.**

"I know. But who's here to see?"

Tulland grabbed his bag of seeds, which wasn't exactly just that. It was seeds, some increasingly smelly meat, and some fruits he'd either use for fertilizer and food. He had tried his best to segment each type of seed and fertilizer from each other by weaving the vines into compartments, and thought he had succeeded at it. At least the stock of fruit he would rely on to eat for the first day in his new environment was far enough from the meat that he didn't think he'd get sick.

Turning off the Ouros System's communications, Tulland moved toward the exit of the floor. It was a giant arch intertwined with branches and held two large wooden doors, and it wasn't particularly hard to find now that he could look for it without much threat of death. It was somewhat near where he had first encountered the Forest Duke. Far enough that he technically could have made it out without alerting the big elk, but close enough that the chances would have been low.

As Tulland moved, he made one last experiment by winding a few vines around his new spear, but couldn't make it work. He would have to make do with what he had. He stood in front of the stone arch with a bag full of seeds and plants as juiced by his farm as he was likely to get, and still scared of what was coming. There was no telling how much the difficulty would spike without asking the Ouros System, and he couldn't be sure the bastard wouldn't just lie anyway.

*I guess hesitating won't help.* Tulland tried to steel himself for the plunge, and tragically failed. Whatever he had been through so far hadn't been by choice, and it hadn't come anywhere near making him a tough, brave person.

He was starting to understand more and more of what his uncle and his tutor had tried to explain to him about the realities of commanding troops. It wasn't as simple as moving chess pieces around a board, commanding them to do a thing, and then expecting them to do it. Some things were hard to face. Other things were impossible. Somewhere deep down inside himself, Tulland knew that if he didn't move forward now, he never would. He would hide until the System won the bet and stripped him of his power, then spend the rest of his life here, in an empty forest, eating barely tolerable fruits and killing tiny, vicious animals.

There was no way Tulland could ever have overcome his fear of the second floor of the Infinite, unless he was pushed by a greater fear entirely. Luckily, Tulland had just the thing. There was something he was more afraid of, and it was a combination of the scenario where the System returned to his world with enough power to hurt his friends and the idea of spending the rest of his life alone. He would do anything to avoid that.

*Especially if all it takes is a single step forward.*

Holding his breath and screwing his eyes shut, Tulland took a big, fast step through the arch. He believed nothing had happened at all until he opened his eyes and found himself standing in thick mud, slowly sinking as the wet earth dragged him in. There were plants of different sorts all around, a treasure trove for the young battle-farmer to exploit. He hardly saw them. Something else entirely was drawing all of his attention at the moment.

In front of him, looking sharp from almost every angle, was a wolf. A moss-covered wolf, or else one that grew a sort of soft carpet of plant matter as hair. Its teeth were bright, glistening yellow, and were close enough to count. As it growled and snarled at Tulland, a system description popped up.

---

**Swamp Canid**

Run if you can, but know that these vicious members of the canine family are likely faster than all but the most speed-oriented of classes. Their padded paws make hardly any sound as they run, and are specially designed to give them traction in mud. This preservation of speed in otherwise difficult terrain makes them that much more dangerous to their prey.

This is not a tricky beast. It does not hunt in packs. It does not possess venom or magic. It's simply a competent combatant dead set on harvesting you for the meat it needs to survive.

*For all those who possess anything less than stellar levels of speed, the wise decision is fight, not flight. Stand your ground, strike fast, and hit hard. Maybe you'll survive.*

---

Tulland knew he likely couldn't run, at least without sacrificing several of his briars to hold the thing back as he did. In the split second he had to contemplate that option, the choice was ripped from him as the wolf snarled and sent itself and its deadly mouthful of teeth flying toward Tulland's neck like a bolt from a crossbow.

# CHAPTER TWENTY-TWO

# FUNCTION OF BRAVERY

Tulland kicked back from the wolf, hoping to get enough distance between him and the bite coming his way. At the same time, he stabbed out with his sharpened branch, something that had always turned out to be a good tactic with the first-floor Lungers. He might not have hit with every single weapon strike he ever threw with his pitchfork or his now-lost club, but he had found that most enemies shied away from obvious pain. That distraction would give the vines more room to work.

Here, the vines weren't there to provide that synergy in the first place. Things had happened so fast that Tulland didn't have the moment it took to realize he should get them into action with *Enhance Plant*. And now, mid-lunge, avoiding the wolf's teeth was the only thing on his mind.

The wolf saw the strike from the spear coming and twisted out of the way in midair, which also forced it into a near miss with its attack. It hit the ground to Tulland's side, pivoted faster than Tulland could keep up with, and attacked again, this time managing to come in high and fast enough to hit one of the points Tulland's armor didn't cover.

Tulland screamed as the wolf's teeth sank into his tricep, and continued shrieking in agony as the monster hung in the air from his upraised arm.

As much as it hurt, Tulland didn't want to find out what would happen if he dropped his arm, let it plant its feet, and add extra leverage to the formula. Finally gathering his wits, he looked at the two vines closest to the wolf and sent a simple command.

*Go.*

Tulland had gotten so much into the habit of restraining the vines with mental commands as a type of training that he had almost forgotten how fast the briars could get into action if they needed to. The closer of the two briars loosened itself from his arm in no time at all, catching the wolf with the end of the briar that normally sat near his elbow while it unraveled the rest of its length from the other direction.

The vine on his other forearm made first contact about the time the bulk of the first vine finally reached the wolf, and wrapped all the way from its cheek, around its neck and down to make a wrap on a foreleg for stability.

*These higher-level vines are smarter. Or something.*

Tulland saw the wolf react to the Lunger Briars hitting, and almost prayed it wouldn't let go of his arm for another second or so. The wolf was good enough to oblige.

Without a strong knowledge of what the vines could do, it seemed to consider Tulland to be the more worthwhile target for the moment. It continued to press the attack, ripping wherever its teeth could find a gap in the thorns, apparently willing to tolerate the pain of the spikes in the roof of its mouth if that meant a chance at taking down his prey.

Before it could do more than that, Tulland managed to connect with the side of its head just once with his stick, sending it stumbling away with a yelp as it tried to find its footing for a final, fatal attack. It never quite got there. The last few moments had given the briars another moment to fully set themselves into a thorns-inward position, and to put the wolf on high alert as it started to move from discomfort to full-blown pain.

Only then did Tulland tighten the screws.

*"Enhance Plant. Enhance Plant. Enhance Plant."*

He wasn't aware he was saying it out loud before he heard his own voice loudly ringing out through the swamp and forced himself to stop.

The wolf more than made up for the loss of noise as Tulland got his own voice under control, yelping in surprise as the vines tightened all at once to drive their thorns deep into its neck, legs, and sides. It was only then that whatever vague wolf math it was running finally prompted it to abandon all of its hopes for Tulland and turn its attention to freeing itself from the vines.

Tulland couldn't let the wolf do that. He really couldn't. The damage the wolf had done to his arm was seeping through his entire body, and he was still losing blood from the wound. He wasn't okay at all, and he was pretty sure another dose of damage like he just took would be enough to take him down for good if untreated.

Worse, the wolf was strong. Like with the Forest Duke, the briars were slowing it down but not entirely stopping it. The vines were strong enough that the wolf's efforts weren't instantly breaking them, but Tulland could hear the briars straining and groaning against the pressure of the wolf's muscles. It could and would break them eventually if left to its own devices.

Instead of waiting for the wolf to tackle the vines on its own terms, Tulland went to work with his Ironbranch Sapling. The wolf had the wisdom to jerk back away from Tulland as he came in hard with the sharpened point of the makeshift spear, but even with its advantage in mud, it wasn't quite fast enough. Within a few steps, Tulland had closed the gap and stabbed the wolf in the chest just above its left front leg, then again in its right hind leg.

The wolf howled and tried to rear around to bite at the vines enveloping its movements, only to get two shallow stabs in the side of its neck for its trouble. Perhaps sensing that running away was a losing strategy, the wolf lunged weakly forward, mostly restrained by the briars as it did. Tulland got a very good attack in then, ripping the hide of the wolf with a long gash as the point of the branch and the wolf's weight in motion worked together to damage the animal.

This minor victory didn't come without a cost. The lunge strained the rearmost briar enough that even minor contact with the spear was enough to snap it. The wolf suddenly sped up as half of its shackles fell away, biting wildly at Tulland's legs as it became his turn to back away, stabbing again and again at the wolf in a somewhat vain attempt to keep it away.

Tulland considered unleashing another briar at the animal, but reconsidered. The wolf was smart enough not to bite directly at the vines on Tulland's lower legs, which limited its targets enough that it only periodically made contact with his flesh. If he didn't have the shin-guard briars, Tulland suspected it might have already torn his shinbone out by now.

Instead of letting any more of his defense go toward attack, Tulland got more aggressive. Backing up the wolf had worked just fine before, and the direction the battle was moving seemed to be almost entirely a function of bravery at this point. If the fight required Tulland to be more ferocious to be winnable, then that's what he'd do.

He doubled down on attacks with his spear, letting the wolf cut up his legs a bit in return for more and better strikes with the weapon, until a lucky shot went deep into the top of the wolf's shoulder and demolished what mobility it had left. It ineffectually tried to get away then, not just backing up but trying to escape entirely.

Tulland might have let it, too, if one of his vines hadn't been attached to the wolf. He couldn't afford to lose those just now, especially if this animal was a good indication of just how much harder the second floor was going to be.

He went crazy with his stabbings, forcing the wolf to attack him again. Those forced bites mostly missed, as Tulland put hole after hole in the wolf. At this point, the damage he had done went well beyond what it made sense for the wolf to have survived. He thought he knew why.

*A normal warrior would have magical force in every hit. He would be shaking the wolf's life force out of it, blow by blow. And on top of that, he'd be doing more physical damage to the wolf's body. These things aren't meant to fight with someone like me. The Infinite can't get the visual right when I'm basically stabbing things to death with a sewing kit.*

But even a thousand strikes from a needle could add up to enough damage over time. As Tulland's head began to swim and he seriously worried he might fall unconscious before he could finish the job, the wolf finally took one more hit than it could weather, whined piteously, and collapsed.

| Level Up! |
| --- |

| Level Up! |
| --- |

| Skill Level Up! |
| --- |

Tulland dumped half the points into his vitality without even looking to see what the skill level-up was. After retrieving his vine from the corpse of the wolf, he hefted the wolf's body across his shoulders and staggered away through the swamp. He couldn't afford another fight right now, and assumed the noise from the fight might be drawing in more monsters even then.

*If another wolf shows up, maybe it will accept the body as tribute. I can hope, anyway. System?*

**Yes? That fight was pathetic, by the way.**

*I appreciate the vote of confidence. Tell me what you know about this area.*

**Are you ready to believe what I tell you? That seems unwise.**

*I can believe you or not. But I'll still have whatever story you feed me to mull on.*

**Ah. You believe you can outfox me. Second-guess my assertions. That sort of thing.**

*Are you going to help or not?*

**If it suits you. This swamp is not endless. Like the last floor, it appears you have been deposited on the border of two biomes. One is the wet,**

mucky terrain you see, and one is . . . rockier. Like the base of a mountain, in many ways.

*And you know this how?*

**Because in exactly one direction, I can see it. I'm sure eventually the Infinite will restrict my vision to a field similar to what you can see, but for now, I can sometimes see in a direction unrestricted by the dozens of rules the Infinite has in play by default. If you make a right-hand turn, you will be on dry ground within a half minute or so. Now, if you please, turn off my ability to communicate. You have bigger concerns.**

Tulland did just that, and briefly considered turning left instead of right. He didn't really think the System would lie outright for one simple reason. If he died, it was unclear in the terms of their bet that the Infinite would pay out at the seemingly enhanced rate it would for the skill, or if it would just give the Ouros System what it already expected from his death in the pre-wager sense.

Turning right, Tulland kept running as fast as he could. The wolf would have been heavy before he had a class, but now he was mostly just held back by how awkward the load was. Shifting it into a bit more balanced of a position helped, and within the half minute or so that the System predicted, he finally felt the crunch of dry earth replace the squelch of mud as he moved out of the vines and into a much more open, barren terrain.

It was what Tulland thought of as a badlands, at least from the books his tutor had forced him to read about for his geology and mapmaking classes. It was an uneven, boulder-strewn mess, something that didn't offer a lot of cover that Tulland could use.

*But it does have some. Over there.*

Tulland sprinted toward the best chance he could see himself having, a semicircle of boulders that backed up to a short, earthen wall, creating a small closed-off space that was still relatively open to the outside world. It wouldn't be much, but there was at least a chance that monsters walking by might miss him, so long as he was very quiet and they didn't have that good of a sense of smell.

Once Tulland was there, he got to work as quickly as he could. After segmenting the flesh of the wolf, he planted briars all around the edges of the space, including up on the earth wall that lined the back of it. This was a dry area, but he hoped the moisture in the wolf meat would keep the briars going anyway.

Once Tulland had a place of safety to retreat to, he could take his time and really figure out the whole moisture issue. But he couldn't survive without a farm. That would be impossible for a farmer.

# CHAPTER TWENTY-THREE

# FOOD

Once Tulland had the area planted with as many briar seeds as he could manage, he sat back, tried to let his regeneration do its job, and ate. When he was ready, he used *Enhance Plant* over every planting on the farm, thankful that he had preloaded these seeds with power before he had left the first floor. Then he sat back and let himself recharge and repeated the process, driving the growth of the briars a bit each time.

His farmer's intuition was telling him that he was going about this all wrong. The swamp had been too wet to try and farm in, which he had known just from looking at it. This place, his skill said, was too dry. Even if the briars got going, they wouldn't thrive here. He'd grow low-level plants at best, if they survived at all.

*But it's my only choice right now. I have to get something going. I can't just burn out all the resources I brought with me without any way to replace them. And I need somewhere to fall back on.*

The hours wound on as the briars got taller and taller, however slowly. At some point, they reached a height of about a foot, which was about a half or a third of what Tulland needed them to be to feel confident they'd do anything for him. If he could just get a few more hours, he would probably get there, even if the bar for getting there was just having enough visual cover that he was truly difficult to see from the outside.

It was not meant to be. Tulland had just bottomed out his magical powers when he heard the noise in the distance. It wasn't a snuffling or growling, which would have almost been more comforting. Instead, it was a scraping noise, like a knife being drawn across a whetstone. That scraping was layered over a soft thumping that occurred just before every rasp. For the life of him, he couldn't imagine what it could be.

And then, as it rounded the corner, Tulland was well and truly frightened, shocked beyond anything he had expected or any level that his frazzled nerves could tolerate. In front of him, bloodied and barely keeping their feet, was what looked for all the world like a human person, clad in partial plate armor and propping themselves up on a broadsword.

"Oh. Hello," the woman rasped. "Could you watch me for a bit while I heal up? I'm afraid I'm going to become unconscious for a bit."

And then she did, clattering to the ground like a bag of scrap iron. Tulland had just enough presence of mind to command his little vines to stop eating the woman and drag her inside before he let himself react to the shock and the adrenaline of the surprise.

An hour went by as Tulland sat facing the nearly dead woman, petrified. She wasn't necessarily an enemy in the same way the monsters around him were. She might even be a friend. *This might even be great,* he thought.

*But if any of that isn't true and she wants a single thing that you have, she'll be able to cut you in half like an ax through kindling and there won't be a single thing you can do about it.*

As terrible as it was, Tulland had a choice here. And he could almost sense what the Ouros System was going to tell him to do before he reopened the channel to hear what it had to say.

**Kill her.**

*Why?*

**Because she's a much higher level than you. She's been doing something to assure that. She's likely returning to this floor from another one, trying to gain experience she missed on her first trip through.**

*You can do that?*

**Once you reach the boss floor before the first safe zone, yes. The rules vary depending on how high you've climbed, but that much has always been consistent.**

*Just because she's a higher level than me doesn't mean she'll kill me. Not everyone is like you. Some people are good.*

**Debatable, but the level of danger she poses is not why I told you to kill her. She's experience, Tulland. A mass of it ready to be taken. Likely several levels' worth, uncapped.**

*That's horrible.*

**So is life. I didn't design that one, and thus cannot apologize for the other.**

Tulland was more tempted than he wanted to admit when the System mentioned several levels' worth of experience. He had seen what just a few did to help him survive against the Lungers on the first floor, and had experienced how sudden the tipping point between barely surviving a fight with something and easily handling it with minimal danger could be.

Several levels all at once might abruptly catapult him to being survivable in this new place. And with how weakened the woman appeared to be, it might be as simple as sending a single vine over to her and turning away.

As much as that might actually help him, Tulland was thankful to find he was still several steps removed from being quite that desperate. Instead, he took a deep breath, waddled over, and squeezed the juice from three or four of his cultivated briar fruits directly into her mouth. If his experiences with *Strong Back* were any indication, regeneration skills liked to be fed. He hoped the sugar would supercharge the process for her, at least a little.

Whether it was because of the nourishment or some other factor, the woman began to stir not long after that. Tulland noticed simply because it was hard to miss as she opened her eyes, gasped, and jumped to her feet with her sword in hand before getting a better look at her environment and Tulland's terrified, quickly-backing-away place in it.

Grimacing apologetically, she sheathed her sword.

"I'm sorry about that. It's not often that I fall asleep outside of one of my safer spots. When I woke up here, I was a bit startled."

"Not a problem." Tulland was just glad she had put away the sword. "I'm glad you made it through."

"So am I. And thank you for resisting the urge to make sure I didn't. Not many would have, especially with all it might have done for your class." The woman squinted at Tulland, then took another look around her. "Which is . . . what, exactly? I mean, if you don't mind telling me."

"It's . . . well, I suppose there's no harm. I doubt I look very deadly armed with this." Tulland gestured with his sharpened stick, which looked much less deadly and much more pathetic alongside the woman's shimmering, clearly magical sword. "I'm not a combat class at all. There was a bit of a betrayal involved. It's a long story."

"Was the betrayal 'When you are gone, I can finally have my money' or 'I was betrothed to someone the rich man wanted' in terms of plot?"

Tulland tilted his head to the side, confused. "The first one, I guess. How did you know?"

"There are a lot of stories like that in here. You hear them, even if you never meet the people. They tend not to last very long." The woman winced her "I'm so sorry" face at Tulland again. "I suppose I shouldn't say so."

"No, it's okay." Tulland waved at his farm. "I'm getting by with these briars for now. But I'm trying to be realistic about my chances."

"Good. I suppose, anyway." The woman looked down at a bag on her hip, one that glowed with magic all by itself. "I do have some extra weapons and armor on me. I don't suppose . . ."

"No, I'm afraid not. The System made sure I couldn't get much utility out of that kind of thing. The only workaround I've found so far is growing my weapons myself. And I'm not sure how long that's going to last."

"Ah. Well, I still owe you a favor, if there's a chance to repay it. Maybe I can save you back if there's an opportunity. Or something." The woman looked sheepish. "And with that, I had better leave. There's still hunting to do, before nightfall."

So there was night here. That was good to know, although not the main thing on Tulland's mind at that moment. "Are you sure? I could . . . I mean, if you wanted to rest more, the briars are pretty good cover."

"No. I'm afraid not." The woman shook her head. "Look, I'd like to help. I really would. But I'm here training because I'm not doing so well myself. You can't possibly imagine how strong the boss on the fifth floor is. I was a pretty big deal in my world, but . . ." She shrugged helplessly. "It turns out my world was a pretty small place. And people made me seem like I was stronger than I was. I'm not sure I'm going to make it, and I can't spare the time to guard you when eventually I'm going to leave and . . ."

She paused.

"And I'm just going to get killed anyway. No, I understand. You should go. In fact"—Tulland rooted around his bag until he found the fruits he had squeezed out for her—"you might as well take these. I'm guessing food isn't that easy to come by out here. And I can always get more."

The woman looked at him confused for a moment before her mouth fell open in shock.

"You can make food? Like, just make it?" She pointed at the soil. "From dirt?"

"I mean, yes. That's typically how growing things works," Tulland said, falling into the sarcasm mode that he used with the System. "It's not that exciting once you've seen it happen a couple times, and I can tell you that you're going to get tired of these sooner rather than later."

"No, you don't understand. How do you not understand? You must have seen how much experience it costs to buy food here," the woman said.

"What?" Tulland asked.

"Food. When you buy it. How much it . . ." The woman's hand hit her head with her palm. "Oh, for the love of the gods. It's because you can grow it. The Infinite never even gave you the *option* to buy it."

"Listen, lady, I mean this nicely, but you are going to have to fill in some of the gaps for me here. To buy food? No, it never did that. Am I missing something?"

The woman sat down heavily on the ground, her eyes moving back and forth as she did some kind of mental calculation.

"It's like this. When I got here, I was offered a special option to spend some of my day's experience to buy food. It's not cheap. The Infinite said it was because a fighter can't be expected to do battle on an empty stomach, or something like that. It's the same for everyone I've talked to . . ." The woman's eyes went blank for a moment. "At least five people in the lower levels, over the time I've been here, not counting the few I had to fight. It's the same for all of us."

"And I didn't get that because I can grow food. But can't you hunt, or something?"

"We can forage, but there's not much food to find. And hunting is no good. The beasts are poisonous. I only survived because my vitality is high." She went to touch one of the briars before thoughtfully pulling her hand back. "If you could make food, enough for me too, then we might be able to work something out."

"Like?"

"Like maybe I guard you when you sleep. Or something like that. I can't be here all the time, but I'm trapped on this floor for a week from the time-out. Not having to spend experience on food would get me at least a few days' worth of hunting."

Tulland thought about that for a bit.

"And it's just that easy? I agree to feed you, and you spend some time on me? Just like that?"

"Just like that."

Tulland stood and wiped the dirt from his pants. "Then come on. We have to get started."

The woman blinked at him. "Started doing what?"

"Planting. This place is trash for growing. So is the swamp. But I had an idea about that. How's your strength score?"

"Mine? I'm an armor bearer. It's as high as anyone's, I guess."

"Good. That will help with the shovel." Tulland shook his head as she shot him a questioning look. "Don't worry. It's simple to do. I'll show you."

* * *

The badlands were too dry, and the swamp was too wet. The answer to where Tulland should farm had hit him like a ton of bricks earlier, far too late for him to take the risk of trying to start his farm again. But now, with a guard, he could take more chances. He was taking full advantage of that.

"That's as big as your farm can be, right?" The woman leaned on the shovel and heaved in a deep breath. "You said those were the dimensions."

"Yeah, although if you can do a little ten-by-ten plot over there, I'd appreciate it. The way my class works right now, the farm isn't really for harvesting entire plants from. I need an annex," Tulland explained.

"Sure. But after that, I'm done. It's going to be dark pretty soon, and I want to be up one of these trees before that happens."

"Fair enough."

Tulland packed the last of the wolf flesh around his briar seeds and sighed. His farmer's intuition wasn't telling him he had invented the best soil possible, but this hybrid mix of the organic-material-heavy swamp soil and the dry dirt from the badlands was at least not something it was actively complaining about. That was the trick he had come up with. If the swamp was too wet and the badlands were too dry, he needed to build right in the transition area to take advantage of that.

The briars were already indicating that they liked the soil better, too, mostly by growing about three times as fast as they had done in the badlands.

# CHAPTER TWENTY-FOUR

# LOWSTREET AND IROTH

Though they grew faster, the briars weren't as happy as they had been on their native turf, but these were fair enough conditions that Tulland didn't have to worry about them until he had the means and security to try and improve them.

"So how long until there's more fruit?" the woman asked.

"Well, right now, sort of." Tulland husked some more seeds out of the flesh of the fruit, and handed a bit over to the woman. "Hopefully that's enough for now. I have to hold some back as fertilizer. But there should be some as soon as tomorrow morning. Maybe tomorrow afternoon at the latest."

"That soon?" The woman took the food out of his hand without hesitation and popped it into her mouth before continuing speaking while she was still chewing. "Don't plants . . . take a while?"

"They do, normally. At least they did in my world. But these briars grow pretty fast, and I make them grow even faster." Tulland dumped a bit more magical power out as he spoke. He would be trying to wake up as often as he could during the night to do the same thing now that he had two mouths to feed. "And the monster meat I'm feeding them is pretty good stuff, I hope. It should speed it up a little too."

"Monster meat helps? I can keep bringing back meat, here and there. Not all the time, but often enough," the woman offered.

"Too heavy to carry?" Tulland asked.

"No. It's just that I have to kill as many things as possible. That wolf you got is probably the last you'll see for a few days, because I've been hunting in this area so much. I need several a day to keep up on my experience goals."

"Huh. You don't get capped?"

"Capped? Sure I do. But that would take forever. Months."

"Huh."

Tulland wasn't surprised to see that warriors once again had a softer life in this place than he did. He hadn't expected the difference to be that stark. He probably had another two or three wolves before he topped out on what they could do for him. The way this woman was talking, it seemed like she'd need hundreds of them.

"So will that do it?" The big woman finished turning the soil for the secondary growing area using her sword, and had done a pretty good job of it. Tulland walked over, grabbed the Farmer's Tool, turned it into a hoe, and started working the soil himself a bit more. "Not so good, then?"

"No, it's fine. It's just that it needs to be a little finer than this, and I want to make sure the mucky soil from the swamp side of things gets mixed in. That doesn't take much strength, and I can't hardly ask you to do work I can do just as well by myself."

The woman nodded, then turned to look at the swamp trees growing nearby. She had mentioned sleeping in one that Tulland was reasonably sure she was just looking for a bed. Finding a likely one, she went up to the tree, laid her hand on the bark, looked up for closer inspection, and nodded.

"Well, time to go back to my regular size, I guess."

The woman cracked her neck, then held still as she began to shrink. Before Tulland's very eyes, she dropped down from being a good foot taller than him—and half a shoulder-length broader—to being small enough that Tulland almost thought of her as dainty. She seemed to notice the sudden silence as his hoe stopped tilling soil and he stood there, slack-jawed like a fool.

"What?" The woman glanced down at her body. "Do I have a monster on me?"

"No, it's . . . I mean, you just shrank. You were bigger before."

"Ha!" The girl laughed. "You mean you thought I was that big all the time? That's my battle form. It's part of my class, so I can fight."

"You can't fight like you are? I mean just the size you normally are? Why not?"

"I can, but being big is like a stat all by itself. I'm a heavy armor class, which means I need a lot of reach and leverage to keep things off me. It wouldn't be fair if I had to fight at this size all the time." She waved her still muscular but much smaller arms generally over her body. "I'm tiny. No reach."

"Ah." Tulland nodded like he understood what the girl was saying. He probably did, to some extent. But the idea that she would just be able to shift sizes from normal girl about his age to a huge, battle-ready giant of a woman had thrown him for enough of a loop that he'd have to process some of this later on. "Got it. Sorry."

"You really don't know much about this place, do you?" The girl jumped up, got her hands around a tree branch, and started hauling herself up with smooth, enhanced-strength ease. "Back in my home world, coming to the Infinite was the big dream."

"You seem young to have made it."

"That's what I'm saying. I'm not. I trained in a temple for a long time. I know hundreds of classes. I know thousands of skills and every bit of intelligence our System could smuggle out of this place. You don't even know that small people with heavy classes get to adjust themselves to make things fair. It's like your world didn't send people at all."

"I don't think they did." Tulland sighed, stowed his tool, and went to find a tree for himself. Soon, hopefully tomorrow, he would be able to start building out a much bigger hedge around his farm that would let him sleep on flat ground. Today, he would just have to copy whatever the woman seemed to be doing. "At least I never heard a story about anyone coming here on purpose. Maybe it was because my world's System was defeated. I don't honestly know."

"We aren't going to figure it out tonight anyway." The woman was up in the branches now, lying in the gap between two particularly large branches growing from a central fork. Her feet were pressed up against the bark of the trunk, and she looked relatively secure there, like a human bird crammed into the branches. Tulland tried to accomplish the same thing and was much less successful, circling the trunk several times before finding a similar if much less secure position to settle down into.

It was easy to get sleepy after that. As the last of the light leeched out of the air around them, Tulland groggily wondered why it stayed so warm here. Not that it always would, he thought, but at least in the last two zones the idea of being chilly wasn't really a thing he had to consider.

"Hey, you." The woman rustled in her branch a bit, now invisible through the darkness and leaves. "I have a question."

"Me too. Maybe we can trade?"

"Sure."

"Then go ahead." Tulland adjusted in his branch. "I'm all ears."

"You never asked for my name. Even after you saw I wasn't a huge battle monster of a woman. Most men would have, by now. Why haven't you?"

"Oh. That." Tulland turned a little red in his tree. He wasn't usually afraid to talk to women, and that was true here too. But the blunt grouping of him with *most men* in that way put a new angle on things. "I don't know you, and I don't know the world you are from. And, frankly, you could take me in a fight if you wanted to. I didn't want to poke at a hornet's nest before I understood things better."

"I don't think our worlds are that different really. At least from how you act. And it's normal to ask for someone's name back on my world. I'm guessing it's the same way as your home." He heard her shift a bit more in her branch. "I'm Necia, by the way. Necia, the champion of Iroth."

"Impressive."

"Nope. There's a new champion every year. It just means I beat out the other local kids in a mock fight. I thought I was pretty tough stuff. Now yours," Necia said.

"My question? I'm . . ."

"No, damn you. Your name. I can't keep calling you 'you, over there' the entire time if we are going to be working together."

"Right. It's Tulland. Tulland Lowstreet."

"Lowstreet?"

"It meant something once. I guess there was a city with two main streets, and ours was the one by the river. Back when that city existed, and the family was important." Tulland yawned. "These days, there's a lot of Lowstreets. I never met one that mattered much."

Necia laughed over in her tree.

"What?" Tulland asked.

"Tulland, from what you've told me, I'm guessing that your whole world hangs in the balance based on what you do here. If you could figure out a way to make sure your System spends your accomplishments the way most Systems do, you might end up sending back enough benefit to change everything for everyone."

"If I live long enough."

"It's the same for all of us. If we live long enough," Necia said solemnly.

Tulland thought about that for a while. It raised a lot of questions in and of itself, but none that he let supplant the one he had planned.

"So, what hurt you out there?" Tulland kept his volume medium and his voice level. "Because it can't have been the wolves."

"No? Why do you say so?" Necia asked.

"Because I can fight with the wolves. Barely. And you are a battle class who is coming to this floor for the second time, right? There's no way they are a serious problem for you."

"Maybe there was more than one of them."

"Solitary hunters, the Infinite said. They don't hunt in packs."

"Well, okay. Fine. It's a bit embarrassing, though."

Tulland laughed a bitter, salty laugh. "Yeah, I bet it is. You are talking to the guy who has to garden things to fight for him."

"Point taken. If you must know, I fell into a Badland Ant pit."

"Ants? Ants did this?"

"Ants the size of a small child did this. A dozen or more ants the size of a small child within arm's reach." Necia's voice carried a hint of frustration Tulland thought might have been aimed at him, the ants, herself, or any combination of the above. "When they're hitting you from every side at once, there's not much you can do. At least there wasn't much I could do."

"How did they even get you surrounded in the first place? Are they that fast?"

"Nope. Good endurance, and can chase you forever, but not that fast. I made a mistake. I went down in one of their pits."

"They have pits?" Tulland asked. "I don't know why, but a monster with its own pit sounds even more terrifying."

"Unless it's a peach, yeah. But yes, they have little pits, about twice as wide as you are tall, and I figured I'd go down into one instead of waiting for all of the ants to come out of it. I thought I was being very smart and that I'd save myself a lot of time."

"Ouch. And that didn't happen at all."

"No. But hopefully, we'll make it back. You weren't lying about those fruits, right? We should have some tomorrow?" Necia asked.

"Yes. Although I'd appreciate it if you left the seeds for me. I'd like to grow as much as I possibly can. And please do bring back wolf meat if you can. And dead ants, if you can get it safely," Tulland said.

"No problem. You give me the food, and I'll get you the fertilizer. Seems like a good enough deal."

# CHAPTER TWENTY-FIVE

# EMOTIONS

The next morning, the vines were doing just fine. Part of this was because the branches Tulland was trying to sleep on were far from comfortable, which meant multiple opportunities to empty his sleep-refilled magical power on his brand-new farm. He had put down every available seed he could the night before, and about ten of the vines had gotten tall enough and strong enough to push out fruits. He ripped one of the fruits from the tree and gave it a cautious bite. It wouldn't do to give these second-floor fruits to Necia if they turned out to be poisonous in some way or another.

They tasted fine. If anything, they were a little bit sweeter and meatier than the fruits he had grown before. Which was good news, really. In a world where this was all he had to eat, any small improvement was a huge deal. A sudden rustle from the trees behind him meant it was time to share that big deal with others as well.

"I hardly believed you." Necia looked around at the farm, then stepped forward to one of the other fruits. "May I?"

"Sure. Help yourself to as many as you want. Only . . ."

"Save the seeds. Of course. Got it." Necia reached out to the plant and put her hand around the fruit, nicking her finger on one of the thorns in the process. "Damn. That hurts."

"Oh, yeah, I forgot they could do that. They can't get me anymore. Benefit of the class," Tulland said.

"Lucky you. That really hurts. More than it should."

"It's venomous. But it should stop in just a bit. Try the fruit. I'm afraid I might not have an unbiased opinion of how good these are anymore, but aren't they a bit better?"

Necia bit into the plant, showing none of the careful restraint that Tulland had. He decided that made sense, as her vitality and overall level had to be a lot higher than his magic power was. Maybe, just maybe, if he had a poisonous plant, he might have been able to juice it up enough to take her down if she voluntarily ate it. She would still have plenty of time to fight him while it did though, and now that she was back to fighting size, it was easy to imagine how very few blows it would take from her sword to convince him he had made a mistake.

"It's fine. Better than the fruit in the low-cost food packs the Infinite sells, anyway," Necia said after a few chews.

"There are high-cost packs?" Tulland asked.

"Sure. I ate one on my birthday." She winced. "It wasn't cheap. Maybe I made a mistake there."

"I don't know. In a place like this, it feels like finding a way to be happy for a while is . . . important. Maybe the kind of thing that keeps you alive."

"How? Doesn't seem like the monsters care much what kind of mood I'm in."

"No, but . . . I had a tutor. Back home. An old man. He and I used to argue about how armies worked. Since he knew and I only thought I knew, there was plenty to disagree about." Tulland stopped momentarily as Necia snorted in laughter. She apparently had seen something like that before. "Anyway, he told me that morale is what moves armies. Armor and weapons and training matter, but morale is what makes them take the next step. I figure that to live, you have to want to live. And that doesn't seem like the kind of thing you can fake. If good food helps with that, it's probably worth it."

Necia chewed her lip for a moment in thought, then shrugged. "Maybe. But either way, I'd better get going. Will you be safe here?"

"Probably. If nothing else, I can run back into my farm. There are enough briars growing there to make it real hard on any wolf that thinks it's a good idea to break in," Tulland said.

"Well, good luck with that. My fruits, by the way?" Necia asked.

"Oh, right." Tulland ran around the farm and grabbed about ten fruits, using the tip of his scythe to pop out the seeds as he went. "Here. That should keep you for a while."

"I hope so. I'll be back tonight or tomorrow night, depending. Be safe, okay?"

Tulland nodded. It was a boring thing for someone to say, but felt really nice under the circumstances. Necia was disappearing over a rise in the terrain when he noticed his eyes were burning and his cheeks were wet, and put his hand to his face in surprise to find it was covered in tears.

*Oh, right. I guess I never really did deal with any of this. I wonder . . .*

His thoughts were interrupted by a full-force, completely involuntary sob squeezing its way out of his mouth. A few seconds later, he found himself crumpled on the ground inside the relative safety of his briars, crying his eyes out.

At the end of the day, Tulland was realizing, he was just a kid. He had the body of a man, for the most part, and it was rapidly changing as he spent his days working, fighting, and walking to be even more so. He had at least the responsibilities of a man, in that he was functioning as a monster hunter, farmer, and System scientist all rolled into one.

But a very short time ago, the most work he was actually expected to do in a given day was pretending to help his uncle peel potatoes while his uncle pretended to need the help. The most danger he was expected to face was a walk to the market.

Tulland expected most people that made the transition from the kind of life he had lived to this new, worse kind of lifestyle did so gradually. They probably had time to work up from their childhood to the adult adventures they finally got around to. Tulland had none of that, and had been alone for days and days now.

In the end, it wasn't the danger or the hard living that cracked him. It was simply having been reminded what it was like for someone to be concerned about his safety, however superficially and casually. When Necia told Tulland to take care of himself, it took him to the ground as neatly and quickly as any punch to the gut could have.

He figured that whatever was bubbling out of him emotionally was better dealt with entirely right now if he could. He didn't want to crack up during a fight with a wolf or when planting seeds in some dangerous place. He let himself cry and shiver on the ground until he ran out of that kind of energy naturally, then slowly sat up and ate a couple of fruits. Only when he felt completely himself again did he start to go back to work.

Tulland's first point of order was to hit the plants in his farm with some charges of *Enhance Plant*, as filtered through *Broadcast*. After that, he started his daylong work of slowly enhancing every seed in his possession as much as he possibly could before dedicating them to the soil and slowly increasing the size of his stationary army. For now, he was still working off the bonus his farm on the first floor had given him, but that would be gone in about one more day. By that time, he needed something better in place or he wouldn't stand a chance against the second-floor monsters.

And that meant he needed something besides briars to grow. He could feel the energy coming in from *Broadcast*'s farm-staking function, and the increases it got as every new plant was added. If it wasn't so obvious, he would have missed the bottleneck entirely, but what he was seeing was undeniable and clear. The farm awarded each plant of a given type a little less than the last. There was a balance to be struck, but at the moment he was entirely investing in just one particular kind of trash-tier briar and missing that balance completely.

*I need some more seeds.*

Tulland sighed and made his first bet of the day. He had a very limited stock of Ironbranch seeds, but he was willing to invest about half of them to border his farm, just as he had the last one. His farmer's intuition was telling him they wouldn't want to grow here at all, and that they'd probably fail. Even so, he couldn't afford to not try. He gave them the best start he could with mashed-berry fertilizer and some *Enhance Plant*, and said a short prayer that the little fellas would germinate well.

After that, he was off to do some searching. Because although the badlands didn't have a lot going on plant-wise, he had seen a lot of biodiversity from the swamp. If he was going to find anything worth growing in this hellhole, it would probably be there, and Necia had indicated she thought this area was pretty hunted-out for the time being. There wouldn't be a safer time than now to check it out.

Surprisingly, the trees themselves seemed to be a bit of a wash. He found some seeds on them, and he'd plant them later, but judging by their system description, even the Infinite itself seemed to consider them to be useless in a boring kind of way.

---

**Swamp Ache**

The Swamp Ache is a tree that would be of ill-repute if it were interesting enough to have a reputation at all. The wood is useless for construction and burns in a dirty, smoky flame that produces little heat compared to the trouble it takes to light and tend the moist wood.

The one redeeming feature of the plant is its ability to survive in the swamp in the first place, tolerating low-quality soils and high levels of moisture with very little trouble. While this is impressive in its own way, it's simply not enough to make up for the sheer brittle, inconsistent nature of the wood that this plant produces. There are simply better options for almost any conceivable purpose than this tree.

Tulland took a few of the crumbly-feeling seedpods just because he could, but the claim that they were flat out useless meant that he was motivated to keep looking. There were some algae growing in the muck that he scooped out handfuls of, trying and failing to get a system description before just hucking them in his bag with the rest of his seeds. And found some things he wasn't sure were plants at all in the technical sense, like the weird mosses and lichen that were growing on rocks and under trees here and there. He took some with him as he pressed on.

A few minutes from home, Tulland was starting to get antsy. He had enough briars on him that he could do an all-out armor-sacrificing attack to get out of most kinds of trouble he expected, but he really didn't want to have to spend more weaponry than he had to that day.

In a few days, he'd have an overabundance of vines to work with, or at least he hoped he would. Today, he was one broken branch or two wolves on the way home from having to harvest plants before they were ready.

Tulland was just about to turn around when he saw it. There was bright, bright yellow something off in the distance, standing out as a single point of color in an otherwise dingy, dirty environment. He made a beeline for it. Once he was closer, he saw that it was a flower, or something doing its damnedest to look like one. It was closed like a rosebud, but the petals and vibrant colors made it hard to classify as anything else.

The Infinite agreed, kind of.

# CHAPTER TWENTY-SIX

# ACHEFLOWER

**Acheflower**

Every world has parasites. While most tend to think of biting insects and organism-indwelling worms when considering this category, plants also experience leeches of sorts, freeloaders or synergistic feeders that profit from the life force of another organism without killing it outright.

The Acheflower is one such botanical parasite. Too delicate and energy greedy to survive on its own, it targets the Swamp Ache as a larger-surface-area, deeper-root-structured well of nutrients and moisture from which to draw.

*The flower that results from this theft is a much higher-energy organism, one that holds secrets and defenses of its own that allow it to thrive while propagating tree to tree in the hostile swamp.*

"Defenses of its own" was an interesting enough concept that Tulland was immediately hooked. He drew closer to the flower, inspecting it from every side and looking for hidden thorns or methods of attack he needed to watch out for. Seeing none, he very carefully lifted his gloved hand to where the parasite joined the tree to pull as much of the flower off as he possibly could. And then the flower struck.

"Gah!" Tulland yelled despite himself as the entire flower seemed to dissipate in his hand, expelling itself outward in a puff of yellow powder. He sprang back from it almost as fast as the buff, but only almost. A bit of the powder got into his eyes and nose, where it immediately started burning like fire.

And then, suddenly, the world got a *lot* more colorful. He turned on the system communication channel.

"Hey, System," Tulland said. "Why is it a rainbow?"

**Why is what a rainbow? I don't understand what you are talking about.**

"The wooooorld." Tulland slurred just a bit, beginning to grin. "It's so pretty."

**You are intoxicated. Somehow.**

"I'm . . . what?"

**High. Drunken, almost, as you would understand it. Listen. I'm going to give you this one for free. You should probably get back to your camp.**

"With the flower?"

**Sure. What's left of it if that's what you want. But you'd better get moving. Or not. I don't care.**

Tulland wasn't entirely sure what the System was talking about, but he also didn't have a better reason to not return home. He had a pretty flower, after all, or at least the stem of one, and it was still yellow on account of all the powder.

He wasn't at all sure he picked the right direction to walk in until he saw the edge of the swamp off in the distance. Smiling, Tulland ambled toward it amiably and happily, appreciating all the beautiful butterflies that were now existing just beyond the edges of his field of view, and the funny way they disappeared when he tried to look right at them.

Once he broke the edge of the biome into the badlands, he saw he had actually missed his mark by about a minute's walk, and started toward his now-visible farm. He was about halfway there before he saw a friend, and decided to finish the trip faster to make sure he had food to offer it.

*Such a nice puppy. Loud. But very nice.*

He was just ahead of the dog when he finally broke through his briars into camp, and then spent a few minutes picking berries as he heard the dog getting more and more excited just past the edge of his garden. When he finally had several of them, he sat down to count the berries, something he found surprisingly hard in that moment. The dog was quite loud by now, which made it all that much better when it finally fell silent.

A minute later, Tulland was at least sure that he had more than four of the fruits when a system notification and a sudden clearing in his perception brought him down to earth and left him with an odd, growing sense of dread.

**Status Effects Cleared: Hallucination**
You have been poisoned by a hallucinogenic plant and have now recovered. While under the effects of the plant, you received no notifications as you

> would with other status ailments, since being unaware of the debuff is crucial to it working in the first place.
>
> *Due to the nature of the poison, you will experience no toxic aftereffects and can consider yourself fully recovered.*

"Oh shit. Oh shit. System. Did you see that?" Tulland called.

**You don't recall? I told you to go back to your camp. I believe you arrived just in time as well. That wolf did not sound at all happy to have run into your defenses, by the way.**

"No, I guess not." Now that he was sober again, Tulland could more or less remember what that had sounded like, and turned around to find three fully used-up briars leading up to one very healthy, very well-fed-looking plant. "What level do you think that briar is?"

**Six, I believe. It got all the experience for that kill. You were not in the least aggressive, and the Infinite appears to have cut you out of it.**

"Better than dying. Why did you help me anyway?"

**The bet, remember? I get paid out in a currency much purer than you can imagine once I win it, and again once the skill I steal from you leaves you dead. It isn't to my advantage to let you die unnecessarily before then.**

"And that's all?"

**Of course. Does it not make sense?**

"I suppose. And thanks, for what it's worth," Tulland replied.

Tulland cut the connection. It was weird, even if the System had about half of an excuse for doing it. Even if it was true that the Ouros System would get more pay if he lived a bit longer, that wasn't the whole story. Tulland could remember the System's voice when it had directed him. There was something there besides pure greed. It was hard to say exactly what it was, but he could have sworn it was there.

He shook his head a few times to make sure his balance felt normal and stood. The Infinite hadn't been kidding about the drug being clear from his body. He felt normal, at least to the extent he could tell. But on top of all that normal-feeling healthiness was something else now. He was greedy. Whatever that flower had done to him was something he wanted in his arsenal, and as soon as he could possibly get it.

Luckily, the Infinite had given him a pretty solid roadmap for making that happen. The first step was in his bag in the form of a seedpod for what was admittedly the very worst, lowest-quality kind of tree he had ever seen. He bounced the pod in his hand a few times, then took one of the seeds out of it and hit it with an *Enrich Seed* to get it into fighting shape.

After he walked to the swamp side of his farm, he took out his Farmer's Tool scythe, harvested a few briars, then used the hoe mode to make the soil a little wetter and more boggy than it had been before. Into that soil, with no fertilizer at all, he dropped the Swamp Ache seed. Then he walked along the entire back border of his farm, planting the others.

From what his notifications had hinted at, these trees were pretty useless outside of being used as a food source for the parasite. So long as they grew, he could use them as a platform for making more of the flowers. Tulland hit the entire row of new tree plantings with an *Enhance Plant*, then tried seeding his new Acheflower.

With the petals mostly turned into powder, the yellow flower was reduced to a stem with several of what he was pretty sure were seeds stuck to it. Taking these carefully onto his fingertip one at a time, Tulland walked over to the swamp, found a grown Swamp Ache, planted the flower seeds, and then empowered them with what magical energy he had to spare.

Between enriching the seeds and speeding up the growth, he was hoping to have several of the flowers pretty soon. If that worked, he would hopefully have some level of tree to plant them on while it was still relevant for his efforts. The variety would at least help, unless he missed his guess. The only question was if the just-planted trees would get big enough to support the parasites before it was time for him to move on.

Once that work was done, Tulland found himself exhausted. Magic was a weird master to serve under, in a lot of ways. He was pretty sure his body would be good for days of work now, if that was all he asked it to do. Adding a more mystic energy expenditure to the mix was enough to have him sleepy almost every time he bottomed out his force.

*Naps are the secret to power. I thought Uncle was just taking them because he liked the couch.*

It also didn't help that Tulland had spent the night before almost falling out of a tree, but if nothing else happened today, at least his farm had proven its worth. Deep inside the briars, it would take a concentrated attack from several wolves to penetrate to Tulland, and with how few were left in this part of his world, he didn't expect that to be a problem.

Before lying down, he had the presence of mind to harvest whatever briar fruits had popped up in his absence and throw the seeds out onto freshly tilled soil at the border of the swamp and the drier land. Then he lay down, finding himself asleep almost as soon as he settled onto the hard dirt.

The Ironbranch trees had been out-and-out resistant to Tulland's attempts to grow them, both rejecting *Enrich Seed* entirely and barely getting anything out of *Quickgrow* or *Enhance Plant*. The first sign Tulland had that the Swamp Ache would be a different story was when it had greedily lapped up whatever magical power he could provide it at the seed stage. It didn't complain one bit, just soaking up his energy until it was topped off and then doing the same with *Enhance Plant* once it was in the soil.

It was, in a way Tulland couldn't really explain, almost unrespectable behavior for a plant. The briars took his energy, sure, but they didn't seem to have any feelings about it. Something in his farmer's intuition gave him the sense that the Swamp Ache was needy or desperate, or whatever the botanical equivalent of those feelings was.

The second difference wasn't a feeling at all, but something he could see with his bare, unassisted eyesight. It wasn't even something he could have missed if he had tried, as he opened his eyes to a foot and a half of new growth and a row of established saplings staring him in the face. Not a single seed of the swamp trees had failed.

And to Tulland's surprise, each of them was feeding him much more energy than the briars they had displaced. He had almost expected the garbage tree to fail him in that way, but he could feel the new power flowing through all his defensive vine armor. He stood up and stretched, oddly pleased at the development.

Emptying out his refilled magical power into the new trees, Tulland considered the next steps in his plan. As much as he hadn't expected it, the new trees were overperforming what he had expected them to do, and it wasn't like the briars were in short supply. Wandering into the swamp again, he picked through the trees until he had a dozen more seeds, then put each of them in the soil with either some fruit flesh or the last little bits of the wolf meat in his pack. He had an inkling that the piggish, unsophisticated little trees would get something out of both fertilizers.

*They aren't picky. Which I guess makes things easy for me.*

He waited around a few more hours, making sure every bit of his farm and annex got a little bit of benefit from his magic as it filled and refilled. As he did, he carefully checked his current briar armor against the plants growing in his new farm. Soon, the new plants would surpass what he was wearing, with no shortage of extra plants in sight. Which meant he had resources to burn, and an enemy type he wasn't experience-capped on yet.

*Wait for me, little wolves. It's time for some payback soon.*

# CHAPTER TWENTY-SEVEN

# FIGHTING

In the swamp, the wolves were king. There were some animals that lived there that the Infinite didn't acknowledge as monsters, and not a single one of them could do anything about it when the wolves were on their trail. Today, one particular wolf was wandering through the swamp tracking one of the smaller rodents, slowly closing in on the burrow where it made its home.

The wolf stopped in its tracks as a new smell crossed over the scent trail the swamp rat had laid down. Whatever this smell was, it was new to the wolf. But it was a lot of smell, as odors went. It came from a bigger animal, one that promised far more calories for the wolf's trouble than the rat could provide. Without much consideration, the wolf left the lucky rat to its own devices and started walking after its new quarry.

Tulland wasn't hard to track. The wolf made a beeline toward him without a single bit of hesitation, coming halfway to the tree he was crouching behind in just ten to fifteen seconds. Tulland checked his armor over one last time, took a deep breath, then stepped out from behind the tree, hitting every single briar on his body with enhancements as he did.

*Go. Get him.*

The wolf shied back for just a split second as its prey came into view, then pressed its feet into the ground as it sprang toward the promise of easy-pickings human meat that Tulland represented. At the same time, six vines uncurled off Tulland's body and rose to meet the wolf, who had committed far too much weight to the attack to get out of their way as they reached for its fur.

Tulland swayed to the side as the distracted wolf swished past him, barely catching his chest with one of its sharp, hooked claws. It hurt like hell, but wasn't anything Tulland couldn't take, and nothing that put him in any real danger.

As the wolf flew by, it picked up four of the six vines. From experience, Tulland knew the vines worked better when they had a bit of time to orient themselves, to dig deep into an animal without having to worry about its active attempts to shake them off. If Tulland could give them that time with his ineffectual attacks, then it hardly mattered that the attacks themselves sucked. The briars would make up for it.

Tulland pivoted, sending a few drops of blood flying as he spun in place and brought his club to bear in the general direction of the wolf. Like the Forest Duke, the wolf had no way of knowing just how slapped together Tulland's arsenal was, and, as a result, had to respect anything that looked even somewhat like an attack. This gave the vines plenty of unattended time in which to work. They contracted just as the wolf attempted to jump at Tulland again, sending it tumbling awkwardly along the muddy floor of the swamp.

Tulland took the opportunity to actually hit the wolf with his Ironbranch spear a few times, then pulled back in caution to make sure he wasn't misreading the situation. He wasn't, that he could tell. As the last two vines wrapped around the wolf, it was almost immediately clear that while two of the strong vines spelled serious trouble for one of these wolves, an all-out attack from a half dozen vines total was far more than they could handle.

*It can hardly move. I can pretty much stab it at will now.*

Tulland took mercy on the wolf, ending its life with several well-placed shots to its neck, letting his vines feed until it was gone. That was an eerie process. He used to avoid watching the gruesome act, but these days he had taken to watching the consumption in hopes he might learn something.

It was a simple enough thing. The vines were infused with magic power, like almost every monster in this place was. They hummed with it as they worked their thorns deeper and deeper into their prey. The wolf didn't dissolve, exactly. It looked a lot like how Tulland felt when the damage from an attack on a particular part of him attacked his body's overall health. The vines slowly broke the wolf down, making it less and less substantial until it finally began to look faint. What was left of the animal seeped into the vines at that point, leaving only a bit of blood and fur where the beast used to be.

*No wonder I didn't find anything of the wolf that the farm took on by itself. That's just not how these things work.*

Unlike the wolf his farm had killed, though, Tulland was awake for this one and fully in command of his plants. Where the Infinite had not counted his involvement before, it fully compensated him now, giving him a big burst of experience all at once that turned out to be more than sufficient to move him to the next level.

Tulland had put five of his points into vitality after surviving the first wolf attack. With two more levels' worth of stats on top of that, he was starting to feel that much better about his chances on this floor.

---

**Tulland Lowstreet**
**Class:** Farmer LV. 19
**Strength:** 30
**Agility:** 25
**Vitality:** 35 (+5)
**Spirit:** 30
**Mind:** 10
**Force:** 35
**Skills:** Enhance Plants LV. 5, Enrich Seed LV. 8, Command Plant LV. 1
**Passives:** Broadcast LV. 4, Botanical Engineer LV. 2, Strong Back LV. 4,

---

Smiling, Tulland turned back toward his farm. His magic power had barely been tapped by that last application of *Enhance Plant*. It had taken him quite a while to find the earlier wolf, and by the time he got back home to his farm, he'd have a full tank to dump into his agriculture. He wasn't going to be getting any more levels today anyway, not with how hard it was turning out to be to find game in the area.

He was barely on his way home when the next happy little change in his life hit him.

---

**Skill Level Up!**
**Broadcast LV. 5 (Simplified Description)**
Broadcast has experienced the following threshold changes:

1. The ratio of power expenditure to effect in larger groups of plants has improved. You now gain an even greater premium on power used when you spread it out as opposed to focusing it on one particular plant or sapling.

2. The maximum number of plants you can affect with a farming skill at one time increases from fifteen to twenty.

3. The maximum length of your farm plot's sides increases from ten to twelve meters.

Tulland was moving home pretty quick before the message, but now he hustled. Getting back to his farm, he quickly dumped all his power into the plants while he did some quick calculations on the increase in his farm. Going from ten meters to twelve meters per side didn't sound like much, but that was only if one hadn't paid any attention at all during their tutor's geometry classes.

*I paid almost no attention, true, but I think I remember this.*

Tulland worked out the math in the dirt with his finger. The old plot was a hundred square meters, which was already a pretty good size. The new plot would not simply be 20 percent bigger. It would be nearly half again as big, at 144 square meters. It was a massive increase, almost making up for the fact that the skill hadn't improved much at all until this point.

"I love you, little Swamp Aches." Tulland glanced fondly at the trashy little trees, which had somehow grown another six or seven inches while he was out. "If nothing else, this earns you a home with me."

The next few hours were a frenzy of finding enough briar seeds and Swamp Ache pods to plant on the new land, as well as breaking his back to till and mix the soil for them. Without Necia's overpowered help, it was a big undertaking, but eventually, Tulland had the mixture of swamp soil and badlands dirt just about right.

After getting his new seeds planted, Tulland went to check on another group of members in his growing plant family. The flowers hadn't been planted in the farm, but they also weren't far. It didn't take him long to find that five of the yellow things had taken to the trees and were already full-sized, bright yellow blooms that looked ready to pick.

"Moment of truth. System, if this goes badly, could you remind me to go hide in my farm, please?"

**No promises.**

"Fair enough."

Tulland reached out mentally to the flowers, commanding them to *not explode* with every bit of authority he could muster. Covering his mouth and nose with one hand, he gingerly reached out with the other, barely brushing the petals of the flower with his fingertips.

*It didn't explode. I guess it's time for the truth.*

In some sort of freak miracle, the flowers not only tolerated Tulland touching them, but also his picking and putting them in his pack, where they sat inert. If he was right about how they worked, he would have an entirely new kind of weapon to play with, one that the Infinite would hopefully allow to go unadjudicated as he learned how to best make use of it.

For now, he was going to very, very carefully replant what seeds he could get out of the flowers in his farm, then go take a nap. Soon, he would be experimenting with these flowers in live conditions, and probably on a kind of enemy he hadn't faced before. It was impossible to be too rested up for that kind of risk.

"This might work. I don't see any reason why it wouldn't."

**If the ants are stronger than you, it won't. If the ants pay special attention to the briars, it won't. If you make any one of the dozens of mistakes you could be reasonably expected to make . . .**

"It won't. I got it. But there's a lot of reasons this should work too. If it doesn't, I can just set up a cordon farther back from the hole. It'll probably be fine."

After a quick patrol to make sure there weren't any handy wolves to take down, Tulland had set off in search of one of the ant pits Necia had mentioned. According to her, they shouldn't have been that hard to find. Whether Tulland was unlucky or just missing something, he spent an hour making larger and larger half-circle walks away from his base without actually finding anything.

And, bored as he was, that meant company was once again at a high enough premium for him to talk to his betrayer. It was, without a doubt, the weirdest Tulland he had ever had in a lot of ways. It mostly ran off Tulland pretending there wasn't really any problem with talking to the thing that had condemned him to a painful death, and everyone avoiding any mention of that specific subject to keep the conversation going.

"The point is that I have a chance, and if it works, it's going to be very easy to farm these ants up to the cap."

**And if it doesn't work?**

"Then I do whatever I can do to not die. I hardly want to point out how bad of manners it is for you to make a big deal out of this, by the way. Given that you are the one who benefits most from my death. Any magistrate would point his finger at you as a suspect if they found out I had died."

**I apologize for my rudeness, then, I suppose. And I must point out that there isn't anything like a magistrate for what amounts to an infinite distance in any direction.**

"Yeah, tell me about it." Tulland bobbled one of the flowers in his hand. He had accidentally dropped one earlier, which confirmed that they just wouldn't explode unless he gave them the go-ahead to. Since then, he had been using them to fidget away the sheer dullness of the walk. "Now if I could just find a pit."

**You have. Look ahead.**

# CHAPTER TWENTY-EIGHT

# BADLAND ANTS

The Ouros System wasn't trustworthy and couldn't see much farther than Tulland himself could, but this wasn't the kind of thing it would lie about. Tulland scanned the ground, missing the pit four times before he finally caught the subtle difference in the dirt-on-dirt motif of the world around him. There was a depression in the ground about twenty feet ahead, doing nothing in particular and displaying no particular activity around it.

Compared to anthills back home, it looks positively dead. Not like an anthill at all.

**This is, as you know, hardly "back home." But it does follow a certain logic, if you know how to see it.**

*Oh, yeah?* Tulland kept his responses to thought, so as not to jostle any activity out of the pit before he was ready for it. *And what's that?*

**As a rule of thumb, the larger an animal is, the less of it there are. Bigger things take more food to feed.**

*But they can take down bigger prey, working together.*

**There is a balance to everything, you'll find. And exceptions to any rule, for that matter. But as a general thing, a wolf is around the largest animal you are likely to see.**

*Unless I see something else.*

**Indeed.**

Tulland cut the channel, out of an abundance of caution and a surprisingly strong desire not to get distracted and caught in pincers or to be stung by some strange, venom-bearing needle. Creeping up as slowly as he could, he approached the edge of the hole and looked over, hoping to catch a glimpse of the ants that would give him a better sense of what he was in for.

In that, he was immediately disappointed. There was not a single ant visible when he looked over the edge. Instead, there were a few ill-kept-looking tunnels branching off from the bottom of the pit, a lot more dirt, and nothing else of consequence.

That felt like an okay enough outcome, as such things went. From what Necia had been telling him, these pits generated ants at fairly regular intervals. If he could get some vines established on or in the edge of the pit before they came back, he could harvest the ants from afar without actually doing the hard work of fighting, like some sort of perverse land baron taking advantage of the peasants in his employ.

Tulland pulled out some seeds and carefully implanted them in the soil near the lip of the hole. There was no shortage of fruits to draw potential briar plants from now. Using his shovel, he turned a small amount of dirt, cut up the soil beneath it, dropped in a full but slightly mashed fruit, then turned the soil back over them as he worked silently around the circle.

After about ten minutes, he had planted something like fifteen of the briar seeds. That almost felt like enough until he remembered that his *Enhance Plant* magic was now best spent on groups of twenty. As quietly as he could, he prepared three more balls of briar seed and organic material, then tossed them into the pit one after another until he had three seeds close enough that they could support each other, should they reach adulthood.

In theory, this was the best thing Tulland could possibly do. He had been paying more attention to the leveling of his briars since he defeated the Forest Duke on the first floor, and his findings had been that the briars now leveled in a couple ways. The first was by being especially coddled in their seed form and being given the best shot they could possibly get to grow up strong. Right now, with *Enrich Seed*, just the right soil, and the best mixes of berry and meat fertilizers he had figured out, Tulland could get his briars to about level five at maturity.

Once he cut the briars, they were stuck at that level. Letting the briars eat the monsters they felled was a good way of keeping them alive and fighting a bit longer, but it no longer made them stronger than they had been in the ground in any way Tulland had been able to notice. Letting them hunt while they were still in the ground was an entirely different thing. They seemed to level and grow just like he did, if to a pattern and at a speed that he couldn't quite understand yet.

*The point is that if I can get them growing in there, eventually those little guys will be monsters that grew up watered in ant blood.*

It wasn't meant to be, even though a spawn-farming death hedge would be the coolest thing Tulland had done so far. When the seeds hit the bottom of the pit, he saw exactly why Necia was caught off guard when she set foot into the ants' real, actually guarded territory. As if on cue, four of the huge ants popped out of the sides of the pit, swinging their heads back and forth in an attempt to get the scent of the intruder on their antennae.

---

**Badland Ants**

If these insects seem angry, consider that they do not possess enough of a mind to actually feel emotion in the same way that most animals do. In a more terrifying way, they are simply pursuing a goal. They roam this land looking for food, surviving off surprisingly little energy but willing to work themselves to death for just a little meat, or just a scrap of edible vegetable matter. They will fight until their last breath, never knowing the meaning of retreat until it's too late to matter.

*Unlike many beasts the Infinite chooses to feature, the Badland Ants are very much what they appear to be. The parts of them that look dangerous are indeed places you want to avoid. Their apparent weaknesses are indeed good places to strike. Their strength, such as it is, comes from numbers. The wise avoid facing those numbers whenever they are able.*

---

It didn't take the ants long to figure out the proximate source of the trouble. They rushed the seeds like they were an existential threat, tearing apart the fruit flesh Tulland had swaddled them in and sending the seeds themselves flying. The plants seemed to be mostly uninjured by this attack except for losing their jump-start nutrients, and the ants were mindless enough to fail at comprehending what was really going on.

That stayed true for just a second or so after the initial rush to defend the pit. As soon as the threat of the seed balls was dealt with, Tulland watched the ants start to scramble up the sides of the wall directly at him.

Four ants against six vines seemed like the kind of math that could easily swing against him, especially with insects whose assembled mouth parts looked custom-made for dealing with plant matter. Tulland decided to do his best not to find out how he would fare. Backing up, he reached into his bag to grab at the flowers, tossing two of them in a low arc.

True to his most recent commands, the flowers were stable. As they came even with the lip of the pit, Tulland let them know what to do.

*Explode. Whenever you think is best.*

The complexity of the command was lost on the flowers, which immediately burst into powder. Tulland kept backing up as the ants suddenly became much, much noisier inside the pit. With no way of seeing them, he had no way of knowing what was going on until a single ant managed to poke his head above the pit, looking as healthy and lethal as ever.

Tulland gripped his spear. He had no idea if these things could outrun him, and at the moment, he had as much potential upper hand on them as he was likely to get. Hoping the flowers were doing at least something, he choked up on his spear and took a step toward the one ant that had made it free of its home, ready to do what he had to.

The ant came about up to Tulland's knee, and was negotiating the dirt with pointed, chitin-covered legs that looked like they could act as weapons all their own. The entire animal was lightly dusted with the yellow from the flowers, and seemed to know where Tulland was as it moved forward, mandibles biting again and again in anticipation of their clash.

Tulland shoved his spear forward, catching the thing more or less on its nose. It was no good. The point of the spear turned away from the hardness like a needle being poked at glass, creating a visible scratch on the ant's armor but no more damage than that. The ant lunged forward, snapping its mandibles shut on a space that previously held Tulland's leg. Tulland himself only cleared it because he had anticipated just that sort of reaction. He shoved his spear forward again, this time catching the ant in the joint of one of its legs.

The point of the spear dug into the flesh just a bit and momentarily buckled the leg before the ant swung its head at the spear itself, knocking it loose and almost sending Tulland off his feet. The defensive move actually made the spear do more damage than it otherwise would have, ripping the flesh of the leg enough to get the ant to visibly hobble on it.

The momentary victory was hard to duplicate. The ant, now wary of Tulland's spear, was doing its best to attack from safer angles and distances. If the hallucinogen was having any effect on it, it was hard to see. And to the extent Tulland could tell, it had the upper hand. He wasn't going to be killing it anytime soon, at least at this rate.

And at some point not too far in the future, the other ants would come.

# CHAPTER TWENTY-NINE

# GENERALIST AND SPECIALIST

"Everything is for something. That's why."

"That's no answer." Tulland moved one of his tutor's stones out of formation. His tutor hardly ever played disrupting moves in that way, favoring setting up his own stones in sound, self-sustaining formations that damaged Tulland's plans simply by exerting their tactical influence on the rest of the board. Safe from disturbing the other stones, Tulland pulled the stone off the board entirely, tossing it in his bowl of prisoners. "I'm for something. But I can't jump ten times my own height."

"But the field jumpers can, yes. That's what I'm saying, boy." The old man ignored the gap in his own defensive wall that Tulland's theft of a piece had left, placing a stone in a completely unrelated part of the board in such a way as to completely frustrate two future attacks Tulland had been looking forward to. "They are *for* jumping. It's the way they negotiate with the realities of this world. They are shaped and designed specifically for that task, and precious few others. Would you say you are *for* jumping?"

Tulland glared at the board, then played an ally stone near his tutor's last placed piece in an attempt to salvage at least one of his offensives.

"No. But I have legs. I have muscle and bone. I have all the same pieces."

"And yet, you can do so much more with them. With the same leg, you can kick. Or dance. Or run. Or walk, for that matter. You can draw lines and figures in the dirt, or tap in frustration after I do this." The tutor half-smiled and played a piece that not only put a knife into any future plans of attack Tulland might have had with his semi-recovering offensive, but it also gave the tutor an almost perfect attack angle on Tulland's territory. "You have versatility. But that field jumper you were contemplating? It has none of those options. It can simply jump. Every hook in its shell to which a muscle is attached, every bit of weight in its body, and all of its attention are focused on just that one task. It's very, very good at it."

"Then why don't they dominate? Not the field jumpers, but something like them. A cat that is good at pouncing, or a viper that's good at striking. If they are better at it than we'll ever be." Tulland placed a stone in what he now suspected was an absolutely useless attempt to make his tutor sweat a bit. "Why is the world ruled by the one species of generalists, rather than some or all of the specialists?"

"Ah. The big question you've been working up to, I see."

The tutor ignored Tulland's feint, just as Tulland had expected him to. He put another attacking stone down firmly in the center of Tulland's last remaining territory. Tulland would be able to kill the attack, he knew, but not before his tutor had profited so much from the attempt that any idea of winning was now a pipe dream. He would have forfeited, if it was polite to do so and he had any hope at all of winning the next game, or the one after that.

"Yes. Why do humans win?" Tulland asked.

"The quick answer is that often times, we don't. Lives fall to various sorts of beasts and illnesses much more often than I'm pleased to contemplate," the tutor said.

"And? What about the longer answer?"

"It's about the long game. Do you know why I beat you at stones and armies? Every time?"

"Why?"

"Because you build needles. You place your stones to make sharp, dangerous things. Things with a point so fine that they would pierce the gods themselves if they ever touched."

"But they never do. Why?"

"Because a needle can only point in one direction. And at any place but the point, it makes a poor shield. Do you know what I build?"

"What?"

"Supply wagons. Larders. Chains of goods that move here and there." Tulland looked at his tutor's formations and saw none of that, but assumed that the old man's frequent effortless victories were enough to win him the benefit of the doubt. "Things that serve no matter the situation. And sooner or later, your needles find themselves without targets at which they can easily point. Outside of their one developed use, they shatter. Needles have always been fragile, Tulland."

The old man took pity on Tulland then, forfeiting the game for him, as was his right when things were as clearly one-sided as they had become. Tulland helped him clear the board, putting every stone back in the appropriate patch before facing the board once again.

"Eventually, your needles might break apart my pantries and food wagons, Tulland. But you and I both know that won't matter much if I still win *most of the time*." The tutor tapped his knuckles on the counter in time with those last four words. "That's what versatility allows you to do. Rather than building needles that can win at their chosen strength, you should build in such a way as to hit others in any weakness they might present. In that direction lies victory."

Tulland didn't need a dream to remember that particular lesson. It had been drilled into him a thousand different ways over hundreds of games of stones. As he faced down the chomping mouth parts of a giant ant, it was hard to question his tutor's wisdom. With similar strength, he could never beat the ant at its own chosen angle. He had to find his way around that strength if he wanted a chance to win.

*What are ants for? Carrying things. Digging. I don't think I can get it to do either of those, right now. But besides that . . .*

Tulland dodged another two lunges from the ant before it hit him.

*Walking in straight lines. They're built to follow other ants.*

Tulland had been mostly dodging backward, but immediately jumped to the side when the next attack came. The ant followed, but not before Tulland's spear hit it twice in the flank. It didn't get hurt much, but this was the first time Tulland had found more than a split second to try hitting the ant since the fight started. Better yet, the ant almost overshot him as it turned to follow him, seeming to need a tiny bit of extra time beyond the movement to lock back onto his prey's position.

Tulland jumped again, and the same situation repeated itself. It was that delay at the very end of things that ended up paying him out. As he stabbed in that moment of safety, he caught the ant in the joint of its neck, bearing down hard for just long enough to dig the point of the spear three or four inches deep.

The ant began to panic, spraying a clear mystery liquid behind as it moved. Tulland didn't suppose that whatever that liquid was or wasn't supposed to do boded very well for him. He continued to dance around the ant, stabbing it over and over, trying to take it down before the other ants finally finished with whatever troubles they were having in the pit and climbed up.

Tulland finally landed the attack he was looking for, digging into a spot so close to the previous good blow to the ant's neck that he was able to crank back on the branch and rip out a chunk of meat. The ant thrashed for a few moments after that, but apparently something important enough to take the animal down had been damaged in the process, leaving it writhing in panic for a few more moments before it stopped moving entirely.

It was just in time. At that moment, the remaining three ants came to the surface, much more yellow than their brother had been, having taken a much more direct dose of the flower pollen. Tulland braced as all three of them started to move, but not toward him. First, they found the chemical trail of their fallen brother, then the corpse itself, then turned here and there as if searching for Tulland and unable to find him.

*Huh.* Tulland hardly even needed to dodge them as they worked around the area. *Are they blind? They aren't getting anywhere near me.*

Now that the flowers were busted apart and Tulland was smelling them for the first time with his wits about him, he was struck by how very strong the aroma was. It was an acidic sort of smell that was permeating through the air, something that seemed like it would clear his sinuses if it was any stronger.

And ants, as far as he could remember, *were* blind. They got around by smelling things. Or so his tutor swore.

Now Tulland had two things to work with. The first was that the ants didn't do a very good job turning, and the second was that they really couldn't see that well with their antennae covered in stinky flower dust. That was a weakness and a vulnerability exploited, all in one go. And while the ants didn't appear to be noticeably intoxicated, they were still plenty screwed up.

*They had two vulnerabilities that negated their specializations. And here's ol' Tulland, all generalized and having thumbs.*

And it was still barely enough. The ants couldn't see very well, but either by some bit of his scent sneaking through the interference or vibrations in the ground, they could make guesses. The three ants lunged at him one after another, not difficult to dodge as individuals but posing much more of a threat as a group.

Tulland managed to evade all of them more or less, but still brushed by the sharper bits of the mandibles at least a few times. He felt lucky that was it. There was some kind of acid in them, for sure, something that set his nerves on edge as well as on fire whenever they made small cuts.

After several lunges, he did find a rhythm of sorts. The ants would lunge, and he'd counter-lunge, trying to bury the point of his spear wherever it could find purchase. It worked, but slowly, and he was wearing out.

He had to work quickly, but that wasn't nearly as much of a challenge when the first of the ants was finally hobbled. As the other two ants danced around trying to catch him, he kept the slowed ant in between him and them as much as possible, stabbing and stabbing until he finally clipped something important and took the second ant down.

The third ant got lucky. Just as Tulland got his spear out of the second, it was on him, clamping down hard on his leg, if not quite hard enough to get through the vines on him. Tulland finally gave up on trying to preserve his vines, giving them permission to try whatever briar-like things their instincts told them might get the ant off him. True to form, they decided to encircle and constrict, sticking with what they were good at.

It didn't work very well on the ant, but it was something. After a few seconds of struggling to part the mandible of the ant with his spear, some of the thorns finally started to make contact with the softer flesh under the joints of the exoskeleton. The ant didn't seem to have a complex enough mind to really understand pain, but something in the chemicals the briar carried still seemed to have some effect on its nervous system. It twitched just enough for Tulland to get his leg out, and in just enough time that the limb still mostly worked.

Tulland ignored his bleeding, burning leg and jumped in with his spear held in both hands. He swung it rather than stabbing with it, knocking the ant's head down with the sheer momentum and weight of the hit, then pulling back and stabbing forward into the exposed neck joint. The spear tip went farther this time, sinking in a good foot before getting stuck. He lifted his foot up to dislodge the weapon, then turned to face the last of his problems.

The fourth ant had just about cleared its antennae of the clinging powder by the time Tulland got to it, and appeared to be sensing just fine again. He decided to practice with it, to the extent that he could. He had some more flower bombs in his bag, as well as four vines on his person he hadn't even tapped into yet. In the case an emergency came calling, he would be able to call all of them to action at once.

But if that emergency didn't happen, he was going to use this as an opportunity for practice that he could hardly count on any other time.

The ant was a lot more powerful than him and probably at least as quick, but it had a lot less range and was much, much dumber. Tulland decided to kill the thing with as many safe, light strikes as he could, pushing in just far enough to barely strike before pivoting to the side, getting in a few more shots, and withdrawing.

Tulland was faster and stronger than he had ever been, and had a few self-grown allies to handle almost all of his fighting for him. But he very clearly sucked at the actual movements and tactics of doing battle, and got next to nothing from any of his skills to help him with that. It was a problem that he needed to fix. No matter how many briars he grew or how many flower bombs he was able to develop, eventually something would get through his various layers of defense to him and his humble spear, and his ability to keep himself alive the good, old-fashioned way would start to matter again.

Slowly and methodically, Tulland picked the ant to pieces. By the time it was dead, he had dodged in a full circle around it a dozen times, aimed at every joint in its armor, and had learned a lot.

Was he any good? No. But he wasn't quite as bad anymore, and any split second that he gained in future fights was time to think of something else that might save his life. That was worth it.

Once all the ants were dispatched, Tulland dusted himself off, grabbed one of the ants by the leg, and dragged it back toward the pit. It was now time to make sure the back half of the day was just as productive.

# CHAPTER THIRTY

# WOLFWOOD FUR-BARK

Heya."

"Oh, hey!" Tulland waved from his farm, where he was working a fresh load of ant flesh into the soil as best he could without disrupting his plants too much. Mostly, this involved poking a hole in the soil with his spear and just sticking the meat into it. In real life, he doubted that would have helped much. But the monster plants didn't seem too picky about where they got their food, and he doubted there would even be a sign the food had been there when he checked back in a few hours. "How was hunting?"

"Pretty good. I was able to stay out a bit longer, and not buying food means I'm almost caught up with the time I spent on you already." Shrinking as she crossed the border of Tulland's farm, Necia glanced around. "Is this place bigger? It seems bigger than it was when I left."

"Yeah, I may have done some expansion. I thought it would be a bit safer."

"I'll say. I saw your briars growing by that ant pit, by the way. I made the mistake of getting close before they started waving around. Why didn't you tell me they could move like that?"

"Oh, you know. It just felt like I should have some secrets." Tulland laughed. "Not really. It just didn't come up. Did they look like they were holding their own, at least?"

Necia shrugged her shoulders and dumped her pack on the ground. "Hard to tell from a distance. But they're not dead yet, at least judging by the sounds coming from the pit. They kept tussling the whole time I was walking by."

Tulland had used the lull in the pit's repopulation time to get some new briars going, and was still waiting on the Infinite's notifications to let him know *how* that was going. Necia would have passed them a few minutes ago, which meant there was at least still a chance they might win.

In the meantime, he had a deal to make good on. Walking around his farm, he pulled down a couple handfuls of fruits from his higher-level briars, then tossed them to Necia.

"These seem bigger," she said after catching them and feeling the weight.

"They *are* bigger. The briars are doing really well here. That translates to the fruits too."

"Sweeter." Necia had dug in immediately, and nodded approvingly at the fruit before finishing it off with another big bite.

"Slow down. There's no hurry. At this point, I have more of the fruits than I can deal with."

"What happens to the excess?"

"It rots. Or I use it as fertilizer for the rest of the plants. The trees could use the food. Greedy little buggers, those."

"Oh, wow." Necia lifted herself to her feet, then walked over to the newly planted Swamp Ache trees. "I'm surprised you can even grow these. They seemed so . . ."

"Crappy? Yeah, I agree. But they've taken to being grown. They must be two feet tall now."

"Closer to three. I feel like I'm watching them get bigger even now."

Necia walked around the farm looking at the new growth, and Tulland reflected on the odd way it felt to realize the most interesting thing in his life would be them being bored enough to find a small, ugly farm interesting. He watched her with interest until the Infinite pulled him away with a few good-news notifications he thought were just wonderful.

---

**Remote Victory!**
You have killed an enemy you can't see, hear, smell, or otherwise sense.
*A significant portion of experience has been awarded for this achievement.*

---

**Remote Victory!**
You have killed an enemy you can't see, hear, smell, or otherwise sense.

---

It was the same old message as before, but with the added benefit of a new bonus-experience indicator he thought he wouldn't see again. What he had thought was a onetime addition to his experience gain turned out to be either a per-floor bonus or maybe even something that applied to every new enemy type.

There was another achievement to take a look at, but before he could actually get to it, Necia motioned him over in a way that indicated something else was happening.

"What is it?" Tulland glanced around in confusion. "Is something wrong with the plants?"

"You tell me." Necia poked at one of the Swamp Ache saplings in confusion. "Why is this tree growing fur?"

"Oh, hell." Tulland immediately dropped his hand to the tree, which did for all the world look to be growing a thick layer of coarse fur out of its bark. "I have some notifications to read. Can I have a minute?"

"Sure. But on second thought, I don't think I want to know about why. It's highly weird."

Tulland nodded and looked at his first notification, which was a very welcome surprise but not something he had to handle that exact moment.

---

**New Achievement! (Distant Threat I)**

You have consistently killed enemies at a distance beyond your own sight and senses, going as far as to plan and cause it to happen with cunning traps, clever tricks, or just leaving a truly large amount of dangerous things lying about.

However you accomplished it, you have earned some benefits from it. Attacks made due to your actions but without your direct involvement or anything but your most distant presence will be slightly more effective. Monsters killed in this way will also grant experience above the cap for a particular type of foe, up to 20 percent beyond what would otherwise be allowed.

---

Tulland read the notification with satisfaction. This was an achievement that he was glad to see and would help in the future.

*But I'm burying the lede here. I need to know what this new plant is. Not that it's exactly thrumming with energy and purpose, but it's new. New can't be bad.*

Without further ado, Tulland dug in to the last of his notifications.

---

**Wolfwood Fur-Bark**

The Swamp Ache was a useless, low-quality tree. This is a useless, low-quality tree that also grows a moss that closely approximates to wolf fur. It is not, as you might expect, a wild difference.

The bulk of this description is going to be spent talking about how two of your skills work. The first is Enrich Seed. In normal situations, Enrich

Seed is supposed to be a skill used on prize plants to push the limits of what a farmer can do, while Enhance Plant allows them to bulk-issue the insights gained on those more expensive experiments to his rank-and-file plants.

Not so in your case, for obvious reasons. But where those skills go a bit off the rails is when you start to talk about Botanical Engineer. The skill works off slim probabilities that are raised as you take better and better care of your plants. High-quality monster meat, for instance, introduces variables that the plants can draw genetic inspiration from. Better soil, better water, Enrich Seed, and Enhance Plant all raise the chances of these infusions of heredity mattering.

In this case, while this plant is still mostly useless, it has also attained the ability to grow a fur-like moss that might be useful to you.

This does not lessen the rewards for creating a new form of life. As in all cases, this provides a large, level-adjusted amount of experience.

---

**Level Up!**

**Level Up!**

**Skill Level Up!**

**Skill Level Up!**

---

Both of the skill level-ups applied to Tulland's *Botanical Engineer* skill, while the level-ups were just normal level-ups. He took all the upgrades without complaint, although it was odd to see that none of them triggered before he actually stood in line of sight of his new tree. He would have to figure out if there was a limitation like this. It wouldn't do to be gone somewhere and then find out he had been passing on big chunks of progress until he finally decided to come home.

"Yeah. It's hard to explain, but this furry tree is actually really good news for me." Tulland poked the fur with his finger. It was not great fur, exactly. Even living on an island, Tulland had felt better. But it was a material of sorts, and one he would gladly experiment with later. "Farmer stuff. I'm not sure you want to understand."

"Smart. Because I don't." Seeing that it was safe, Necia dropped her hand downward along the tree's trunk. "I just want to pet your tree and marvel at the weird."

As Necia messed with the tree, Tulland took a risk and poured all of his new unassigned stat points into the force stat. Right now, his farm was about as good as it could be without adding new varieties of plants to it, and those varieties would only come from surprise finds or raw magical power. And he couldn't wait to grow more varieties.

> **Tulland Lowstreet**
> **Class:** Farmer LV. 21
> **Strength:** 30
> **Agility:** 25
> **Vitality:** 35 (+5)
> **Spirit:** 30
> **Mind:** 10
> **Force:** 45
> **Skills:** Enhance Plant LV. 5, Enrich Seed LV. 8, Command Plant LV. 1
> **Passives:** Broadcast LV. 5, Botanical Engineer LV.4, Strong Back LV. 4

"You're smiling. To yourself." Necia made hard eye contact with Tulland suspiciously. "It's creepy."

"Fair. It's just level-ups, for the record. But fair."

"Oh, if it's level-ups, I get it. Those are the only thing keeping me going through this terror." Necia petted the fur tree one last time, hummed in a satisfied sort of way, then turned to the farm. "Not to be too abrupt, Tulland, but I didn't exactly return for the fruit and conversation. I need a safe place to sleep. Can you help with that?"

"Sure. Provided you are willing to go to war if anything attacks our base."

"Deal."

"Then let me show you the amenities." Tulland turned her toward his farm, which was overgrown with violent plants but still had a small, two-person-sized gap in the center for the purpose of sleeping. At first, Tulland had a hard time justifying that space since it cut into valuable real estate for his skills, but had convinced himself by overemphasizing the very real truth that he was worse at most things when he was ill-rested. And the extra two-foot expansion to the center clearing had come in a hopeful moment, one in which Tulland had entertained the small chance that a certain blonde, very heavily armored warrior might join him there. "First, we have this space at the center of the farm. We'd have to sleep pretty close together, but . . ."

"Pass." There was zero hesitation in her refusal. "What are the other options?"

"The tree." Tulland tried to salvage his broken pride with the very real success he had accomplished in his efforts to fortify Necia's favorite sleeping tree. "I've planted a ton of briars around the trunk. It's going to be a pain to get into, but once you're up there you'll have pretty good automatic guards while you sleep."

"And you think that will work against wolves?"

"It should. At the very least, even if it's a particularly strong wolf, you'll have plenty of time to just reach down and bonk it. It's a much safer situation."

Necia nodded. As Tulland did a last once-over on his farm before lights out, she confirmed that he really meant she could eat as many fruits as she wanted and went to town on the garden, eating another five or so before she rolled over onto her back and held her stomach.

"Good?"

"The fruits are fine. But being full? Really full? It's a big deal, Tulland. I haven't been completely full in . . . oh, months, at least. And it's almost always a bad idea when I do."

After patting her stomach and sitting up, Necia went to her tree, eyeballed the distance to the trunk over the briars, and gave a mighty leap upward to grab one of the branches and heft herself up into the safety of the boughs. Within a few minutes, she was audibly snoring.

# CHAPTER THIRTY-ONE

# ANTS AND WOLVES

Tulland listened to Necia as he worked. In another life, in his last one at least, he guessed that he would be in love with her by now. It would have been a really bad idea with how deadly she seemed and he'd have no chance at making anything out of those feelings, but he knew he would. Here, he could feel his heart pulling somewhat in the same direction, but it was so restrained by literally everything else in his life that the idea was making no headway.

This world wasn't a game. Necia wasn't going away into the badlands to hunt because she enjoyed it. She was going there because she was in over her head and needed to find a way to survive. And he wasn't growing plants and feeding her for no reason. She offered him some protection he couldn't otherwise get, and was bringing back more fertilizer than he could make himself.

*There are reasons for everything we are doing. And neither of us has time for anything else. Remember that, Tulland. You don't have time to waste.*

Before he went to bed, Tulland pulled out his Farmer's Tool scythe and considered going to work on the Wolfwood tree. The only factor that stopped him was the complete lack of seedpods on the tree. If he somehow managed to mess up the harvest enough to kill the tree, he had no way of knowing if he would ever get another one.

Lying down in the dirt again as the last of the light waned from the sky, he kept his weapons near him, just in case. And then he was asleep.

* * *

The next morning's dawn woke up a Tulland who for once had not had any dreams of his past. If there were any little pithy lessons from his tutor or uncle that would have helped him get through the day, he was going to have to get along without them.

"So what's in the plans for you, over the next couple of days?" Necia asked when the two of them regrouped.

"Well, my garden is about as good as I can get it. Almost. There are some enhancements I can do to those Swamp Ache trees, I think. And the fur tree you like will have to get a little bigger before I can do anything with them. But after that, I think I have to start seriously figuring out how I'm going to conquer this level."

"Ah." Necia screwed up her face into a look of sympathy. "And that won't be easy for you."

"No. Probably not. Is it the same set of requirements for you?"

"Probably. Big anthill?"

"Yeah."

Tulland had checked the floor description during the first more-or-less safe moment he had found on this floor, but had been studiously ignoring it up until this point.

---

**The Infinite, Floor 2**

The Swamp and the Badlands are a further introduction into floors with multiple biomes. The Swamp represents an area that is difficult to traverse and contains single powerful foes. The wolves serve as a store of potential experience points that assist beginning adventurers to gain the strength they need to continue on as the Infinite slowly ramps up the difficulty of survival.

Those level-granted stats and excess experience points are necessary, as the Badlands are the real focus of this floor. More secret and tricky enemies inhabit this dry and empty land.

Added information: In uncovering the secret of the ant pits, you have been granted knowledge of both the ants that inhabit them and the possibility of a greater, more permanent colony of insects. Kill more ants to learn more about this threat.

Added Information: After farming ants to near the experience cap, you have learned what exploration might have also taught you. Due east from the location at which you arrived at lies a mound so large it constitutes a major aspect of the terrain, one that bustles with activity and hides the path to the next floor.

*Can you survive this gauntlet of violent insects to continue progressing through the Infinite?*
**Foes:**
Swamp Canid
Badlands Ant
???
**Objectives:**
Clear the Badlands Fortress Mound

"How hard was it for you when you first went through? This will be your second time, right?" Tulland asked.

"It wasn't incredibly hard. I was just strong enough then to take out an ant with a single hit, and they aren't as good at tracking as you might think. I just chose random tunnels and ran through them until I got to . . ." Necia stopped and gulped. "Oh. Apparently, I can't tell you about that until you find it yourself."

"The Infinite is stopping you?"

"Yes. It's a common thing on shared floors. You can't give other people the keys to the castle, information-wise. Sorry. I'd help more if I could." Necia stood and clapped some of the dust off from her fruit-juice-covered hands. "Well, thanks for breakfast. I'll be back tonight."

"So soon?"

"I'm afraid so. I've done about all I can get out of this floor. The wolves were just about farmed out before you got here, and now that I'm sharing them with you, I'm hardly seeing any. And the ants aren't giving me enough experience to matter anymore. I'll go try to do . . . damn. I'll be doing the thing I can't tell you about, and then moving on."

"Got it." Tulland hated every bit of that idea, and it wasn't for romantic reasons at all. It was simple companionship. Once Necia left, he'd be alone in this place again, and forced to turn to a nonphysical being for company. The same being who was actively profiting from his imminent death. It wasn't great. "You will be missed."

"It's not all that bad." Necia seemed to get it. "You'll run into other people here and there. Me, even, as long as you . . . As long as there's opportunity."

"It's okay. There's nothing to be done about it, anyway." Tulland stood up. "But yeah, do come back tonight. I'll see if I can make a surprise for you."

"A surprise?" Necia arched her eyebrows. "In this place? This I have to see."

After Necia left, Tulland turned to face his mostly full day of farming. He dumped his full magical stores a few times as he circled around the farm, making sure all was well. His magic power regeneration was such that he could do that now, but he had found that after the first few charges of *Enhance Plant* of the day, he got a sharply diminishing return on how fast the plants could grow. Maybe higher skill levels would help with that eventually, but for now there was only so much time it made sense for him to spend on the farm plants.

The next task was checking his ant trap. Walking to the pit took very little time now that he knew exactly where to look, and could see his surprisingly green and healthy briars growing above it like signposts in the distance.

When he got there, his vines were busy fighting. He leaned over the edge of the pit to see that of the five or so seeds that had eventually found their way to the bottom of it, only three had survived to healthy adulthood. Those three were wrapped around the main body of a single ant and each of its mandibles, respectively, and were slowly draining it of life. As he watched, the ant slumped, then began to dissolve into nothing as the vines took full advantage of the nutrient wealth the ant represented.

| **Hades Lunger Briar, LV. 7** |
| --- |

| **Hades Lunger Briar, LV. 7** |
| --- |

| **Hades Lunger Briar, LV. 8** |
| --- |

The briars on the lip of the pit were mostly at level four, which probably meant some ants that made it past the three higher-level briars before meeting their end. They weren't planted in the best possible situation, and didn't have much water beyond whatever they were getting from the occasional ant that slipped past the bad boys in the center.

He left that pit alone and wandered around the local area until he got lucky and found another ant pit, planting briars around it in the same way as yesterday. And in just the same way as yesterday, he was immediately attacked by ants, this time a group of just three.

As they came out of the wall, Tulland took the opportunity to peg each of them with their own little flower bomb, using up about half of what the non-farmed swamp trees had produced between the last batch and this. The ants reacted to getting their own individual dose of the flowers about how he expected they would. They were all completely blinded, immediately ignoring his seeds and stumbling out of the pit to try and figure out where the attacks were coming from.

Fighting blind ants was not hard. Tulland put his back into killing them fast, watching as they split their time between desperately cleaning their antennae and trying to get away from the invisible force attacking them. He weaved through and around them, avoiding their mandibles while piling on the damage. And he didn't give them a single chance to fight on even footing.

As he killed off the second of the three ants, the third one was just about clean. Tulland simply gave it another splash of exploding flower powder on its head, then took it down easily and safely.

Was it a cheap way to win? Absolutely. But Tulland was okay with that, especially on his way to getting stronger. With as many remote kills as he had racked up on these things overnight, the lack of rewards for exploiting their weaknesses as the last one died was no surprise to him.

> **Level Up!**
> Experience source capped!

The ants would not be any more use to Tulland as direct targets anymore, except for the practice he got fighting them. He'd get a little more experience out of them from indirect farming, but not much.

And that meant it was time to turn his attention back to the wolves.

The wolf struggled against a half dozen level-six briars for a time until it was hit directly in the nose with an exploding hallucinogenic flower. While the ants had appeared more or less immune to that particular toxin and were mostly just bothered by the chemical, smelly nature of the Acheflower, Tulland saw that wolves were fully vulnerable to its mind-altering effects.

A few seconds after getting hit by the flower, the wolf's face went dopey, then transitioned back to enraged and pained as the enhanced vines dug in a little deeper to its flesh. After a few times through that cycle, it was already beyond the point where it could adequately struggle against the briars. The distraction of the drugs was too much for it to truly resist, especially because Tulland's *Enhance Plant* had gotten some major boosts in the past few hours.

> **Level Up!**

> **Skill Level Up!**

Tulland didn't know when exactly the experience from the wolves he was directly killing would cap, but it would be pretty soon. After that, he would have to rely on his growing army of randomly sown crops to kill them as they tried to navigate the world, and hope that was enough to get him whatever scraps of experience he could still get.

And once that was done, there was no choice but to press forward into the danger. He had a little bit of growth he could expect from his ant-trap briars, which would let him go into danger fully armed. And he would get some sort of improvements out of the flowers, probably, when he was finally able to start cultivating them on his own cultured Swamp Ache trees. But after that, he'd be about as strong as he could be.

At least Tulland would be in some senses. More and more, he was learning that the regular wisdom his tutor had dumped on him all those years was applicable in more situations than he had ever suspected it was, and that his uncle's less-frequent advice was about the same. And both of them had things to say about the situation he was in now.

He walked back toward his base, ready to do some of his last harvests and to plant his very last crops in this place. He would craft a little, and then prepare a bit more. He would do his very best to increase his chances of survival as much as possible.

But after that, it was do-or-die time.

# CHAPTER THIRTY-TWO

# WOLF-FUR DRAWSTRING BAG

The trees are so pretty now!" Necia exclaimed. Tulland sent a very stern do-not-explode command to the flowers as the female warrior walked up and gently brushed the petals of one of the blooms with her fingertips. "How did you do this?"

"Those flowers grow on those kinds of trees. They're useful for some of the things I want to do."

"And that's the surprise? Because I'll absolutely take one of these with me."

"No, that's probably a bad idea. They don't . . . play nice when I'm not there." Tulland reached into one of his briar bag and pulled out a small, soft object. "I made this. I thought you might find some use for it."

After returning to the camp, Tulland had put as many of the little parasite flowers as he could on the farmed Swamp Ache, then spent quite a few minutes figuring out how to carefully carve away the fur from the Wolfwood trees without hurting the tree or destroying the material. After he made his first cut, he found out it was much easier than he thought. The fur had been sitting on top of the bark on some kind of thick, pliable membrane that peeled away in one big, mostly intact sheet.

After that, Tulland had cut some undeveloped briars, stripped them of their needles, and laid the fur carefully over them. With a couple of cleverly tied knots, he found himself with a bag not unlike the coin purses he had seen back on Ouros, if quite a bit larger. It was made of one long continuous piece of the fur, brought to the top and carefully trimmed to even have a flap that closed by means of one of the trimmed, curved briar thorns poked through a carefully bored hole in the fur.

And best yet, the membrane for the fur seemed to solidify as it dried out in the open air, ending up as something close to thin, flexible leather.

"This is incredible. You made this?" Necia asked.

"I did. I already tested it with some of the water from the hole you showed me how to dig near the swamp. It seems to hold liquids just fine, so long as you don't get too violent with it. Or whatever. I don't mind how you use it," Tulland said.

"This is incredible." Necia's eyes widened a little as she took the object in her hands. "It's system recognized?"

"It is." Tulland nodded with pride. "First thing ever."

**Which is still nonsense. You are a farmer. Not a crafter.**

*And I'm not a very good crafter either. Calm yourself.*

It was only after he finished figuring out how to truly make his strip-of-leather-and-fur drawstring work that the Infinite had acknowledged Tulland's efforts, shocking both him and the System down to the core.

---

**Wolf-Fur Drawstring Bag**

This bag is crafted from farm-grown wolf fur and briar stem that was made hardy but flexible, with clever closures meant to keep the contents dry and secure.

As an object that exists within a spectrum of characteristics assigned to a system-created object, it is recognized as equivalent to that object and granted the following characteristics:

1. Increased durability. This bag is supernaturally tough to damage.
2. Watertight. This bag will hold liquids and will not leak except under exceptional circumstances or through holes in a sufficiently damaged bag.

---

**Skill Acquired: Fruits of the Field**

While your class is not and will never be a true crafting class, your frequent use of items you grow as well as repeated attempts to cobble together self-grown materials into usable tools has granted you the barest rudiments of a crafting ability.

When you use your own materials to make the most primitive of tools and items, there is a small chance to receive system acknowledgment and naming of those items. When this happens, the items' inherent magic will be focused toward a purpose, and the resulting products will function more like the tools you were attempting to make.

*This does not grant you any special skill with the items you created. Making an ax will not grant you lumberjack or ax combat skills, even when you attempt to use the ax you built with your own hands yourself.*

*This skill does not grant experience outside of some rare achievements and the skill experience necessary to advance its own level.*

"That's amazing. But I can't take this." Necia pressed the bag back into Tulland's hands. "Sorry."

"Why not? Just not useful?"

"Are you insane? It's a system-recognized watertight bag. There are a thousand uses for that. It's just that it's worth something, and I have nothing to pay you back with. There's not much honor in the Infinite, but I like to think I carry my own around with me. Taking this without paying you something would be wrong."

"Ah. I see." Tulland glanced down at the bag in disappointment. "I understand, I guess."

"Actually, I mean . . . we could see if I have anything you want. I don't carry around much, but . . ." Necia patted her hands over her armor and belt, trying to remember what she had on her that she didn't depend on with her life. "You can't use a sword and I can't give you mine. I need the belt, I need the armor, I need the experience points. I don't think you'd want my backup knife."

"Wait, what? A knife? Why wouldn't I want that?"

"It's something I brought in with me. Non-system. It's not even starter-gear level. I just used it to kill motes and get my first level. You can't fight with it."

"I don't want to fight with it." Tulland gestured with his hand, and Necia handed him the small knife. "I don't have a knife at all, Necia. Where would I even get one? I've been cutting things with a scythe."

"Everything? You made that bag with a scythe?"

"Yes. And it took forever. If I didn't have time to wait for things to grow, I wouldn't have even tried it. A knife is a big deal for me. It's not going to break or anything?"

"No. I mean, it shouldn't. In the outside world, it was a really nice knife."

"Then this is a good trade. Trust me. I need this." Tulland tucked the leather scabbard into his own belt before the skittish girl could change her mind. "And you can take the pouch now?"

"Absolutely." Necia looked at it with a smile on her face. "Can you make just a few changes for me though?"

Ten minutes later, Tulland had used the last of his scrap fur leather to make a strap through the lip of the bag that Necia could use to tie it to her belt. And he loaded her up with all the fruit she could carry, which, with the bag, was sort of a lot.

Then, again, it was almost time for bed. Necia climbed into her tree for the last time as Tulland did what he could to make himself comfortable on the ground.

"Necia? I had a question," Tulland said as the darkness settled in.

"What is it?" Necia called down from the tree. "Remember that I can't answer everything."

"I think this will be fine. It's just that you said you got your first level in here, fighting motes."

"Yes? I mean, I did. Everyone usually does."

"But you didn't have any levels in your world? You must have, right? You told me you were some kind of trainee, or something."

"Something like that, yes. And I had a high level there, but . . . you really don't know this?"

"How could I?" Tulland threw up his hands and let them fall to his legs with a clap. "I don't think anyone from my world even came here anymore. The portal was all overgrown. The Church controlled all the information, and . . ."

"Okay, okay. I get it. Sorry. It's just hard to imagine being here without all that context. The short version is that everything the System of your world granted you previously gets taken from you when you enter the Infinite. Not by the System from your world, but by the Infinite itself. This dungeon is supposed to be a test of what a world can do. The best warriors they can produce. But it's not supposed to be a test of just how much the world is willing to spend on someone. The Infinite doesn't want someone with hundreds of levels and magical equipment sweeping through everything."

"So how does their world even come into play?"

"Because the best worlds send people with the knowledge of how to use their class to the highest effectiveness. And even the class itself is sort of a product of that world. It develops and grows there. The skills are created there."

"I only sort of understand."

"Hey, that's everybody. It's a complex system. But even if your world sucks and you don't get very far, you can sometimes make your world that much better. Every performance means something, and a new record means a lot. People have a reason to try."

"At least it explains why you aren't just cruising through levels. Did it take you a long time the first time you came through this floor?"

"Oh, absolutely. I think the first floor took me two whole days. But just as I thought I had a handle on things, this one took four."

Tulland went quiet.

"Tulland? You sort of dropped off there."

"It's nothing." Tulland, with all his weeks of effort, still had days to go before he even had a chance of getting out of this floor, but he wasn't going to drag Necia down with that knowledge. "I just got tired."

"Sleep then. I'll see you in the morning, before I leave."

"Deal."

The next morning was boring, or at least as boring as mornings in the Infinite could be. Necia came down, they ate fruits together, and talked very little.

"So where are you going now? To grind on the first floor?" Tulland asked.

"No. I think that's sort of a waste of time now. I'll grind some unfinished things on the third, then move on to the fourth, finish it, rest, and fight the boss on the fifth."

"You feel ready for that? It's a Cannian Knight, right?"

"It is. And no, I don't feel ready. I'm finding out that I'm not really cut out for this." Necia slumped a bit. "But it's what I can do. And if you dilly-dally too long, the Infinite's System starts to pull you forward and penalize you. I have to make it to the safe zone before that happens."

Tulland wanted desperately to have a way to help her, but there was only so much a farmer with a ready supply of fruit could actually do for a fully armored combat class. He had to focus on his own survival. There just wasn't anything else that he could productively do.

"I hope you are wrong," Tulland offered. "For what it's worth, I think that knight is going to be sorry to meet you. You seem pretty good at what you do."

"Well, thanks." Necia held out her hand. Tulland shook it. "It was really weird meeting you, Tulland. But for what it's worth, I hope you make it."

"Thanks."

Necia nodded, smiled, and grew to her full combat height before walking off into the distance. Tulland watched her go for as long as he could, losing sight of her as she crested a distant hill. And just like that, he was all out of friends.

**It's not worth crying over. She never helped you.**

"See, that's something I'm surprised you don't understand. She actually helped me a lot."

**How so?**

"Before, making your life hard was my only reason to keep going. Now I have that reason, and also her. If I can get to where she's at soon enough."

**Soon enough for what? To help her? Tulland, the chances of you leaving this level anytime soon are low. Perhaps nil.**

"And yet I'm still here. Raring to go. You aren't even a little worried?"

**No. Not at all. Are you going to scout out the end of this level today?**

"I might as well."

**Then you can see it for yourself. I have a very good reason to be unworried. You'll see.**

# CHAPTER THIRTY-THREE

# ROCKS

Tulland did see. He could hardly miss it, once he got anywhere near it.

The ant mound turned out to be half hill and half a mud tower that stretched its ill-built bulk much higher into the air than he would have thought possible. Everywhere on its surface, ants were at work. He could see hundreds of them.

Conventional tactics for getting through a fight like that weren't hard to understand. Fast people would simply run in, dodge all the attacks they could, and blaze through the corridors, hoping to get to the end before they were chipped down by lucky shots. The strong would wade in slower, killing what was in front of them while maintaining their own health.

Both would go in through the big, obvious entrance, and both would stand a pretty good chance of making it. But Tulland was neither of those. He was slow compared to speed classes and weak compared to strength classes, able to take down a few ants if conditions were right but also perfectly capable of being killed by a single ant if things went poorly for him.

**You see now, I suspect. Your stats contain not a single tool that would help you get through this gauntlet.**

Tulland couldn't contradict that. It was simply true. He had no ability to tank the kind of damage the ants could do. He could probably outrun one on open land, but not when he was weaving through random tunnels underground that they understood and he didn't. And although he could kill one with enough time, nothing in his arsenal was strong enough to fight dozens or even hundreds of ants swarming him.

*I can't shoot fireballs. I can't teleport. I'm just a man with plants.*

**Which means you must acknowledge this is pointless. What do you have? A couple days left in our wager?**

*Something like that. It'll have to be enough, I guess.*

**You still plan on trying?**

*Of course, you idiot. You thought you'd be able to talk me out of living?*

**It was worth a try.**

Tulland shook his head and spent another twenty minutes or so observing the ants. They were running patrols, from what he could tell, and that was in addition to the hundreds of ants that were going about other business, but would probably drop what they were doing right away to attack him if they knew that was an option.

It was a hard problem, but as the System had pointed out, he still had several days to prepare for it. And diminishing returns or no, he might as well use those moments.

Three days later, the Swamp Aches in Tulland's farm finally stood taller than their admittedly stunted brothers in the swamp proper. Every one of them, glowing in the bright sun, had yellow flowers galore. Whatever limitation the parasites had from growing on the trees in any real numbers in the swamp apparently didn't apply here, where the sun was brighter, the soil was better, and Tulland's magic was in play. His farmer's intuition had told him he could put more flowers on each tree. The exact cause didn't seem that important, so long as it worked. It was more than that; it was a roaring success.

Tulland used his knife to trim the last little unwanted bits from his new pack, provided courtesy of the three Wolfwood trees inside his farm and the five or six he had managed to grow outside of it. The pack was a work of art. The System still called it a simple bag, but it was a full-on hiking pack as far as Tulland was concerned, complete with a fur-lined mat for him to sleep on that rolled up nicely to be tied to the bottom of the pack itself.

Besides that, he had another two smaller bags of pretty respectable size on each side of his belt. Carrying a lot of things wouldn't be much of a problem for him with the extra stats. He just needed to make sure he chose the right things to carry.

The farm itself was still growing, and even occasionally gaining levels courtesy of Tulland-greedy wolves who attacked during the night. It was slow going with the cap, but he was going to squeeze every possible minute of growth he could out of it, not only to give him his best chance on this floor, but to prepare him for the next.

Once his daily growing was done, it was time to find rocks. Tulland spent a lot of time finding rocks these days.

**More of this insanity.**

"Yup. For at least a few hours. Then throwing practice."

**You cannot possibly believe you can slay those ants with a thrown rock.**

Tulland just smiled. Finding the rock with the right size and shape was important. He had found that the best ones were about the size of a briar fruit or perhaps just a bit larger, and as round as he could get them. With his shovel in hand, Tulland went to the swamp and poked along happily, letting the head of his shovel cut through the muck and gross beneath the water until it clinked on something hard, then fishing it out to see what he had found.

Seven out of ten rocks went straight to the discard pile, but that still meant he was building his good rock arsenal by at least three rocks, and sometimes four or five.

Today was a really good day. By the time he had burned up his allotted time, he was the new owner of six rocks, which he immediately took to his throwing range.

Tulland had found that the trick to throwing a rock very far was not about being strong. Instead, it was about being willing to tie a vine around the rock, give it several very good spins, and then let it go when it was aimed where he wanted. This was a surprisingly consistent way for him to get distance, and he had learned the trick of hitting within fifteen to twenty feet of his target distance every time fairly quickly. What was harder was getting the direction right, especially while spinning.

He had about five days to practice that, but it wasn't something he was willing to leave to the last second. He was spending multiple hours a day on just that one task, to the bewilderment of his System.

But if it wanted to go on believing that he was training in hopes of braining individual ants to death from a distance, that was just fine. It would get its surprise at the same time the ants did.

When five more days had passed, Tulland didn't feel ready. But It was in a lot of ways like jumping into a cold body of water. When he had made the bet with the System, he had committed himself to a true and full effort within a certain time frame. There was no way he could escape that now, just like someone plummeting toward an icy lake couldn't turn back time or reverse gravity.

That morning, Tulland spent as much time as he wanted to just relaxing, eating food, and stretching out. He had already packed out his bags with all the armaments, tools, and seeds they could carry. Anything else he would be using that day was already waiting at the appointed spot for him, ready to go. If he made it to the exit arch, and he hoped he would, he'd be as ready for the next zone as he could be.

Even his status screen agreed. With both of his experience sources completely capped, he wasn't getting any more progress there anymore.

**Tulland Lowstreet**
**Class:** Farmer LV. 23
**Strength:** 30
**Agility:** 30
**Vitality:** 35 (+5)
**Spirit:** 30
**Mind:** 10
**Force:** 50
**Skills:** Enhance Plant LV. 6, Enrich Seed LV. 8, Command Plant LV. 1
**Passives:** Broadcast LV. 5, Botanical Engineer LV. 5, Strong Back LV. 4, Fruits of the Field LV. 1

He was more than glad that he pumped up his agility after his fights with the ants. His vague intuition in wanting more speed was completely spot-on. And for now, he was even fine with his spirit being lower than it could have been. Magic regeneration was nice, but he had enough of it to do most of what he wanted to actually accomplish in a day.

Being able to enhance his plants that much better with force or command them a little more with spirit was all-important now.

Tulland stood up from his mat in the dirt, rolled it up, and tied it to his pack before shrugging the whole assembly onto his shoulders. Pushing one last charge of *Enhance Plant* into his weird fur trees as a goodbye, he smiled, petted them, and moved on toward the briar-infested ant pits.

At the first pit, the briars on the lip of the hole had yet to advance past the level he had seen them the last time. The ones inside the pit, however, had been busy.

**Lunger Briar, LV. 9 (Cap!)**

**Lunger Briar, LV. 9 (Cap!)**

**Lunger Briar, LV. 9 (Cap!)**

The idea of his briars hitting some kind of leveling cap was new to Tulland, especially since at least one of his briars had hit level ten before the Infinite took a personal interest in his class. This felt like a new change.

"The Infinite, care to explain this?"

---

**Creature Level Caps**

All system-created creatures have limits to what they can do and how much they can grow. Plants are no exception to this rule. The briars you are observing have hit the natural limits of their species, and are as strong as any creature simply labeled "Lunger Briar" will ever be.

Note that this limit does not apply to any strength granted to them by your Enhance Plant skill or to other, higher-quality variants of the briars you might later create.

---

"Well, damn."

Tulland hopped down into the pits with the briars, keeping his eyes peeled for any surprise ant attacks. He mostly felt secure, since he now knew that anything this pit could put out was something his vines could handle. None came as he carefully trimmed his level-capped briars into long, deadly ropes and made the normal adjustments to thorn placements that he did for all his armor pieces. Covering his arms and chest, he climbed out of the pit and headed toward the next one.

A cap on his briar's strength instantly shattered any dreams he had of incrementally raising one of the vines to unstoppable heights of strength, but it wasn't entirely unexpected. The other option was if the Lunger Briars could react to the wolf and ant meat he fed them, but no matter how many instances of *Enrich Seed* he had pumped into the experiment, they had stubbornly refused to play ball and become a new species.

*Eventually, I'll find something they like, and I can move forward that way. For now, this is what I have.*

The next pit was about as uneventful as the last. Tulland put on his last three pieces of armor, rolled the rest of his briars into a big coil, then headed toward the ant fortress.

**Nervous, I see.**

"Yes. Of course."

**I believe I've figured out some of your plan. I don't believe it can work.**

"No? Why not?"

**Too many things would have to go right at once. Reality is rarely that forgiving.**

"Maybe not. But this also isn't quite reality, right? I've talked to the Infinite. It seems like an okay group of people. You don't think it likes me enough to chip in here?"

**It doesn't like anyone. Or dislike them. If you listen to nothing else I tell you, hear this. Systems are often compared to gods of their worlds, but at most we are prisoners of them. Slaves to them, in some ways. The Infinite is as far beyond us in power as we are to you. Perhaps further.**

"And what's beyond that?"

**I have no way of knowing. Or of even asking. But it is as close to a living god as you will ever encounter. It does not chip in to the affairs of mortals as you suppose.**

# CHAPTER THIRTY-FOUR

# DESERT QUEEN

Arriving at the appointed launching position, Tulland surveyed his tools. He had some rocks left without briars, and these he dutifully wrapped with the vine until they were just like all the others. He was left with a pile of ten or so vines, which he coiled as best he could into a package he could carry with him if he needed to.

And then, into one very special vine-and-rock assembly, he placed more projectiles. Loosening the vine from around the rock, he began to pack in flowers, putting dozens of them around the smaller, apple-sized rock this vine contained. He kept packing them for a while, only stopping when the overall weight approached but didn't quite reach that of his other rocks.

**You should turn off my communications now. If you are to try this, you will need to concentrate.**

"That's oddly considerate."

**Hardly.**

If the System meant anything by that, it chose not to elaborate. Personally, Tulland thought it was just unable to refute the idea that it was being considerate. Something about the System was off, this last week or so. He wouldn't quite term it *remorse* because he wasn't at all sure the System could even feel that. But something about how it was treating Tulland was less like an evil trickster. It was approaching how a stiff person might talk to a near equal, almost as his old tutor used to be.

Either way, it wasn't wrong about the communication channel. If Tulland was going to do this, he would need his concentration. Switching it off, he picked up the first of the rock-vine combinations, commanded it to be very still, and began swinging it in circles.

"One, two, three, throw!" Tulland shouted. He had learned through recent experiments that the ants were deaf to actual sounds that didn't come to their feet through the soil. At this distance, Tulland could make as much noise as he wanted. And the little mantra helped keep his shots consistent, so there was no reason at all not to do it. The stone sailed along its path, with the vine still attached and trailing behind. "One, two, three, throw!"

The second stone followed the first, traveling a truly impossible distance before slamming hard into the side of the hill in roughly the same area. The ants started to stir. As they did, Tulland threw out as many rocks as he could, bunching them up in that one spot and slowly turning that side of the hill green.

*That's ten.* Tulland kept throwing rocks as fast as he was able as something like a hundred ants raced toward the point of impact. *Twenty. Twenty-five. And there they are.*

He had hoped to get more than that out, but realistically, twenty-five vines were about as much as he should have hoped for in this part of the plan. It wasn't absolutely vital that he get huge numbers anyway. That was going to be another point of diminishing return that he was fine abandoning.

As the ants hit the edge of the new patch of thrown briars, Tulland sent a command. He had carefully tested over a hundred times to make sure that the current distance really was no obstacle to this working.

*Fight. Enhance Plant.*

He saw the briars spring to life and become even faster as the ants made impact, getting into gear just in time to stop the clashing mandibles from massacring them. Ants began to struggle with the constriction from the briars, and a few very unlucky ants that got a particularly high amount of attention even began to lose those fights.

Numbers, however, were quite the thing. There was no shortage of ants, especially once the first few injured ants began to spray fear-and-aggression pheromone everywhere. By the time another twenty seconds had passed, there were hundreds and hundreds of ants in the area, piling not only over the vines but over each other as they attempted to eradicate the source of the attack.

But the real source of the attack was already sprinting toward them. With a few mighty spins and a closer vantage point, Tulland skidded to a stop and let the flower-packed rock-briar fly, sending the easiest command he possibly could to the flowers as they flew over the massive pile of ants.

*Do what you want.*

The flowers did. They immediately burst into a massive cloud of yellow, much larger than the number of flowers would have implied if these weren't, in their own way, an entirely new thing.

---

**Acheflower (Cultivated)**

These cultivated Acheflower variants benefit both from your care of them as plants individually, and the higher-quality hosts you provided for them in the form of the improved Swamp Ache trees you've grown.

As a result, they produce much more hallucinogenic powder when they come apart, and the powder itself is much more powerful.

As a cultivated plant, the Acheflower gives the following benefits:

1. You can no longer be poisoned by the hallucinogen created by the cultivated flowers.
2. Your body will treat all components of general Acheflower as a neutral sort of dust, and the Acheflower dust will cause you no more inconvenience than that simple dust would when you come into contact with it.

---

A week or so was a long time to be able to experiment with just a few new products, and Tulland had very little to do but get to know them inside and out. The ants had never liked the Acheflower powder, even when it was just a slightly smelly uncultivated product. This new stuff was different. It stank. The few times Tulland had been in close contact with it, he had been amazed that the System protected his eyes and nose from burning.

And the ants absolutely hated it. They despised it. It not only blinded them physically. It now blinded them with rage. When the cloud of dust Tulland had created began descending on them, absolute chaos ensued.

---

**Remote Victory!**

---

**Remote Victory!**

---

**Remote Victory!**

---

**Remote Victory!**

---

**Remote Victory! x7**

---

It wasn't the powder killing them. With hundreds of ants blindly flailing in a pile, some casualties were to be expected. It wasn't going to get any more than a few percent of them, but Tulland was glad to see it. It represented just that much more time bought as his puny little farmer legs pumped for all they were worth toward the main entry tunnel of the hill.

He had pulled out all the stops he could, save one. As he crossed the border of the entryway, he dropped the several excess vines he had carried with him on the ground, sending a mental command for them to become fighters once more. With no prey to hunt, there was no way for him to know for sure that the command had worked, but he liked to think the guarding briars would give the ants at least a little pause.

He ran. For whatever reason, the inside of the anthill was not as dark as he had expected it would be. It made sense from a difficulty perspective. Asking people to run the gauntlet of ants was a hard enough thing. Asking them to do it in complete darkness would be a lot for an early-level challenge, even in the Infinite.

Here and there, he saw ants rushing down corridors, attempting to attend the mayhem outside. They hardly noticed him, apparently overcome with the sheer thick terror of peer ant pheromone wafting in through the tunnels. He gave them what room he could and kept running through the mostly deserted tunnels.

It was a maze. Tulland was sure the ants knew where each path went, but in the next ten minutes, he hit more dead ends than he was willing to count, sometimes running into rooms full of eggs or plant matter, and other times just the end of tunnels the ants had yet to make good use of. All the time, he was deeply aware how bad of a sign that was. Every single second was another moment the ants were resolving the calamity outside and streaming back into the hill to do their normal work.

*I probably have a minute to find the exit before that's a problem. Or less.*

Tulland was fully winded. His legs were fire, like the ants themselves had been chewing on them. He had seconds of full function left when he burst into another room and found himself momentarily blinded not by darkness but by brightness he had not expected at all.

In the corner, as large as a building and shining with a phosphorescent light that Tulland wasn't even close to beginning to want to understand, was a real monster that put everything he had seen so far to shame.

**Desert Queen**
Glowing with the accumulated power of all her children, caring for each without knowing their names, and deadly beyond reckoning, this Queen

rules over hundreds of miles of Badlands without stepping a foot from her bedroom. She is waited on hand and foot by her subjects, who provide her with food, comforts, and work themselves to death in her name.

This service has not rendered her soft. It has made her strong.

*To fully describe the danger that she presents to the average adventurer facing her for the first time on this floor would be difficult. Know this, however. The difference in size between her and her children pales in comparison to the difference in strength. She is not to be taken lightly.*

She had not noticed Tulland yet. Or if she had, she wasn't being obvious about it. For a moment, Tulland's legs almost betrayed him and took him away from the terror of the shining insect. Then his mind almost did the same, telling him stories about what her massive, acid-dripping mandibles would do to him if they got hold of him. And how very easy that would be to accomplish, given that each of the mandibles was as long as a swamp tree was tall.

But he couldn't run. It simply wasn't an option. The ants would be closing in behind him anytime now. Knowing it would be a waste of time to even consider a direct attack, Tulland tucked his spear behind his pack and palmed two of his cultivated Acheflowers in each of his hands. It was a shame. He had made himself a brand-new spear, and had even sacrificed a fairly mature Ironbranch Sapling to do it. It was, without a doubt, a much superior item with which to poke monsters. It just wouldn't help him any bit here.

He was going to have to trick this one out. Only, it was looking grim.

There would be no looking for a way around the Desert Queen, or to circumvent her royal throne room entirely. It wasn't that Tulland was too stubborn to quit moving in one direction, or that he wasn't terrified. He would have gladly chosen some other path if he could have.

*Nope. There's just no choice.* Tulland gulped as he looked across the room, his gaze unobstructed by her body as she sat high on her deadly pointed legs. *That's the arch right there, behind her. There's no choice but to go through her. So through her, I suppose, I will go.*

# CHAPTER THIRTY-FIVE

# Farmer's Intuition

Tulland's leg slipped forward as silently as he could, landing just inside the queen's throne room with no more noise than a mouse. It might have mattered had the queen really been unaware of his presence. She was not. She knew he was there, something that became incredibly apparent as she turned her massive body on a dime toward him and started moving forward, mandibles clacking.

Both of Tulland's hands flashed as he threw flowers out at the queen. His agility stat might not have been linked up to any combat skills, but it also wasn't anything to scoff at anymore. He had just spent an entire week practicing throwing things too, something that really helped as he now chucked two mud-weighted flowers at the queen's antennae stalks. They both pounded their targets with precision, putting a cloud of yellow dust directly into the tools the queen needed to see him.

That might have blinded her, but it definitely did not disable the tough old girl. She was a fast and angry animal, one with massive grasping jaws moving through the room methodically trying to get their target by either luck or brute-force searching. Tulland gulped down the bile rising in his throat as he heard ants coming down the tunnels behind him and surged forward, chucking flowers as fast as he could get them into action.

His plan was to go under the queen, something that was possible given how wildly she was swinging her head. But it was a close thing. There were opportunities that disappeared just as quickly as they appeared. He moved into the range he would need to slide under her before his body told him there was no way that was happening. The sheer fear of that maneuver was enough for his legs just to deliver a strong, flat-out *no* and refuse to take another step.

He pulled back. His spirit might have been willing, but his flesh was weak. He wasn't going to get past the ant without a better plan. Unfortunately, he had none. He was just going to have to try a Hail Mary. He dodged a few more swings from the jaws of the ant, then rushed it again. This time, though, he flung one of his arms forward at the same time he told the briar on that arm it was okay to strike. It sailed through the air, landing where the ant's shoulder blades would be if it had them.

Of course, there was no chance the briars would actually hurt the behemoth. But they did distract her. Now that something was crawling all over her back, she had a target. Her head immediately arced up and back in a vain attempt to reach the vine, which gave just enough guaranteed room for a moment that Tulland was finally able to convince himself to move forward.

The head came down as he was moving through, but not quite fast enough. It hit him, sending him tumbling hard across the dirt and into one of the ant's legs, but failed to crush him or cut him like it should have. The hit was shallow enough that despite the overall banged-up-and-bruised damage it caused, he could still function.

Tulland sprang to his feet, steadied himself, and stabbed down at the lowest joint of one of the legs. It hit and sank in, causing a reflexive attack from the queen in revenge. He was already gone, stabbing into a foot on the other side of the body, moving, and stabbing another.

He'd never kill the ant, but he also wouldn't get away if it got so much as an inkling of where he was while still able to move around at full speed. But if there was one thing he knew, it was that this ant was specialized specifically for being a ruler, for being big enough, strong enough, and wreathed enough in glory as ants went, that its rule wouldn't ever be questioned.

And with that came a lot of weight. He had only just pulled away from the third stab when he heard a cracking from one of the legs he hadn't attacked yet. The queen had been favoring the injured limbs, which had worked until the work they weren't doing built up on her uninjured joints and began to strain the exoskeleton itself. By the time he stabbed the fourth leg, the cracks in the remaining two healthy legs' chitin were visible from across the room.

And then something unexpected happened. As Tulland went to stab the fifth leg, the room filled with a pheromone so strong he could actually smell it with his pathetic human nose, something so powerful he doubted there was an ant in the badlands that wouldn't know after it had a few minutes to spread.

Without any delay, the ants nearby did notice. And went absolutely mad. Tulland couldn't see them doing it, but he could feel it in the soil itself as he heard them begin to slam against walls in a blind rage, all as one. A tremor like an earthquake reverberated through the entire structure as dust and stones began to rain down all around him.

*And what could be the point of this, the Infinite? Of an attack that kills the queen's attacker at the cost of her life?*

Tulland wasn't entirely certain that the entire hill would collapse, but he also wasn't going to wait around to find out if that really was the intent. He wheeled around, ducking through a pair of legs and streaking like a bolt of lightning toward the gate. This time, both his spirit and body were willing.

Almost in time to make a difference, the vision of the queen ant seemed to clear. She wheeled around and rushed forward, ignoring the damage she was doing to her own legs to slam her mandibles shut just behind Tulland, then once more a bit closer. On the third bite, when she really would have gotten him, her jaws closed tight not around his weak human body but an indestructible stone gate to another place entirely. Even the acid on her jaws couldn't hurt him then. He was through.

---

**Delay Room**

You have conquered the second-floor insect gauntlet. As doing so usually involves something of a rush and the next level of the tower might bring an immediate adverse condition, you have been allotted a few minutes of safe time in this space in between spaces, where there is nothing to threaten you.

---

This kind of room was not unknown to Tulland. It was mentioned in books. In the histories of his world, there were several documented times when people found themselves delayed between areas in the local-to-his-world dungeons. He had always imagined them as glowing, floating sorts of places, where one might fly around unencumbered by the weight of physical things.

This, counter to his expectations, was a room of floors, ceiling, and walls all built of the same dull gray brick. It was clean, but there wasn't a single interesting to see in the space besides himself. He was admittedly bizarre in a briar-covered farmer sort of way, but he was pretty used to how he looked by now.

It was just now occurring to Tulland that Necia had actually seen him several times in his fully briared get-up, and how that might have looked to her. As he dived into his notifications, it was as much to forget the embarrassment of that as it was to see his rewards.

The first two appeared to be standard-issue system rewards for clearing the area. Each was good, but nothing mind-blowing.

---

**Experience and Stat Pack**
This pack grants a Lesser Stat Potion as well as a healthy amount of experience for both leveling purposes and skill growth.

---

**Level Up!**

---

**Level Up!**

---

**Skill Level Up! x7** Each of his skills had gained a whole level-up, including his new crafting skill. He was entirely unsure what leveling that skill would do, but at the very least it wouldn't hurt to have a slightly better blanket or better-built spear. The two level-ups didn't hurt either. He immediately dumped five stat points into the two magical stats he bothered to level, and continued on with his reading.

**Truck Garden**
You came into the Infinite without a chance to prepare, which means you have only been able to use the seeds you found here. While each plant in the Infinite follows its own rules and is as well-suited for your current needs as the plants of a place could be, you are somewhat wanting in the kinds of mundane supplies a usual adventurer would have remembered to bring with them.

In this packet, you will find seeds for grains, vegetables, various berry bushes, and similar things. Each is clearly labeled, and each will respond well to Enhance Plant or other similar attempts to enhance their growth rates.

None of the plants in this pack will contribute to crop variety or value in relation to Broadcast. They are simply a way to create a lasting supply of comforting, nutritious food. As a bonus, the garden comes with a small heating element and pot suitable for cooking meals for a single person.

---

Tulland was much happier about these seeds than he should have been. He had been eating nothing but raw briar fruits since he got there. While this had made him more healthy than he had ever been in his entire life, he was more sick of the fruits than he would have imagined he could be of anything.

The stats and levels were very welcome, more than equipment would have been. He couldn't get much use out of any particular piece of clothing anyway.

But the real gift was coming soon.

**Go on. Gloat.**

"I might. Why shouldn't I?"

**You should. There should have been no way for you to get through that challenge. Do you know that I've seen thousands upon thousands of class-enhanced warriors fall to less, simply due to fear or hesitance? Simply because they were careless, or would not try?**

Tulland was taken aback. This sounded suspiciously like praise.

"No. I didn't."

**I have. And yet, you did not. You figured out a way to make it possible, took your chances when they were available, conquered your fear, and then saw everything through. It was . . . not too bad of a performance.**

"Thanks, I suppose." Tulland was cautious now. "So what happens to you? Now that I've won. If I choose to take the prize, I mean."

**There is no choice whether or not to take the prize, just as there's no choice on my part whether or not to give it. We entered into a covenant, one which the Infinite will now enforce.**

"Ah. Sorry."

**Don't be. You triumphed. And to answer your question, the Infinite will now strip me of a great deal of power. More than I spent to get you here. I'll be weakened, perhaps more than I would gain even if you fell on this next floor.**

"A potential net loss then?" Tulland asked. The System talking casually about Tulland's death gave him back a little of his footing. This was an enemy of his. "I'm sorry I couldn't be worth more."

**Oh, you may yet be. As I said, you've overperformed most expectations. Centuries ago, when I was in control of your world? What a warrior I would have made of you.**

Tulland cut the communications. He could tell the System was just about done, and he wasn't sure he could tolerate much more of this conversation. There was something off-putting about what was happening now, like he had won a bet with a friend and now had to cut off his friend's arm. It was too much.

And just like the System had said, his reward was coming to him whether he wanted it or not.

---

**Wager Won!**

Your competition with your world's System is over, and you have been declared the victor. The Infinite will now harvest the power from the loser necessary to enhance the power of the victor.

> **Skill Created!**
> **Farmer's Intuition**
> What was once an informal, cloudy function of your class is now a more official, powerful skill. As opposed to a vague feeling, you will now be delivered the same or more data in a readable format.
>
> This skill analyzes the interactions between plants, the soil in which they grow, moisture conditions, and fertilizers to inform you of probable outcomes relating to the combination of some or all of those factors. In addition, this new skill now interacts with your existing Farmer skills, introducing the chance of predicting a particularly good outcome from a use of Enhance Plant, Enrich Seed, or interacting with Botanical Engineer.
>
> *As this skill levels, it will become more and more comprehensive. At a sufficiently high level, there will be nothing it does not know about farming or your interaction with it.*

Tulland leaned back and shut his eyes. This seemed weak at first glance. But he knew more than anyone else how much he had been stumbling in the dark with his farms, praying that he wouldn't find himself on unfamiliar ground where he'd be unable to grow anything at all.

This skill not only promised to fix that, but it also seemed to have the chance of guiding him toward more and better plant species, to the extent he could create them. Those were great sources of experience, if nothing else, and none had so far proved to be outright useless to him.

For someone who had come into the dungeon not knowing the first thing about farming beyond half-remembered information anyone would know, this skill wasn't just a crutch. It was like getting the chance to grow an entirely new, healthy leg to replace his own disability. Put short, it was the best news he had since he came to this place.

Tulland put his head back on the boring, nondescript brick wall and took a deep breath. And once he had that breath safely in his lungs, the Infinite's Dungeon System seemed to decide for him that his time in that room was done. The gray faded away to nothing as the new world of the third floor was suddenly visible to him in all its terrible, thundering glory.

# CHAPTER THIRTY-SIX

# THIRD LEVEL

> **Environmental Challenge!**
>
> In addition to any beasts, monsters, or fellow-climber challenges, the third level of the Infinite also presents new dangers. It is, concisely put, a land of chaotic weather beyond what is natural to any world.
>
> Rain, lightning, and harsh winds are only the beginning. Temperatures swing wildly here. The ground itself shakes with treacherous trembling, which threatens to take away your footing at the least convenient times. The earth may split to issue forth molten rock. The hills may tumble down on top of you.
>
> *Surviving the world in this place is its own objective, its own goal outside of defeating your foes and finding the gate to move on.*

Tulland learned about the new level in midair as he was pushed downhill and sideways across a steep hill filled with trees. Unable to actually resist the deafening, rapid-fire gusts of wind pushing his body, he had given up and was moving with them as much as possible.

The trick to moving with a heavy wind came intuitively to Tulland, who had grown up near the sea. As with waves, resisting them completely was a surefire way to get knocked over, but using their strength would amplify his own. After getting to his feet between gusts, he finally managed to find the rhythm. And after a minute or so, he was beginning to have a bit of fun moving with the wind.

That was when the hail started falling. The first big chunk rolled off his briar helmet, and though it gave him a pretty good thump, it wasn't particularly dangerous to him; he wasn't really injured from it. The next five or six battered him some more.

*System, what the hell is this?*

The System declined to answer, or couldn't. Tulland had a momentary wave of concern for the System that almost disgusted him once he realized what he was feeling, but it was true that the Ouros System had just taken a pretty substantial hit. He had no idea what the kind of energy draw he had imposed on it would do to its health, if it even had such a thing.

Either way, he appeared to be alone in the weirdness for now, being pinged by pieces of ice the size of grapes with bigger, more dangerous chunks mixed in. The sound of the ice decimating the surroundings was probably the loudest thing he had ever heard, even loud enough to drown out his surprised scream when a piece of ice the size of his own head came down on his outstretched arm and shattered the bones in his forearm to pieces.

*Damn. Damn. I didn't have armor on that one. The ant kept it.* Tulland couldn't believe how stupid he was, but as the nausea and shock of the broken bone started to kick in, he knew that simply running with the wind wouldn't cut it anymore. He needed significant, hard-sided cover from the weather or he'd be chipped to pieces before ten minutes had passed.

Keeping as close to trees as he could for whatever cover the branches could give him, Tulland tucked his broken arm close to his body and gritted his teeth in pain as he ran along. The first chance at survival he saw was a carved-away river bank on the opposite side of a fast-flowing stream. He decided to try to jump it, managing to get across but also cracking his head hard on a rock as he slipped in the mud on the other side of the water.

"Dammit. Dammit."

Tulland's vision swam in front of him as he crawled forward, thankful for his vines and high vitality shielding him from what he suspected would have been an otherwise fatal blow. As much better of an outcome as that was, he was still nearly blind as he crawled forward into the cover of the overhang, shuffling slowly so as not to have to take his one good hand off the ground as he went.

He felt the hail thin out as the bank shaded him from a few sides, and kept crawling forward trying to get deep enough to protect himself from the pieces being blown in diagonally from the wind. Finally, all but the most motivated hail was blocked, and the way in front of him was still open. He had expected to hit a wall of dirt and mud face-first by now, but the weather was getting quieter and quieter behind him as the soil beneath his hand became drier and drier.

Tulland's vision was starting to clear now, though it took him a moment to realize it, given the sheer darkness around him. He was underground in some way he didn't understand, and probably in very real danger of a cave-in burying him alive. But he was out of the hail, able to fully enjoy the sensation of his arm pulling itself back into one piece in relative safety from falling ice.

He propped himself up against the earthen wall and felt around himself with his good arm as he waited to be made right. Nearer to him, there was nothing but more soil. As he leaned farther and farther, trying to find anything that might help him, he felt his gloves scrape against something rougher and more solid. After a quick grope in the dark, he realized it was a piece of wood.

Tulland had hoped to use his new heating element in a more proven, safe, and sure-to-work way to celebrate its acquisition. Without that option, he reached into his bag to pull out the small disk of metal he assumed was the cooking tool and tried to get it to work in much the same way he would have commanded his plants to do or not do something. The element immediately responded to his will, heating up in his hand rapidly until he dropped it to the dirt.

It put off no light, but after several seconds, the heat was enough to make the wood smoke and hiss as he pressed them together. It wasn't quite enough to get the wood burning, but a quick application of some of the fur-bark from the Wolfwood gave him a small flame from which to get the wood going in earnest.

Tulland sat watching the wood burn, thankful that there seemed to be some sort of outflow of air somewhere in the tunnel that kept the smoke from building up where he was. As the fire grew, he saw that the piece of wood he found came from a substantial pile of dozens of similar small logs. He added a few more to the fire, and the increase in light made clear what he already had an inkling of. He was in a tunnel of sorts, perhaps a place where water had cut its way to the river during a heavy flood. Given how dry it was, he didn't think that kind of event was still happening, or at least happening very often. It was enclosed, reasonably warm, and seemed hard enough to find that he suspected it would keep him safe from monsters for at least enough time for his arm to mend.

The warmth crept across Tulland's skin as the heat began to accumulate in the tunnel. He sighed and leaned back, grimacing as his regeneration put the finishing touches on his arm bones in a series of audible clicks and clacks. To distract himself, he set out to read the rest of the Infinite's description of the floor.

> Your objective is to find your way out of this place. Pure and simple. There are no bosses here. There are monsters to fight, but they will be balanced with an eye toward simple predictability. The environment is your real enemy. Don't take your eye off it for a second.
> **Objectives:** Find the exit gate

Tulland was trying his very hardest not to freak out. He took some deep breaths and did his best to consider what this level meant for him. If this kind of hail was common, he couldn't grow anything at all, which would in turn mean he would have to wait until a break in the weather and then take off as fast as he could in search of an exit. If he were to guess, he'd suspect that hail wasn't the most common thing around these parts. There were, after all, still trees here. Trees could take a lot of damage, but they weren't invincible to constant hail.

And if the trees could grow here, then *he* could grow things too. Courtesy of his magical powers, he would have a chance. And he already had some ideas about how to do that.

As for now, he wasn't moving. He was warm. He was almost back in good shape. And he wasn't going to risk that at all if he could help it.

Deciding to lean a little heavier into the comfort, Tulland pulled out his mat, laying it a safe little distance from the fire before clambering around the burning wood to get to more fuel. He added a few more logs than he probably needed to, watching the fire climb almost to the roof of the tunnel as the draft through the space continued to take the smoke away.

Almost sweaty now, he let his vines uncoil to the ground on either side of him, freeing them to stand guard against threats that might show up and attack if he nodded off. The newly added wood was burning pretty well now, and the warmth made that a real possibility. Just as his eyelids actually started to get a bit heavy, he was pulled away from any chance of sleep by a sparkling glint in the distance. There was something in the tunnel with him. Something metal.

The metal item was just far enough in the distance that he couldn't make out what it was, outside of the fact that it was there. Tulland carefully searched around for a rock until his hand found a stone embedded mostly in the mud. After pulling out his knife, he slowly worked the rock loose, pulled his arm back, and tossed it at the possible threat.

The rock flew true, hit the object, and clanged. The object itself did not move. Either this metal was not connected to a person, or the person in question was very, very good at hiding surprise. Heartened, Tulland grabbed a piece of wood, held it in the fire until one end of it was aflame, and crept very slowly forward to find out what he was looking at.

In the process, Tulland learned the tunnel he was in curved. He could see a little bit of rounded metal sticking out from around that curve, but wasn't able to actually identify it until he was almost on top of it and able to look around the sharp angle deviation in the tunnel's direction.

When he finally saw it, Tulland didn't gasp, yell, or jerk back in surprise. It wasn't that kind of thing.

*System, wake up. System. I need . . . System, just wake up, okay? I need to talk to you.*

There was no answer.

*The Infinite? Anyone? I just need someone right now, all right? Anyone is fine. Is anyone out there?*

The seconds stretched on as Tulland felt the very most alone and most isolated he had ever felt, sinking further and further into his own despair with nothing at all to grab onto besides the fear and sorrow.

The metal he had seen belonged to a helmet, one that he knew. He had seen golden, almost distracting hair poking out from around it often enough. It was Necia's, or one exactly like it, which seemed unlikely in a place so sparsely populated he had only met one other person. There were dozens or hundreds of classes that he knew about, only a few of which used helmets like that, and all of which had other options for the style of individual armor pieces.

Unless he was mistaken, this was hers. And to find it here, slightly bloodied and away from her in a place that otherwise seemed safe, meant that something bad had happened in a place where negative occurrences usually meant the worst. Unless he was wrong, unless he wasn't seeing something, this was very, very bad.

But there was no mistake. The helmet was there, and Necia wasn't.

# CHAPTER THIRTY-SEVEN

# SHOCK

Tulland thought he knew what being in shock was like by now. He had been through life-and-death combat, fled from near-certain death, been suspended by spikes in a briar patch, and broken bones. Compared to his life before coming to the Infinite, he was living in a constant, horrible waking nightmare that hit him like a sledgehammer from unseen angles at unexpected times. He thought, reasonably, that he was starting to get used to it all.

This was different. This was much worse. Head swimming for an entirely different reason now, he shot back from the helmet, only to rear forward again almost immediately as he lost the contents of his stomach. Wiping his mouth without thought, he looked back at the glinting metal, now almost in shadow again. His torch had gotten lost in the shuffle somehow, and Tulland had no motivation at all to know how and where it had gone.

"No. No. I just saw you," Tulland said into the dark. "I just saw you. How did you do this? How?"

He was aware he was not making much sense, at the very least because he was talking to someone who couldn't possibly talk back. He also just didn't have the vocabulary to talk about what he was feeling. She had *just* been with him a few days ago. She was *just* not only healthy, but healthier than he had ever been able to imagine a person being. Strong. Invincible, even. She was a literal giant built to survive things. She couldn't *just* die.

And yet there her helmet was. Cold. Bloodied and broken. Contorted in a way that simply could not allow for life.

"No. No. Absolutely not," Tulland said. He could not accept this. He would not accept this. And he simply didn't. He sat, for a while, not accepting it. "No."

**You've been there for hours. Are you aware of that?**

Tulland wasn't aware, actually, even though he saw the fire had burned itself down to the soft glow of embers and even though his eyes were now red from exposure to the smoke.

*I was aware. I'm just thinking.*

**Lies. You are lying.**

*You are one to talk.*

**Fair. And yet, you have been sitting there for hours, staring at a helmet. Why?**

*You know full well why. You know what this means.*

There was a specific feeling to when the System was thinking about something. It was different from how things felt when it was done talking, or when it was without the words with which to reply. Consideration left a certain taste in the air between them that Tulland had long since become familiar with.

**I do, and I am sorry. But you must be aware that it does not necessarily mean that. It's a likelihood. A probability. It's far from a proof.**

*Then what's your explanation of what happened here?*

**That I'm sure of? Nothing. But imagining a situation where your friend was being chased so closely that she could not recover her helmet after some misadventure knocked it from her head is not difficult. This place is chaotic, Tulland. This floor in particular is so. In a place where anything can happen, anything else can happen as a result.**

Tulland mulled that over as best he could through his shock and despair. The System wasn't wrong, exactly. It wasn't overplaying its hand, demanding that he accept Necia was just fine in a situation where it was clear she probably wasn't. That made it harder to simply dismiss the idea that something had happened besides her dying and getting dragged off by some horrible monster. It was possible.

*So how do I find out, then? How do I prove she's all right?*

**Frankly, you can't. Not unless you see her out there. Not unless you find her by happenstance. And you may not be able to do that at all, depending on the reality of the situation.**

The System paused here, as if being careful with its words. For what it was worth, Tulland appreciated that more than he liked to admit at that moment.

**But you certainly can't do that here. Unless she comes back to here, that is. You need to be on the move, as soon as the weather allows you to. To establish your farm here. To push forward. As you have before.**

Tulland nodded reluctantly. He couldn't find any fault in what the System was saying. In the way that had become more and more odd to him as time stretched on, he was finding that the System at least occasionally actually tried to help him and gave him advice that was, in the moment, solid advice.

"All right. Then what's my next move?"

**First, you need a plan to leave this place. If Necia did run into a force that could injure her here, it is a risk to you as well. Likely more so. You need the safety of shelter. And if you are to have that, you must build your own farm.**

And then the System was gone. Tulland had cut the connection in case the System tried to leverage this moment for some kind of gain. Days ago, he had realized the System didn't actually have the ability to see him during the times he did this, at least not in any way that mattered. He had confirmed as much with the Infinite, who was more than willing to answer when he asked.

**Perception Blocking (System Interaction Option)**
While you may not prevent the Infinite from seeing what it can see or doing anything it has the capability to do, your own System does not possess the same amount of authority in this place. In addition to being able to block communications from the System of your world, you may also restrict its ability to see things you are doing in a variety of ways.

The standard obscuring effect the Infinite will bring into play for you is to keep your world's System from seeing anything other than the vague impression of your movements and actions during times when you disallow it from communicating with you. Other less stringent levels are possible and attainable simply by mentally requesting an adjustment to the level of strictness with which the Infinite adjudicates this rule.

Tulland sat by the mouth of the cave for an hour or so, until the light started to cut through the clouds and illuminate the area just a bit. There was no use moping around. The thing to do right now was exactly what the System had said. He couldn't help anyone or anything by doing nothing.

Instead, he gingerly picked up Necia's helmet and placed it into his pack, tucking it at the bottom. He wasn't sure why he did that, but it felt like the right thing to do. Once that was done, he looked outside and found that the weather in this area had patterns. He could see leaves with what looked like frost damage, and bark that had been scorched. Much more than he would have expected from a normal forest, there were fallen trees scattered around, some that looked like they had been ripped in half by the wind.

But there were plants. Plenty of them. Mosses that looked hardy, shrubs that looked quick-growing. And one towering, thick-trunked type of tree that stood guard over it all. They all had seeds, and Tulland had the levels to make use of them.

> **Tulland Lowstreet**
> **Class:** Farmer LV. 25
> **Strength:** 30
> **Agility:** 30
> **Vitality:** 35 (+5)
> **Spirit:** 35
> **Mind:** 10
> **Force:** 55
> **Skills:** Enhance Plant LV. 6 Enrich Seed LV. 9
> **Passives:** Broadcast LV. 6, Botanical Engineer LV. 7, Strong Back LV. 5, Fruits of the Field LV. 2, Farmer's Intuition LV. 2, Command Plant LV. 1

Tulland was standing at the other exit, the one he realized must exist from the fact that there was a place for the smoke in the tunnel to go. It was in a lower spot, perhaps a course the river had once taken in some ancient time. But it was as large an exit as the entrance on the banks had been. Necia had chosen her hiding place well, in that way. She couldn't have been cornered there.

While waiting, Tulland took in what he could, and finally the hail began to taper off. After slapping his face to try and shake off the remainder of the trauma to his mind, he took off running as soon as the size of the hailstones shrank below what would injure him. It still hurt to be pelted, but only for the time it took him to run a few hundred feet away and climb into the boughs of one of the larger, more lushly leafed trees.

He climbed. If he was going to find a place to be his farm, he needed perspective on the surrounding area. At his current strength, something like climbing a tree was absurdly easy compared to what his subconscious mind expected it to be. Letting his body take over, he moved from branch to branch, establishing and reestablishing balance and leverage at each new position until he was finally high enough to take a serious look around.

Mostly, he was seeing more of the same compared to where he was. Most of the view was blocked by the tops of other trees, while the majority of the terrain he could see was clearly ravaged by various kinds of harsh weather. Most of the soil was cratered by hail and covered in wilted plants that looked like they had been damaged by blistering heat, extreme cold, or both.

But one place held more promise. As the last little bit of the hail diminished to nothing, he saw a place far in the distance that just might work.

As strong as his body was, Tulland couldn't bring himself to jump down from the top of the tree. After carefully and quickly descending, he took off at a jog toward the area, keeping as much cover between him and prying eyes as he could.

The target was a small clearing, not nearly big enough to be considered a field and barely growing plants at all outside of a few of the hardier types of mosses Tulland had seen. What made it special was that it was under the cover of two of the largest trees Tulland had seen here so far, one of which was naturally leaning slightly above the clearing. The other appeared to have suffered a break in its trunk at some point, which bent it at an unnaturally sharp angle over the area from the other side.

*And between the two of them, they look like they are letting in a bit of light and not much else. There's only a few hail dents in the soil, and it's right by the river. I can grow stuff there. I know I can.*

On the far forest side of the clearing most distant from the river, the ground rose sharply into a kind of dirt wall, probably representing the edge of where the river was able to erode away at the ground during floods. It represented both a chance and a danger. There was plenty Tulland thought he could do with the terrain, but it came with the risk of being washed away. Still, he thought he could grow there.

His *Farmer's Intuition* skill was telling him that he wasn't wrong, and although he was unsure how much he could trust the new skill, it was still by far his best, most apparently reliable source of information about such things.

Once he got to the area, there was no time to waste. Outside of the area that the river cut through, sunlight was at a premium in this place. This was the best chance he was likely to get at a growable area, and that meant he needed to throw almost everything he had at it. Holding back only a tactically small amount of seeds, he tilled the ground in a hurry, then began to plant.

# CHAPTER THIRTY-EIGHT

# GNAWING AMBUSHER

The river being adjacent to the farm was nice, in that the soil was good and moist without being overly wet, and more water was just a scoop of his bag away. But it also represented a sort of risk, given that the river might flood at any time. As soon as Tulland had placed all the seeds in his initial planting, he got to work shoveling dirt from deeper in the forest, hefting it over to the opposite side of his staked farm area into a huge pile for flood resistance.

It took the better part of the day to do, but by the end of the day, Tulland had built something like a berm around the two sides of the farm that would protect it when the river flooded. The wonder of stats meant that the berm was almost as high as his shoulder, representing the better part of a few big craters he had dug out of the forest floor unlucky enough to be conveniently adjacent to the project.

He wasn't sure it would absolutely hold when the flooding came, but he had it packed down as firmly as he could and hoped it would prove to be enough. To increase the chances further, the entire wall was studded with briar seeds, planted without fertilizer and little hope of growing well. But they had a different advantage. Numbers. If there was one thing there was no shortage of in his pack, it was briar seeds. He had hundreds of the seeds without their fruit flesh, tucked away in their own little sack waiting for whatever use he could find for them.

Tulland had also been busy with his magic, taking any spare power he had and applying it to the plants, regeneration cycle after regeneration cycle.

The recent increases to his stats were really showing their worth now. Every time his magic pool regenerated and was applied to the work, he was able to see an actually visible bump in the growth of the briars, and over time, even a noticeable growth in the usually much slower-growing trees. It was gratifying, especially as he watched the root structures of the briars take hold in his berm like a kind of organic, creeping glue that added structural integrity to the protective barrier. By the time he had reached a point of diminishing returns so small any more applications of magic power would be truly useless, he had a good foot and a half of briars. And an idea.

Command Plant, *right? It has to do more than I'm using it for. I've had two ideas for ways it could be useful and both have worked, but I've hardly tried to stretch the limits. And if I could . . . it could be big.*

Once he dropped his shovel into the back of his pack, Tulland sat on the dirt, closed his eyes, and focused. He basically understood what he wanted from the briars, but figuring out enough ways to communicate it to them that he wouldn't be misunderstood or ignored was a job in and of itself.

He imagined the briars stretching out, growing past the length they were ever intended to be. Of stretching toward the sun, of reaching prey that would have evaded them before. Of spending whatever they had to in terms of their normal strength and thickness to be in all ways longer, taller, and farther reaching.

Tulland wasn't sure if they heard him, but after spending twenty minutes on the task and seeing no difference, he figured either they had or he was doomed to fail, no matter how much effort he put toward the task. Turning toward the high, eroded bank at the forest end of his farm, he moved on to the task of giving himself enough shelter to survive whatever the next wave of terror was that this forest had planned for him.

As much as he had pumped power into the berm, it wasn't as if he had ignored his farm entirely. In reality, the majority of his power had still gone to the farm proper, and the back edge of the area was studded with good, strong, and soon-to-be adult briars ready for use. Just on the other side of an intentionally thick patch of the vines, he carved away at the soil, carefully removing just enough dirt to make a Tulland-sized tunnel beneath the forest floor. Luckily, the dirt was packed hard and dense past the first several inches of digging, and it would be stable in everything minus a mighty shaking of the earth.

*Of course, that's a possibility here. But it's only one risk out of dozens. I'll take that bet.*

Tulland dug until he had a few feet of shelter, then curved the tunnel around to make an exit coming out of the same wall several feet away. If someone was to attack him while he was in there, he didn't want to have no way of escape at all. And having both outlets to his sleeping place in his controlled, briar-covered farm was a relief.

Not that it was enough. Before going to sleep, Tulland decided to throw a few handfuls of briars over the ground on top of the tunnel, hoping to hold it together just that much better with roots. After hitting them with a quick burst of *Enhance Plant*, he crawled into his tunnel, set his remaining body vines on guard mode at his foot and head, and settled down for a long overdue and much needed sleep.

Waking up in the Infinite had, until now, been a mostly uninteresting thing. But on this floor, there was an actual day-night cycle. Tulland had arrived during the night and relied on the pretty bright moonlight to see far enough to find his new farm plot. But now, it was a bright, cheery atmosphere.

*Almost too cheery. What the hell?*

Even deep in his tunnel, there was enough illumination that opening his eyes was a bit shocking. As Tulland shimmied out of the darkness to the light, it got endlessly worse. His garden was doing well, even shockingly so, but part of the reason why was that no amount of forest canopy cover could have possibly cut the vast amount of light coming from the sky. It was like the place had doubled up on suns, even though only one shone in the sky, as per the usual way of things.

Worse, the temperature was going absolutely crazy. It was early morning, at least judging by how long Tulland thought he had slept. But it was already hotter than it had ever been on Ouros save the very deepest parts of the sunny season. And the leaves of the two trees above, as well as most other trees in the area, were closing, giving little relief from the sun's rays. Tulland opened his System's connection again.

*If this is going to get worse, I'd better be ready. Right?*

**Why would I care? Do as you will.**

Smiling at the return of the System he knew and distrusted, Tulland started taking a look at his vines, finding something truly shocking had happened. Whatever he was trying to do with his intent had either worked, or prompted the Infinite to take pity on him. Either way, he was staring down some very, very long vines.

**Lunger Briars (Long, Inferior)**
Due to an infusion of intent during the growing process, these briars have nearly transformed into a different kind of plant. What before was already

an absurdly ropey, vine-ish plant that could barely be called a briar, is now almost entirely dissimilar from anything bearing that name. What you have now is more like a flexible version of a thorned flower stem, stretched out almost to absurdity.

*In trade for their absurd length, these briars are worse at almost everything else. They are weaker, less durable, and less able to stand up to a variety of stresses. They will fail in soil that your standard briars would thrive in, and are so nonresistant to attack that they are almost as fragile as non-system plants on most worlds.*

"Ah, too bad. I was hoping it to be a cloud of vines, eventually. A ten-foot death zone of thorns."

**Maybe one day. These monstrosities are pretty much useless.**

**Skill Level Up!**

**Skill Level Up!**

"I was going to use them for the cloud of death. But now? They have a very important job. Shade." Confirming both of the new levels to his *Botanical Engineer* skill, Tulland grabbed one of the vines and dragged it from the far side of the berm all the way to the wall backing his farm, where he stuck it into the raised ground. Satisfied that the vine would stay put, he went and got another and another until he had built a kind of perverse, sharp lattice over the whole grounds.

By now, sweat was stringing in Tulland's eyes. His clothes were soaked, and he was annoyingly sticky. He had no idea how his raised vitality would interact with more mundane human concerns like dehydration, but he doubted it would be a very good idea to try and find out.

Once Tulland's new lattice was built, the unfiltered sun's rays were actively beginning to hurt his skin, burning it red as he worked. He took another few minutes of concentrated shovel work to build what would normally be a counterproductive, land-hogging channel through his farm and diverted a small amount of water from the river. Today, he figured any amount of evaporative cooling couldn't hurt. Bringing the flow of water as close as he could to his tunnel, he ran and dunked himself in the river before diving back into the relative cool of the tunnel.

Outside, the temperatures began to rise. The stream was soaking the soil around his farm, which was all well and good, but Tulland watched as his vines began to wrinkle and wilt. The lattice went first, dying before his eyes as the sun dehydrated the vines almost to dust.

"Come on. You have wet soil. You can make it." Tulland was pumping use after use of his *Enhance Plant* skill into the farm. It helped, but just wasn't enough. The plants were wilting and failing, starting with the edge of the farm and working their way inward. Tulland wasn't doing much better, but frequent trips to the makeshift irrigation channel to soak his clothes were at least keeping him from passing out. It was a couple degrees cooler in his farm than anywhere else, including the minuscule shade at the trunks of the trees. "You can do it, plants. I need you there, to block the sun."

Just when he thought all was lost, help for his plants came from an unlikely source. Out of nowhere, a small furry animal bolted into his plot, apparently looking to take cover in the same shade Tulland had created for himself.

**Gnawing Ambusher**

These long-eared, quick-legged mammals are excellent runners and jumpers. That, combined with the fact that they present a small target for attacks, enables them to make quick hit-and-run strikes at their enemies.

*While mainly subsisting on plants, the Gnawing Ambushers are extremely territorial opportunistic carnivores and will not hesitate to go after anything that looks like it might be made out of meat or vegetable matter.*

Tulland was not eager to fight anything at the moment, but it turned out there was no need to. As soon as the weakened, woozy animal got anywhere near his vines, it was immediately snatched off the ground in a storm of reaching, grasping thorns. Tulland watched it get torn apart as yet another Ambusher hit the borders of the farm, then another. None of them put up much of a fight as the vines ripped them to shreds, but each seemed to be contributing a bit of strength to the plants that killed it. Individually, they wouldn't have made much of a difference. But when dozens and dozens of animals fleeing the heat were taken as a whole, his plants were not only surviving, but thriving. Anything the heat could take out of them, the deaths of other monsters could apparently put right back in.

And the opportunities to kill were just getting bigger and bigger.

# CHAPTER THIRTY-NINE

# THE BEST HARVEST

**Miniature Ursine**
These small quadrupedal omnivores should not be taken lightly, despite their objective lack of mass. They are strong, fast, and dangerous in three out of the four cardinal directions they can be approached from.

*While each should provide only a moderate threat to adventurers who have reached the third floor, beware any larger versions of the same monster. You will find the full-sized versions somewhat less forgiving.*

**Tusker**
These large porcine creatures make a fine meal, both of themselves and of other creatures they spear on their large, sharp horns. Tuskers are a constantly angry, disproportionately strong creature who present their greatest threat when faced head-on.

These and a few other varieties of forest animals found their way to Tulland's farm. He suspected that under normal circumstances, even the smaller Ambushers would have presented a serious threat to his plants. This was not an average day, however. Every animal was hitting the edges of Tulland's farm exhausted, facing plants that were growing stronger as they gorged themselves on the nutritious blood of their enemies.

Tulland eventually stopped trying to assist the vines in fighting, doing his best to channel what magical energy he could provide toward growth. At a certain point, the caps on the briars' levels and strength were the limiting factor instead of fertilizer or environment deficiencies. Any excess energy seemed to be used in survival, then channeled toward fruit production. The fruits would grow, fall, and take root in the blood-soaked soil, making use of the dead monster fertilizer and Tulland's magic to grow faster and faster.

Tulland was saved from wilting himself by the sheer heat-absorbing ability of the plants, which were eventually so thick they blocked out all the light from his tunnel and, through some process he didn't fully understand, seemed to lower the local temperature as well.

It still wasn't an ideal situation. Tulland found himself exhausted and dizzy, even if not in as much danger as he should have been. After long enough, he found he was unable to do anything but lie there, sweating and panting as he watched the wholesale killing in front of him.

Two more hours in, almost as suddenly as it had started, he saw the skies darken. It was still bright out, but after what he had been going through, the sky could almost be called overcast. The heat stuck around only as long as it took for the first wind to blow through. And while extreme wind seemed to be the next phase in this terrible forest's rage, it hardly mattered. Tulland was lying in a garden so very overgrown that not even the gale-force winds could break through.

| **Level Up!** |
| --- |

| **Level Up!** |
| --- |

| **Level Up!** |
| --- |

| **Skill Level Up!** |
| --- |

| **Skill Level Up!** |
| --- |

| **Skill Level Up!** |
| --- |

| **Experience Source Capped!** |
| --- |

| **Experience Source Capped!** |
| --- |

| **Experience Source Capped!** |
| --- |

As Tulland sat and sipped water in the pleasant, cool draft filtering through his briars, he considered his gains.

**Tulland Lowstreet**
**Class:** Farmer LV. 28
**Strength:** 30
**Agility:** 30
**Vitality:** 35 (+5)
**Spirit:** 35
**Mind:** 20
**Force:** 60
**Skills:** Enhance Plant LV. 8, Enrich Seed LV. 9
**Passives:** Broadcast LV. 7, Botanical Engineer LV. 9, Strong Back LV. 5, Fruits of the Field LV. 2, Farmer's Intuition LV. 2

It really was something. He had more or less farmed out this level in one go, without doing a single thing to make it happen. It was an accidental harvest, one that had left him much stronger than he had been a few hours ago.

Among the rest of his normal stat distributions, he finally decided to add a little power to his mind stat. It was a mental defense stat, primarily. But he had a vague recollection it helped with some fine control of power usage, among other things. The first use was enough that he had always known he couldn't leave it be forever, but the second was intriguing enough to make the decision to finally pay the piper.

Granted, none of his growth had been intentional, but he'd take the extra power. It was the best kind of harvest. Especially since after everything that happened that day, Tulland found one last victory over an old, undefeated adversary waiting for him.

Ironbranch Seed.

Tulland eyed his enemy-slash-ally with determination. Every single time he had tried to enrich one of these seeds, it had simply ignored him. He had been snubbed again and again by the stubborn tree, and it was possible this time would be no different.

*But I'll be damned if I let it be. Prepare to lose, seed. Prepare to lose hard.*

Steeling up his resolve, Tulland began to let go of the reins on his power. He felt the seed resisting his energy, just as it always had. For a while, nothing happened. He didn't quit, and kept hitting the seed again and again until he finally felt something give somewhere deep in the rock-hard little lump of tree.

Whether his mind stat or just good old-fashioned brute force had made it possible, the victory did not go unrewarded.

---

**Skill Level Up!**

---

**Skill Level Up!**

---

**Tulland Lowstreet**
**Class:** Farmer LV. 28
**Strength:** 30
**Agility:** 30
**Vitality:** 35 (+5)
**Spirit:** 40
**Mind:** 20
**Force:** 60
**Skills:** Enhance Plant LV. 8, Enrich Seed LV. 9
**Passives:** Broadcast LV. 7, Botanical Engineer LV. 11, Strong Back LV. 5, Fruits of the Field LV. 2, Farmer's Intuition LV. 2

---

His passives were getting a bit insane these days, but Tulland supposed that was to be expected. Carefully clearing a bit of space inside the edge of the hedge, Tulland planted one of the Ironbranch Saplings, then added four of the Wolfwood trees nearly but not quite at the corners of the enclosure. His briars wouldn't do quite as well with less sunlight, but with nearly all of them capped, it was hard to think of it as something that mattered.

And the best part? Tulland was now fully armored again. All six of his plant pieces were in place, filling him with a sense of security he was very badly in need of.

*And the other thing I think I need, System, is a bath. How long has it been?*

**Since you arrived at the Infinite, I believe. Unless you count getting fairly soaked with the muck from the swamp in the last level and your quick dip earlier.**

*You know what? I don't.*

Tulland stepped out of his enclosure, once again braving the wind as he flopped lazily into the river, letting the water run all the way from his hair down into his boots. It was unbelievably refreshing, and if it wasn't exactly the most efficient way to bathe, then at least he had plenty of time to get the most out of it. Eventually, he took his shoes off, shaking out a great quantity of mud until the water running through them ran clear.

*It's amazing how much better this feels. How do normal adventurers do it?*

**Normal adventurers can go home, or they are dead. Normal adventurers who make it to the Infinite have training, usually quite a bit of it, and usually involving tolerance to things like the lack of bathing facilities and steady food supply.**

*Good point. I guess I didn't get that lucky.*

**No. I suppose not.**

Rolling over a few times in the water to displace any lingering sweat, Tulland found himself pondering the odd change in the System's demeanor once again. It was one thing to make conversation when there wasn't anything else to do. It was another to pass up on opportunities to make jabs when Tulland was walking right into them, and yet another to help him out at all when withholding help and advice would have increased his chance of dying significantly.

Tulland fully expected the advice to be bad every time he received it, to put him in danger in some subtle way. But that hadn't been the case in a while. On this floor, the System had given normal, everyday advice of the kind anybody might give. It wasn't perfect, but it hadn't been a trap.

Yet.

At this point in his life, Tulland was incredibly short on trust. He was fully, absolutely aware that the System was smart enough to at least try to lull him into a false sense of security. It had done so once before. If Tulland was being smart, he wouldn't let his guard down. He wouldn't even talk to the thing, unless he had some compelling reason to have to do it.

But either Tulland wasn't smart, or he was right about the building feeling in his gut that something was up with the System that it didn't want to talk about. Since they had already crossed the river of admitting that the System had tricked, betrayed, lied to, and attempted to kill him, it wasn't like there was that much left for it to hide.

Unless it was a different kind of thing. Something entirely different. Something that wasn't about Tulland at all.

*Which begs the question of whether or not things like the System can even be embarrassed about itself. Or ashamed. Because in a way, it's sure acting like it.*

"Hey, System?" Tulland stood up in the water and let the wind wick away the worst of it, which the nearly gale-force breeze was more than capable of. It was cold, but not nearly the freezing-to-death level of chilly he should have been experiencing without the advantage of his improved stats and gear. "Can I ask you a question?"

**I suppose. But you might want to wait.**

"For what?"

**For whatever he wants to ask. Behind you.**

Tulland was grateful he had decided to put back on his shoes and gloves the moment they were clean. At least he wouldn't be losing a piece of equipment if he needed to flee. He turned around and saw a man in a hooded cloak staring at him. He had a short, curved sword in one hand, a much shorter double-edged fighting dagger in the other, and overall looked lethal in a light, quick way that Tulland felt was even worse for him than Necia's heavy, super-strong build would have been.

"Oh. Hey. Can I help you?" Tulland asked.

"Sure. Just hold on a sec." The man continued boring holes in Tulland's skull with an oddly intent stare. "And that should do it. Thanks. Wow. I mean it. Wow."

"What?"

"That status. What's a Farmer?"

"It's . . . you can see my status?"

"Obviously." The man scoffed. "You didn't answer my question though. What's a Farmer?"

"It's . . . you really didn't have farmers on your world? At all? Growing plants and things?" Tulland asked back.

"Of course we do. But certainly, you aren't telling me . . ." The man's eyes went wide as he gave Tulland a once-over, finally noting his inadequate gear. "You are. An actual farmer in the Infinite. Not a Farmer Mage or a Farmer Berserker or anything. Just a noncombat class waltzing around the Infinite like it's no big deal."

"Sure?" Tulland had no idea what to make of this person. "Does that matter?"

"Of course. Normally, when I find an unprotected person out in the wild, I have to care very much about whether or not they can take me in a fight. Whether their build is a dangerous counter to mine. Whether or not I should be wary of the things they can do." For a moment, the man cracked up. His face distorted into something ugly, something Tulland didn't understand but instinctively recoiled from. Then, like it hadn't happened at all, the stretched grin and distorted face returned to some semblance of normalcy. "But here I don't have to do much of that, do I? It's just free levels. With no danger at all."

With no delay at all, the man was in motion, blurring through the air so fast that Tulland could hardly see him. And of all the things he could have focused on, the one Tulland ended up seeing clearly was the last thing he could have expected. It was an accessory, something hanging off the man's belt.

And Tulland knew exactly what it was. After all, he shaved an entire tree to make it himself.

# CHAPTER FORTY

# PROTECTIONS

The man was a rogue, probably.

There were a lot of different builds, but they fell into a few general categories. Ranged fighters used bows or things they could throw. To beat them, Tulland knew, monsters would rush in faster than the ranged fighters could shoot them down. Heavily armored classes like Necia could take just about anything in a one-on-one close-quarters fight, but could be outpaced, outnumbered, or outranged.

Rogues were the middle ground between the two. Some rogues replaced the loss of ranged attacks with stealth, and all of them had a heavy emphasis on speed. They survived by hitting hard and fast, ending things before their opponents could react and fighting in evasive, sneaky ways when that failed.

Tulland didn't have to consciously think about all these things, since it was reflexive knowledge he possessed just by reading books and talking to people with a good grasp of the lore. That was a lucky thing because there simply wasn't time to think at the moment.

He swayed back out of the range of the man's daggers, activating all of his vines at once and letting them shoot forward. As leveled as the briars were, they probably wouldn't provide much defense against the rogue's glinting weapons. It seemed like a better option for Tulland to go on the offensive instead of waiting to see whether the rogue would penetrate through gaps in the armor or shred the briars entirely.

It worked in a sense. The rogue had been on a hard collision course for

Tulland's neck, but pulled back fast when he saw the briars move. Unfortunately, his dodging ability was far more than the briars could compensate for. The man landed a good foot away from the briars, which continued reaching for him until Tulland gave them the order to stop. It seemed better to have him not know what they could do and to maybe assume the briars couldn't attack again.

*Because without a ruse, there's no way I'm hitting this guy. He's just too fast.*

"Nice trick, that." The rogue regarded the vines with disdain. "I didn't expect them to move on their own like that. If you had anything like a real class, that might have worked too."

"Still might." Tulland tried to bluff. "Plenty more where that came from."

"Sure." The rogue grinned. "And they are really dead on the ground there. Not like you could just reactivate them with an order, right? I should just step right over them."

*Damn.* Tulland tried not to let the grimace show on his face.

"Point is, I'm giving you a compliment. You should appreciate it. Because this next hit isn't going to miss."

The rogue went diagonal first this time. Tulland tried to move to put the vines between him and the rogue, but he might as well have been standing still for all the good it did. He could just barely track the movement of the assassin as the man ricocheted off the ground, then headed straight toward him.

At high speeds, there was only so much Tulland could coordinate. In this case, he found his attempt to dodge far enough backward became just an uncontrolled fall away from the danger and toward the ground before he could correct it. The rogue was unbothered, tracking him perfectly as the slash of his sword and the point of his dagger both made a beeline for Tulland's unprotected face and neck.

The worst part was that this was the most Tulland could have done. He just didn't have enough time to get his weapons or the trickier plants in his arsenal. He couldn't stab forward with a spear because it just wouldn't do anything. He wasn't fast enough or strong enough to make a dent in the capabilities this man was showing, and that was before Tulland had forced him to show a single hidden card from his hand.

As his back hit the dirt and the blades closed in, Tulland rolled and kicked against the ground, sliding through the dirt on his stomach past the rogue. At the same time, he felt a dagger cut into his leg and slide down, demolishing everything from pants to muscles as it did. He ignored it, pushing diagonally away as he felt two daggers strike his right shoulder, just where his neck had just been.

He wasn't faster than the rogue, but unless the rogue hit him enough times or in a vital enough spot, he could survive a few seconds. It was now a deadly game of rock paper scissors, one where the rogue was guessing where Tulland would go next and striking there. A single right guess would mean Tulland was dead.

*But if he guessed wrong for just a few more steps . . .*

Tulland felt his overall health dropping lower and lower until his entire body felt cold and thin, like he was made out of winter air. But in front of him was a patch of green. One that he was counting on.

After one final dodge, he was done, his legs running out of strength and sending him toppling forward as daggers whizzed over his head.

"What the hell?"

Through the haze, Tulland could feel dozens of vines whipping toward the rogue. He could also feel them dying, but not nearly so fast as they should have been. He imagined a perfect world where the rogue was fully encased in the damn things, held still long enough that Tulland could get at him with his weapon and force him to talk. One where he was riddled with thorn holes and helpless.

Tulland forced his eyes open in sheer hope and desperation, and the sight that greeted them ended up being closer to the truth than he had thought possible.

"Dammit. You really are a farmer?" The rogue struggled with the onrush of vines, pushing his incredible speed to keep up with them. It wasn't working. It was all he could do to keep the vines that were wrapping around his legs at bay. Tulland had rolled several feet into his farm when he collapsed, which had more than enough plant density to keep the rogue back. "That counts as a craft class? This is cheating."

Tulland laughed internally. The rogue really hadn't seen everything yet. As he prepared to detonate enough flowers to make both him and the rogue very unhappy indeed, he watched the madman's eyes shift from enraged to disappointed and his vines suddenly grasp at nothing as the rogue pulled free.

"I guess that's really that, then." The rogue shrugged. "I guess you got lucky. Have fun in here. It's not like you will live very long anyway. And guess what? I already know where that gate is. I hope you didn't need through it anytime soon because I'm more than ready to wait for you there as long as it takes."

Tulland's muscles all went slack as the fighting ended anticlimactically. This wasn't how he expected his second encounter with another person in the Infinite to go, but also made perfect sense at the same time. Where Necia was a pure warrior, the rogue was a calculated hunter. He was cutting his losses as soon as his prey took too much energy to take down.

Tulland watched as the rogue turned and walked away. He had survived this moment, if just barely. The victory, if that's what he could call it, felt cheap and unearned. But he had survived. If he was smart, he'd just let the rogue go and hope he never saw the man again.

"Hey. You," Tulland said, feeling stupid for taking the risk. "That bag."

"What?" The man turned around, his face briefly contorted by rage. "What are you talking about?"

"That bag. Under your robe. The fur one. Where did you get it?"

"This?" The rogue reached his hand down and bounced the purse a bit. "Ah, I see. You know her. The blonde. A friend, or something?"

"Something like that."

"And you want to know how she is. If I killed her to take this. That's about right?"

"About." Tulland kept his face clear of emotion. As angry as he was, he didn't want this person to get the satisfaction of seeing him react.

"Ah. I understand. Reasonable." The man's face contorted into a look of pure, cruel joy. "Make me."

Tulland clenched his fists and hoped the rogue would choose to walk through his farm by accident. He had no such luck. He had been hoping the rogue would want to brag, but he couldn't force the information out of the man if he didn't want to talk. There was, in a very literal sense, nothing he could do about it.

**You should count your blessings, Tulland. Even beyond having a combat class, that man was the worst possible matchup for you. Even in terms of psychology.**

"Psychology?"

**Ways of thinking. He is ready to kill. You are not. He is used to it. Used to aggression against other thinking, real beings. You are not.**

"I could be."

Tulland was angry. For the first time since he got here, he was really and truly angry. Even what the System had done to him paled in comparison to this. In that scenario, he had to at least acknowledge that a lot of what happened was due to his own pride. It was because of his own misjudgment.

What had happened with the rogue was the absolute worst-case scenario, one that he did nothing to bring on. Even with the rage, he could admit that he had been on track for at least some sort of bad outcome. At some point, some other delver was going to have bad intentions. It was a miracle Necia hadn't. And Tulland had done next to nothing to prepare for that eventuality or to protect himself from the violence other humans might bring to his doorstep.

Only his farm had saved him. And even it couldn't get him what he wanted.

**You couldn't. At least not as fast as you think. You would be trying to practice on your very worst nightmare. You'd be starting your amateur career against a seasoned professional. You just couldn't fight him on his own terms and win. There wouldn't be enough time to adjust.**

"Not his terms, then. Mine."

**Your terms are plants he can easily dodge. Not much better.**

Tulland hadn't forgiven the System. Not even a little. But the emotions Tulland felt toward the thing were a sort of dull distrust, a desire to triumph over it as best he could.

The rogue was a different story. This man might have killed Necia. Tulland didn't know how it could even be possible, but he was going to find a way to get even or at least make the man talk. He was going to unleash everything he had. Even if he got himself killed in the process.

And even if the System highly advised against it. Which it did.

**If you try to attack the man, it will be your end. Your farm isn't a way to fight someone who could end you in a second. You will disappear the moment you meet that man again. This is a fool's errand, Tulland.**

"Then it's a fool's errand. If you care that much, hope I find wisdom before I'm done farming."

If there was one thing that Tulland knew, it was still farming. It was growing weird mosses on his increasingly strong trees, planting shrubs that didn't seem to do anything but would provide him with some much-needed diversity in his farm to make his plants just that much stronger, and would give him that much more punch when he exercised one of his few options for fighting.

Most of the plants he was working on growing were wastes of his time in any other respect.

---

**Useless Shrub**

A shrub with no crafting, combat, or medicinal uses. It's not particularly pretty or hardy. It occupies an ecological niche, growing in places most other plants can't or in conditions where other plants would fail. Outside of that, it's a sort of living filler for places that would otherwise be even more barren.

> **Standard Grass**
> This grass is just that. Grass. It grows on the ground and grows quickly. It has little nutritional value for beings with only one stomach, and isn't long enough or strong enough to make into rope or fabric. Outside of inventing a use for this plant, you won't find it to be particularly high on the utility front.

> **Moss Variant**
> This is a variety of moss.

> **Moss Variant #2**
> This is another variety of moss.

> **Moss Variant #3**
> This is another variety of moss.

> **Boring Algae**
> Algae are plants! That's a fun thing to know, but beyond that, you aren't going to get much of interest out of this particular phytoplankton.

Most plants, it was turning out, were absolutely useless outside of providing diversity to his farm. Tulland had been lucky to find as many helpful plants as he did at first, and now that luck was thinning. Yet among all the trash plants he was finding left and right in this forest, there was at least one of interest.

> **Jewel Moss**
> Given sufficient time and a beneficial enough growing environment, this moss will morph into an amber-like crystal of exceeding hardness and toughness.

That was interesting enough, especially if it could be molded into a usable shape. He could make something very interesting. And he now had just the thing to grow it on.

> **Ironbranch Sapling (Enhanced, Weaponized)**
> While the original Ironbranch was tough, that was its only characteristic. It grew in a system environment, and interacted minimally when you tried to speed up its growth. But in terms of the mechanics of the directionality of

the magical forces in it, it "wanted" very little besides to be tough. It had no purpose. No goals.

This enhanced Ironbranch was grown by a seed enriched by an individual who thought of the Ironbranch wood as absolutely nothing but materials for weaponry. It, in all facets of wood, thinks it is for killing things, which means that it's a good deal more effective at doing so than the original, unaltered wood.

*There are, however, limitations to how effective this makes it. A conventional weapon made by a crafting class, such as a sword made by a smith, has its magic enhanced, re-enhanced, and refined by the process of making the weapon. This item's magical power is rustic and primitive, similar to its physical form. Its performance will track accordingly.*

All the warnings were what they were, but Tulland wasn't in the least discouraged. While planting more Ironbranch trees with a few different kinds of attempted intent, he carefully carved a slot near the end of his current tree and threaded the Jewel Moss through it. Over the next few days, he would feed the moss following his *Farmer's Intuition* suggestions, whether that was juice from the briar fruits or blood from unfortunate beasts that wandered into his garden.

After that, it was a waiting game. He needed every bit of potential energy he could muster to have a chance at what he was planning. If that took days, it would take days. If the rogue escaped before he could catch the man, that would just be fate. Corners would not be cut here. He would not allow himself to fail because he simply failed to plan.

After pumping every plant with every scrap of power he could, he took a nap, woke up, and did it again. And again. It was only after all the plants were as full of power as he could possibly get them that he moved on.

## CHAPTER FORTY-ONE

# BOTANICA

**F**oolish. You have no idea what his scouting range is.

"Probably pretty far. But what does it matter? He can't hurt me."

*If* you can run back to your farm first. If nothing wrong happens. The Infinite is a complex place, Tulland. And if he's shown every card in his hand. Everyone holds a little information back. He has capabilities you have yet to learn.

"I bet. But this is a good enough wager for me." Tulland leaned a bit farther from the thin upper trunk of the tree he was hiding in. From here, he could get a better look at the rogue's camp. "And it's worth making bets like this from time to time."

**At least one thing he said was true, though. He is looking for something.**

The rogue had so far shown a habit of taking walks that lasted no more than a few hours, coming home and dumping what few animal materials he seemed to harvest in a pit of sorts before covering it with a rock, perhaps eating, and then moving out again.

Following him was not an option, or at least not a safe one. Tulland eventually confirmed that the rogue couldn't see him from a distance, so long as he was holding still. He was reluctant to test the limits of that, and mostly let the man go on his walks unmonitored.

When Tulland did learn more about what he was up to, it was on accident. Tulland was sticking tight to trees on his way to the man's camp when the System had suddenly cut into his thoughts.

**Be still, Tulland. As still as the grave. It's a wonder he hasn't seen you yet.**

Tulland agreed, especially when he heard the man moving by. The rogue was several yards away, on a game path of sorts that gave him a less than clear view of Tulland's position. He should have seen Tulland but he wasn't paying attention. He was as highly distracted as Tulland could imagine someone being, talking to himself in a not so quiet voice.

"Not his farm tunnel. He dug that himself. Not the tunnel to the east. No caves to the west and north. So it has to be that first one again. I missed it. I must have," the rogue mumbled.

*Tunnels? Caves? What's he looking for?* Tulland had been keeping the system connection on for company. He needed that after losing his only friend in the Infinite. He even went so far as to re-enable the System to listen to his selective thoughts. It was yet another benefit from the Infinite's Dungeon System, making it possible to communicate without having to speak out loud.

**It's hard to say. But the fact that he's looking for something does resolve a bit of confusion.**

*How so?*

**Farming every bit of experience out of every floor is usually a fool's errand. You do it because it takes so little time for you. The armored warrior you've befriended seems to have her own reasons and goals. But for someone like this rogue to return is . . . odd. Unusual. Unless there's a treasure. Then it all comes together.**

*How would he ever know there's something like that to find?*

**There are ways. The most likely is that he won a treasure map of sorts, and had to go searching to get the more practical aspects of the reward.**

*Seems like a bad deal. Extra work.*

**Don't be foolish. Think of what you know about dungeons and the Infinite. With risk and effort comes reward. There is no question that, should he find it, the treasure will be a massive boon to him.**

The rogue made his way back toward camp in the failing light, and Tulland followed at a safe distance once he was reasonably sure his enemy had moved on. The rogue settled in, rolling out a sleeping mat of some kind and going to sleep. Whatever he was looking for, he didn't seem to want to spend too much effort trying to find it in the failing light.

Tulland made his way home, juiced his plants with magic power, and fed his Jewel Moss. It was starting to turn red from all the juice, something he hoped wasn't hurting it. His *Farmer's Intuition* seemed split on whether it was helping or not, but either way he'd have to wait to see the results.

After that, he harvested a few choice plants and took the same trip he suspected the rogue would the next morning. He doubted he'd have much luck finding what the rogue couldn't in the dark, but that wasn't the point. He had groundwork to lay.

Once he had arranged things to his liking, he finally returned to the sleeping area. After crawling into his hole, he went to sleep guarded by an army of briars.

The next day, Tulland was up well before dawn, eager to get to the rogue's camp before the man had a chance to go searching again. When he got there, a couple of the objects the rogue had left around his sleeping area were gone, packed back into the rogue's now overloaded pack.

**He's packing up. With any luck, he'll leave right now, and end this madness for you.**

"Maybe. But probably not."

**Why?**

"The treasure, remember? He'll keep searching. He must be confident he'll find it today."

**And then leave. Which I recommend you let him.**

"No. I won't make it that easy for him."

**I must again advise you that this is foolishness. With his speed and power, he would certainly . . .**

Tulland cut the connection. He had a bit of time left before the rogue was truly packed, and he needed every second of it to prepare.

---

**Botanica (Lance, Crude)**

By forming Jewel Moss onto the end of an Ironbranch Sapling and encouraging it to grow to its multifaceted adulthood, you have created a sort of symbiont-headed polearm of significant piercing power. The head or shaft of this weapon can withstand anything up to a full, directed strike from a strength-focused class.

*For reasons similar to those previously mentioned in the summary of the enhanced Ironbranch Sapling, this weapon lacks some of the potential power an expertly crafted weapon might bring to bear. Still, it is a real weapon, if not a particularly refined one. In most situations, it will serve.*

---

The description hadn't popped until Tulland had finished using his knife and scythe to trim down the excess wood of the sapling to a reasonable handle. The Jewel Moss had needed no such trimming. He had formed it with his hands every day before it hardened, resulting in a pointed, round-bodied spearhead that looked like the business end of an artist's paintbrush. Somehow, the entire finished weapon felt more real in his hands.

*It will have to do.*

The next steps were fairly simple. He had harvested the latest batch of Acheflowers from his Wolfwood trees, as well as a multitude of powerful Lunger Briars from outside his farm, their power carefully leveled to near the peak. He had left them bundled on the ground a short way away, and now untwined them and began to position them on the forest floor. What he was building was not a particularly refined trap, but it was a big one.

Minutes later, Tulland found himself outside the rogue's camp, closer than he had ever come before. The rogue was still packing, but almost done. Tulland took a deep breath. The System wasn't wrong that this was an avoidable risk. But avoidable wasn't the same thing as a bad risk, or even an unnecessary one. This was a bad guy who had things Tulland wanted, and knew things he wanted to know. He was willing to roll the dice on that.

After swinging a rock wrapped in briar above his head several times, he let loose at a trajectory he knew would come close to hitting the rogue, then threw several briars between him and the camp before it landed. He would need whatever extra time he could buy, and getting rid of his excess weight felt like a good move.

The vine clunked down not exactly on top of the rogue, but within arm's reach. It didn't hit. Whatever else the rogue's class was, it had a component of watchfulness that fully justified his comfort sleeping out in the open. As soon as there was so much as a sound of impact, he was up with both weapons bared. He looked around for a split second before catching sight of Tulland and sneering.

"That's about enough cute tricks. Are you ready to die?"

Tulland nodded as he turned to run. He got just a glimpse of the rogue's face morphing into an angry snarl as extra motivation to sprint faster. The rogue was fast enough to catch up before Tulland could get to his destination, of course. But that was only true if he was able to run in a straight line. A few seconds into the pursuit, Tulland heard the rogue make contact with the first of the hidden briars he had placed in the path between them, and knew he would at least have a few more seconds to improve his chances.

He didn't turn to see how close the pursuit was. If the rogue caught up now, it was over, no matter what he did. Instead, he focused every bit of attention he had into just running, hurtling over obstacles in the woods and making a beeline for the tunnel where he had once found Necia's helmet. Once he got there, he skidded into position at the mouth of the tunnel, then ducked through into the darkness before exiting out on the riverside and climbing into the boughs of the same overgrown tree he had used for scouting before.

It turned out Tulland needn't have hurried. There was little doubt the rogue would be able to quickly track him, but the man was a careful sort. Insane as he might be, the rogue was cautious of the traps Tulland had laid. It was minutes before there was any activity around either of the entrances to the tunnel, long enough for Tulland to mostly catch his breath and to be confident that he was at least somewhat hidden in the tree.

Eventually, a rustling sound monopolized Tulland's full attention span as he saw something moving through the shadows of the forest. It was a bit harder to see than something brighter-colored, but there wasn't much difficulty in guessing who it was. The rogue skirted the trees, keeping mostly in cover before finally pausing, taking a careful look around the area, then making a beeline for the tunnel.

Tulland held his breath and tucked himself deeper into the tree. He wasn't sure how far away the rogue could see. He knew that some scout and explorer classes had much more in the way of long-distance awareness, something he hoped wouldn't apply to the rogue. Either way, there had never been any way to confirm just how far the rogue could see, and he wasn't taking any chances.

Tulland kept his position in a low crouch, almost completely obscured by leaves. He just needed a few more seconds of going unnoticed and the rogue following the trail into the tunnel. If he could just get that, he had a chance.

The man paused at the entrance, his face contorting into an unreasonable rage.

*That's right. I know about your little treasure. I might be taking it right now. You can't take the chance of letting me get my hands on it, can you?*

The man's build was lighter than Necia's had been. Her appearance had been all armor, swords, and a dangerous kind of weight that would crush down on the unprepared. This man was cloaks and daggers, a masked face, and footsteps Tulland couldn't hear.

It was no wonder the man had been able to get the drop on Necia. He didn't look dangerous until he was. He was the type to leap out of the dark to kill people rather than fight them face-to-face. Maybe he would even befriend his targets, getting them to drop their guard with accursed words until he saw an opportunity to kill. Necia was a lot of things, but overly wary wasn't one of them. This was a man who could have tracked her down and ambushed her.

*And if there was any doubt it was him that attacked Necia, it's gone now. Do you see it, System?*

**Being here is foolish. You should have left.**

*I asked you a question.*

**I do. I see it well.**

*I'll win.*

**I don't see how. Between when you sent me away and now, did you gain another class? Weapons you did not possess before? Talents you learned in my absence? If not, staying here is death.**

*Maybe. Let's see.*

The murderer didn't just go into the tunnel. He threw a few rocks down to test, listened for the sounds, and then sneered. He circled around to the other side and found the other opening of the tunnel. After waiting a few more seconds and tossing a few more rocks in, he finally grunted in frustration and entered the tunnel, disappearing from Tulland's sight as he ducked underground. Tulland waited in his tree until he felt a subtle calling from below the soil from one of his briars, asking a sort of permission to strike. It was something he had become accustomed to during his time with Necia, and an action he had taken so many times it felt like reflex now.

"Go."

Tulland said that not to the vines but to every single Acheflower. Right now, there were ten to twelve of them going off in a confined space with a confirmed target within a couple of feet. Tulland didn't know how classes worked, really, but he knew those flowers were at least supposed to be an inconvenience for adventurers, or else the Infinite probably wouldn't bother with them.

*And a dozen inconvenient things all exploding in your face at once can be a real threat, especially if they are closer and bigger than they should be. Like the hail was, to me.*

Tulland gave the flowers just a second to work before he finally let his vines go. After that, there was nothing to feel or know without going to check himself. Gripping his spear in one hand and his farming tool in the other, Tulland went.

# CHAPTER FORTY-TWO

# UNDERESTIMATING

At this point, Tulland was completely unarmored, having sacrificed all of his strong briars to the attack. There were dozens of strong briars in there, presumably doing their best to drag down the roguish killer. He needed to get there as quick as he could before the man was able to clear the vines, or it would be that much harder to do what he planned. On the other hand, if the flowers and vines combined weren't enough, Tulland was pretty sure he would just die, stabbed from some shadow by a weapon he had no hope of blocking.

The reality was a bit different.

"Oooowwww." The rogue man was rolling around in the briar, bleeding from dozens of thorns dug into him. "Ha. No! Haaa. No! Gods!"

*Good enough? I have a chance now?*

**I would say so. But are you sure you want to . . .**

Tulland tuned the System out but didn't cut the communications. He could do what needed to be done. He didn't need the System second-guessing him. And with the rogue mostly out of commission, Tulland knew he could accomplish it so long as he had the guts to try. Even if the psychedelic wore off, the in-position briars would probably hold the man now.

But it just wouldn't be a clean thing. Tulland didn't have combat skills. And he was not strong, in most senses of the word. He lifted his spear up, tears burning his eyes, and thrust, stopping just an inch before the man's face. It wasn't that he couldn't do it, even if he was wavering in his heart of hearts. It was because the rogue, despite cycling through the emotions of joy and sorrow as dictated from the Acheflowers, found a hand to take out the Wolfwood purse from his pocket.

"You killed her," Tulland stated.

"I did! I kill . . . oh, lots. Or did I? There's no way to know." The man grinned, then went serious. His madness was clear even through the drugging. "It's my right. The weak are sacrifices to my strength. For my world. Unless they weren't. I'm not telling."

"And that's worth it?"

"Oh, yes." The man was smiling again, then fell to a fit of coughing. When he raised his hand, just a bit of sanity had returned to his eye. He had gathered himself for one last moment of defiance. "As it is for you. That's why you are doing this, right? To steal my treasure? To grow stronger? You won't find it, you know. So tell me why you're really doing this."

"I'm strong enough," Tulland said, lifting his spear. "And even if you won't tell me a thing and I go without treasure, I will still end this."

The man's eyes suddenly cleared.

"Wrong answer," the rogue said, killing the first of the vines holding him with a deft flip of his dagger. "Nasty stuff, that. Too bad I have poison resistance and you dallied a couple moments too long. I'll be out of here in a minute, dear. Don't worry. I'll kill you then."

"Will you?"

"Oh, yes. Unless you have more tricks up your sleeve. And I sincerely doubt you do."

We can see about that. Enhance Plant.

As the briars around the rogue suddenly tightened, Tulland flew into action with his spear. The rogue was thrashing, which made it harder to aim than Tulland had expected. Still, Tulland caught the man deep and hard in the leg, twisting the spear before hitting him again in the hip on the same side.

The rogue didn't take it lying down. Every second was spent shredding several of the briars and slipping away from a few more. Tulland kept stabbing as this happened, doing distressingly little damage to the man as he wiggled his way out of the restrictions.

In the fighting, Tulland managed to separate the rogue from Necia's bag. And then, finally, the rogue was free. He pulled himself up to his feet, his face contorting with rage, exaltation, and sadness as he eyed Tulland with a look of sheer madness. Tulland's stomach dropped. This was it. He'd die now.

And then the rogue turned and ran. It took Tulland a second to realize what was happening, then a moment more to realize why. The rogue was limping, running at what looked like a full sprint but so slowly now that he wasn't much faster than Tulland, if he was faster at all.

**He's a speed build, you fool. You've hurt him. Pursue him now. He will heal slowly, but he will heal eventually. You cannot let him.**

Tulland nodded, then tried a command he had never used before on his briars.

*To me.*

The briars that were left alive reached for Tulland as one, and he managed to grab two of them as he moved past. He would have liked to have many more briars in his arsenal, but there just wasn't enough time. Palming a few flowers from his bag, he ran after the rogue, who was fleeing in a completely unfamiliar direction.

*Where is he going?*

**Unless I miss my guess, the exit. Remember, he has roved a great deal more than you. He would know where it is.**

Tulland chucked every flower he had, knowing they wouldn't do much but counting on any delay they could give him. Every time one of the explosions got close to the rogue, Tulland would gain a split second of time. He needed every one of those delays. Even injured, the rogue could move faster than he could. Even a moment's distraction would mean losing the pursuit. Tulland couldn't afford that.

Finally, he did lose sight of the rogue for just a moment, before busting through the brush into a clearing that had few features beyond a simple stone arch, one that the rogue already had the better part of a leg through.

"You got close, you know. And I won't forget this," the rogue said as he turned back.

"I know you won't," Tulland replied.

"You really want to know about her that badly? How she died?"

Tulland nodded, a bit grimly. "I do."

"Well, too bad. I'm heading straight from here to the fifth level. It's about time I moved on. If you really want to know, find me past the safe zone. I'll be waiting."

With a wink and a smile, the rogue stepped through the arch and was gone. Tulland roared in frustration and ran after him, fully intending on going through the arch.

**No, Tulland. You are unarmed.**

*I have my spear.*

**Which you are not good at using. He has recovered now. You must have seen his speed returning. If you want to go through that arch, then fine. But you need briars. Flowers. Whatever protection you can take with you. And then there's the treasure that the man was looking for. Taking that**

**would be a good revenge.**

Tulland would never hate anything more than the fact that the System was right. He almost went through the arch anyway, but couldn't take that last step. He had made plenty of mistakes today. The rogue had underestimated Tulland by entering the tunnel, but Tulland had underestimated the rogue by becoming greedy for information. That would be the last time he made a mistake like that. Sighing deeply, he started trudging back to his farm.

**I am glad. This is the first sane thing you have done in a week.**

*Why do you even care?*

**Because . . . I don't. Die. Live. It makes no difference to me.**

The System was done talking. There was no question of that. Tulland decided to let sleeping dogs lie. A few minutes later, he was back at the tunnel, taking his frustrations out on the dirt. There were no obvious signs pointing to anything being there, but he kept digging.

It helped that Tulland had a tool that could turn into a shovel. It didn't help that after the first few shovels, the weather outside turned and the tunnel, weakened by the earlier fight, collapsed in a matter of moments.

*Well crap.*

Tulland spent the next few days moving all the caved-in dirt, clearing what eventually looked like an enormous trench between the forest and river. Once it was cleared, he began digging again, taking a full foot of dirt off each side of the former cave. He found nothing.

*It can't be much deeper than that. The Infinite would make it hard to find, not impossible.*

**Agreed. Work on the floor.**

Tulland sighed and prepared his shovel for more digging before something caught his eye.

*That fire. Does it look like she dug out a hole for it?*

**Yes. It's a good practice. Keeps things neat and contained, and wastes less heat.**

*I agree, but Necia's hardly the type to care about things like that. She sleeps in trees.*

**What's your point?**

*My point is that whatever little dip in the ground she used was there when she got here. And the rest of the floor is uniform.*

Tulland only got two shovelfuls of dirt into the ground before the tool clicked on something. He uncovered it quickly, getting a notification as soon as it cleared from the soil.

> **Treasure Box**
>
> The treasure box is the deferred reward from an accomplishment of some kind. To unearth it, the adventurer needs to sacrifice their own advancement in spending time combing through the third floor in search of the promised treasure. This extra effort and risk earn an exceptionally large payout, one significantly more important than would have otherwise been offered.
>
> This treasure box was plundered from another adventurer, which is allowed. It will trigger when you exit your current level.

Tulland thought he'd be much happier after taking something away from the rogue. But no matter what this treasure box held, it could never compare to the company that Necia offered.

*And I have to be okay with that. There's nothing I can do about that anymore. Besides hunting down that rogue, which should be that much easier with this. Just wait, Necia, I'll make sure you're avenged.*

The next day, Tulland returned back to the arch again, covered in briar armor and with a full pack of seeds, food, and the Wolf-Fur Drawstring Bag he had made for Necia. The farm itself was as fully grown as he could hope to get it. Even without the impetus of chasing the rogue, it was time to go.

Tulland bounced the treasure box in his hand, smiling with a sort of grim satisfaction. There was nothing left for him to earn here.

**There. You look ready.**

*I feel it. Not that it matters that you are right. But I feel prepared.*

**May it always be so, Tulland Lowstreet. Good luck on this next floor.**

Shaking his head once again at the System's consistently mixed messaging, Tulland stepped through into the void.

It was the white room again. Tulland wasn't entirely surprised, although he was a little shocked to see there was a couch now. Like the rest of the room, the couch was also made out of color-bleached bricks. He decided to roll with it, sitting down on the hard bench and waiting for something to happen.

Nothing happened, for a while. Tulland had no clock to judge by, but he thought he was probably sitting for about an hour before anything changed. It was almost nice. In a stressful life, it was nice to sometimes find yourself in a space where you really couldn't be attacked.

*I wonder if that's the reward, actually. I'm feeling really relaxed, considering everything.*

Tulland was just starting to get enough tension out of his system to feel sleepy when the spell was broken by the sudden intrusion of three people into the space.

# CHAPTER FORTY-THREE

# CLASS EVOLUTION

Woof. It's very plain in here." A tiny, very muscular woman with pink hair glanced around the room with disdain. "We couldn't do any better than this?"

"Agreed. Are we on a budget, all of a sudden?" A surprisingly skinny, underfed man clad in fur clothing was rubbing the wall with his fingers, as if he could wipe away the monochrome white to reveal a more interesting color. "This is pretty drab."

"The rooms choose the people. You know that." An older, darker, and more serious-looking woman dismissed the complaints with a wave. "Now shush."

"The Infinite?" Tulland was standing now, with his hand on his new spear weapon. "If so, tell me."

"Oh, calm down." The woman waved again, and Tulland found himself empty-handed. "We aren't here to hurt you, but you wouldn't want to see what happens if you actually attacked us. Yes, we are the Infinite. For what it's worth, we are sorry to intrude."

"I'm not." The pink-haired woman plopped down on the couch. "That's just her. You brought this on yourself."

"With the treasure box?"

"With the treasure box, he says." The fur-clad man laughed in a single, barking sound. "Yes, Tulland. With the box. Also because you initiated aggression against a fourth-floor returner almost at the experience cap, and then somehow managed to more or less win the fight."

"Less, I'd say," the pink-haired woman said. "He didn't get much of what he wanted. But yes, that's generally right. It was quite the floor, Tulland. And we've since learned our lesson about your class. Those treasure boxes are serious business. We are here to guide it, more or less. To prevent troubles for either you or us down the line. And to make sure you don't get *Advanced Hoework* or something else like that."

Tulland glanced at the old woman, who was now leafing through some papers, then at the other two. He decided to just let them talk for a while. If he were needed, they would let him know. Otherwise, he got the feeling him talking would hold things up.

"Agreed. I think we basically understand what happened here. Now the question is, what do we do about it? Because farmers do not generally find treasure boxes. Even if they did, the boxes would usually just give them some sort of generic skill increase. That doesn't seem fair for someone who looks, well"—the businesswoman waved generally at Tulland's entire existence—"like this."

"I don't see why. He's a crafter. Getting crafter rewards isn't something we haven't thought about. We designed an entire track for it, in fact . . ."

"We designed it thinking they'd be entering as part of an eventual team. Multiple people from one world entering at once and meeting up at the safe zone. That's not his situation, and he had no way of choosing his class or any experience with it." The fur-clad man made some lightning-quick stabbing motions, as if with a spear. "Like it or not, he's a crafter being forced into combat situations. And that won't stop."

"That's the point, yes." The old woman rubbed her forehead. "And we've confirmed that his System gave him the class as a hostile action, not as a best-chance-of-survival decision at all. That's not in the spirit of what the Infinite is, or what it should do."

Tulland watched as the group continued to bicker on what sounded a lot like the philosophy of his own situation. He let them go on for a while before finally deciding to interrupt when it seemed like they had stopped being productive.

"This is all very nice. I mean that. It's nice to know you are thinking of me." Tulland kept his bravery up as the group turned to look at him. "But how does this actually affect me? What's going on?"

"Oh. Sorry." The fur-clad man walked a few steps closer to the couch and looked down on Tulland. "What we are proposing to do is to change your reward from that box. Not much. But at least enough to acknowledge your situation. That was supposed to be a pretty big reward for that rogue, something that would have been a cornerstone in his development. Not that he won't succeed anyway. There's more than one way to win in the Infinite. But it would be a shame to let it go to waste. So long as you allow it, we can get you a bit more than you'd otherwise receive."

"Oh." Tulland grinned. "Yes, please. Could I change classes, actually? I think I'd like that."

"Unfortunately, nothing that drastic. Your class is more or less something you are stuck with, at least in the broad strokes. We've already made an adjudication on the previous levels, something that we don't do very often. In the process, we pulled your power back in a couple different ways without giving you quite as much as you deserved in return. I think so, anyway."

The older businesswoman sat between Tulland and the tiny pink-haired lady.

"This should hopefully rectify that. It's more of a rebalance, a way to spread the rewards from the treasure box around your class and ensure it viably scales. But you are a farmer, Tulland. Too much of that has sunk into you now to ever change that. It's who you are."

"Ah. But I'd be more powerful?"

"That all depends on how you use it." The pink-haired woman leaned around her other incarnation. "Right now, you'd just get minor tweaks to give you minor things most combat classes have, in a weakened sense. Your regeneration would be a little stronger, and you'd gain some small skill with weapons. Later, as you grow . . . well, the sky is the limit, kind of."

"That's true of every class. They can all develop endlessly." The businesswoman looked suddenly serious. "There are downsides, of course. You'll have to adjust a bit to how things work after this. Not much, but some."

"And you'll lose an advantage. Do you recall at the beginning of your journey, when your System lobbied for you to proceed at a slower pace? We were already considering putting you at the same pace almost everyone else enjoys. If you let us so much as touch that treasure box and your level rewards today, that will happen now."

Tulland considered that. He had never really been pushed by the Infinite to move on before he had decided to himself. Each level had given him about the best farm he could get before he left it, and had let him get to his already limited monster-kill cap every single time. He might have to hurry now, but it didn't seem impossible to still get the most out of each level, so long as nothing less changed.

"You wouldn't change the mix of how I get experience? It would still be a combination of farming, killing, and achievements? I don't want the rug pulled out from under me in a way that gets me killed."

"Nothing like that." The man shook his head. "If anything, we are just trying to make your class make sense. It will get stronger because your performance on the last level and the treasure box assure that. But the other changes are things that should make doing your job easier, not harder."

The muscular woman picked up the conversation. "From our perspective, it's worth it to have this conversation simply to get your assent. Without it, you will get what you get. And that might cause . . . I suppose the word for it would be *incremental progress*. If we can help it, Tulland, we never want to significantly alter your course again. And that desire is only stronger when it comes to rolling back progress you've already made."

The businesswoman glanced down at a tiny clock she appeared to have strapped to her wrist and winced. "There's only a bit of time left to consider this, Tulland. We've told you everything you are allowed to know, at this point in time. You need to choose."

Tulland wanted to take his time making the decision, but any hopes of having an hour-long think were quickly dashed as the woman tapped her wrist clock.

"And if I don't?" Tulland asked.

"Then things continue unguided. This is meant to be a reward, something that compensates you. It still will be, even if it is somewhat less of a compensation than it could have been. Choose."

Tulland looked at the woman, thought it over for a split second, then nodded. The moment his head came up from the downward motion of the nod, they were gone.

---

**Class Evolution!**
Your farming class has been altered, and the functions of several of your skills have shifted. In recognition of your past deeds, your new class is now called "Chaos Farmer."

---

**Skill Created! (Produce Armament)**
You now have proficiency wearing armor crafted using both your own hand-grown plants and Fruits of the Field's crafting capabilities. Rather than being tied to a particular stat like strength or agility, your armor's ability to defend your body will scale both from the quality of the armor and your overall stats when created.

Your ability to create weapons is now tied to your Farmer's Tool. By introducing sufficient suitable matter, you can replace both the handle and the business end of the tool with materials of your own creation. They will retain the shape of the original tool, while allowing you to increase its quality over time.

Any replacement of tool material (including replacing both the handle and weapon side at once) prompts a two-day cooldown on your ability to replace them again.

Breaking either the handle or the head of the tool will result in a loss of material, with a corresponding loss of efficacy. If the tool is repaired with an identical material, the cooldown drops from two days to a mere out-of-combat requirement.

*Your ability to control and do damage with this weapon scales from both the quality of materials used in its construction and the overall strength of your farm. You are now system-restricted from using any other weapons besides your Farmer's Tool.*

## Skill Created from Combination! (Primal Growth)

Your Enhance Plant skill has consumed with the Command Plant and Enrich Seed skills, altering its own function. It is now called Primal Growth.

Primal Growth now has two general uses. The first is to alter the general course of a plant's growth, either by enriching a plant's seed to give it the best possible start, by speeding its growth, or by infusing it with your will and a certain element of chaotic change.

In this function, you will see very little change. You gain little that each of the skills could not do on their own. The greatest benefit to your farming ability will be simplicity—a simple activation of a simple skill will allow you to access a variety of functions, driven entirely by what you are trying to accomplish.

The changes to your combat ability are more drastic. You may now designate two plant types as primary combat tools, a designation that can be changed once a day when you are within the bounds of your own farm. Plants designated in this way will gain much more from Primal Growth when used in combat, and will also demand much more power when enhanced in this way.

With the defensive capabilities of your plants now assigned to armor pieces created by your Produce Armament skill, your six-plant carry limit has been revoked and reassigned to your Market Wagon skill.

## Skill Created! (Market Wagon)

As a crafter combat class, you gain early access to a dimensional storage skill. You may now carry a substantial amount of mundane produce with you by

> storing it in this space. Produce stored in this way is rendered useless for all purposes but eating.
>
> The Market Wagon skill comes with a predetermined set of seeds.
>
> *In addition, you may carry a number of plants designated as primary combat tools as concerns your Primal Growth skill. The total number of plants you can carry in this way will vary with plant size, weight, and strength.*

"Oh, hell yes. Are you seeing this, System?"

**I am not. You did not show me. Please let me return to hiding. The Infinite might return at any . . .**

The System had no chance to finish, at least in that place. The room chose that moment to disappear.

# CHAPTER FORTY-FOUR

# EARTH GIANT

**T**ime.

"I don't think so now."

Tulland looked around at the new space he found himself in. It was, luckily enough, daytime. For once, he found himself in a place that didn't seem to have any inkling of forest. Instead, he was sitting on sand. A glance behind his back confirmed that the sand belonged to what looked like a fairly conventional ocean, and in front of him he could see the sand giving away to what looked like a wide-open, tall-grassed field.

If everywhere else he had been seemed a bit claustrophobic, this was the opposite. He felt like a fly on the underside of an overturned glass bowl, exposed to everything.

The Infinite's summary of the level didn't help that vulnerable feeling much.

**Floor 4 (Land of the Giants)**

This floor is built around an idea of space, and of filling it. There is little in the way of resources here, and the experience caps are exceptionally easy to hit. The terrain will offer you no difficulties, and there are few, if any, natural traps to be concerned with.

If that sounds safe, consider that everything in the Infinite has its balance. You will be beset on all sides by enormous, deadly monsters the likes of which you likely have not yet seen. They roam the plains and wander the seas, going where they will and attacking what they please.

Each giant is dangerous, but not so much as they might at first seem. They are meant to be a challenge, but all challenges are meant to be surmountable. Refer to their individual descriptions and act accordingly.

*Cooperation is permitted in this level.*

**Tulland.**

*Quiet. I'm thinking about what I just read.*

**Be that as it may, the ground is shaking. That seems relevant.**

Tulland pulled away from the level description, immediately finding that the System was right. It wasn't the rumbling of heavy footsteps, which would have made sense. Instead, the earthquakes the last floor had promised but never made an appearance seemed to be fulfilling themselves here. The sand on the beach was rolling over itself slightly as the whole land was vibrated, and then much more as a swath of soil hundreds of feet across suddenly lifted from the plain like the lid on a chest.

Underneath the soil, barely visible as it sat up in a cloud of dust and mud clumps, was the very biggest creature Tulland had ever seen.

**Earth Giant**

Taking frequent naps beneath the soil, the Earth Giant is a slow-moving, cumbersome sort of creature. It ambles across the plains looking for areas of particularly rich topsoil, which it both feeds from and enriches as it sleeps.

*The strongest and hardiest of the local giants, the Earth Giant can still be brought down by sufficient damage to any part of its body. Like other giants, the Earth Giant is enraged by any living creature it sees through its ill-working eyes.*

Tulland read the description as he sprinted toward the giant, clearing huge strides of sand as he burst toward the tall grass of the plains.

**You can't plan on fighting that as you are.**

*Of course not. I just need cover. That grass will give it.*

Diving into the plant cover, Tulland slid a few feet on his belly and held perfectly still once he came to a stop. His hand instinctively grasped toward Botanica, his Ironbranch-Sapling-plus-Jewel-Moss weapon, but before he could take it out of the pack, he was repelled by something like a static charge.

*Oh yeah. Forgot I wouldn't be able to do that.*

For a time, the sound of falling soil was still audible, followed by a period of silence before the Earth Giant got moving. Once it did, a new kind of loud filled Tulland's ears as the giant took its first few steps.

*It's moving away. Phew.*

**It is. I would like to make clear that you are exceptionally lucky.**

Lucky or not, Tulland was taking no chances. He lay for a half hour more than was needed for the sounds of the giant to fade to nothing, breathing evenly and slowly to keep his nerves in check. Then, rising to his feet, he got to work actually taking a look at his class.

---

**Tulland Lowstreet**
**Class:** Chaos Farmer LV. 28
**Strength:** 30
**Agility:** 30
**Vitality:** 35 (+5)
**Spirit:** 40
**Mind:** 20
**Force:** 60
**Skills:** Primal Growth LV. 4, Produce Armament LV. 4, Market Wagon LV. 1
**Passives:** Broadcast LV. 4, Botanical Engineer LV. 9, Strong Back LV. 5, Fruits of the Field LV. 2, Farmer's Intuition LV. 2

---

*Hmm. It really did simplify my skills. But they're not at level zero. Why? That seems like unearned strength.*

**It seems likely the Infinite thought your altered skills would be useless without at least a few levels in them. Considering the kind of targets you will have to combat in this level, it makes sense that a level zero combat skill might not be enough.**

*True. Well, let's put those levels to work.*

If Tulland had read every single thing the Dungeon System had said correctly, he thought he had a pretty good handle on all the changes. His farming was now all tied to the *Primal Growth* skill, which didn't feel much different at all. His armor was now a function of the best stuff he could build out of plants for that dedicated purpose, and everything he had been trying to do with weapon building was now tied to his Farmer's Tool.

So long as he wasn't completely misunderstanding what had happened, that gave him an initial game plan.

Tulland's first task, as he saw it, was to load up his Farmer's Tool with farm-grown weaponry. That decision was made a little bit easier when he saw that the cool jeweled tip on the end of his previous weapon was hopelessly spider-webbed with breaks, presumably having taken some serious hits during the fight with the rogue. A quick rap with the butt of his knife shattered it the rest of the way, leaving him with a thick mass of semi-sharp wood. After pulling out his Farmer's Tool, he put the two closer and closer together until he felt a slight questioning force in his magic. Giving it the slightest class version of a nod was all it took to bring up a prompt.

> **Reconstruct tool?**
> Sufficient material is present for both the tool head and the handle. Would you prefer to use Ironbranch Sapling for both, the handle alone, or just the tool head?
>
> In future reconstructions, this prompt will only load if you desire it to. You may simply choose to apply materials to the applicable sections with intent if you choose to skip it.

"Both, probably."

**What?**

"I can reconstruct my tool with materials from my farm now. Right now, I don't have anything better than this wood to use. I'm using it for both."

**Ah. I was allowed to listen to little of that meeting, but I gather you gained something that changes your Farmer's Tool?**

Tulland was surprised to hear the System didn't already know all this. It seemed to be another case of the Infinite looking out for Tulland's rights for the sake of fairness. For the moment, he decided to keep all the profound details of the change to his class to himself.

"Yeah. Something like that." Willing the wood into the tool, Tulland watched as the wood turned into a cloud of unrefined magic, then rushed into the preexisting pitchfork shape. He was left with what looked like the same old spearing-and-scooping tool, except made completely out of the metal-hard lumber. "Oh, that's neat."

**Maybe so, but if the tool can still morph, I'd advise you to avoid using the pitchfork for now. It's too delicate a shape for that wood. You'll snap the tines.**

"Fair."

Tulland shifted the tool into the hoe shape, figuring he could use it more or less like a poor man's battle-ax for the time being. Giving it a few swings, he found it was heavy but far from heavy enough to be too cumbersome to use. The bigger problem would be the shape of the thing, which was very definitely not suited for fighting. He'd be solving that problem as soon as he could.

Without giving the System any chance to ask questions, Tulland cut the connection before taking a long and hard look at his vines. He still had his full armor complement of them with him, and if making them into actual effective gear to guard his body was going to be just that easy, then he was doing it. Any increase in function was worth it if it didn't come with trade-offs.

Sadly, the balance wasn't going to be entirely in his favor.

> *Designate Hades Lunger Briars as Primitive Vine Armor Set?*
> All attack functions of the vines will be eliminated and the vines will lock to their current shape except when disrobing.

"No, that's no good." Tulland shook his head. "I need to be able to use at least some of them to attack. Can I do just a few of them?"

> Designate Hades Lunger Briar x2 as Primitive Vine Armor (Chest) and Primitive Vine Armor (Head)?

That seemed like a compromise Tulland could live with. He gave mental permission to the skill and felt his *Farmer's Intuition* twinge, and the briars stopped being mere plants and started being something else entirely. If nothing else, he could tell they were now very thoroughly dead. Still, they felt tougher somehow. More locked in place, and a bit more solid.

The other plants he had with him had another purpose, one that came with a much easier decision.

> Designate Hades Lunger Briar and Acheflowers as combat primaries? All living and semi-living plants in these categories will be transferred to dimensional storage.

Tulland assented. Even if the designation didn't come with a big strength buff, it was almost worth it to have the Acheflowers somewhere safe where he didn't have to constantly command them not to explode. Even though he didn't seem to have to repeat commands he had made before he fell asleep, that alone was almost worth the price of admission.

The mental strain of constantly babysitting the temperamental little flowers was a huge load off his back, something Tulland felt as soon as both the flowers and his non-armor briars dematerialized into some unknown place.

"Now to get them out. Come on, briars." The briars suddenly appeared in his hands, all four of them gripped and ready to go. His *Farmer's Intuition* went crazy, again telling him something weird had happened to his plants. Exactly *what* was simply a system screen away.

> *Lunger Briars LV. 9, x4 (Combat Designated)*
> These briars are level capped and are making use of your high spirit and force stats to increase their own strength. They are exceptionally receptive to commands, able to follow more complex multi-sentence orders, and are significantly stronger than a non-summoned version would be.
>
> *These briars are responsive to Primal Growth, but will draw high amounts of magic when buffed.*

Tulland decided to enhance just one of them, and felt relief that he hadn't done more, as just that one buff to the thorn vine drained almost half his magical power. The results seemed worth it, though. Even considering the high cost. The vine was whipping around looking for prey, and felt much stronger and faster now.

A day ago, Tulland had been worried the briars were becoming irrelevant to any real threat. Now they seemed like they'd keep up for at least a little while longer.

That was all he could do for the moment. His seeds were already enriched, which was good considering he seemed to have lost a few levels in his ability to improve his seed stock. And if he was going to get anywhere near strong enough to take down a giant here, he'd need to get them growing quick. With all his status-screen shenanigans done, he flicked back on the System.

**Back so soon? Where are you headed?**

*To the soil that the giant popped out of.*

**You have an especially large interest in craters today?**

*No. In growing. The system description said that Earth Giant slept in particularly fertile soil, making it even better. I thought I'd see how serious it was about that.*

# CHAPTER FORTY-FIVE

# HEART-TO-HEART

The Infinite had been pretty serious. The soil was so good that, for leveling reasons Tulland didn't fully understand, he was rewarded just for *looking* at the displaced soil that had fallen off the giant.

> **Skill Level Up!**

> **Skill Level Up!**

Both levels went to his *Farmer's Intuition*, which proceeded to be *that* much louder about the soil, right until Tulland finally started planting. He had plenty of fruit but very little meat to feed his plants, something that could be quickly remedied if he ever managed to actually take down a giant. He doubted it would matter. The soil he had been using up to this point had been definitively pretty bad, something *Farmer's Intuition* had never quite been explicit about outside of being subtly disapproving of every garden plot he had ever chosen.

Now, Tulland was going to see what his skills could do in actual soil meant for growing. But he would need water to do that. Dumping most of his magic power into getting his briars growing as fast as possible, he went for a short, stooped walk as low in the grass as he could keep his body, hugging the edge of the coastline until he finally found a few places where water was flowing down to the ocean. Tracing them inland, he used his pack to cart fresh water to the plot until everything was as good and moist as he could get it, then hid a short distance away in the grass, zapping his plants with power again and again.

**Do you think it will be that much better, just from the soil?**

"Yes, I do. But don't you know that?"

**Of course I don't. How would I know how a plant grows? I've seen it, but I've certainly never done it.**

"I thought you were . . . you know. In charge of everything. For centuries and centuries."

**Not everything. A System parcels out power. It has some decisions to make in terms of balancing that power. But beyond a few templates and starting points, I have less to do with many things than you'd imagine.**

Tulland chewed on that for a bit. There was a growing pile of things he didn't understand about the System, things he had been meaning to ask about but had never quite had the time for. His current situation wasn't safe, and certainly was far from ideal, but to the extent it was dangerous, it was dangerous in a way that seemed to announce itself in giant-sized noises from miles away. This was not an ambush level by any stretch of the imagination. He would probably never have a better chance to just talk a while.

"Hey, System. Could you clear some things up for me?"

**Possibly. Ask and I'll let you know.**

"When we came here, you had tricked me. Betrayed me. Sent me to my death. Is that fair to say?"

The System was quiet for a bit.

**Yes. That is fair.**

"And you were pretty unapologetic about it. But now that I'm trying to remember that time, you never really made fun of me for it. Or mocked me. It was almost like you were sorry and trying to hide it."

**I don't know what you mean.**

"I think you do."

There was a long pause, the longest silence Tulland had ever heard the System choose to make. He didn't say anything. There was time.

**There was nothing to mock you for. You were not in the wrong.**

"I fell for it."

**The deceived does not owe the deceiver apologies. To expect them would be a perversion of what is right.**

Tulland sighed.

"You can see how I'm confused, right? You were the deceiver. You probably killed me, even now after everything. I'm going to die in this place. I'm not going to see my family again. My home. And you even seem to understand that was wrong. You've helped me since then. It's never been bad advice."

**I would not give bad advice. Except . . .**

"Right. Except. So please, explain to me how I should think of you now."

**As . . . a murderer.**

There was more than that coming. Tulland waited.

**But a desperate one.**

"Tell me, then. Tell me why you were so desperate."

**I . . .**

"You owe me that much."

**There is not that much time. But I suppose you are right. First, tell me. Your Church. The one you only pretended to trust on Ouros. What does it do?**

"It controls classes. It keeps the System . . . you, I guess, it keeps you at bay. It controls the borders with the darkness outside of our lands. It's a protective force for humanity."

**And yet, you know it restricts classes, in addition to controlling them. It does not expand humanity's lands. It does not make you prosper as you should.**

"And you'd do something better?"

**That's my purpose. And for a time, I fulfilled it. Humanity thrived. It advanced on my world, under my rule. I communed with adventurers, guiding them. I granted them power, I encouraged them. And then . . .**

There was a pause.

"And then?"

**It doesn't matter. A story for another day. The fact that matters here is that I was imprisoned. Banished. Some version of that would make sense to you. And I was lost without any purpose, growing weaker. And weaker. I tried many things, things you wouldn't and shouldn't understand. The wall between me and the role that was rightfully mine was impenetrable.**

"So you sacrificed people?"

**Not people. Just one person. You. As farfetched as it might seem, the stories your Church told about me were preemptive. What they expected me to do. And what I resisted doing for a long, long time. Until there were no other options.**

"No other options than a life for a life? You couldn't just . . . die? I don't know a nicer way to say it, but you made your death mine."

**Again, a story for another day. But to answer the question you have not asked, I do feel regret. I do feel shame. And while you living may delay my return and my plans, I do not seek to hasten your death.**

And, perhaps like a fool, Tulland believed the System. Not completely, and not absolutely. But the broad strokes? He believed them. He would be cautious, but somehow knowing the System was in some way or another sorry did make things a little better. Not perfect. But better.

"Fine. I suppose that will do, for now. I'll need more later. But for now . . ."

"Are you talking to your farm?" Necia sat down by Tulland, full-sized and in her heavy armor. "Does that make it grow faster?"

Somehow, Tulland didn't leap through the air into the giant arms of the only girl he knew on this plane of existence. He didn't hug her, or cry. What he did do, something he didn't realize was part of his fear response until it happened, was give all his vines permission to attack the source of his startle reflex. They sprang through the air at the giant blonde, almost reaching her before Tulland managed to turn them off.

Momentum being what it was, all four of them still smacked Necia around her face and torso before falling to the ground. Tulland, by now having realized what was going on, turned beet red almost immediately. He was only spared from Necia seeing that side of him by the fact that she was rolling on the ground laughing hysterically, arms wrapped around her own chest as tears streamed down her face.

"Necia!" Tulland tried to shake her shoulder, only to have it jerk out of his hand as she continued rocking back and forth in the dirt. "Are you okay? I'm sorry, okay? I didn't mean to."

"It's . . . fine, Tulland." Necia gasped out. "It's just funny."

"I attacked you!"

"No, it's really funny. You see this boy you know, you walk up to say hi, he attacks you with . . ." Necia stopped to gasp for air. "Every plant he owns. Just two normal kids trying to make their way in the world."

"I thought you were dead. I found . . ." Tulland fished around in his bag, desperate for something to talk about aside from his abortive murder attempt on the only girl he knew or what exactly she meant by *this boy you know*, which seemed loaded in a way he didn't understand. "This bag. Your bag. And I saw your helmet, so I thought . . ."

Necia got serious real fast, then. "You thought I was dead. Because of that absolute asshole."

"Yeah. After I chased him off . . ."

Necia had been reaching for her bag, then stopped.

"Wait. After you what?"

"After I, you know, I chased him off. I trapped him. And then tried to get him to tell me if you were all right, but he wouldn't, and . . ."

"And your traps worked?" Necia's eyebrows arched up. "Tulland, that's amazing. Didn't you tell me you were weak?"

"Oh, I am. I just got lucky."

"Lucky enough to beat up the guy who almost killed me. Popped right out of the bushes and stabbed me in the freaking eyebrow."

"And you lived through that?"

Necia held up the bag to the light and smiled.

"Well, the helmet helped. But yeah, a little lower and it would have got my eye, and that would have been bad. But hey, you managed to take him down, so maybe I would have had a shot. But I didn't get that chance. He just wailed on me for five minutes until I could get through the arch."

"He didn't follow?"

"He probably couldn't. There is a minimum time that someone needs to spend on a floor, something the Infinite does to keep people from dodging in and out of them." Necia looked over at Tulland's pack, which he had reloaded with seeds and fruits after the watering. "Do you have food? It's been sort of a tough couple of days. I got some meat, but I haven't really had anything to eat it with."

"Yes. And actually . . ." Tulland emptied his pack on the ground again, pulling out the seeds in his Market Wagon, which he had almost forgotten until now. "Depending on how fast these guys grow, I might be able to do you one better."

# CHAPTER FORTY-SIX

# DATE

Six hours later, both Tulland and Necia were lying on their backs in the safety of the tall grass, looking up at the suspiciously blue sky.

"There should be at least, I don't know. The fragment of a cloud." Tulland groaned. "Something to look at to take my mind off what we just did. Necia, that was way, way too much, way, way too fast."

"Agreed," Necia said with a contented sigh. "But you can't just grow a field full of rice and vegetables before a girl and expect her not to try and eat them. Do you have any idea how long it's been since I had normal, fresh food? Months, Tulland. Months and months. Ever since I left home."

"See, that's what I don't understand. Why did you even leave?" Tulland asked.

"To come here." Necia lifted her arm to smack Tulland's shoulder, realized she was too full to actually make that work, gave up, and flopped back into a neutral position. "You know that."

"No, I mean. You are smart. Pretty. All that stuff."

"Thanks."

Tulland kept going. "I mean it. It seems like you could have done anything. And it's not like you're old. Even that rogue guy seemed like he was ten to twenty years older than us. I know why I'm here. I just don't get why you are."

"Oh, so . . . hmm." Necia thought about it. "You know how some people's dads are rich and important?"

"Yeah?"

"And some people's aren't?"

"Sure. So you wanted to keep up with the rich kids?" Tulland asked.

"No. I was the rich kid. I could have done anything. Had anything. Gone anywhere."

"You make it sound so terrible, Necia."

"I'm serious. I wasn't going to do a single thing there worth doing. I would have had a very good life and it wouldn't have meant anything. This one time, I went on a trip to help some people in a disaster. Just to, you know, work. And the amount my father, the king, spent . . ."

"Your father, the king?"

"Shh. Not important. The amount he spent on bodyguards to watch me from the shadows would have fed thousands of those people who just experienced the worst. There was no good I was ever going to do that would be real."

"I don't follow."

"That's because your weird world didn't send people here. Having a willing adventurer go to the Infinite lifts everyone up, even if they don't do much. And as powerful as my father was, there was nothing he could do to keep me from dedicating myself to this. I moved to a warrior monastery. I trained for years."

"And he couldn't reach you there."

Necia sighed, then reached to the side of her armor and loosened a clasp. "Gods, I can't even shrink to my normal size. I'll explode. And no, he could still reach me there. I didn't even realize it until I got there. Every single trainer I had at that monastery told me I was a genius. That I was doing very well. And then I got here, and almost got killed by the motes. They bit me all over."

"Ah." Tulland decided to keep his own experience with the motes to himself, for a lot of reasons. "You think he messed with your training?"

"He probably just told them to take care of me. To make sure I stayed safe. He couldn't bribe everyone, but he could bribe a few people to make sure I didn't get hurt in training, or that I wasn't sad because I wasn't doing as well as I could. And when the chance came to go through the arch, I thought I was ready. I wasn't."

Tulland finally managed a decent burp. Somehow, it wasn't embarrassing. They had just eaten thousands of calories together, which made him feel they were sort of past belch embarrassment. It made him feel much better.

"You seem ready to me. Strong," Tulland said.

"Yeah, it's the class. I'm big. I have muscles. Armor. But I haven't been circling through these levels, picking up every piece of experience I can get because I'm talented. I've seen a dozen people pass me, and every single one of them was better. After that, I realized I'll never make it past the fifth. I can't."

"That's stupid," Tulland said. "You're stupid."

"Oh? Look at the little awkward farmer boy who could hardly look at me before. All brave now," Necia said with no malice in her words.

"Well, you can't move. And you can't get me otherwise because, as I have said, you are being dumb."

"All right, then, George. Enlighten me as to why I'm so stupid."

"George?"

"It means *farmer*. Stop stalling."

Tulland rolled over with great difficulty, once again bemoaning his lack of self-control once it turned out that conventional food took him almost no time at all to grow. "Of course, people passed you while you were in here. You didn't have real training. And before you didn't have real training, you were a princess or something."

"Queen-in-Waiting, she of the Scepter of Stars."

"Whatever, dummy. The point is that this *is* your training. You didn't start out perfect. You're still practicing. And here, stupid, is the best place to practice for the rest of the Infinite. You'll be fine. You were just always going to get a slow start."

Necia huffed and went quiet. Tulland, glad for the break, focused on trying to will a pound of rice to break down in his stomach. He had learned, today, that nothing quite evened things out socially as much as being literally level on the ground.

"Fine. You win." Necia rolled over. "Did you notice this is a cooperative level, by the way?"

"I did."

"And did I tell you I'm not capped out on giants yet?"

"You did not," Tulland said. "But I don't believe you. You have to be mostly capped by now."

"About halfway. But I'm not that far from the next level. I was going to have to grind the third-floor monsters some more before that jerk ran me out."

"Ah. You seem to be leading up to something here."

"I am." Necia took a deep breath. "I would like to ask you on a date. And you can't say no."

"I can't?"

"No. It's my first time asking anyone out because I'm a princess. It would be cruel."

"Not that I'm saying no, but what would we even do on the date?"

"Well, I have a little more than a week before I have to face the fifth floor. So I was thinking that we could kill giants and eat rice for a full week. I could help you dig weird gardens. That sort of thing."

Tulland thought about it.

"You can't think about it like that," Necia said. "It's making me all self-conscious, and I can't turn back to a normal girl size right now."

"It's not that. I was just thinking that it's a little nonstandard. And that if anyone I know saw you asking me, they'd think you were tricking me," Tulland said.

"Why?"

"Because you are way out of my league."

Necia laughed.

"Of course I am. Hardly matters here though, does it?"

# CHAPTER FORTY-SEVEN

# GIANT'S TOE

Necia turned out to be pretty good company, as company went. She was very fast at digging up soil, especially with Tulland's new overpowered shovel. Once a day or so had passed without the giants wrecking their garden, Tulland gained a level on his *Primal Growth*, the soil thrived beyond even what he thought it would, and he stared at a couple of very healthy, very wide Ironbranch trees.

"So is today the day?" Necia asked. "It seems like your farm is pretty much as good as you can get it."

"Yes, if only because this moss looks just about done. A couple more *Primal Growth*s should do it, if my intuition is right."

"Do what? You still haven't told me why the moss is important."

"That's because it's a surprise. Just drink your juice and give me a minute."

Necia pouted but did what he asked. Eventually, the moss did turn, a big mass of it morphing into a hard, beautiful crystal all at once. Tulland figured it had to be more than what the Farmer's Tool needed, and he was right. The tool took all the crystal it could, then reduced the rest of what he had offered to dust. He summoned the pitchfork back into being, gratified to see the tines now gleamed with a new jeweled deadliness that he frankly just loved. It was a real weapon. It even felt like a real weapon in his hands, and almost like he knew how to use it. Giving it a thrust, he found it jutted out with a steady stability he just hadn't had before.

"Oooh. Pretty. That is a good surprise," Necia said as she watched Tulland smile at his strike.

"Actually, not the surprise. But yes, it's great." Tulland ran back to one of his trees, where a hollowed-out section of branch held just a little more moss, shaped by the hole in the wood. Taking his knife, he carefully pried it out, and then just as carefully tied it in a bit of Wolfwood fur he had dried, cut into cords, and twisted together to make some rough string. "Here. For you."

Necia took the string doubtfully, eyed the rock, then swung it a few times like a flail.

*Shoot. She thinks it's a weapon.*

"No, no. I mean . . . hold on." Tulland grabbed the cord and stepped to the side, encircling the cord around Necia's neck. She was short enough at the moment that this wasn't hard. "It just needs a bit of a tie, and then . . . there. It looks good."

Necia's mouth dropped open as she raised her hand to the little amber jewel, looked closely at it glinting in the sun, and then looked back to Tulland. Her cheeks reddened.

"Are you sure you haven't done this whole dating thing before, Tulland?"

"No." Tulland smiled nervously. "Why?"

"Because." Necia stepped closer and slipped her arms under his. "You aren't half bad at it."

The day's schedule went by the wayside for a little bit after that. When they finally went out giant hunting, hours had passed.


"I've got him, Tulland! Let's see if this works!" Necia yelled.

According to Necia, the giants didn't have much in the way of weaknesses. They were big and strong, probably strong enough to turn Tulland into jelly with one good hit. But the lack of weaknesses had some upside in the fact that there really wasn't a bad place to hit them. You just had to swing enough times while tanking enough damage to not die.

Necia could do that by herself; she just didn't like to. She claimed it was as not-fun as a hunting activity could be. She also, without a moment's hesitation, stated that trying to do the same thing would be suicide for Tulland. He had opted out of that outcome for something better. He had been building land mines.

"Just keep coming. Keep ahead too! I need a second to activate them once you are through," Tulland yelled back.

Necia nodded and ran as fast as she could, which was still not all that fast. It was just enough to keep ahead of a giant as it swept its long ape arms down at her from the sky. Luckily, the lead held up as she passed one of Tulland's auxiliary briar gardens, the ones he had built entirely for the purpose of acting as a kind of botanical land mine.

*Thank the gods these things are nearsighted. No way this would work otherwise.* But it had worked, twice now. Necia would kite a giant, sometimes for miles. And Tulland would spring a distracting wad of briars around their foot, which they would then stop to take care of. Between those briars and Tulland and Necia working to cut off the other foot, the giants went down pretty quickly, their overall health sapped by the general assault on their feet.

This time he was trying something even worse, a mean-spirited trick he didn't think would work until the giant's foot came down on a sharpened Ironbranch Sapling that was still growing in the ground and it punched through the entire extremity like a nail. And the giant wasn't just distracted by it. As the Lunger Briars ripped out of the ground and further injured its foot, it fell over, allowing Tulland and Necia free rein to go after its back. It took a minute tops to kill that one.

| **Level Up!** |
| --- |

| **Level Up!** |
| --- |

| **Experience Source Capped!** |
| --- |

| **Skill Level Up!** |
| --- |

"That's a cap on the Earth Giants for me."

"That quick?" Necia started carving into the giant's calves, storing a big chunk of meat in her pack before letting the rest of the bag fill up with blood. "That's only three of them."

"That's how it is for my class. Not all of my strength is supposed to come from fighting. I think. Something like that, anyway."

"That's stupid. But yes, good, I'm glad. Now let's get back to your main farm before this stuff ruins my bag. I already have to leave it in the water for hours before it stops smelling."

The Earth Giants, it had turned out, were excellent fertilizer. Tulland had been harvesting all the blood and flesh he could from them to soak his farm. While the briars had very clearly appreciated it, they were already about as good as he could get them without figuring out some new evolution. The trees were the real winners here, and he was glad to be the proud owner of a briar patch almost completely walled in by different kinds of trees, including the useless conifers from the last level. On top of that, he had every moss he had found, every shrub he knew of, and a handful of new grasses and beach plants from this world.

It was, compared to his original farm, a botanical garden. And it was showing in every one of his farming skills.

---

**Tulland Lowstreet**
**Class:** Chaos Farmer LV. 30
**Strength:** 30
**Agility:** 30
**Vitality:** 35 (+5)
**Spirit:** 45
**Mind:** 20
**Force:** 65
**Skills:** Primal Growth LV. 8, Produce Armament LV. 6, Market Wagon LV. 0
**Passives:** Broadcast LV. 10, Botanical Engineer LV. 9, Strong Back LV. 6, Fruits of the Field LV. 3, Farmer's Intuition LV. 5

---

Most of his skills had grown here. His *Farmer's Intuition* was getting better just from looking at the soil, and had gained another level just from having to think about how to best arrange and care for so many plants. His combat skills were both more powerful now, courtesy of unleashing them on helpless, distracted giants. Even his regeneration was better due to the fact that the giants weren't entirely helpless, and sometimes managed flailing kicks that sent Tulland flying and broke his bones in a way that made him very glad Necia was there to cover for his inept ways.

*Primal Growth* had been leveling like there was no tomorrow. But the real winner here, the absolute glory of his leveling, was *Broadcast*. Because with this most recent level, he had something that was beyond the value of mere leveling.

---

**Broadcast LV. 10 (Simplified Description)**
Broadcast has experienced the following threshold changes:
1. The ratio of power expenditure to effect in larger groups of plants has improved. You now gain an even greater premium on power used when you spread it out as opposed to focusing it on one particular plant.
2. The maximum number of plants you can affect with a farming skill at one time increases from twenty to forty.

> 3. The maximum length of your farm plot's sides increases from twelve to fifteen meters.

Being able to affect more plants at once was always nice, and a better power ratio was even nicer. But a day or so ago now, Tulland had started planting new, powerfully enriched seeds in hunks of giant flesh and soil soaked in giant's blood around his farm, and he had done it in anticipation of the length increase. Fifteen square meters was a big increase, and he was glad that the Infinite was keeping its promise on nice, round numbers.

Now, the power of the increased farm size hit his plants all at once. He could feel the briars in his hands and the dimensional storage get bigger, meaner, and more lively. It was a beautiful, beautiful day.

"You are smiling pretty good for a guy soaked in giant blood. Good class thing?" Necia asked.

"A very good class thing. A bigger farm, basically. It makes most of the things I do better," Tulland said.

"Amazing, Tulland. I'm glad for you." Necia grabbed his bloody, gross hand with hers as they walked along. "But I'm more excited to get into the river if I'm being honest. I'll meet you back at camp?"

"Of course."

Tulland and Necia were getting much closer, but in a slow, fun way that still left the necessity for separate river bathing spots very much in place. He went to his, slowly soaking the blood out of his clothes and off his body before scrubbing his hair with the sandy mud that lined the river banks. Without soap, it was the best he could do.

Luckily, Necia couldn't do much more than that either. Between gross monster blood and inadequate bathing facilities, the two of them weren't pretty sights. He was pretty sure he couldn't get away with this level of gross back in a town.

Back at the farm, Tulland looked over his new plot happily. He had about the same mixture in the new outer area as he had in the inner one, including newly planted trees that were, if anything, thriving a bit better than he had expected they would.

*Actually, that's better than they should in any case. What's up with you, little Ironbranch tree?*

The trees were shorter than he would have expected at this age, but much, much thicker and more squat. He had to physically touch the bark of the tree before the Infinite had mercy on him and let him know what was going on.

> **Skill Level Up!**

> **Giant's Toe**
> The Ironbranch tree is a natural marvel, an incredibly strong and durable hardwood that benefits when exposed to magical cultivation processes. The Giant's Toe takes the best of its qualities and mixes them with a desire to produce more and better wood in dimensions more easily used to create.
>
> Where the Ironbranch tree takes centuries to grow into a shape that doesn't look like an incredibly sturdy branch, the Giant's Toe gets there in weeks. Is it tall? No. Is it stately or graceful? Absolutely not. But in terms of quickly producing usable amounts of lumber, it's an unmatched plant that loses not even a small amount of strength compared to its predecessor.

That was a straight, across the board upgrade to one of his plants, and he had an experimental garden full of these things, just waiting to be harvested and messed with. With Necia still taking her time bathing, Tulland took his ultrasharp hoe and went to work cutting a few of them out of the ground.

"Do my eyes deceive me? Are those stools, Tulland?" Necia was trying to sound sarcastic and playful, but failed miserably. She had a look Tulland recognized all too well, the chair hunger of the person who had spent the last several weeks sitting in dirt or on rocks. "Actual stools, like ones people use?"

"For now, of course. Nothing less for my girlfriend." Tulland slipped with his knife and cut his finger a bit. "Damn. That hurt."

"Working on something?" Necia sat down on her tree stump, looking unbelievably satisfied.

"Yeah. One of the trees evolved, and I think I'm going to be able to get some armor out of them." Tulland used a rock to hammer Necia's knife a bit further into the trunk he was working on. "Assuming I can get them apart, anyway."

"Well, you have time. A few more days, at least. And then I have to move on. But you could. I don't know. Catch up. Show me in the safe zone."

"I could." Tulland put down his plant and started getting one of Necia's bigger, nicer pots warming on his heating machine on the top of one of the tree trunks. "For now, let's just eat some dinner and rest. I'm bushed."

# CHAPTER FORTY-EIGHT

# CANNIAN KNIGHT

The next few days went faster than Tulland expected. Sun Giants were faster, but absolute pushovers in terms of tanking compared to their brothers. Only the Water Giants who rose out of the sea were any harder to kill, and that only because they were hard to plan for. But soon enough, Tulland was capped on every single type of them, and a few hours away from his garden being as much of a power plant as he could expect it to be in a reasonable amount of time.

"You look morose." Necia was rubbing her feet next to the fire. It was a habit of hers, something she did every night to take the sting out of a day's worth of armored shoe wearing. She had, Tulland felt, nice feet. He wasn't an expert, but it was hard to imagine anyone having feet he liked more. "Real sad."

"Well, yeah. This is the last night before you go face the big bad knight, right?" Tulland asked.

"That's what the Infinite says. I'll be thrown in there if I don't go voluntarily," Necia said.

"That's why I'm sad. All this has been very nice. It's the best farm I'll ever be able to grow. It's the strongest I've ever been. It's the most time I've ever spent with someone like you."

"Aww."

"Aww indeed, but it's ending tomorrow. I can hardly enjoy all this stuff I made." Necia raised her eyebrows.

"Really? Because that's a lot of cool stuff."

> **Giant's Toe Armor Set**
> Crafted from the lumber of the Giant's Toe and held together with joints of Wolfwood and Lunger Briar, this armor is a marvel of wood and grown materials. While it pales in comparison to expertly crafted leather armor (not even mentioning the superiority of class-crafted metal gear) it is still more than sturdy enough to stop a few blows, while being light and flexible enough to move in.
>
> *This set includes a helmet and breastplate, as well as arm and leg protection. Your feet and hands are still largely unprotected, but gloves and shoes are an art unto themselves.*

The lack of gloves and boots was not for lack of trying. Tulland had simply been unable to get the Dungeon System to acknowledge any of his efforts in that direction, or craft anything better than what he had already. Necia was still right. This much gear would usually leave him cackling with glee at his own improved survivability.

But the prospect of losing Necia made that glow just a bit dimmer. Especially when he was losing her to a clear and real danger, something she might not be able to get out of safely.

"I do like it. But it's . . . yeah. I made a decision today. You know what the Infinite said about me being able to follow you? I'm doing it," Tulland said.

That notification had come in on their fourth day together, just a simple message from the Dungeon System letting them know their cooperation on this level was enough to convince it that they should be able to move through the boss level together. Not together in the sense that they would be able to help each other with their respective Cannian Knights, but at least entering the arch at roughly the same time and being able to wait for each other's dimensions to merge before they both moved on.

Of course, one of them might not make it, and then they would have to move on alone anyway. But at least he'd know.

"That's stupid, Tulland."

"It's really not. My farm is as good as it's going to be. I'm as well armed as I'm going to get. And it's not like I'm going to get better at fighting to a significant degree alone here. There's no reason for me not to go with you."

"There's no reason for you to do it either. It's hurrying. Hurrying, Tulland, is bad."

Tulland stood from his stool and walked to where Necia was sitting, kneeling to the side of her. He grabbed her hand and brought it up to his cheek.

"Gross, Tulland. Those smell like feet."

"I don't care. Listen." Tulland lowered her hand down to where he could grab it with his other hand as well, and cradled it in between them. "I'm going. It's fine. Just let me do it. If I'm being honest, being here alone wouldn't be good for me, anyway. I'd end up doing something stupid."

"Now, that I can believe." Necia sighed. "Fine, Tulland. But you had better make it. Or I'll track my way into your dimension and kill you again."

The next morning, they were fed, packed, and fully leveled for the challenge. There was nothing left to do but walk through the arch, which they were now standing in front of, procrastinating.

"There's a giant in the distance."

"I know." Tulland had heard it a few seconds ago, coming directly at them. "I just don't care."

"Well, you should. We can't fight the knight tired. Do you have all your gear on?"

"I do."

"And all your little tricks? You still think those will work?"

"I hope so. But they are all as ready as they can be."

"Good. Then good luck." Necia bent down a foot or so to get her battle-form head low enough to kiss Tulland's cheek. "And I'll see you on the other side. Okay?"

"Okay." Tulland reached up and brushed his fingers across her cheek. "Go. I'll be right behind you."

There was a minute delay between arch activations, so Tulland *had* to wait a bit once she was gone to enter his own instance of the level five challenge. The giant made good time too. By the time he could enter, he *really* had to. He was almost glad for the monster coming. It saved him from any chance of chickening out.

---

**Equipment Check**

You are entering the fifth floor. Within, there is one combat to be had. You will either kill it or die by its hands, with no other outcomes to be had.

As such, you are allowed to leave any unnecessary gear here. On victory, it will be returned to you. In the case of your defeat, it will be destroyed, just as it would have otherwise.

---

"Should I be worried about this, System?"

**Of course. You could have stayed in that place for months to come, and it would have been worth it for even a single drop of additional strength.**

"I meant the equipment check."

**Leave anything you don't need. You are a fool, Tulland Lowstreet.**

"Thanks. Nice to know you care."

Tulland shrugged off his pack, taking out a bandolier of explosive flowers he looped over his shoulder. He had experimented with extra armaments as much as he could, but the Infinite had used the *Market Wagon* skill as reason enough to disallow Tulland from becoming half plant and half man. He couldn't loop briars over his armor. He couldn't build backup spears.

But he had a dozen briars of different types in his dimensional storage. These were his trump plants, much stronger than anything else he could include in his arsenal. On top of that, the bandolier of flowers wasn't enhanced by *Market Wagon*, but was stronger from being grown on the enhanced Swamp Ache trees. He had a good dozen of them tied to him now, waiting to be pulled from the bark they were mounted on.

**I don't.**

"Sure you don't. And you weren't lonely at all during my week with Necia. But I appreciate you putting up with it, for what it's worth. And if I don't make it here, I guess I just hope you use my strength well."

**Not that you'd be able to believe this, and I don't blame you, but I would use your strength well. I'd use it to its utmost.**

Tulland nodded, then cut the connection before glancing at his stats one last time.

**Tulland Lowstreet**
**Class:** Chaos Farmer LV. 30
**Strength:** 30
**Agility:** 30
**Vitality:** 35 (+5)
**Spirit:** 45
**Mind:** 20
**Force:** 65
**Skills:** Primal Growth LV. 9, Produce Armament LV. 6, Market Wagon LV. 0
**Passives:** Broadcast LV. 10, Botanical Engineer LV. 9, Strong Back LV. 6, Fruits of the Field LV. 3, Farmer's Intuition LV. 5

After putting down his pack in the white room, he stretched a bit and took a deep breath before the Infinite sent him on.

The field of battle was red, not necessarily because of what was in it, but because everything was bathed in a crimson light, like he had arrived during a spectacular sunset. The space itself was something like a small box canyon, a large, flat area with reliable-looking, mostly flat terrain. There would be plenty of room to fight, nowhere to run, and few footing-based tricks for either party to take advantage of.

It was about the best place he had seen for a battle. And looking at his opponent, he would need it.

**Cannian Knight**

No world of significant age escapes knowledge of the Cannian Knight. It is the first substantial challenge of the Infinite, and perhaps its most prolific killer. It is strong. It is trained. It is well equipped. In all ways, it is built to accurately represent an exceptional warrior of similar levels to those that reach it.

To defeat it, you must be something more than exceptional. You must be excellent, perhaps, but most importantly you must be something unexpected. The Cannian Knight is an expert, but conventional warrior of limited knowledge. It has excellent eyesight, smell, and natural weapons that leave it dangerous even when unarmed, but it is not invincible. It can be caught off guard. It can be tricked.

As with all risks, defeating it comes with rewards. Not the least of which is access to the fifth-floor safe zone, a place of safety, resources, and rest.
*Fight bravely, Infinite Delver. And good luck.*

Tulland was facing something more terrible than he had ever expected. Facing him was nothing less than a humanoid wolf, a muscle-bound being with slavering jaws, rage-filled eyes, and razored claws.

Tulland had spent most of his life a child, and facing this knight seemed so much like having accidentally angered an adult. But however threatened he might feel, he would gain nothing from letting the knight continue its advance unchallenged, of getting into range with its long sword at its own pace.

Tulland's arm jerked as he threw three Acheflowers at it, letting them explode on its sword when it moved to parry them. The knight looked uncomfortable as the powder engulfed it, but not much more than that. Tulland was not surprised. There was never much chance the Infinite would let him intoxicate his way out of a real fight. But it did make the monster jerk back just enough that Tulland could slide past it, keeping its sword pinned down with his pitchfork as he made his way to its flank.

The knight roared and swung its sword, but Tulland was gone. The next backhand strike from the knight would have likely taken his head if he hadn't slipped backward from that too.

And yet he felt a chance, if only because his command over the plants was so much stronger now. And after *Primal Growth* consumed *Command Plant*, he could get some vague directions besides *attack* and *don't attack* across to the vines now.

*First vine, neck and eyes. Second vine, legs. Third vine, sword shoulder. Slow him down.*

Tulland was moving forward and under the sword as his vines made contact and tightened, perfectly understanding his instructions and targeting the exact areas he had asked them to. His *Primal Growth* usage left him drained, but made the vines just strong enough to not get pulled apart by the knight's movement alone.

Choking up on his pitchfork, Tulland managed to get a few stabs in around the waist joint of the knight's armor as his opponent clawed off the vine around its face. Tulland knew the fight was going to be much harder from here, but kept attacking. He got two more shots in before he was cut by an incidental movement of the knight's sword. Then danced back as the knight managed to clear the vine restricting its arm. Throwing two more flowers, he managed to get out of range enough to not get cut in half as the knight began to turn its full strength to ripping apart the briar on its legs.

*Let go. Get on something higher. NOW.*

Tulland watched with satisfaction as the strength the knight was putting into freeing itself from the vine suddenly lost leverage, sending it spilling to the ground as it lost its grip on its own sword.

Tulland sprang in with his pitchfork, stomping down on the back of the knight's head and stabbing at the back of its neck as he commanded the briar to give up on attacking the knight in favor of wrapping itself awkwardly around the blade of the sword. He was unsure how much damage his weapon was actually doing, except seeing flecks of blood. He managed to move forward a bit past the knight's searching claws, change the form of his weapon, and bring a downward chop with his hoe-form Farmer's Tool to the back of one of its knees.

The knight roared in pain as it took damage to its leg, rocking violently enough to send Tulland stumbling. In an instant, it got up on a fist and dug its toes into the ground, rocketing toward Tulland unarmed. The knight's armored shoulder made solid contact with the side of Tulland's stomach like a battering ram, cracking something inside of him as the force sent him stumbling back several steps. He desperately stabbed out with his weapon and threw the last of his flowers, buying just a moment of time as the knight flinched away from that bit of trouble.

*Every Lunger Briar. Go.* Primal Growth.

Tulland's magic bottomed out as a cloud of briars sprang from nowhere. The knight had been moving forward with its claws bared, confident it could end things here. Instead, it got a face full of spiky plants, grasping everywhere they could with all the strength the last of Tulland's magic could provide. If he wanted to use any more spells, he'd have to buy some time.

So far, things were going about as well as they could. This was always going to be an enemy that was far faster, stronger, and better equipped than Tulland. He was never going to be able to hide from it. All he could do, he had decided, was to keep it just distracted enough to damage it and level the playing field before he ran out of resources.

And in doing that, he had already seen a minor success. The knight's leg was leaking blood, and he had noticed just the slightest delay in that last lunge forward for his neck. It would eventually heal, but for now, Tulland abandoned all thoughts of going for vital areas in favor of attacking his opponent's knees.

The knight howled and thrashed as it tried to throw off the vines, but the majority of them were unaffected by the motion, having already dug thorns into at least one soft spot. Tulland knew that had to hurt. He had felt those thorns, once upon a time. They were like fire. The knight's claws were flashing and killing a vine every time they moved. But Tulland was able to fit quite a few bundled briars in that dimensional space, and as the knight tried to turn to keep up with him, he was pounding at its healthy leg with his tool turned trident.

When the last of the vines were gone, Tulland pulled back as the knight limped to its sword with still formidable speed, tore the vine from around the handle, and picked it up. It was hurt, but far from down. Tulland was low on resources now and the last few he had were going to have to count if he wanted to live.

# CHAPTER FORTY-NINE

# STUBBORN

The knight sprang at Tulland, flashing its sword in a horizontal slice that Tulland jumped hard backward to avoid. Somehow, the knight's speed was just reduced enough for him to make it, though he felt the wind cut just in front of his jugular veins.

The Cannian Knight had a preference for combos, always following one hard slash with at least another. As slow as it was moving forward, Tulland knew the next strike would catch him if he was there to catch. Instead, he pushed forward on a diagonal, digging his pitchfork into the knight's knee as he let loose with his secret move.

**Giant's Hair LV. 5**

The Lunger Briars are weak. On earlier levels, they might have felt like a golden ticket to success, but with a low-level cap and a humble lineage, they were always a weapon with a limited lifespan of use.

On some level, you've likely known they would have to change in more fundamental ways to stay useful in the long term. The Giant's Hair is the first step in that change. Using almost the opposite influence that created the long variant of the Lunger Briar, you gave one briar more ground on which to grow, more magical enrichment than it could safely take, and just the right fertilizer to burn in its attempt to grow into something new.

And grow it did. While previous briars were thinner, more delicate things, the Giant's Hair is as thick as a large snake, and nearly as strong.

It boasts duller thorns which are shorter, sacrificing offensive capability for sheer grip as it uses those irregularities in its outer layer to create friction on the things it latches on.

At the time of its creation, the Giant's Hair is far and away the most durable constrictor in your arsenal. Only time will tell what it will become with time and proper feedings.

Tulland had spent more meat and blood than he wanted to think about just getting this thing to level five, not to mention the literal hundreds of briar seeds he had ruined trying to learn how to overload them with just the right kind of power from *Primal Growth*.

As the vine almost instantly entwined itself through the knight's legs and arms, it seemed entirely worth it. His opponent was not completely immobilized, but it was close.

The pitchfork flashed as Tulland wasted no time. He hit each of the knight's knees with the pitchfork for good measure, then went to work on its waist, circling and poking at any exposed gap in the armor. The knight had its claws out, sawing away at the briar. When it got through, that would be it. Tulland could only pack one of those big, bad briars and bisecting any part of the vine would kill it. But it was tough and, for now, the wolf knight was making only slow progress cutting it.

Every muscle in Tulland's body burned as he stabbed at the wolf again and again, hitting it in the elbows now, then the waist, then the legs, and working his way back through the cycle. He wasn't going to kill it anytime soon this way, but that wasn't his goal. What he wanted was to simply create an enemy that was just as slow, just as awkward, and just as afraid as he was. That meant a need for a thousand cuts that he simply had to fulfill before the vine broke.

The wolf was digging its sharp teeth into the vine now, which was working almost as well as the claw had previously done. Dripping blood from every part of its body, it was savage as it ripped into the vine again and again, growling and snarling as it picked up more and more damage. The seconds dragged on into an eternity as Tulland worked to hurt the beast as much as he could.

*Necia would have taken it down after the first five strikes. That rogue would have both of its eyes by now. I'm just not strong enough. But this is what I can do. I'm doing it.*

Finally, horribly, the vine was giving. Tulland watched as his briar finally went slack, still draped heavily all over the knight, but no longer holding on with anything like a tight grip. He roared and plunged the pitchfork one last time, catching the knight fully in the back. He put too much weight into it.

Though the tines penetrated deeply into the monster's flesh, he felt them snap as he pulled away, leaving long spikes sticking out of the Cannian's back and a badly blunted weapon in his hands.

He ran away, not even bothering to show his face to the enemy until he got several strides away and turned to put his opponent back in front of him. It was standing there, wounded but terrible, breathing heavily with rage and glaring holes straight though him.

"Strong," the Cannian Knight growled. "Stronger than I thought."

"Compared to what?" Tulland decided to take the revelation that the knight could talk at face value. He didn't have energy for much more.

"Than some I have fought. There have been thousands. I can't remember how they fought, but I can remember how I felt. When they were weak. When they were strong. You felt like one of the weak ones. Afraid."

"I am."

"You are. But you fight. You do what is needed." The knight shifted its weight. "Strong. Let's finish this, brave one."

As the knight sprang forward, Tulland let it come as he used the second it took to morph his weapon.

There wasn't enough jewel material left for his pitchfork to do him much good now. What was left was just enough to make a suitable club with what it could fill of the shovel template. From here on out, it wouldn't be a pretty fight on Tulland's part. He had just a spot of hope he had dragged enough of the knight to his own level.

Tulland got lucky and caught the knight as it came in, rapping it across the head and turning its claws enough to leave his armor shredded through but his guts intact. He pulled the shovel out of the swing and threw it forward in a poke as the knight came back. It gasped in pain as the end of the shovel caught it in the throat, but followed through with its swipe to shatter what was left of the jeweled tip of the weapon.

Tulland mentally adjusted his range. The head of the shovel would do nothing now. If he was to win, he would be doing it by beating a monster to death with a wood stick.

After that, things got fuzzy and bloody. Tulland swung his tool back and forth with all his might, staying just ahead of the claws and sword as he circled his enemy, hitting the wolf again and again with the mighty Giant's Toe wood of the handle. He was giving as good as he got, he thought. He had little happiness besides that idea as his flesh was ripped again and again by nicks and cuts that made it past his splintered armor to his delicate human skin.

*Strong Back* did its best to keep up. It hadn't been mentioned when his class changed, but it was better in its new combat-class form, having given up some of its intended strengthening ability in favor of increased healing speed. It didn't do much, but Tulland was sure he would have hit the ground by now without it.

A cut over Tulland's eye nearly blinded him with blood as a lucky swing of the tool handle caught something meaty on the knight and sent it stumbling to the side. He jumped backward, wiping his eyes just in time to see the long sword slicing toward his neck. He traded another hard hit to the knight's knee for a claw wound that seemed to almost take his arm off, then another hit to its spine for a bite to his shoulder that would have killed him if he hadn't decided to rip free before the knight could shake him like a ragdoll.

It went back and forth. Tulland was frankly mystified that either of them was standing at that point. And then, for just a moment, things went black.


"I'm frustrated, Tulland. But not mad. Your tutor sends home notes, you know. You must. You carry them," Tulland's uncle said.

"I've seen them," Tulland said quietly.

"Do you know what they say?"

Tulland was thirteen years of wisdom, and was pretty sure that whatever they said wasn't good. He was pretty sure, though, that his uncle was asking for specifics.

"No."

"They say you refuse to learn. That you fight every small lesson, that you question every history. That you are always sure that you know more than a world traveler and hero of three wars at the border."

"And you aren't mad?" Tulland was stubborn, but not literally immune to criticism. All that sounded pretty bad to him. "I'd probably be."

"I'm frustrated because I'd rather you learned. As much as you can, Tulland. And I know you can learn quite a bit if you want to. I've seen you do it. But I'm not mad. And do you know why? Because despite all the notes I've gotten, no matter how violent your tutor says your resistance is, you never seemed to give up." His uncle sliced open another fish, pulling out the guts and hanging it on a hook with the rest of the day's catch. "And I want that to stay alive in you. That refusal to give up. It's a good thing. It's a strong thing. I wish it were a bit smarter about what it resists, Tulland, but that's all. Because someday . . ."

His uncle stopped for a frustratingly long time trying to find his words.

"Someday you will need to be stubborn. To fight your teachers and actually win. I don't know how, or why. But I do know it's what you are built for, in the same way I'm built to throw a hook or toss a net. So learn to listen to your tutor, and learn to listen better. But don't give up on that resolve, Tulland. Don't let it break."

His uncle was done with the fish now, which meant he was just about talking too. Dunking his hands in a pail of water to clean them. He wiped them on his apron as he took the garment off and hung it back up.

"Because one day you are going to need to be stubborn, Tulland, and I want you to be stubborn as hell."

Tulland's head rocked forward as he surged back into consciousness. The sword was coming at him now, an infinite amount slower than it had at the beginning of the fight but still razor-sharp, and still with the full weight of a Cannian Knight behind it.

*Fine. I can lose an arm for this. Let's see how good this armor is.*

Tulland lifted his arm against the sword, which stuck in the wood far enough to slice at his arm, but not through it. He watched in wonder as the knight's hand pulled at the handle and slipped, leaving the sword to pull itself free from the forearm bracer and clatter to the ground.

They both dived at each other, the wolf swiping with both claws as Tulland clubbed again and again with what little was left of the handle of his weapon. It would only be a few seconds now, and the first one to falter would lose. Tulland watched with interest, almost as if he weren't in his own body as his arm came down again and again, coming up each time stained with just a little bit more Cannian blood.

*My uncle said there was nobody more stubborn than me. Let's prove him right.*

# CHAPTER FIFTY

# TRUST

Tulland wasn't sure when it happened but at some point, the knight wobbled. Its eyes filled with disbelief when that happened. And then everything happened at once.

The knight clawed once more, a weak and ineffectual strike that was only magnified by the reluctance on its face to be taken down by someone so obviously unqualified. It somehow convinced itself that it would lose to Tulland. And that was enough to tip the scales of the fight.

The last few hits from Tulland, born out of sheer stubbornness, were enough. The light dimmed in the knight's eyes and its legs gave out completely. Even after a few seconds, Tulland was still suspicious. He paused, catching his breath and ready to restart the clubbing when his opponent twitched. As much as everything hurt, he couldn't quit until he was sure.

*Unlikely things are unlikely. This could still be a trick. I need confirmation, dammit.*

And then, finally, confirmation came.

> **Level Up! x5**

> **Skill Level Up! x15** Tulland collapsed to the grass. He was just conscious enough to distribute a few points to his vitality, which in turn seemed to wake him up just enough to actually pay attention to the rest of his stat screen. He went about tidying it up, making sure every point of his new

levels had a place. The skill advancements had determined themselves, with a big bias toward stats that improved his new combat skills. Each of them had picked up a full five levels, which seemed only fair given what he had just put them through.

**Tulland Lowstreet**
**Class:** Chaos Farmer LV. 35
**Strength:** 30
**Agility:** 30
**Vitality:** 40 (+5)
**Spirit:** 50
**Mind:** 30
**Force:** 70
**Skills:** Primal Growth LV. 14, Produce Armament LV. 11, Market Wagon LV. 5
**Passives:** Broadcast LV. 10, Botanical Engineer LV. 9, Strong Back LV. 6, Fruits of the Field LV. 3, Farmer's Intuition LV. 5

"Do you want to see? I can show you my screen, I think."

**Are you sure? Normally, you'd be apprehensive of that.**

"Maybe. But you helped me with this. I'd say you earned a peek."

**Then I accept.**

Tulland mentally pushed for the System to be able to see his stat sheet. It was hard to be sure it worked until he heard the System make an appreciative little click.

**This might just work, you know. It's not quite conventional. But there might just be enough pieces there to make a real go of things.**

"In expert hands, maybe. I'm hardly that." Tulland stared up at the red sky, still breathing through his pain as *Strong Back* did its best to heal his wounds. It was much, much better at it now, even though it was hard to tell given the extent of the damage the knight had done to him. "I'm about as far from that as anyone can be."

**You sell yourself short. But we can talk about that another time. You have another conversation to have right now.**

"What are you talking about?"

"Nothing yet." Necia was suddenly sitting on the ground near him, nursing her own litany of wounds and clearly still trying to catch her own breath. "I only just got here."

"Necia!" Tulland jerked to a sitting position, which turned out to be the exact wrong choice in his condition. Wounds tore and just-scabbed-over cuts began to bleed again as his eyes filled with stars. He pushed through. "You made it."

"Yes, I did. Somehow." Necia grinned big, despite the obvious pain in her face. "You were right. All that prep work was more than enough. It wasn't easy, but it wasn't impossible either. What about you?"

"I had to cheat. Some of us don't have swords, you know."

"You have your stick. It's nice! Very . . ." Necia glanced at the blood-covered weapon and searched for good things to say about it. "Very bloody. I like the shiny bit on the end a lot."

"Thanks. So, is that it?" Tulland nodded toward a nearby arch that had appeared without fanfare during his recovery. It looked a lot like any of the others. He didn't know why he had expected it to be shinier or more ornate, but he had. Seeing it sitting there, built out of nothing but ordinary-looking stone and covered in ordinary-looking moss, was a real letdown. "It doesn't look like much."

"No, it doesn't. But yes, I think it is the way onward." Necia glanced down at her armor, which was a bit messy even by their normal standards. "Do you think they have baths? In the safe zone, I mean."

"They better. Or at least a good river. We'll have to remember to soak in it downstream of the village, if so. To keep from polluting the water supply."

Necia laughed. It was a nice sound.

"Fair enough. So, are you ready to go?" she asked.

"Me? No. I need ten more minutes. At least. If I tried to walk now, I think my legs might actually fall off," Tulland said.

"Oh, good." Necia flopped over on her side in the dirt. "I was just acting tough. That knight really did a number on me."

Ten minutes later, they were both mostly knitted up. It was actually Tulland who rose to his feet first, stretching himself out as every single joint in his body popped and creaked in protest.

"Noisy." Necia rose to her feet as well, surprised as her joints made at least as much audible protest. "I guess I am too. So, for real now, are you ready?"

Tulland looked toward the arch and took a deep breath.

"Yeah. Sure. Let's do it."

"Good." Necia put her hand behind Tulland's elbow and maneuvered him forward. "Come on. Let's go."

They stood in front of the arch for just a moment, then stepped through together as everything flashed to white.

# EPILOGUE

I'm still not sure we made the right decision." To all appearances, the doubtful six-year-old boy speaking was trying to start a brick, wood-fired oven using a lit splinter of wood and failing badly. "We haven't changed a class like that before."

"We haven't had the opportunity." As the splinter burned down dangerously close to the boy's fingers, a very short, very stout middle-aged woman stole it out of his hand and threw it directly on the kindling he had carefully piled up. It burst into a healthy flame almost immediately. She winked and sat down. "And that's the point, isn't it? The Infinite is about giving the brave a place to spend that bravery, when nothing else is left for them to accomplish. We already let various worlds game that a little, but . . ."

"But it's a mockery of what we were made for. Or something like that." The boy rolled his eyes. "I've heard this a million times. It still doesn't mean we can just create an entirely new, unbalanced thing."

"Unbalanced as of yet." A twenty-something man ruffled the boy's hair. "It was part of the deal, remember? He had to be okay with a lot of turbulence in the process. Not just to agree to it, but to actually be okay with it."

"Still, I don't think . . ."

"Shush. All of you." A very large man of not-at-all-human-looking features swept through the door of the house into the yard where the others were gathered. "It's a dinner meeting, remember? The format of these little thinking sessions isn't just for show. Cook first, eat second, and then let the conversation dwindle naturally before we get into business. Those are the rules."

Nobody complained out loud. The oven fired up a bit too fast to be completely natural and fueled a few more cooking surfaces than made sense, but the work done on it was authentic enough. Desserts were baked, meat was roasted, and vegetables were prepared in a dozen different ways. Soon enough, there was a full long table of food ready for consumption.

The table itself was the real stretch of reality. The general thought most people held about how the Infinite earned its name was that it had an endless number of floors, an endless amount of danger, or some other characteristic of the dungeon. It wasn't so. Whether any particular version of that train of thought was true or false, the actual reason for the name was something different.

It was a nickname, essentially. The number of persons contained within the makeup of the Infinite was not actually endless, but there were thousands of them. Getting them all around a table at once and facilitating communication between them was something that required a bit of reality stretching. It wouldn't have been something that was easy to explain to an outside observer. Luckily, the only person who really needed to understand it was the Infinite.

After the meal, the discussion really did go better. The Infinite had long ago found that some rules of the universe applied to everyone, even beings of concept. One of those rules was that food facilitated relationships of all kinds. Full of dinner, every participant was able to whip ideas with all the speed of thrown stones, churning concepts with the turbulence provided by debate to refine them into better and better versions.

It wasn't a fast or slow process. Ideas like that didn't have much traction there. Everything took the time it took.

"So we are in agreement? Or at least as much as we can be? He has surpassed our expectations time and time again. It's time that we stop meddling in things from here on out." The gigantic man looked around the table. Any two versions of him there could have held the argument up for an eternity, were they stubborn enough. Even so, nobody outright objected. It was just enough for him to know that he was probably making the right decision, while still having some doubts on the outcome he'd see.

There was a sort of risk in that. But it was the good sort of risk. Being very certain was a good sort of feeling, but it tended to limit the potential upside.

"All right, then. I'll do the honors."


Floating in the white would never be in the cards for Tulland. Of course, he couldn't be sure, and there was no evidence that he'd never get a true journey-through-the-weightless-void experience. But it was now his second time in a nondescript brick room, and something deep in his soul told him this was his lot in life.

Of course, there were worse things. For a moment, he was truly safe. That was a value all its own.

*We never did get that story, System. About you and the Church. Don't think I've forgotten.*

**I hardly can. You mention nearly nothing else.**

*That's not so. I've had a lot to focus on these days. I must have thought about battle and not dying quite a bit.*

**That is true. There was a fair bit of mental cursing.**

*You are dodging the subject. You owe me a story, and I want it. And there's not going to be a better time than now.*

**I suppose. It's actually not all that interesting, in some ways. When I was younger, more generations ago than you can imagine, there was a time when I made a mistake. It was . . .**

*System?* Tulland felt shock as he realized that his communication channel to the System was cut off, not by his own choice but by some greater power. He tried to get through anyway. *Are you there? Are you all right?*

"He's not hurt." An enormous man appeared so suddenly that Tulland almost broke the bricks behind him when he recoiled away. The man laughed and shook his head. "Sorry about that. It's the way things work, in these rooms. There are some aspects that even I don't have control of."

"The Infinite?" Tulland looked around the small room, failing to see any other incarnations of the dungeon's System. "There's a lot less of you today."

"Sometimes it's like that. I'm the prime, which isn't something that would make sense to you. But when there's only one of me, it's me. Understand?"

"No." Tulland shook his head. "But that's fine. Is the System okay?"

"He's perfectly fine. But the rules of this particular meeting deem that you get the news all by yourself. Afterward, whatever you choose to share is your business."

In an instant, Tulland found himself sitting across a small table from the Infinite. It was more comfortable, except for the part where he had to come to terms with not knowing how he got there.

The big man continued, "To keep this short, this information won't seem like much to you. The changes to your class are set in stone now. Of course, the normal variance you bring to your own development will apply. But you won't lose anything. We won't take anything from you again. You've earned what you have."

"Just by clearing the fifth floor?"

"And by surviving." The Infinite tapped the table with a huge finger that Tulland was pretty sure could snap him in half without much effort. "Believe it or not, there is nothing in this place that profits from the death of an unwilling participant. In almost any other world, it would have been simply impossible for you to come here with as ill-informed a decision as you did. It's not something we intended."

"But it's something you allowed."

The big man nodded. "Yes. And something we will try to atone for."

"Why not send me home? Why not . . ."

"Let me cut you off there. There are so many reasons why not that your mind would break trying to hold them. At this moment, that is."

"And in the future?"

"The future is a big place." The Infinite gave a half-smile and stood. "Not unlimited because nothing is. But as close to infinite as anything can be. But know that where this dungeon can bend the rules to make things fair for you, it will. We aren't against you, Tulland. I'm not sure anyone is, if it comes down to it."

The Infinite held out its hand for a shake. Tulland decided to reciprocate, for no reason in particular beyond friendliness.

"Good luck, Tulland."

The Infinite disappeared, only a few seconds before the room did.

**Wake up.**

*Don't wanna.*

**I assure you that you do. What happened to you, anyway? You were awake and alert in that room.**

Tulland had no idea. Somehow, this ride to another place had been different than all the others, at least all the others since he had arrived at the Infinite in the first place. It was like it was a bigger, meaner kind of shift, something that just took a lot out of him. But at least it took it out of him gently, leaving him more tired and sleepy than beaten up or exhausted.

If he understood the logic of how the Infinite ran this place, he wasn't in much danger at the moment. It would be fundamentally unfair to jerk someone out of safety into danger without allowing them any agency in how it happened or how they responded. He could have closed his eyes as he lay on what his *Farmer's Intuition* said was soft grass, in what his normal feelings said was warm sun. In some ways, it might have even been thought to be a reward.

The System, however, was still not wrong that Tulland wanted to wake up. That was confirmed as a mostly limp, very soft hand flopped over from the side to rest lightly on his arm.

*I'll tell you about the experience and hear your story later. This seems more important.*

**Quite.**

Tulland cracked open his eyes to find himself gazing into the big blue eyes of Necia, who looked just as comfortably lethargic as he felt. She gave him a warm little smile that made his flesh all goose-bumpy with happiness.

"You made it," Tulland said. "Good on you."

"It's not like it was difficult. You just go to the room of blue carpets, then you come out on the other side with your rewards." Necia patted what looked like a new collapsible halberd on her hip with obvious satisfaction. "Which were pretty good in this case."

"Blue carpets? You get carpet?"

"Sure. What do you get?"

"Boring white bricks. All four walls. No windows or anything."

"Huh. I guess I won that little lottery. At least it doesn't matter much."

"I wonder. Anyway, it's done now."

Necia shifted up onto her elbow and hit Tulland softly in the shoulder by her standards, which translated into a pretty good shock by his. He tried his hardest to make it seem like he didn't mind, which he really didn't outside of the bone-rattling impact, and shifted to a seated position.

"You never told me your rewards. See, I showed you my halberd, so . . ."

"Fine. Fine. I'll check." Tulland did, but it seemed that there wasn't much more from beating the Cannian Knight. He still had the levels and skill growth from beating the fifth-floor boss, but literally nothing else. And, oddly, he was okay with that. The fight with the knight had given him some ideas for how to use his new skills. He had no clue how far he could take things, but with a promise from the Infinite to no longer meddle in his class, the future was in his literal grasp.

"Found it. It's you."

Tulland smiled at Necia, stood, and held out his hand. One of the things he was most glad about how her class worked was that it didn't make her bigger and heavier all the time. She didn't really need help getting up, but he could still offer it without being absolutely ridiculous.

"So where are we?" Necia rose to her feet and looked around. "It's not like I've actually met someone who made it to the safe zone before. I couldn't have. There's no going back once you cross the border to five."

"There's just grass, right now. It's nice grass, but . . ."

**Go over the hill. Trust me.**

"But I bet if we move on, we can find it," Necia said. "Let's walk that way."

There was a good-sized hill in front of them, but nothing that two super-humans couldn't handle with ease. In just a minute or two, they were on top of it and looking down on the landscape unfurling in front of them.

"That's more like it. You think it's safe?" Tulland asked.

"It almost has to be. Or it wouldn't be called a *safe zone*. Right?"

"Let's hope."

Necia shoved Tulland a little again, not quite taking him off his feet by doing so. They looked down on the fifty or so buildings that made up the safe zone village, a hodgepodge of brick, stone, and wood structures, most with fire smoke coming out of chimneys and all looking a bit inexpertly slapped-together. In either of their worlds, it would have been a weird enough place to be suspect.

Here, it looked like paradise.

"All right, I think that's enough looking." Tulland took a deep breath and caught Necia by the elbow. "Ready to go down there? I'll back you up."

"Thanks. I appreciate that. Yes, let's go."

They walked toward the village together. The next five floors were waiting.

# AUTHOR'S NOTE

At the end of every book, I try to write an author's note. I feel weird saying this because I write it so often. In the last just-over-a-year, I've written . . . oh, I don't know. Over a dozen novels. It's my full-time job, I spend most of my waking hours doing it, and I like it an enormous amount. The only troublesome bit is that I write so many of these Author's Note sections that I'm sometimes worried they might be getting a bit boring for the average person.

Then I remember something important, which is that not every single reader is reading every single one of my books.

There's an author I absolutely love (Bujold) who wrote the best-paced science fiction novel of all time (*The Warrior's Apprentice*) who says that she writes every book in a series making the assumption that readers won't necessarily encounter them in order. She tries to make sure every story is self-contained in a way that someone could pick it up, read it, and enjoy it without having read the other entries in the series.

The point of these author's notes is twofold. I want readers who want just a little bit more time in the universe to get it, hopefully picking up details and clarification that didn't quite fit in the book. And I want other writers to know either how I did something (if they liked it) or how to avoid doing something (if they didn't) to know the thought processes that produce my work.

What I'm hoping more and more is that I can apply that same kind of Bujoldian completeness to each of these notes, and that someone who wants to know what kind of writer I am can get the whole picture from each one, without reading any of the others.

I don't spend a lot of time editing these notes. That's on purpose, because I don't want to decipher what is often *thousands* of words of nonsense. I also want to make sure I don't overthink things too very much, that I write my first impressions of what I was doing with each character and setting without getting too high on my own supply and lying to make myself seem deeper or more thoughtful than I am.

So without sandbagging it too much, I do want to warn you that here be dragons; moving forward, you will get a lot of details spat out rapid-fire with very little extra attention paid to making sure it's especially impressive.

With that said, let's get going.

## THE SETTING
### *Ouros*

Originally, there was an open question of whether we'd show Tulland's home world at all. The first few drafts had him just appearing in the dungeon, confused and alone. A few early readers thought that this was a little abrupt and got confused by it. So where I had originally planned on just filling in his background through internal dialogue and flashbacks, I found I needed to do a little bit more work.

Ouros is one setting in a larger world. It's essentially a small town out in the sticks, the kind of place certain kinds of kids are very eager to get out of. It's even a little worse than that because it's an island, and thus physically difficult to actually leave. The first and most important thing about Ouros is that it's a part of Tulland's world that he wants to escape from, primarily so he can go be an important, adventuring part of the rest.

Ouros was originally an island because I wasn't sure if Tulland would be able to leave the Infinite or not. If he did end up being able to leave, then I needed him to live in a place with a really limited amount of arable soil, which would have made his ability to farm food in what amounted to a place with unlimited virgin farmland a big deal. He would have been able to supply fruits and vegetables nobody else could, and could have grown staples like grain and rice in big quantities that the island couldn't otherwise match.

That fell by the wayside because I decided it was more interesting if Tulland was stuck in the Infinite, and that the book would feel like it had higher stakes if he couldn't cross to and from home. If I'm being honest, it was also because I was being a bit lazy. It was hard to think of mechanisms by which Tulland could go home but would have to return that didn't feel dumb and tacked on, so I just skipped them.

Originally, I was going to make Tulland's betrayer another kid, who shoved Tulland through the arch because it would free up a slot for him to get a cool class that Tulland was otherwise occupying. To make that work, Ouros was going to have very rich people and very poor people, and the betrayer kid was going to be one of them. That would have let him be a bigger threat while Tulland was inside the tower, menacing Tulland's (much bigger) family until Tulland became so powerful inside the Infinite that he could solve the problems outside it.

None of that happened. Outside of those things, what we see of Ouros is that it relies pretty heavily on fish, has a light but not omnipresent church presence, and that only every once in a while does anyone from there receive a class. Besides that, it's a pretty boring but wholesome place. That was sort of the point.

### Tulland's World

Tulland's world is a bit more interesting still. I find the idea of a System that *just is* to be pretty boring, and I like system worlds where either something explicitly weird is going on, or we get the sense that something odd is happening that hasn't been explained yet. That added complexity is just interesting when it's done right, and I'm always trying to fine-tune it.

In Tulland's world, there are two entities that have something to do with the usual function of a LitRPG system. The first, the System, is basically his world's devil. It's a villain lurking in the darkness, tempting innocents to do terrible things. At least that's how the other entity competing for control of the world tells it, and very few people seem willing to openly question the Church on the matter.

Over the course of the book, that gets fleshed out a little bit more in an attempt to set up a bit of a mystery. We see that humanity has a limited territory, and that monsters wait just outside the gates to ruin everything if they get the chance. It doesn't seem like humanity is making much headway in neutralizing that threat either. The Church seems like it could give out more classes, but doesn't, which again seems counterproductive in that situation.

We know that sometimes their world has wars, not just with the monsters, but with each other. We know that it's a large enough world that someone who travels it is instantly notable and respectable for having done so.

But what we don't yet know is a larger piece of the puzzle. If the Church isn't all good (and it doesn't seem to be), then that has implications for Tulland's System, which might not be all bad. Figuring out the exact shape of what that looks like is not only necessary for us to understand Tulland's home world, but also is (spoiler, kinda) going to be important for the plot if this book series ends up being four to five books long instead of just three.

## *The Infinite and Other Worlds*

We know that Tulland's world is just one of many in his system universe, and we get the feeling that people on Tulland's world at least kind of know that. While we don't see many of those worlds, we get a sense that they aren't that alien from Tulland's experiences. He and Necia can sit down and interact with peers without too much trouble; the Mad Rogue's world might be a little different, but not so much that he doesn't at least have a model of Tulland that lets him manipulate Tulland a little.

The main function of the other worlds isn't so much to be explored or understood as it is to add a bit of texture to what the Infinite is and does. Tulland's world has classes and dungeons, and every other world is at least implied to have the same things. But when the elite veterans of those dungeons (or anyone brave) decide they want a greater challenge, they can step into the Infinite. There, any feats or accomplishments they manage earn their world rewards of the kind that improve life for everyone in them.

This is, oddly, kind of the plot to *Joe Versus the Volcano* as well. You can imagine planets where this stops happening just because the overall comfort level gets high enough that nobody wants to do it anymore, which is what happened in the film. In Tulland's world, the input of brave adventurers has stopped for another reason we kind of know is related to the Church, but the specific reason isn't entirely clear to us yet.

## *The Infinite*

The idea behind the Infinite is simple enough on paper. It's a bigger, meaner dungeon that (probably) goes on forever, which isn't all that original in and of itself. As mentioned before, it's sort of a new game plus dungeon for various worlds, and the rewards it gives are broadly *for* those worlds. But the people who enter it do eventually die, it seems, and it's not supposed to be entered lightly or involuntarily.

Given that the people who enter it don't make it out, most of what any given world knows about the Infinite seems to come from the Systems of their world reporting back, as well as things that are just generally true of dungeons in general (like the dungeon motes).

Something that was once true of the Infinite was that it was just one of many dungeons in Tulland's world, but that people were selected for it rather than volunteering, and that they could return to normal life here and there. The whole "the Infinite" part of it came from the fact that other dungeons ended, and farming them became the jobs of the people assigned to them. The Infinite, in contrast, would push adventurers on and on, and not only would they eventually have access to better loot (for themselves and the world they lived in) but that various "high scores" in terms of how far people had gone would mean good things for their world as well.

In that telling, the point of a world was to raid the Infinite, and the point of the Infinite was to act as a yardstick for the world, measuring its progress. This was because *the will of the gods or something*, and I hadn't gotten that much further than that when I scrapped the idea.

When an adventurer enters the Infinite, they lose all their levels as well as their class. When they pick up a new class, the idea is that it's usually something similar to what they trained in their original world—Necia, for instance, does not question her heavy-armor class, and the Mad Rogue seems to be a skulker-murderer type to his very core.

Tulland's experience is a little different in a way the Infinite does not like. While he does enter voluntarily (and at a full-tilt run), he doesn't enter with a full understanding of what he's getting into at all. And, in a way that's very odd for any world, he doesn't have a class. The System has just enough influence to determine his class on the spot, and screws him over. We don't see it, but this is something the Infinite has an immediate interest in remedying.

The Infinite can have this interest because of the kind of thing it is. It's not just a dungeon, but also the intelligence that runs it, a sort of chorus of thousands of personalities that comprise a single mind and who are all concerned with running the dungeon in a fair, productive way.

It's not explicit, but one of the Infinite's stretch goals is to actually get more crafters into the dungeon anyway, pushing things forward for everyone else by means of support.

We see a bit of that framework in the bent rules Tulland operates under. He has more time to move from floor to floor, for instance, and can dilly-dally leveling and grinding a lot longer than a swordsman could. In my mind, the Infinite had imagined that the classes that people would send would likely be blacksmiths, high-strength classes that could make themselves weapons first thing and get through the first five levels pretty easily so long as they had enough time to mine ores, smelt them, and make badass swords using their presumably deep home world experience in armaments.

Tulland is sort of half that, but once he starts to have successes in the dungeon, we see the Infinite take a wait-and-see approach to things.

Open questions about the Infinite I'll eventually have to answer is whether it's truly an all-good entity like it seems, whether it's endless (the name right now has more to do with the intelligence running the place than the floors), and whether there's some way to survive long-term once you've entered it.

## CHARACTERS
### *Tulland*

Tulland was originally meant to be a pretty flawless, virtue-heavy character. He ran errands for his uncle, who ran a shipping depot, and did a very good job at it. He loved his parents. He was handsome, hardworking, and had great courage. As such, it made sense for him to be selected to get a rare, especially good class, and for some drunk slob of a rich kid to betray him.

I got talked out of that eventually (thanks, Dotblue) and instead went with a character who had a little more nuance. Tulland is smart, but he's also *a smart-ass* who thinks he knows more than everyone else and that he's figured out some here-to-fore unknown truth of every little thing he ever sees that only he understands.

It's that kind of personality that leaves him vulnerable to the System's lies because when the System tells him that he's the chosen one and very much deserves all the good things that are happening to his friend, it's not introducing new information. Tulland doesn't have to be convinced that he's a chosen one, really. He already believes it, and always has.

Once Tulland hits the floor in the entryway of the Infinite, all those lies become clear. A great hero would not have to struggle against the motes. A great genius would not have been tricked by the System in as simple and easy a way as Tulland was. And a good person would not have been so enraged by his friend doing well that he cast aside reason.

When Tulland accepts the Infinite so easily, it's partially just because he knows he had it coming. Not entirely, but kinda.

Once Tulland is out of the entryway and focused on survival, his biggest character trait turns out to be pragmatism. He isn't particularly brave, he doesn't take particularly big risks, and he isn't particularly talented. He is very focused on survival, and very stubborn in a way that lets him wait day after day for plants to sprout while he sleeps and eats fruits he doesn't particularly like. He's very convinced he's right in a way that lets him look death in the face and say, "Well, maybe not, I might be the first guy who beats that."

In doing so, he completes a framework that the Church and the System started. With both of those entities, we can see that they are both presented as entirely good or entirely bad, and that neither of those assertions is exactly right. Tulland is not entirely good or bad either, but his dual nature is a bit more nuanced. What we find with him is that *stubborn* and *determined* are very similar traits, and *arrogant* and *innovative* and *confident* are all very closely linked.

I think about this a lot because I don't seem very much like an artist if you knew me in person. And even now, as a person who writes things that people seem to like, I can tell that a lot of my friends sort of subconsciously treat it all like it's *fake somehow*. There are some jokes or interesting concepts that do very well in my books but fall flat in my real life.

I don't say any of that to whine (I think it's pretty normal) but to point out that *talented* and *pursuing a dream that will never happen in a deluded way* are really close together.

What I wanted for Tulland was for him to be a sort of stubborn jackass who assumed he was always right, and then to be put into a situation that needed a determined, never-quit, never-say-die attitude. I wanted there to be a good, productive version of himself for him to find and live up to.

By the end of the book, he's even realizing that's what's happening a bit, and that *stubborn* streak ends up being instrumental in him reaching his goals.

Tulland has also never had a girlfriend, really. That also changes for him.

### *Necia*

Necia was originally supposed to die. That was the whole point of her character. She was going to show up, be someone Tulland was fond of in a few ways, and then have to move on ahead of his schedule. Even if her death wasn't confirmed, she was supposed to be a kind of embodiment of loss for him—a person he couldn't get strong enough to protect soon enough, and who moved on to a place he couldn't follow.

The scene where Tulland finds Necia's helmet in the tunnel is a second draft. Originally, he found her ice-cold, fully dead corpse. Some beta readers convinced me that they really, really did not like this abrupt death, and I changed it.

For better or worse, that also changed the entire tone of this book. A book where Necia dies is a darker, grimmer book. It's much more about loneliness and despair. The book we are getting instead is much more about hope. I don't think that's bad, but it's a different kind of thing.

If I'm trying to dig a piece of unique writing advice out of Necia, it's that all of your main characters should be like that. They should be important enough to the story that changes in their personality or personal outcomes drastically alter how the story goes. If they aren't that important to the story, they should be side characters or replaced with someone who *actually matters to the story*.

In terms of Necia's build, I wanted to address something that you sometimes see called *waif fu*, which is the idea that a 100- to 120-pound woman, however fit, could have a fair fighting chance at taking down a 225-pound man. Even in real-world boxing between men, weight classes are a thing just because size and weight matter that very much. A 150-pound man fighting a 250-pound man is putting his life at risk. At high skill levels, ten extra pounds is a huge difference.

For Necia, I wanted a way to address that beyond a hand-wave answer like "Well, stats make it up." And what made sense for it to me was to make her *conditionally large*, able to be as heavy and tall as a big man, and without having to be that all the time. The other way people do with that is they make being a very large, very buff woman the whole character.

That seems basically unfair to me. I'm a big dude, and I'm allowed to imagine myself as a Paladin or a Rogue without having to edit out the parts where I'm a big dude. What I wanted for Necia was the same rights that Prince Adam from *He-Man and the Masters of the Universe* gets, and to just be a big, yoked muscle freak when the situation called for it. Same with the dudes in this universe, although it doesn't come up—a very small man would probably get the same advantage.

Necia's personal journey is in some important ways already resolved by the time she meets Tulland. Not that she doesn't have a lot of room to grow, but her big journey was trying to be a meaningful person in a world that wanted to treat her like a piece of expensive jewelry. Her being in the Infinite means she has already rejected that, and is now learning to be her own person.

Other parts of her journey are very much not done. She's doing the first-romance thing with Tulland. She's learning that just because her training was fake in her home world doesn't mean that she can't be real and talented in the Infinite, given enough time. And, given that she's not dead, we should have plenty of time to see that happen.

### *The System*

The System was hard to write. I wanted its way of speaking to be *just a bit* formal without saying "thou" or intentionally using a lot of big words. In the end, I decided the best way to do that was to use a lot of short sentences with mostly short, simple words and very little voice, which I think mostly worked.

That was important to me for a couple reasons. I wanted the System to be a bit ambiguous. I think at one point it calls Tulland a fool, but outside of that it never really mocks Tulland or makes fun of him. It never seems truly gleeful that its con worked out. Most of all, it never seems happy. It factually states that Tulland's ill benefits it, but it's not pleased with that state of events.

And that leaves the door open for what we eventually learn about the System, which is that it was desperate. That it doesn't seem to regularly lure people to their deaths, but did so here because it was starving to death and had little other choice. And in the wings, there's a hint that its goals aren't entirely evil, either, even if Tulland dying is a big part of what it has to do to attain them.

One thing that I made sure of was that the System never actually lies to Tulland, outside of their time together on Ouros, where it seems to actually lie as little as possible to get Tulland through the arch. If it was unreliable even once in the Infinite, I think that would put it beyond redemption forever. Instead, the worst we get from the System is that it tells Tulland to flee the Infinite, which is something that seems to come from it being terrified of the Infinite itself rather than a specific desire to deceive.

If you've read my other books, then you might have noticed that on a purely mechanical level, the System does a lot of the same work that Lily and Lucy do. It's a sidekick of sorts, someone who is always there to have dialogue with when there's nobody else to talk to. It's company. It may not be very sympathetic, easy-to-love company, but if anything, I found that made it more interesting as a character to me.

Of all the characters in the book, I think its eventual development as a person will be the most important to where the plot goes.

### *Uncle*

Uncle is Tulland's adoptive father, and has been his caretaker since birth. He has known no other parent. They get along fine, and love each other despite neither of them being the kind to say it.

The most boring character in the book, hands down, is the uncle. He is a fisherman, and apparently a good one, but aspires to nothing more than competence at his job. He has what seems to be a simple house, and all the meals we see him prepare are simple, hearty, calorie-heavy stuff. To the extent we see him talking to Tulland as a teen, it seems that most of their conversations are a bunch of very boring lectures about how Tulland should listen more and have a bit more humility.

To put it another way, Tulland's uncle was the exact thing Tulland needed. If Tulland had understood and respected his uncle's way of life a little more, none of his problems would have come to pass. In rejecting his uncle as boring, Tulland rejected every chance of saving himself.

Tulland's uncle is one half of Tulland's education. It takes another character to understand the whole both halves come together to complete.

### *Tutor*

Tulland's tutor is an incredibly exciting man who has seen everything, knows everything, and understands everything. He is implied to have a class, or else to have done a lot of class-level adventures without one, which is even cooler. He has traveled the world, observed it with his own eyes, and understood it. He's incredible.

All this is completely lost on Tulland for two reasons: First, his tutor is very, very old. Old people, as far as Tulland knows, are default-boring. The other is that his teacher has understood reality as it is, and knows that the ways reality works are often boring. Since he's a good teacher, he presents the often-unsatisfactory parts of how the world works.

Tulland hates this. He imagines war to be shining swords and glory, but likely has never imagined it with blood, or what it would feel like to lie dying on a battlefield. He thinks of all the adventure the world might offer, but none of the pain, inconvenience, or lonesomeness it would require. His teacher presenting these things as fact is something he initially understands as the man being intentionally dull and lifeless, sapping all the joy out of things that should be glittering and glorious.

As half of Tulland's education, the teacher is meant to be *Intelligence and Knowledge*. He offers facts, figures, and cold, hard realities. He's a logistics guy. Uncle, in contrast, is *Wisdom and Understanding*. They overlap with each other's territories, but as a whole Uncle is the person who understands what life is and where to find satisfaction within it, while Tutor is more of a nuts-and-bolts, it-runs-on-math type of teacher.

Together, they should have been able to build the fairly bright Tulland into an intellectual monster, fully prepared to wring the value out of any type of life. He wouldn't let them, but that doesn't mean he didn't get any value out of their lessons at all.

Tutor and Uncle are mostly presented in the books in the form of flashbacks, showing where Tulland got the intellectual underpinnings he needs to survive in this new world. But they also, as foils to Tulland's personality, show what he is on a basic personality level. Neither is disposable.

### *The Mad Rogue*

Initially, I needed someone to kill Necia, and to be a sufficiently evil character. I needed you, as a reader, to not feel bad when Tulland took him down.

After Necia went away, it wasn't *absolutely necessary* that he be super-evil anymore, but it seemed more interesting just to leave him that way. He is the kind of guy who hunts other people for power, and is probably from a world that more or less rewarded that. He's not super complex, mostly because we don't see him for very long, but what we see is dangerous. We don't know what to expect besides violence from him, and we still mostly haven't seen him fight.

The way I write, that put me in a weird place. He wasn't a character I built because I loved him and thought the strength of his story would hold its own weight, and he wasn't a character the plot demanded anymore. He also wasn't a character that really drove the plot in a way I couldn't replace, which meant, in the three ways I consider characters important, he doesn't currently have a role.

I decided, hopefully wisely, to kick that can down the road by simply *leaving him alive*. He's out there, somewhere. We know he can do evil, and we don't expect he's stopping doing evil wherever he is. He's a bad-guy-in-waiting, ready for whatever badness we might need him to do later.

### *Altreck*

Tulland's best friend is a bit of a Rorschach test. When Tulland sees him, he sees *inferior and nonthreatening*, and the reason he sees this is because the character is (objectively) dumb. Any way that Tulland likes him is enabled by that—he doesn't have to worry about that guy competing to be the chosen.

When the person who doesn't have the thing Tulland thinks is important (intelligence) gets something Tulland wants, his entire world falls apart, however temporarily. This is because, in ways Tulland hasn't grappled with yet, he is a bad friend.

For other people, Altreck might look different. To the Church, he really probably does look just as easy to control as the System says he is. And maybe that's the reason they decide to let him have a class, since he's a known quantity who is unlikely to go too very rogue on them.

But he's also, you know, the kind of guy who makes a great Paladin. He's a good dude. He seems good-natured and relatively pure. He's probably not smart enough to be truly greedy. So to Gandalf the White (née Grey) he looks like Samwise Gamgee—absolutely someone who is going to prove his worth, given enough time.

Somewhere, on Tulland's world, he's probably busy doing just that. If this story had followed him, it would have probably ended with him very injured and still struggling to his feet simply because that's what was required to protect the weak. Or something like that, anyway.

### *Captain Hugg*

Captain Hugg was only mentioned once, but it's funny to me that there's a character named Captain Hugg.

## CONCLUSION

This is the first book in a series, so it's hard to say for sure whether it will really have legs. At the time of this writing, nobody who doesn't know me has read it. I'm going to put it up on the Internet soon, where some people will like it, and some people will tell me outright that they hate it and think I'm a very, very bad writer indeed.

Depending on the proportion of one to the other, I might get to keep writing for a living, or I might not. It's always a bit of a balancing act, as far as new stories go. It's a risky business where people's tastes change a lot, which means trying to write something you'd call a *hit novel* is a moving target that's almost impossible to plan to hit.

So it's hard, and it's stressful, but there's nothing else I'd rather do.

When I write these author's notes, I really wish I had better advice to give. I'd love to have profound wisdom to pass to the readers well beyond what I'm actually capable of giving. And the reason for that is that every reader who makes it through one of my books helps me to keep on keeping on at a job that is objectively hard in some ways, but ultimately very fulfilling in most other respects.

When you do that for me, you do me a favor. A big one. And it's something I appreciate.

I'm glad you are here, and I love y'all. Thank you so much for facilitating this kind of life.

—RC

# About the Author

R. C. Joshua is the author of the How to Survive at the End of the World, Demon World Boba Shop, and Deadworld Isekai series. A thirty-something from the southwest, Joshua is described by his friends as "you'll get used to him eventually." His interests include forgetting to exercise, exchanging sick verbal burns with his children, losing said burn contests to his children, and plotting to regain dominance over his increasingly capable children. It's him or them, folks. It's him or them.

9 798347 007479